P9-DGL-232

# PRAISE FOR BRIAN FREEMAN

"Must reading for crime/mystery fans."

—*Pioneer Press* on *The Voice Inside*

"Freeman's writing style is so smooth that the pages just turned themselves as I drove towards the exciting finale."

—*Bookreporter* on *The Voice Inside*

"Sure to seize readers and not let go . . . Gripping, intense, and thoughtful, *The Night Bird* is a must-read."

—*Romantic Times* on *The Night Bird* (Top Pick)

"This one will keep you guessing, but read it with the lights on."

—*Publishers Weekly* on *The Night Bird*

"Stunning . . . Wow, what a finish . . . Another one you simply can't miss."

—*BOLO Books* on *Alter Ego*

"If there is a way to say 'higher' than 'highly recommended,' I wish I knew it. Because this is one of those thrillers that go above and beyond."

—*Suspense Magazine* on *Goodbye to the Dead*

"Thriller fiction doesn't get much better."

—*Bookreporter* on *The Cold Nowhere*

"*Spilled Blood* is everything a great suspense novel should be: gripping, shocking, and moving. Brian Freeman proves once again he's a master of psychological suspense."

—Lisa Gardner, #1 *New York Times* bestselling author, on *Spilled Blood*

"Brian Freeman is a first-rate storyteller. *Stalked* is scary, fast-paced, and refreshingly well written. The characters are so sharply drawn and interesting, we can't wait to meet the next one in the story."
—Nelson DeMille, #1 *New York Times* bestselling author, on *Stalked*

"Breathtakingly real and utterly compelling, *Immoral* dishes up page-turning psychological suspense while treating us lucky readers to some of the most literate and stylish writing you'll find anywhere today."
—Jeffery Deaver, #1 *New York Times* bestselling author, on *Immoral*

# THE CROOKED STREET

# OTHER TITLES BY BRIAN FREEMAN

## The Frost Easton Series

*The Voice Inside*

*The Night Bird*

## The Jonathan Stride Series

*Alter Ego*

*Marathon*

*Goodbye to the Dead*

*The Cold Nowhere*

*Turn to Stone* (e-novella)

*Spitting Devil* (e-short story)

*The Burying Place*

*In the Dark*

*Stalked*

*Stripped*

*Immoral*

## The Cab Bolton Series

*Season of Fear*

*The Bone House*

## Stand-Alone Novels

*Spilled Blood*

*West 57* (as B. N. Freeman)

*The Agency* (as Ally O'Brien)

# THE CROOKED STREET

Bestselling Author of *THE NIGHT BIRD*

BRIAN FREEMAN

THOMAS & MERCER

This is a work of fiction. Names, characters, organizations, places, events, and incidents are either products of the author's imagination or are used fictitiously. Any resemblance to actual persons, living or dead, or actual events is purely coincidental.

Text copyright © 2019 by Brian Freeman
All rights reserved.

No part of this book may be reproduced, or stored in a retrieval system, or transmitted in any form or by any means, electronic, mechanical, photocopying, recording, or otherwise, without express written permission of the publisher.

Published by Thomas & Mercer, Seattle

www.apub.com

Amazon, the Amazon logo, and Thomas & Mercer are trademarks of Amazon.com, Inc., or its affiliates.

ISBN-13: 9781503900943 (hardcover)
ISBN-10: 1503900940 (hardcover)
ISBN-13: 9781503902336 (paperback)
ISBN-10: 1503902331 (paperback)

Cover design by Rex Bonomelli

Printed in the United States of America

First edition

*For Marcia*

It takes your enemy and your friend, working together, to hurt you to the heart.

—*Mark Twain*

# 1

Denny Clark emerged through a cloud of steam into the cold darkness of Chinatown.

The fragrance of ginger and jasmine, and the spitting sizzle of hot oil, chased him into the alley. His shoes tracked footprints outlined in pig's blood onto the stone. He slammed the metal door behind him, silencing the chorus of voices bellowing in Mandarin from the restaurant kitchen. With sweat on his forehead, Denny breathed hard and nervously eyed the shadows. On either side of the walkway, brick buildings rose six stories over his head, and fire escapes clung to the walls. The alley-front shops were barred and padlocked. It was ten o'clock on Friday night.

He'd come here to deliver a warning, but he was too late. Mr. Jin was already gone. So was his son. No one had seen or heard from them for three long days.

Denny squinted at the faces in the alley. Two Chinese teenage girls chirped to each other as they zigzagged toward him in short skirts and high heels. A hooker serviced a bald client in the doorway of a massage parlor. Barely ten feet away, a homeless man bared his yellowed teeth and banged a copper mug against the pavement. Denny threw him some change from his pocket.

He clutched a phone in his damp palm. He'd written the number for Zingari on the back of his hand because he knew he might need it later. He struggled to read the numbers; the moisture on his skin had made the ink run. He dialed and waited as the phone in the busy Tenderloin restaurant rang and rang.

Finally, an impatient voice answered. Denny could hear a clarinet warbling jazz in the background.

"Is Chester there?" Denny asked.

"What?"

"Chester," Denny repeated loudly and urgently, trying to cut through the noise. "I need to talk to Chester."

"Hang on."

The noise of the restaurant disappeared. He was put on hold, and he gripped the phone tightly as he waited. Maroon 5 kept him company, and he listened to "Payphone" all the way to the rap by Wiz Khalifa before a new voice came on the line.

"This is Virgil. Talk to me."

"Virgil, it's Denny Clark. I was looking for Chester."

"Well, well, Denny. It's been a long time, stranger. How come you haven't had me out on the boat lately? I'm hurt. Devastated. In need of tequila."

"I'm sorry, but this is important. I need to talk to Chester right away."

*I need to warn him,* Denny thought.

"Well, you're too late, amigo," Virgil replied.

"What? What do you mean?"

"Chester decamped. Disembarked. Departed. Hit the highway. He decided San Francisco wasn't cosmopolitan enough for him. He moved to—are you ready for this?—Pocatello, Idaho. As if that's even a real place. He texted the manager yesterday and said he wants to be closer to his parents. Appalling. Not even a farewell drink."

Denny squeezed his eyes shut. "Are you sure?"

"I'm staring at the bar now. The new bartender is some scary brunette with a lot of ink."

"Okay. Thanks, Virgil."

Denny hung up the phone. He squeezed his hand into a fist and pushed it against his forehead. Everything was crashing down around him. He knew Chester hadn't moved to Idaho. He'd hung out with Chester since high school and knew that his parents were both dead. The text was a lie.

Chester was gone.

Mr. Jin and his son, Fox, were gone.

So was Carla.

Carla, his ex-wife, who'd been in and out of Denny's life for a decade, who'd loved and hated him in equal measure. They'd gotten her, too.

Denny had taken BART under the bay three hours earlier to visit Carla's apartment in Berkeley. The police were already there with squad cars and an ambulance outside the building. Suicide, they told him. Her roommate had found her in the rose-colored water of the bathtub. Carla had cut her wrists in two deep vertical slashes and bled out.

Another lie.

Carla hadn't killed herself, not like that. As long as he'd known her, she'd been scared sick of the sight of blood. Even if she'd intended to kill herself, she would have chosen another way. And she would have left a note to make sure he felt guilty about what she'd done.

No, she'd been murdered. Just like the others. Carla, Chester, Mr. Jin, and Fox. To Denny, that meant only one thing.

He was next.

Denny hurried north through the Chinatown alley. Red-and-black graffiti painted the brick walls, and empty paper bags made cartwheels along the pavement. Banners with Chinese characters snapped like flags in the stiff breeze. He passed a Christian mission. A tea shop selling herbs and ginseng. A fortune cookie factory. Ahead of him, protesters pounded a war beat on their drums.

When he was almost to Jackson Street, a sixth sense made him spin around. He backed into a doorway out of the neon glow and watched the kitchen door of Mr. Jin's restaurant. Something was wrong. Something had changed in the seconds since he'd walked away. Then he realized: The homeless man with the copper mug had vanished. He'd disappeared after Denny left.

There were no coincidences now. Denny was being watched. His enemy had eyes everywhere.

He waited for a gap among the pedestrians, then burst from the alley and ran. He weaved uphill, dodging past fruit markets and dim-sum restaurants. He veered across Jackson, drawing horns from the cars jammed up at the intersection. At the corner, he stopped and looked over his shoulder. The faces of the people on the sidewalk glowed red under paper lanterns hung over the street. He watched for someone breaking from the crowd in pursuit, but he saw no one. He turned and quickly walked away, head down. Two blocks later, he turned again. And then again. He kept going until he found another alley where the neighborhood was quiet and deserted.

He made a second phone call.

"It's Denny," he said.

"Denny? What's up? Are you okay?"

"They're all dead, you bastard. He *killed* them. Even Carla. And now he's coming after me."

There was a long pause on the line. "Slow down. What are you talking about? Who's dead?"

"Everyone, all of them," Denny replied. "Except me. I'm the last one. You think he's going to let me walk away?"

"Where are you right now?"

"Chinatown."

"I'll come get you."

"You?" Denny said. "No, I don't think so. You got me into this."

"Look, find a place to hide, and I'll be there in half an hour."

Denny didn't reply. The only noise on the street was the raspy whistle of his own breathing. He stood next to a secondhand clothing shop and peered around the corner at the empty block. A streetlight illuminated the sidewalk close to him, but the opposite side was dark. Then a tiny flame came and went in the shadows, and the wind carried the smell of a cigarette across the asphalt.

He wasn't alone. They'd already found him again.

Denny stared at the phone in his hand. "Are you tracking me?"

"What?"

"You gave me this phone. Did you tell him where to find me?"

"Denny, don't be crazy. I can protect you."

"This was a trap all along, wasn't it?" Denny insisted. "You're working for him. You planned this whole thing from the beginning."

"No, stop, listen to me—"

Denny threw the phone sharply to the ground, where it smashed into pieces. He sprinted toward the far end of the alley. When he got to the next street, he shot a glance over his shoulder. In the same place where he'd made his phone call, a lone silhouette watched him from between the buildings. The man made no move to lay chase, as if he knew Denny had no way to escape. Denny ran anyway, as fast as his pounding heart allowed. He crossed Powell Street and climbed the next block to Mason, where cable car tracks stretched along the pavement. He'd left Chinatown behind him. He was in the Russian Hill neighborhood now. From here, the streets climbed into the sky, as steep as mountains.

Muscle cramps tightened around his stomach and legs. His thighs quivered. He couldn't run anymore. As he doubled over with exhaustion and grabbed his knees, a puff of air whipped by him, so close to his head that it ruffled his hair. A tiny ping of shrapnel struck the concrete wall behind him. There was no fire, no smoke, no gunshot, but someone had just shot at him and missed.

He looked back. Halfway down the block, a small man hiked calmly toward him through the darkness. The man carried a pistol with a strangely elongated barrel. An air gun. Silent. Lethal.

It was just the two of them on the street. Denny and the man who was going to kill him.

He staggered toward a dead end above him, where steps led through parkland to the heights of the Russian Hill neighborhood. Behind him, careful, measured, unhurried footsteps closed the gap between them. Another low pop and a strange puff of air filled his ears, and this time, he felt a pinch on his neck no more painful than a bee sting. He slapped his skin the way he would to kill an insect. When he looked at his fingers, he saw a smear of blood. Just a little bit, not the gushing flow of a bullet wound. He stared down the hill and saw the man not even twenty yards away, watching him calmly.

Waiting.

Denny rubbed the blood between his fingers until it dried. He took a breath in and out. He told himself that he was fine, but somewhere in his mind, he knew that he was not fine at all. He was going to die like the others. It was tempting just to sit down on the steps and accept the inevitable. The peaks of Russian Hill loomed like Everest above him, and he had almost no strength to go on.

Even so, he knew one person who lived up there, practically in the clouds. Once upon a time, the two of them had been like brothers, but they hadn't spoken in years. He couldn't call him a friend anymore, but he didn't need a friend right now.

He needed a cop.

Denny climbed. Each step was a stab of torture. He wheezed in and out and realized he was struggling now to find the air his lungs needed. But he climbed. He made his way up the slope to Taylor Street, where there was another hill, steeper and more intimidating than the one before. And still he climbed. The higher he rose, the more the night-time city opened up in a panorama of lights. He saw Coit Tower. He saw the pyramid of the Transamerica building. A ribbon of white lights marked the Bay Bridge.

He didn't know how much time had passed since the sting. It might have been only a few minutes; it might have been half the night. The man who'd shot him hadn't even bothered following him. Why follow a dead man?

Denny began to notice strange things happening to his body. His lips felt numb. His tongue grew thick and swollen. Drool ran down his chin. His head throbbed, and he swayed with each step, feeling the world spin. When he reached the last cruel set of stairs up into the trees, he found his limbs growing stiff, as if he were Pinocchio morphing back into wood. His body became a sea of tremors.

Every time he sat down to rest, he was sure that he wouldn't get up. But he did. He climbed and climbed, and finally, he broke from the trees onto the summit, where the house was. He'd been here before. Half a dozen times in the past two years, Denny had come here to make peace, and each time, he'd driven away without even having the courage to go to the door.

There were no lights inside. For all he knew, the house was empty, and all of his labor was for nothing.

Denny collapsed on the sidewalk. His forehead hit the pavement, his glasses broke, and blood trickled down his face. He couldn't walk anymore, so he crawled. He put a hand forward, then a knee, over and over, until he reached the front steps of the house. He slithered toward the door like a snake, and when he was there, he somehow willed his paralyzed body to stand.

He rang the bell again and again and again. And he waited.

A few seconds later, the outside light went on, and the door opened. There was his old friend, staring at him with horrified surprise.

"Denny?" Frost Easton said. "My God, what happened to you?"

Denny had so much to say and no breath with which to say it. His frozen knees caved beneath him, and Frost caught him. Denny was dead weight, but Frost held him under his shoulder blades, and they stood there locked in each other's arms, face-to-face.

Two old friends who weren't friends anymore.

Denny found one last word at the bottom of his throat. Someone needed to know the truth. Someone needed to know who'd done this. He gasped it to Frost before the fog closed over him.

*"Lombard."*

# 2

"Most homicide investigators have to go out into the city to find their victims," the pathologist from the medical examiner's office commented as he knelt on hands and knees over the body in Frost's foyer. "It certainly saves time when they come right to your house. I'm very impressed."

"And you thought advertising on Craigslist was a waste of time," Frost replied dryly.

The pathologist, whose name was Dr. Walter Finder, snickered from behind a polypropylene mask that covered most of his face. He was in his forties, with wild Albert Einstein hair and a pencil mustache. "Murder victims wanted? Apply in person?"

"Something like that." Frost stared down at Denny's body and then added in a low voice, "Actually, I knew him."

"Ah. I'm sorry. Friend of yours?"

"Not really, not anymore. I hadn't seen him in years. You're sure this is a homicide, Walt? It couldn't be some strange disease?"

The pathologist's gloved hand turned Denny's head sideways. "Oh no, he was murdered. See this little wound on the neck? He was shot with something. Probably some kind of dissolving gelatin pellet because there's nothing inside the wound now. Was your friend a spy?"

Frost shook his head. "Denny? Are you kidding? He ran fishing charters for tourists. Why would you think he was a spy?"

"Well, his death looks to be the result of a rare kind of poison. I won't know more for sure until I run tests in the lab, but based on the look of the body, I suspect it's tetrodotoxin or something along those lines. It's the kind of weapon you typically don't see outside of Cold War political assassinations. Sticking people with lethal umbrellas, that kind of thing."

"Denny Clark wasn't a deep-cover CIA operative," Frost said. "He was just an ordinary guy with a boat."

There was a long stretch of silence between them. Then Dr. Finder shook his head, as if Frost couldn't be more wrong. "Oh, believe me, there's nothing ordinary here, Inspector."

Frost frowned and let the pathologist continue his work. He found it hard to identify the man he remembered from his youth in the face of the corpse at his feet. It wasn't just the effects of the poison. More than a decade had passed since he'd seen Denny Clark, and his former friend had changed. Denny had put on weight and shaved off his fisherman's beard. The man who'd never owned a shirt with a collar in his life wore a trendy Italian-made pullover. He'd traded contact lenses for cool lime-green glasses. Even so, he still smelled like the sea, the way he always had.

The sadness that Frost felt wasn't really grief. It was more like regret for how things had gone down. He'd known Denny in high school, but they'd lost touch while Frost went to college and law school. Then, when Frost was deciding what to do with his life, he'd hooked up with Denny again and spent a year living with him on a boat at Fisherman's Wharf, taking tourists out on the bay. For eleven months of that year, he'd had the time of his life. The twelfth month was a different story. They'd broken up badly over a girl named Carla, and it was the kind of breakup that friends don't come back from.

Now they were both thirty-five years old. Frost was a cop. Denny was dead.

Dr. Finder looked up and read the emotion on Frost's face. "I don't mean to make light of losing someone you were close to."

"We weren't close," Frost replied, too sharply. Then he went on, as much to himself as to the medical examiner. "I'm just saying it was a long time ago. Denny and I used to drink beer, steam crab, and listen to Nickelback, I'm ashamed to say. Every kid in his twenties should live like that for a while. We didn't make a dime, but we didn't care about money."

"Well, Mr. Clark is doing considerably better now," Dr. Finder replied. "Present circumstances excepted, of course."

"What do you mean?"

Finder tapped the body's leg. "He has cash in a money clip in his front right pocket. Looks like several thousand dollars."

Frost's lips pressed into a frown. Money and Denny Clark had never gone hand in hand, at least not for long. He found it hard to believe that his old friend had changed that much, even after ten years apart.

"I'm going to check on the investigation outside," he told the pathologist. "Do you have everything you need?"

"I do. Although since I'm here, I was hoping to meet the famous Shack."

Frost grinned. Everyone associated with the San Francisco police knew about Frost's cat. They were an unlikely team, and on most days, Frost wasn't entirely sure which one of them was in charge. "I had to put Shack in an upstairs bedroom, or he probably would have started the autopsy without you. I'll introduce you before you go."

"Be sure you do," Dr. Finder replied.

Frost stepped around the body to the open front door and walked down the porch steps to Green Street. The road was crowded with police vehicles lighting up the cul-de-sac at the top of the hill. He saw plastic numbers on the sidewalk, marking evidence. In this case, it was Denny's blood. He walked to the concrete railing that overlooked the rocky tree-lined slope and imagined the effort it had taken for Denny to climb the stairs with his last breaths.

All to give Frost a message that made no sense at all.

*Lombard.*

To San Franciscans, Lombard was simply an east–west street heading across the city into the Presidio. Tourists knew the name Lombard because of its zigzag route down one of the sharp peaks of Russian Hill. City guides called it the crookedest street in the world.

Frost shoved his hands in the pockets of his black jeans and blinked away his tiredness. He wore yesterday's blue-checked button-down shirt, untucked. The wind riffled through his swept-back hair, which was a mixture of gold and brown and cut short on the sides. He had a high forehead, small ears, and a nose that made a sharp V on his face. His eyes were dark blue. His neatly trimmed beard hid his chin. He was almost six feet tall but a little skinny for his height.

He turned around and leaned against the railing. The March night was cold and clear. Using his phone, he did a quick Google search for the name Denny Clark. The search led him to Denny's website, which advertised custom charter excursions on the bay. Frost hadn't kept up with Denny over the years—in fact, he'd deliberately made sure he didn't know what Denny was doing—but he could see that his former partner had upgraded the business. Denny had exchanged their rusted forty-foot fishing boat at the wharf for a luxury one-hundred-foot party yacht docked in the marina. He catered to the San Francisco elite. Based on the cash in his pocket, it paid well.

The name of Denny's yacht was the *Roughing It*. Frost couldn't help smiling. There was more to the name than just its sly irony for an upscale yacht. Frost had named their original fishing boat the *Jumping Frog*, which he'd taken from a Mark Twain story. Apparently, Denny had done the same thing with his new yacht, even though Denny's knowledge of anyone named Twain probably began and ended with

Shania. It made Frost wonder whether Denny had quietly been sending him an apology that he'd never received.

"Inspector?"

Frost looked up to find a uniformed police officer standing in front of him. "Yes, what is it?"

"Captain Hayden wants to talk to you."

Frost nodded. "I'll give him a call."

The police officer shook his head. "No, the captain is here."

"Here? At the crime scene?"

"Yes, he just arrived."

Surprised, Frost checked his watch and saw that it was nearly two in the morning. He didn't understand why the top cop in the major crimes unit—a man who was on track to be the next San Francisco police chief—would be visiting an ordinary homicide scene in the middle of the night.

Then he remembered what Dr. Finder had told him: *There's nothing ordinary here.*

Frost spotted Hayden's unmarked black town car beyond the crime scene tape. He marched toward the car and saw Hayden's right-hand man vaping mist into the air from an e-cigarette as he stood on the sidewalk. The younger cop's name was Cyril Timko. Hayden had plucked him from the officer ranks several months earlier and turned the twenty-nine-year-old into his assistant, enforcer, and chauffeur. Cyril had the tough, wiry look of a runner, all muscle and bone. In the police gym, he made up for his small stature with a reputation as a dirty fighter. He wore his black hair in a buzz cut that made a sharp point on his forehead. He had thick eyebrows and a five o'clock shadow. His blue uniform fit tightly, and his skin was pale white, as if the button of his shirt collar were cutting off the blood through his neck.

"This is a surprise," Frost said as he approached Cyril. "Why the late-night visit? I would have given the captain a report in the morning."

Cyril shrugged. "It's Russian Hill. Lots of rich voters and rich politicians around here. They get nervous about murder. The captain wants to make sure we're all over this one."

"Fair enough," Frost said, but he didn't think that was the real explanation.

"What do you know so far?" Cyril asked him in a voice that had the raspiness of someone who used to smoke real cigarettes instead of the fake ones.

"The victim came up the hillside stairs on foot. We're still trying to trace his movements before that."

"Any witnesses?"

"Not yet, but we'll canvass the area in the morning." Frost nodded at the town car. "The captain's in the back?"

"He is." Cyril exhaled a cloud of vapor and secured the device in his pocket. He went to the rear door of the town car and swung it open. The interior lights were on, and Frost climbed inside.

Captain Pruitt Hayden took up fully half of the back seat. He was huge, like the former Stanford linebacker that he was. His bald black head had patches of off-color skin like dark and milk chocolate mixed together. He wore Franklin reading glasses that looked oddly tiny on his face, and he perused the screen of his laptop with his lips pursed. His fingers tapped along to a piano concerto playing on the car's speakers. Like his aide, he wore dress blues.

A minute passed, and finally, the captain turned to stare at Frost over the rims of his glasses.

"Easton," he murmured in a voice that sounded like distant thunder. He said Frost's name with the expression of someone who had stepped in something unpleasant. Frost and Hayden had never been friends.

"Good evening, sir," Frost said. "I appreciate the support, but there was no need for you to come out here personally in the middle of the night. We have the situation under control."

"When someone gets murdered in one of my detectives' houses, I want to know what's going on," Hayden replied.

"Well, he died at my house, but we don't know where the actual crime took place yet."

Hayden didn't seem impressed by the distinction. "You knew this man?"

"I did, although we hadn't spoken in a long time."

"So why did he come to you?"

"I have no idea," Frost replied. "I'm surprised he even knew where I lived."

"Can you think of a motive for his murder?"

"Not yet. He was carrying plenty of money, but the killer didn't bother taking it. Dr. Finder seems to think that an unusual type of poison was used. He said it reminded him of a political assassination."

"An assassination," Hayden repeated, rolling the word around his mouth like a fine wine.

"Yes, sir. Denny seems like an unlikely target for a professional hit. All he did was run charters from a yacht in the marina. I'll see what I can find on his boat."

"Do that. And keep an eye out for drugs, weapons, or other contraband. If he's out on the water regularly, trafficking of some kind could be a factor here."

"That was my first thought, too," Frost agreed.

"I want to be kept in the loop on this case," Hayden told him. "Copy Cyril on your reports and give him a daily update on what you find. He'll make sure the information gets to me."

"Of course," Frost replied. He waited a beat before adding, "Do you mind if I ask why? No offense, sir, but you don't typically get involved in a specific homicide investigation unless it has some broader political implications. Is there something here that I should know about?"

"When there's something you need to know, I'll tell you." Hayden focused on the glowing screen of his laptop again. "That'll be all for now, Easton."

"Yes, sir."

Frost opened the rear door of the town car. The cool breeze blew in and mixed with Hayden's cologne. He began to get out, but the captain reached out and closed a powerful hand around his wrist.

"Wait, one more thing," Hayden went on. "The victim, Denny Clark. Did he say anything to you before he died?"

Frost heard Denny's voice in his head again: *Lombard.*

He was about to reply, but then he stopped himself.

In his memory, he saw Denny's twisted face as his friend battled for breath. His eyes were wide with the terror of someone who knew he was about to die. He looked as if he'd climbed a mountain and held off the end, just so that he could give Frost one last message.

One odd, puzzling, meaningless message.

Frost wasn't going to say anything about it until he knew what it meant.

"No," he told the captain. "Denny said nothing at all."

# 3

Dawn was still an hour away when Frost parked his Chevy Suburban on the narrow strip of road north of the San Francisco yacht harbor. On his right, the masts of dozens of sailboats bobbed like awkward ballerinas and made a clinking, metallic music. On his left, agitated waves slapped against the breakwater. He saw the lights of the Golden Gate Bridge through billowing fog, the low hills of the East Bay, and the grim outline of Alcatraz. The wind tried to knock him off his feet.

He had no trouble identifying the sleek flybridge of the *Roughing It*, which had its own diagonal slip among the smaller profiles of private yachts. It was as white as a single cloud against a perfect blue sky. The bow tapered to a sharp, aerodynamic point like an arrowhead, and smoked windows stretched along the main deck. There was open space forward and aft where guests could soak up the sun and lean into the spray as if they were kings and queens of the world. Some of them probably were.

The boat's price tag had to be in the high seven figures. Frost wondered where Denny had found the money to buy it.

As he waited near the locked gate leading to the piers, the engine of a golf cart rattled from the cypress trees near the marina clubhouse. The cart parked next to Frost's truck, and a trim, white-haired security guard hopped down to join him. The man had a large loop of keys jangling from his belt. He took a close look at Frost's badge, and then the two men shook hands.

"Tom Hale," the guard introduced himself. He was in his sixties, with a nimble step and an easy smile. "I'm the overnight security man at the harbor. Did I hear you right on the phone? Is Denny Clark dead?"

"Yes, he is," Frost said.

"What an awful thing. Nice man, Mr. Clark. Down to earth. You can't always say that about the people around this place."

"When did you last see him?"

"Yesterday morning. Mr. Clark was usually on the boat every day before the night shift ended. He pampered his baby, that's for sure. Of course, if I had a vessel like that, I'd be good to her, too."

"Was he alone?" Frost asked.

"I think so. I didn't see anyone with him."

"Did you talk to him?"

"I waved. He waved. That was all."

"What about your shift last night?"

"I didn't see him," Hale replied. "The boat didn't go out. It's still pretty early in the season. I don't think the *Roughing It* has been out on the water since Tuesday."

"It's an expensive boat," Frost said. "Did Denny ever say where he got the money to buy it?"

"People don't talk about that kind of thing around here. Sometimes it's family money. Sometimes it's billionaire nerds from the valley. Or sometimes the things are simply in hock up to their flags. I don't know about Mr. Clark, but he seemed to have the right contacts. No one at the marina gave him a hard time about getting a license to run charters out of here. Maybe he had partners with some deep pockets and political clout behind him."

"What about his crew?" Frost asked.

"He'd hire people depending on the charter. Chefs, bartenders, that kind of thing. But Mr. Clark was the captain. He ran her himself."

Frost eyed the boat, which had the proud look of a Great Dane towering over lesser dogs. "What kind of charters are we talking about? Did you see people you know? Celebrities? Anybody like that?"

"Part of my job is not to notice things," Hale replied. "The people that Mr. Clark took out valued their privacy. Most of the time, he'd have me close off the road while his guests loaded. I'd let in a couple limos, but I wouldn't know who was in them. He wanted to make sure gawkers weren't taking pictures."

Frost nodded. "Did Mr. Clark have any problems with anybody? Did you ever hear any arguments? Or did he complain about anyone to you?"

"No, nothing like that," Hale replied. "As far as I could tell, everybody liked him. And that's a tough clientele to keep happy. Powerful people like things a certain way. If they don't get what they want, you'll hear about it."

"But you never heard any negative scuttlebutt about Mr. Clark around the marina? That's hard to imagine. Denny and I used to run a fishing boat at the wharf. The one thing I remember is that the captains unloaded more crap on each other than the seagulls."

"Well, that's the wharf, Inspector. This is the marina."

Frost smiled. "Is that a little slam, Tom?"

"Maybe a little."

The security guard smiled, too, but he didn't add anything more. Frost wasn't sure whether Hale was telling the truth about the lack of gossip or whether the man had been tipped well enough by Denny and others to remain discreet about the comings and goings around here.

"I need to take a look at the boat," Frost added. "We'll be out with a forensic team later today."

"Whatever you need, Inspector."

Hale unlocked the gate, and Frost walked down the ramp in the darkness. He could see a pink glow on the eastern horizon, behind the skyscrapers that jutted like broken teeth over the hills of the city. He made his way along the water to the pier where the *Roughing It* was tied up, and he stepped across the dock onto the platform at the stern. His weight didn't even make the boat sway.

He climbed the ladder to the main deck, which was damp with spray. Cushioned seats surrounded a vast stone-and-chrome fire pit that gleamed with red stones. It was easy to imagine the flames licking at the darkness out on the cold water. Above his head, the overhang of the flybridge was like a flying saucer, and he spotted the octagonal wall of a hot tub.

This was a place for one-percenters. Denny had come a long way since their days on the *Jumping Frog*.

Frost let himself inside the guest quarters, which were equally lavish. The living room was decorated in white leather, with a well-stocked bar, 4K satellite television, and shining fixtures in cherrywood and stainless steel. The area didn't just look clean. It looked sanitized. He pulled one of the cushions from the leather sofa and found that the base of the furniture had been vacuumed so thoroughly that there wasn't even a crumb of food or strand of hair.

The next room was a dining area with tables that could serve at least sixteen people. Steps led down to the crew deck and kitchen. Beyond the dining room was a master suite with a queen-sized bed and mirrored ceiling. The bed was made with brightly colored sheets and a mountain of pillows. Jade sculptures and silk birds-of-paradise decorated the dressers. Soft overhead lights gave the room a romantic glow. Another flat-screen television was built into the wall, and above the television was a geometric wall sculpture made of mirrored glass. The sculpture hung slightly askew, as if it had been recently moved. Frost looked behind it and spotted a small rectangular plastic panel. One corner of the panel was loose. With gloves on, Frost took down the sculpture and pried away the black panel to see what was behind it.

He found the ends of an electrical power cord and a USB cable that ran back behind the wall. Neither cable was connected to a device, but when he shined his light on the small shelf, he could see a circular dust outline. Something electronic had been situated here and recently taken away. Based on the size and location, facing the bed through the mirrored glass, Frost had a suspicion about the missing equipment.

A video camera.

If Denny had been spying on his elite guests, that was definitely a motive for murder.

When Frost finished upstairs, he returned to the dining room and took the stairs to the lower deck. The kitchen was here, gleaming with stainless steel appliances, and it had the functionality to prepare a gourmet meal. There were other, plainer bedrooms for crew and serving staff. He found Denny's bedroom and office aft, where a locked door led to the boat's mechanical equipment area. He sat down in the comfortable swivel chair behind the desk and tried to get a sense of Denny's life.

The first thing he noticed on the desk was a photograph of Carla. Despite the years in between, he recognized her immediately, tall and slim, with long, straight sandy hair and a sarcastic smirk that was always on her lips. The smirk covered darker, scarier things. He sat there, staring at the picture, and eventually realized that several minutes had gone by while he was lost in the past.

He shook himself out of it and examined the rest of the desk. Like the hidden camera—if it really was a camera—Denny's computer was gone, which likely meant that any video records had disappeared. Probably Denny's ship logs had been there, too. Frost began to think that someone had beaten him to the boat in order to erase the evidence.

He opened each drawer of the desk but found nothing except loose paper clips, open boxes of printer ink, USB cables, and a pair of mini binoculars. There was also a blue box with an expensive Waterman pen that Denny's mother had given to him as a high school graduation gift. Even back in the days of the *Jumping Frog*, the pen had been Denny's prized possession. Some things never changed.

The lowest drawer of the desk felt oddly heavy as Frost opened it. He removed it and turned it over so that he could check the panel underneath.

Duct-taped to the bottom of the drawer was a small brick of cocaine.

Frost leaned back in the chair and shook his head. He'd already talked about the possibility of Denny smuggling drugs with Captain Hayden, and now here was a supply of cocaine to back up that theory. Even so, something didn't feel right to him. The evidence of Denny's yacht business had been carefully removed, but the drugs had been left behind in a way that no one doing a routine search could fail to find them.

Too easy.

He slipped an evidence bag out of his pocket to secure the cocaine but froze when he heard a footstep on the stairs that led up to the main deck. He wasn't alone on the boat anymore. Whoever had made the footstep above him froze, too, as if he knew he'd given himself away. Frost reached into his jacket and slid his gun into his hand. He waited in the silence and then called out, "This is the police. Come down here slowly and show yourself."

The warning didn't work. Instead, the person above him ran. Frost leaped to his feet and gave chase. He took the steps two at a time on the twisting staircase and reached the boat's dining room just as he saw the shadow of a figure disappearing through the doors to the open deck. He crossed the space and burst into the pink light of morning. When he spun around the corner, he saw someone sprinting down the starboard gangway between the ship's railing and the slanting wall of the cabin.

"Stop!"

The man was halfway along the length of the boat when he glanced back and saw the gun in Frost's hands. He weighed his chances and gave up. He froze where he was, turned around, and put his hands in the air.

Frost closed in on him along the length of the gangway. As he got closer, he realized that the man looked more like a boy, probably no more than five feet tall and fourteen years old. He was Asian, dressed all in black in a tank top, cycling tights, and black sneakers. His dark hair was bushy and styled. A gold chain hung around his neck, and one gold stud dotted his ear. His skin had an almost plastic glow, as if he were wearing makeup, and his eyes were alert and suspicious.

"Who the hell are you?" the boy demanded, like a dog standing up to a bear.

Frost smiled. He replaced his gun in his holster and took out his badge instead. "I told you, I'm a cop. My name's Frost."

The badge didn't do anything to ease the boy's suspicion. "Yeah, so? This ain't your boat."

"It's not yours, either," Frost replied. "Who are you?"

The boy set his mouth in a tough line and didn't answer.

"Just tell me your name and what you're doing here," Frost said. "Do you know Denny Clark?"

A long silence passed. The morning sky got lighter as the clouds moved. The boy's eyes darted between the boat and the water of the harbor. "Sure, I know Denny," he said finally.

"What's your name?" Frost asked again.

"Fox."

"Okay. Why are you here, Fox?"

"First, you tell me why the cops are on Denny's boat," the boy demanded. "What's up? Is he dead?"

"Why would you think that?"

"I hear things. Word on the street is that somebody whacked him last night."

"Yeah? Did you get a name?"

"I just heard he was dead." The boy drew his index finger across his throat and made a gurgling noise.

"Why would someone want to kill Denny?" Frost asked.

"No idea."

"So what are you doing on his boat?"

"My father did a job for him," Fox replied. "Now he's missing, and I'm trying to find him. I figured maybe Denny left something behind that would give me a clue about where he is."

"Who's your father?"

The boy said nothing.

"Fox, if your father worked with Denny, I need to talk to him," Frost insisted.

"Why should I trust you?"

"Because I'm here to help. You're not in any trouble. How about you and me sit down and talk?"

Fox shrugged. "Yeah, okay. Whatever."

Frost reached out a hand to the boy's shoulder, but that was a mistake. The next movement happened so quickly and unexpectedly that Frost had no time to react. Fox cartwheeled in place. His leg rocketed through the air, and his shoe crashed heavily into the side of Frost's head. The blow knocked Frost sideways and toppled him over the railing, airborne. A second later, his body splashed into the cold water of the harbor. He sank below the surface and then kicked his way up, coughing and spitting. His head spun as he struggled to stay afloat, and the side of his skull throbbed. His clothes and shoes weighed him down. He swam clumsily around the aft section of the boat and then dragged himself onto the pier. The water gave up his body with a loud sucking sound.

He stood up, drenched from head to toe and freezing. He looked around at the yacht and the pier and saw that he was already alone again.

Fox had vanished.

# 4

"A fourteen-year-old kid dumped you in the water?" Frost's brother, Duane, chuckled to him over the phone. "I'm sorry, bro, but I really wish I'd been there to see that. I'm never going to let you hear the end of it, you know."

"I'm sure you won't be the only one," Frost replied.

He'd draped a towel over the driver's seat of his Suburban, but his wet clothes had soaked through it. Heat blasted through the vents, but the air barely warmed him, and cold drips of harbor water continued to trickle from his hair. He'd been angry at first; then he'd felt like an idiot; now he was finally able to laugh at himself.

It was seven thirty in the morning under a clear blue sky. The Saturday streets were still mostly empty of traffic. He headed south out of the marina, and when he reached the intersection at Lombard, he decided to turn. He was still trying to decipher Denny's message.

"Seriously, are you okay?" Duane asked him.

"Nothing but wounded pride and a splitting headache."

"And the kid?"

"Long gone. I don't know who he is or how to find him."

"Well, when you do find him, run him over to meet the Niners. We could use a kicker like that." Duane laughed again.

Frost heard the metal bang of kitchen pans in the background of the call. Duane was a San Francisco chef who'd sold his brick-and-mortar restaurant several years earlier to open up a food truck in the city's SoMa District. He changed his menus daily to accommodate whatever food was freshest, and the result was long lines of organic-loving twenty-somethings crowding the truck at lunch and dinner. Duane didn't make half the money he once did, but he loved it and didn't seem to mind working eighteen hours a day. Sometimes he slept in his truck rather than make the hike back to his fashionable Marina condo in the middle of the night.

"You should come to dinner tonight," Duane went on. "We haven't seen you in a while. Don't worry, the menu won't be too gourmet for your Oscar Mayer palate."

Frost chuckled. "What are you serving?"

"I'm bringing an Asian-Mediterranean spin to all things Canadian."

"Why Canadian?" Frost asked.

"My new sous chef, Raymonde, is from Montreal, so I figured, what the hell."

"What do they eat in Canada, other than moose?"

Duane snickered. "I'm still working up the menu. We'll have some kind of poutine, I guess. Maybe I'll do a pad thai version. Raymonde's doing smoked meat. It's Canada, so I'll probably have to put a maple glaze on everything. I'm going to see if I can get a Mountie to show up, too. What's Canada without a little Dudley Do-Right?"

"Well, I'll be there if I can," Frost said.

"Perfect. Tabby will be there, too. I want to see her face when you tell her about getting dunked in the harbor by a kid."

"Sure," Frost replied in a flat voice.

He knew there was no way he could avoid seeing Tabby Blaine. She and Duane were almost always together. Even so, she was the most dangerous person in Frost's life. Just the mention of her name conjured the girl in his mind so vividly that she felt close enough to touch. She had lush shoulder-length hair that was mahogany red. She wore her emotions on her face, and her green eyes could go from innocent to wicked to funny to sad like the bay waters changing colors. From the moment he'd met her, they'd connected in a way that was intimate and deep. Talking to her was easy for him in a way that it had never been with any other woman.

That was a big problem because Tabby was Duane's fiancée.

When Frost didn't say anything more on the phone, Duane took that as an invitation to offer extra details about his Canadian menu and the intricacies of some odd pork spread made in Quebec called *cretons*. Meanwhile, Frost watched Lombard Street passing outside his truck. He climbed the hill at Larkin and found himself facing the famous intersection that wriggled down the other side. Apartment buildings stepped down the slope beside the red cobblestones. At this early hour, tourists hadn't mobbed the area yet. He drove across the cable car tracks and down Lombard turn by sharp turn, eight turns in all, past green hedgerows that lined the winding avenue.

When he reached the bottom, he pulled to the curb and craned his neck to look behind him. He shook his head because he hadn't learned a thing. Lombard was famous to outsiders, but it had no special meaning for him. He had no idea what Denny had meant with his message. He drove one more block and turned for home. Driving up and down the peaks of Russian Hill made him feel as if he were in a Steve McQueen movie.

On the phone, Duane was still talking about Canada.

"So, poutine," Frost broke in finally when he couldn't take any more. "That's like French fries with gunk on top, right?"

"Don't let Raymonde hear you say that, but yeah, that's about the size of it. Plus cheese curds, don't forget the cheese curds."

"Well, count me in, eh?"

"Good. We'll see you tonight. Oh, by the way, I heard something on the radio this morning about a murder in Russian Hill. Was that anywhere near you?"

"Inside my front door," Frost replied.

Duane was silent. Then he said, "I'm sorry, *what*?"

"The guy died in my house." Frost waited a beat before adding, "It was Denny."

"Denny Clark?"

"Yeah."

"Were you two talking again?"

"No," Frost said.

"So why was he there? What happened to him?"

"I don't know yet."

"Wow, Denny Clark. That's unbelievable. I'm really sorry, Frost. Are you okay?"

"I'm fine. It's just strange, you know? There was still bad blood between us."

"No kidding."

Frost drove the last hill at Green Street. The yellow police tape still cordoned off the sidewalk, but the squad cars were gone. In the daylight, he could see the dark red of bloodstains running like a thin ribbon from the hillside stairs. Then he looked up at the steps of his house and had to cut off his brother.

"Duane? I have to go. I'll see you tonight if I can."

He didn't wait for Duane to say anything more. He hung up the phone and swung his truck to the curb. Then he got out and ran.

The front door of his house was wide open.

Frost dripped on the white tile as he crept into the foyer. He closed the door silently behind him. His gun was in his hand again. One by one, he checked each room on the lower level. He started at the front of the house in the dining room that doubled as his office, then moved through the kitchen and living room. No one was downstairs. The blanket on the sofa was still crumpled where he'd thrown it off as Denny rang the doorbell in the middle of the night. The glass door leading out to the patio was securely locked. Nothing looked disturbed.

Then his eyes shot to the ceiling as the timbers of the old house groaned over his head. Someone was upstairs.

The hinges of the master bedroom door squealed as the intruder pushed it open. Frost could have told whoever it was that they were making a mistake. He waited. It didn't take long. Above him, he heard the unmistakable hiss of an angry cat and a throaty growl that meant Shack was on the hunt. Someone howled in pain, and footsteps thundered in retreat from the bedroom. A man practically threw himself down the stairs to get away from Shack, and Frost launched across the floor, colliding with the man's shoulder and knocking him to the carpet. He stood over him, his gun pointed at the man's face, which bled in thin stripes from a swipe of the cat's claws. The short, plump man threw his hands above his head in surrender.

"Who the hell are you?" Frost demanded.

The man winced at the stinging wounds on his face. "Holy crap, is that some kind of tiger you've got up there? You should have a warning on your door. That thing could have killed me."

Shack took that opportunity to hop happily down the stairs. He climbed up Frost's soaking-wet jeans and planted himself calmly on Frost's shoulder and began licking his face to welcome him home. The tuxedo cat was full grown but unusually small, barely a foot from nose to tail; he had a black stomach with a single white stripe and white cheeks with a black chin. His tail was short, and he had stubby little ears.

"Meet the tiger," Frost said. "Now, who are you?"

"My name's Coyle. Dick Coyle."

"Do you have ID?"

"Sure I do. Look, I'll tell you anything you want to know, but could you stop pointing that gun at me? I'm not armed. And I'm not a thief."

"Then why'd you break into my house, Coyle?"

"Hey, I'm sorry about that. It was stupid, I know. I rang the bell, but you weren't home. Sometimes I can't resist showing off my lockpick skills. I figured I'd be in and out before you were back."

"And why exactly do you know how to pick locks?" Frost asked.

"I'm a private detective," the man replied.

Frost groaned loudly as he holstered his weapon. If there was one thing he had no time for, it was private detectives. They all thought they were Sam Spade living in 1920s San Francisco. Frost stretched out a hand and helped Coyle back to his feet. The man eyed Shack nervously but didn't protest as Frost steered him to the dining room and dropped him down in one of the wooden chairs.

"ID," Frost repeated.

Coyle pushed his wallet across the table. His driver's license showed that he was twenty-six years old with an address in an industrial section of town. Coyle's dark hair was already thinning, and he had it greased over his head with a part on the side. He had skimpy stubble pretending to be a beard and deer-in-the-headlights brown eyes. His face was full, round, and flushed, and Shack had made sharp cuts down the side of his forehead. He wore a chocolate-colored mock turtleneck and khakis, both in extra-large sizes to accommodate his heavy frame.

Frost went into the kitchen and dampened a towel in the sink. He returned to the dining room and handed it to the detective, who dabbed it gingerly against the wounds on his head.

"Okay, Coyle, tell me why I shouldn't arrest you," Frost said.

"Because we're both doing the same thing. Investigating a murder."

Frost shook his head. Another Sam Spade. "Whose murder?"

"Denny Clark."

"How do you know Denny? Was he a client of yours or something?"

"No, I never met him."

"Then why are you so interested in his murder?" Frost asked.

Coyle pursed his thick pale lips and shot covert glances in both directions. He leaned across the table. "Is this room secure?"

"What?"

"Do I need to worry about bugs?"

Frost was ready to laugh, but then he thought about Denny Clark being killed with the kind of poison that was usually reserved for spies. And about hidden cameras on a multimillion-dollar yacht. And about Captain Hayden showing up at the crime scene in the middle of the night. He decided to indulge the detective's paranoia. He synched his phone to the Bose speakers in the dining room and played Bastille's "Pompeii" at a loud volume.

Frost crooked a finger at Coyle and spoke softly with the music thumping in the background. "Talk."

Coyle used a conspiratorial whisper. "This murder isn't what you think."

"Then what is it?"

"There's a serial killer working in the city," Coyle told Frost. "He's been at it for years, but nobody knows about him except me. He's the one who murdered Denny Clark, and I can prove it."

# 5

Frost needed to get out of his wet clothes. He didn't think that Coyle was going to run, but he wasn't going to take any chances. He handcuffed the private investigator to the iron railing on the patio while he went upstairs to take a shower. When he'd changed, he returned to the patio and released him.

"So is it safe to talk outside?" Frost asked with a sarcastic smile. "No bugs?"

Coyle rubbed the kinks out of his wrist where the cuff had pinched his skin. "I guess it's okay."

"Then tell me what you were looking for inside my house."

It wasn't entirely accurate to call it his house. The house actually belonged to Shack, which made it one of the odder living arrangements in the city. Frost had adopted the cat from an older woman who'd been killed in the upstairs bedroom, and her will had made the house available nearly rent-free to whoever agreed to keep Shack there. So Frost now had a home in an exclusive neighborhood that wasn't really his home at all.

"You won't believe me when I tell you," Coyle replied.

"Try me."

"A snake," Coyle said.

"A snake? Why would you expect to find a snake in the house? And what does this have to do with a serial killer?"

"It's not a real snake. It's a *painting* of a snake. It's not large, maybe a foot by a foot, and it's always done in red spray paint. Wherever this killer strikes, he leaves the same kind of snake painting near the crime scene. It's like his calling card. So far, I'm the only one who's figured it out."

Frost had no time for conspiracy theories. "That sounds pretty crazy, Coyle."

"I know it does. I didn't believe it at first, either."

"How many of these snakes have you found?"

"Eleven," Coyle replied.

*"Eleven?"* Frost exclaimed, unable to hide his surprise.

"That's right. Eleven victims, eleven snakes."

Frost rubbed his beard and studied the earnest naivete on Coyle's face. The detective still sounded crazy, but the number eleven had Frost's attention. "Well, do you have any idea who this so-called serial killer is?"

"No. Some killers like the chase, but not this one. He's smart. He doesn't brag to the cops or the media about what he's doing. I haven't identified any pattern in how he picks his victims. The only thing each murder has in common is the snake he leaves behind."

Frost wandered to the edge of the patio, which looked north toward the city and the bay. A few early morning sailboats dotted the blue water. "Did you find a snake painting inside my house?"

"No, but your cat interrupted me before I was done searching," Coyle said, grimacing as he pressed the towel to the cuts on the side of his forehead. "Look, give me fifteen minutes. We can go over the whole place together. If we don't find anything, fine, I was wrong. But I don't think I am. Denny Clark is the latest victim of this killer. If he was murdered here, there's a snake close by."

"Denny wasn't murdered inside the house," Frost told him.

Coyle's brown eyes widened. "The call on the police band made it sound like he was."

"He died here, but the assault took place somewhere else."

"That means I was searching in the wrong place!" Coyle said.

"And by 'searching,' you mean breaking and entering, right?"

The private detective blanched. "Look, Inspector, I'm sorry. I got carried away. Can we let bygones be bygones? Please?"

"That depends."

"On what?"

"Find me a snake," Frost said. "Get me some proof that any of this is real."

Coyle's head bobbed with enthusiasm. He headed back into the house practically at a run. Below his khakis, he wore neon-yellow sneakers. As heavy as he was, Coyle was surprisingly light on his feet. Frost followed the detective out the front door with an apology to Shack for leaving him behind. At Green Street, Coyle spun in a circle and pointed in different directions.

"Do you know where Clark came from?"

"Up the stairs from Taylor," Frost replied.

Coyle charged downhill with one hand clutching the iron railing. Dense trees filled the slope with shadows, and the hillside was a sea of mud and dead leaves. Apartment buildings with stucco walls were terraced on the north side of the steps. Coyle stopped to peer through the foliage at every exposed section of stucco wall beyond the greenery.

There was no sign of a red snake.

At the base of the hill, Coyle broke from the trees onto Taylor Street and put his hands on his hips as he examined the buildings around them. When he found nothing, he huffed and puffed to the summit of the next hill, where a sweeping view opened up on the eastern section of the city. The day was perfect, and wind streaked across the hilltop. Coyle again made a point of checking every wall and sidewalk for snakes.

Frost glanced at his watch. Half an hour had already passed, and he was growing impatient with the detective's quest.

"Come on, Coyle, we're done here," Frost said.

Coyle wiped sweat from his forehead and upper lip. He pushed down his hair as the wind flew it like a flag. He took a few steps down the hillside that led through Coolbrith Park. "Ten more minutes. Please."

"We don't even know that Denny came up through the park."

"That's okay. Look, you can go home if you want. I'll come back if I find anything."

Coyle lumbered into the park alone with a determined gait. Frost heaved a sigh and headed after him. The brick stairs went almost straight down, with the bay water and rolling San Francisco hills spread out under the sky. There were no buildings here, just landscaped trees, scrub brush, and spring flowers. The steps ended at the base of the park, and two parallel staircases continued on either side of the thick woodland. Coyle, who had a head start, took the steps on the left. When Frost eventually caught up with him, the detective was resting on a low concrete wall at the dead end of Vallejo. His round face looked glum, and his arms hung limply at his sides. He was breathing heavily at the distance they'd traveled.

"Nothing?" Frost guessed.

"I guess I was wrong. I don't understand it."

"Why were you so sure that Denny was a victim of this killer?"

Coyle unhooked his phone from a holster on his belt. He thumbed his way through several pictures and then showed one to Frost. The photograph had been taken aboard the *Roughing It*, and it showed Denny Clark standing between an attractive thirty-something blond woman and a tall, older man in a tan suit. The man's face looked familiar, but Frost couldn't place him.

"This guy next to Denny," Frost said. "Who is he?"

"His name's Greg Howell. He was a big real estate developer."

Frost remembered now. "Okay, sure. Howell died a few months ago."

"That's right. Howell was the last snake victim. Until Denny Clark."

"Howell had a heart attack while he was jogging in Golden Gate Park," Frost pointed out. "He wasn't murdered."

"Well, that's the story, but I don't believe it. I found a red snake on the trail just fifty yards from where his body was found. His death was made to *look* like a heart attack, but I'm telling you, he was killed."

Frost was having a hard time deciding whether Coyle was serious or whether he belonged on the other side of Area 51 with his nose pressed against the fence. "And you've really found eleven of these snakes?"

"Right. Each one was within a stone's throw of some unusual death. I did my research. I talked to neighbors. I found online photos. As far as I can tell, the snake paintings all showed up right after the person died."

"Have you found anything that ties the victims together?"

"Not until now. When I was looking into Greg Howell's death, I found this photo on Facebook, and I identified Denny Clark through the boat. When I heard the police report about his murder, I didn't think it could be a coincidence. I figured, maybe this case would finally give me a clue about who the killer is and how he picks his victims."

Frost took a look at the photograph again. "Who's the blond woman with Denny and Howell?"

"I don't know. I was never able to identify her."

Frost handed the phone back to Coyle. "The snake thing is weird, I'll give you that, but this is San Francisco, Coyle. Nobody ever had to start a campaign to Keep San Francisco Weird."

"At least look into it," Coyle urged him. "Please."

"Right now, my priority is Denny Clark. If I have time, I'll see what I can find about the other victims on your list. I'll keep an eye out for connections to my case. That's all I can promise."

"Thank you, Inspector."

"I have to head home," Frost said. "You coming with me?"

Coyle looked over his shoulder at the steep hill. "I need to rest before tackling that monster again."

"Okay. See you, Coyle. And stay out of other people's houses from now on."

Frost got up and made his way to the stairs that led into the park. Without thinking about it, he headed for the opposite set of steps from the one they'd taken down. The street around him was a mess of cigarette butts, and the mortar in the low retaining wall was pockmarked, as if it had been used for target practice. As he turned the corner, he glanced toward his feet. Then he froze.

He called to Coyle. "Hey, you better get over here."

Frost squatted in front of the wall, studying the bright-red painting he'd found there. He drew a finger across the graffiti. The paint was dry but looked fresh.

It was a snake.

The head was enlarged, with empty spaces to mark its slitted eyes and a forked tongue spitting sideways from wide-open jaws. The braided body twisted and turned all the way to its tail, which ended in the coils of a rattle. The blood-red snake glared at him like a warning. It looked like a harbinger of death.

But Frost realized it looked like something else, too.

The ripples of the snake's body wound back and forth through a series of sharp turns. He counted exactly eight turns from head to tail.

Just like the hill at Lombard Street.

# 6

Frost and Coyle sat in his Suburban near a softball field in Potrero Hill, which was a finger-shaped neighborhood on the east side of the city, nestled between the 101 and 280 freeways. They both ate hot dogs that they'd purchased near the Ferry Building.

"I found the first snake right here three years ago," Coyle told him, licking mustard from his finger. "It was one of my first cases as a PI. The usual thing, wife thought her husband was cheating and wanted to catch him in the act. I'd been following the guy for a couple of weeks. He was a vice cop, so you might remember him. Alan Detlowe."

"I remember the name," Frost said. "He was killed."

Coyle chewed his hot dog and then kept talking. "Exactly. It happened while I was doing my surveillance. The funny thing is, I'm not even sure Detlowe was cheating. If he was, I never nailed him at it. I remember spotting him with this Indian girl at a Peruvian restaurant in Pacific Heights. Weak-in-the-knees gorgeous. I thought, *Gotcha.* But all he did was listen while she talked to him and then buy her dinner and kiss her on the head. It didn't look like anything was going on between them."

"So what happened?"

"Come on, I'll show you."

Coyle got out of the truck, and Frost followed. The grass of the softball field was freshly mowed in diagonal rows. They were near a recreational center with a half-cylinder roof. The downtown skyline was visible to the north.

"Detlowe was part of a Tuesday-night softball league," Coyle said. "I watched him play ball for a couple of hours. I had to go to the bathroom, so I dashed inside the rec center. Let's just say it was one of those visits that took longer than I was expecting. When I came back outside, the game was over, and I didn't see Alan among the guys who were hanging out in the field. But his car was still there. I wandered over and took a look inside, and there he was in the front seat. Dead. Blood everywhere. Somebody cut his throat and did a really thorough job. It couldn't have happened more than five minutes earlier."

Coyle started walking toward the rec center. He led Frost up a driveway that bordered a stand of trees. "I heard somebody over here in the woods. I figured it was probably the killer getting away. I hustled this way as fast as I could, but the guy was already gone. That's when I found this."

He pointed at a concrete wall that bordered the driveway.

Frost saw another red snake spray-painted in a discreet section of the wall that faced the woods. The paint had chipped and faded after three years of rain and elements, but it was otherwise identical to the snake he'd found on Vallejo.

"The paint was still wet," Coyle said. "I figured it had to be connected to Detlowe's murder somehow, but I didn't know what it meant. So I asked around the city to see if anyone had seen a snake like that before. I figured maybe it was a gang symbol, but I never traced it to any of the usual suspects. Eventually, somebody told me they'd seen a snake like that over in Alta Plaza Park. I went over there to search, and I found another snake near the steps on Clay Street."

Coyle showed Frost a new photo on his phone. It was the same snake and a different location, but Frost didn't need Coyle to tell him its significance. He remembered the case.

"There was an Episcopal priest shot in a church near there," Frost said.

"Exactly," Coyle replied. "I could stand where the snake was and look right into the church windows. That's when I started getting curious. It became a hobby for me. Whenever I had free time, I began looking for snakes, and over the next six months, I found five more. Balboa Park. The Presidio. Glen Canyon. McLaren Park. Even a bathroom stall inside Westfield Centre. All of them were near where bodies had recently been found. Mostly homicides, but also one OD. I'm convinced that one was a murder, too."

Frost flipped through the photos on Coyle's phone. He saw more snakes and more crime scenes. Some he recognized, some he didn't.

"Did you talk to the police about this?" he asked.

"Yeah, I talked to the inspector who was working on Alan Detlowe's murder. Guy named Trent Gorham. Do you know him?"

"I do," Frost said. "He used to be in vice, too."

"Well, Detlowe's wife sent Gorham to me so he could look at my surveillance notes. I told him about the snake thing. He wasn't impressed. To him, it sounded like a wild conspiracy. He told me to leave the police work to the police. He even suggested that I was leaving the snake paintings behind myself, like I was trying to get publicity for my detective agency." Coyle eyed Frost curiously. "I'm sort of surprised you didn't say the same thing."

"Oh, I thought about it," Frost told him. He pointed at the detective's hands. "No red paint under your fingernails."

"Well, you can check my car, too, and pull my PI license if you want. Do your homework on me. I'm not making any of this up."

"I know that. So what happened after Trent Gorham blew you off?"

Coyle finished his hot dog. He had an inch of bun left, which he pulled into pieces and tossed onto the lawn for the birds. "I've been on the case ever since. I tracked down a couple more snakes, but the cases were too cold to find anything useful. So I decided to go at it another way."

"How so?"

"Whenever there was an unusual death in the city, I went to check it out to see if I could find a snake. I figured the sooner I knew which ones were victims of my killer, the better chance I had of nailing him. That's how I found Greg Howell. I heard about his body turning up in the park, and I went over there right away. The park police told me it was a heart attack, so I thought it would turn out to be a dead end, but then I found another snake. That's how I knew Howell had been murdered. So I started digging into his life to see if I could explain how and why the killer chose him."

"Did you find anything?" Frost asked.

Coyle danced on his yellow sneakers. He looked uncomfortable standing on his feet for too long. "No. Howell was a big fish. He had his fingers in city projects everywhere. There were too many ways a killer might have zeroed in on him. But that Facebook photo of Howell on Denny Clark's boat has to be important. It's the first time I've found a direct link between two of the snake victims."

Frost leaned against the wall and made sure that no one was nearby. "I'm curious whether you came across a name in any of your research."

"What name is that?" Coyle asked.

"Lombard."

"Like the street? No, it never came up. Why?"

"Well, what does that snake remind you of?"

Coyle bent down in front of the small painting with a notable *oof* from his mouth. He cocked his head as he studied it, and his brown eyes widened in recognition. "Wow, you're right. It looks just like the crookedest street. I never noticed that before. What do you think it means?"

"I don't know," Frost admitted.

Coyle's knees popped as he straightened up. "You sound like you believe me about this."

"I think it's unusual enough to be worth a look," Frost said.

Relief flooded in a flush across Coyle's face. "I've waited a long time to hear a cop say that."

"Well, don't get carried away. It may still prove to be nothing. In the meantime, send me whatever you've got. Victims, photos, anything that I can use to try to figure out why Denny Clark died."

Coyle's lips bent into a grin. "Yeah. Okay."

Frost headed back toward his Suburban, but Coyle stopped him with a hand on his sleeve.

"One thing, Inspector," Coyle said, his face serious again. "You probably think I'm paranoid, but I'm pretty sure I've been followed a few times. I think the only thing keeping me safe is the fact that nobody's been listening to me. Thanks to you, that's changed. If I'm right about this, we should both probably be careful from now on."

# 7

Frost arrived at police headquarters to find Captain Hayden's aide, Cyril Timko, waiting for him outside. The newly constructed headquarters building was located in the Mission Bay neighborhood, close enough to the Giants stadium to hear the shout of the crowds. But it was March, and the team was still basking in the Scottsdale sun for spring training.

Cyril had two takeaway cups of coffee in his hands. He handed one to Frost with a smile that was more like a glare. His face had a skeletal look that showed off his cheekbones and jaw.

"I heard you were coming in, Inspector," Cyril said. "I thought it would be easier for us to talk outside."

"Any particular reason?"

Cyril shrugged. "You know how it is. Cops are a nosy bunch."

Frost tasted the coffee, which was as black as road tar and hot enough to scorch his lips. Some men showed off their testosterone with the grip of their handshake, and others with their Sumatran dark roast.

"Good coffee," Frost told him casually.

They strolled along China Basin past upscale condominiums mostly inhabited by the coders of Silicon Valley. Beyond the residential buildings, he saw the construction site for the headquarters of a Chicago tech company that the mayor had spent two years and millions of tax dollars luring to the city. So much bandwidth hummed through this neighborhood that Frost was surprised the buildings didn't glow.

Cyril, in his uniform, walked with his back as rigid and straight as a pencil. "Any news for the captain?"

Frost choked down another swig of coffee. "I searched Denny's boat, but someone got there before me. There wasn't much left to find."

"Oh?"

"His computer was missing, and I didn't find any paper files. I'm getting copies of his phone and bank statements sent to me, so that may tell us more about who he's been dealing with."

"What about drugs?" Cyril asked. "The captain thought this smelled like a drug hit. Did you find any evidence to back that up?"

"I found a brick of cocaine in Denny's desk," Frost acknowledged.

"Well, that tells us a lot."

"Maybe."

Cyril stopped at the street corner across from the building project, where two cranes swung I beams fourteen stories in the air. The smaller cop's dark eyes studied the work with fascination. "You don't think so? Why not?"

"If someone beat me to the boat, they would have found the cocaine and grabbed it. They didn't. That makes me wonder if they left it behind deliberately to send us down the wrong road."

Cyril rubbed his nose with his fist. "Did you find anything else?"

"I met a Chinese boy who sneaked onto the boat. Probably about fourteen years old. He said his father worked with Denny but was missing."

"Who was this boy?"

"He told me his name was Fox, but that's all. It's probably a nickname. I haven't been able to find anything more about him or his father. But if his father is missing, I'd like to know if there's a connection to Denny's death."

"Do you want help? I can look into the boy myself and see what I can find out."

"Thanks for the offer, but I'm sure the captain keeps you plenty busy."

"He does, but he also said to put myself at your disposal."

"I'll let you know."

Cyril nodded. "So? Is that all?"

Frost thought about Dick Coyle and his snakes. And about Lombard. "That's all for now," he said.

Cyril sipped his coffee. The boom of the construction project rumbled under the sidewalk like an earthquake. "The captain tells me you knew Clark," he said finally. "You two were friends?"

"Years ago."

"Are you too personally involved with the victim? Maybe someone else should handle the investigation."

"I hadn't spoken to Denny Clark in a decade," Frost replied. "There's no conflict."

Cyril nodded. His fingers twitched, and he put down his coffee on the sidewalk and grabbed his e-cigarette from a pocket. The first inhalation of vapor made his whole body relax. "Keep me posted, Inspector. I'll relay everything directly to the captain. This one is very important to him."

"I'd like to know why the captain is so interested in this case," Frost told him.

"He'll tell you himself at the right time," Cyril replied. "In the meantime, don't make any significant moves without talking to me first. And keep this arrangement between us, okay?"

Frost had the feeling that he'd been dismissed by the younger cop. The interrogation was over. He finished his coffee and turned around and headed back down China Basin toward headquarters. Behind him, Cyril didn't move. When he'd gone half a block, Frost glanced over his shoulder and saw the captain's aide still sucking on his vapor cigarette and watching the pieces of the skyscraper come together.

At his desk in the Mission Bay headquarters building, Frost took a close look at the two people who were with Denny Clark in the photo that Coyle had found on Facebook.

The first was Greg Howell, dead millionaire, whose real estate holdings and development projects had made him one of the prime beneficiaries of San Francisco's gentrification over the past decade. The second was a woman with sandy-blond hair who wore a loose-fitting gray sweatshirt and black capris hugging her slim legs. Frost wanted to know who she was.

Her sunglasses covered up much of her face, but what he could see was attractive. He'd originally guessed that she was in her thirties, but when he enlarged the photo to study her skin tone, he suspected that he'd underestimated by a few years. Although her clothes and glasses tried to hide her age, she was probably on the north side of forty. Her red lips were pressed together in a thin, enigmatic line that was neither smile nor frown. Her hair was straight and long enough to wrap around her neck as the wind blew. Each of the men had an arm around her shoulders, but she didn't return the gesture. Her arms hung stiffly at her sides. Her body had a tenseness that said she wasn't happy to be photographed.

Frost studied the picture for clues about the event. Greg Howell had a lowball cocktail in his other hand, which suggested some kind of party cruise, but most of Denny's charters probably fell into that category. The *Roughing It* was out on the bay, because he could see the crown of Mount Tamalpais in the background. The deepening blue of twilight and the lengthy shadows told him it was a late-summer evening. Coyle had found the photo posted on Howell's Facebook page in early August.

The caption on the post was strange: *If I'm lost at sea, here's proof of life.*

Frost called up newspaper reports about Greg Howell and found a lot. Coyle was right. The man had his fingers in everything around the city. He breezed through the *Chronicle* headlines from the summer and fall:

Howell Pitches Controversial Affordable Housing Project

Will Greg Howell Bring America's Cup Back to San Francisco?

Eminent Domain Dispute Pits Mayor Against Howell over Zelyx Deal

Local Real Estate Pro Leads Tsunami Relief Fundraising

City Council Rejects Howell Redevelopment Plan in Dogpatch

And then in October:

Greg Howell, Prominent Developer and Philanthropist, Found Dead

Frost read the article. Howell's body was found near North Lake in a wooded section of Golden Gate Park. He'd been out on an early morning run, and another jogger had found him facedown on the trail at six o'clock. The autopsy gave no indication of foul play, and as a result, there had been no criminal investigation by the police.

There was nothing odd about Howell's death that Frost could see. Except a red snake. When he looked at the photo Coyle had taken of the snake spray-painted onto a boulder in the park, he could see North Lake through the trees and the exact section of the jogging trail where Howell had been found.

Coyle had texted him other snake photos that he'd found around the city. Frost clicked on each picture, and one by one by one they filled his screen, until his monitor was crowded with eleven snakes. Twelve, when he added the snake he'd found himself in Coolbrith Park. All were identical, all blood red, hissing at him from behind empty eyes and taunting him with their secret.

Seven of the deaths that Coyle had identified near the graffiti snakes were homicides. Frost called up the police reports for each case, looking for details that would connect the victims to each other or to Denny. Nothing leaped out at him. The locations were all over the city. The cause of death varied. Two shootings. Two knifings. One bludgeoning. One hit-and-run. One suffocation. None involved poison, as Denny's murder had. The victims ranged in age and occupation.

All remained unsolved.

Frost spent two hours examining the case files until the words and photos began to blur on the screen. There was no pattern, nothing to suggest that one murder had anything to do with another. They looked like the kind of random violent acts that happened dozens of times in the city in any given year.

And then, finally, he saw it.

He'd been so focused on the minutiae that he almost missed an obvious coincidence staring him in the face. The cases were all completely different, but not the homicide inspector investigating them. After the Alan Detlowe case, the primary detective on every one of the subsequent homicides was the same.

Trent Gorham.

Gorham, who'd written off Coyle's snake obsession as a crazy conspiracy.

Frost reached over to his monitor and clicked off the screen so that it went black. He eased back in his chair. A strange sensation of unease pricked up the hair on his neck. Casually, he looked across the warren of messy desks crowded together for the police detectives.

Trent Gorham sat halfway across the room.

And Gorham was staring right at him.

When Frost caught his eye, Gorham stood up from his desk. He stretched the kinks out of his back, then strolled across the office and slumped into a chair next to Frost. The detective wore cream-colored dress pants that emphasized his long legs, black leather shoes, and a burgundy knit sweater. He made a show of idly twirling a pen in his big hands, as if coming over here were no big deal, even though Frost couldn't remember the last time the two of them had talked.

"How's it going, Easton?" Gorham asked him.

"Just another day in paradise," Frost replied.

"Yeah. I hear you." Gorham tapped the clicky top of his pen against his jutting jaw. "That's really crazy about the guy who dropped dead in your house. Everybody around here is talking about it."

"Oh? Are they?"

"Well, it doesn't happen every day, right?"

"I guess not," Frost said.

"You got all the help you need?" Gorham asked. "My desk's not too busy right now. I could lend a hand."

Frost had never felt so popular. First Cyril Timko, now Trent Gorham.

"I'll let you know," he said.

He took a sip of coffee and used the interruption to study Gorham. They were about the same age. Gorham was a large man, almost six foot three, with the powerful build of an athlete. He had blond hair that sprouted from his head like a bristle brush and eyebrows so pale they were nearly translucent. His skin was white, with pink traces of rosacea on his forehead and cheeks, and his eyes were a washed-out shade of blue. His nose was slightly too large for his face, but his overall appearance was handsome. He wore a gullible expression on his face, as if he wanted the world to think he was a dumb jock, but Frost didn't think Gorham was dumb at all.

He decided to poke the hive and see what flew out.

"I could use your help with one thing," Frost added. "I don't know if it means anything."

"Sure, what's that?"

Frost zoomed in on the photograph he'd taken of the red snake near Coolbrith Park. He turned his phone around. "Have you ever seen graffiti like this at a crime scene? I found it not far from where the victim was shot."

He watched Gorham's eyes. The man was cool, and his expression didn't change at all. "Let me guess. Dick Coyle's been talking to you?"

"You're right. He has."

"The Red Snake Serial Killer strikes again?" Gorham asked with a sarcastic twitch of his pale eyebrows.

"Something like that."

Gorham chuckled and shook his head. "That guy never gives up."

"He told me about several other homicides where he found a snake like this," Frost said. Then he added after a pause, "Mostly your cases, I think."

Gorham shrugged. "Lucky me. I guess I catch all the freaky ones."

"You don't think it's a weird coincidence? All these snakes showing up near the bodies?"

"Come on, Easton. Really? This thing should have its own Snopes page. Yeah, it started with a couple unrelated homicides, but then Coyle had to start counting ODs and heart attacks to keep it going. It's crap."

"You're probably right," Frost said.

"You bet I am. Frankly, this whole snake thing pisses me off. Alan Detlowe was a friend of mine. We worked together when I was in vice. Him getting murdered was personal to me. This had nothing to do with a serial killer. It was a drug scumbag getting back at Alan for his busts. I don't appreciate Coyle turning his death into some kind of kooky Internet meme."

"Did you ever track down the origin of the graffiti?" Frost asked.

"I didn't bother. I'm sure you'll find it all over the city. It's probably the logo for some underground band. Or a Japanese anime character. Who knows?"

Frost smiled. "Well, thanks for setting me straight. You saved me some time."

"Happy to do it. No point chasing a dead end, right?" Gorham stood up from the chair. "Seriously, if you need any help on this case, count me in."

"I will."

"And watch out for Coyle. He's nuts, man."

Frost didn't say anything more. He waited as the other detective headed back to his desk, and then he turned on his monitor again.

Twelve red snakes stared back at him.

At the same moment, he felt a vibrating buzz on his phone. He retrieved it and saw that he had a new text message and a photograph waiting for him.

It was from Coyle.

Just found another snake.

Across the bay in Berkeley this time.

That's lucky #13.

Frost studied the photograph that came with the text and saw a red snake spray-painted onto the sidewalk in front of a bridge that led into a wooded community park. The paint looked vivid and fresh. This was new, not old.

Thirteen snakes.

He knew that meant thirteen bodies. Somewhere close by was another victim.

Frost didn't have any of the answers to this puzzle yet, but he didn't think the young private detective was nuts.

# 8

When Frost got home, he found another visitor in his house on Russian Hill, but this time it was someone he knew well. His friend Herb sat in a lotus position in the middle of the living room floor, with Shack curled up asleep in his lap. Nature sounds played from Frost's Echo device, as if he'd wandered into the middle of a tropical rainforest. The patio door was cracked open, but the cold fresh air wasn't enough to erase the aroma of pot that followed Herb wherever he went.

Frost and Herb were an odd couple as friends. At seventy years old, Herb was twice Frost's age, although he had the stamina of someone decades younger. It had been a long time since the era of flower power, but anyone looking at Herb would think the 1960s had never ended. He had long gray hair parted in the middle, with dozens of rainbow beads tied into the strands. He was taller than Frost by an inch but bony and scrawny, with a noticeable limp. He had a long, narrow face and was never without Clark Kent black glasses.

Herb had lived multiple lives in San Francisco over the years. He'd started his career as a biologist, then as a city council member, and most recently as a sidewalk painter who'd become a city tourist attraction in his own right. Most days, he wore paint-smudged overalls and flannel shirts, but today, as he meditated, he wore a flowing robe that he could have heisted from the road show of *Joseph and the Amazing Technicolor Dreamcoat.*

"Sorry to let myself in," Herb told him without opening his eyes. "I needed a quiet space, and the gallery was a madhouse today."

Frost slid to the floor, stretched out his legs, and leaned back against the sofa. "No problem. I'm getting used to people showing up unannounced around here. At least you're not dropping dead or looking for snakes."

This time, Herb opened one eye. "Snakes?"

"I'll tell you later."

Frost patted the carpet beside him, and Shack opened one bleary eye, too. The cat weighed the comfort of his current spot against the obligation to say hello to Frost, and he got up with a slight meow of annoyance and wandered over to stake out his usual place on Frost's shoulder. His purring was like the loud rumble of a sports car's engine.

Herb untangled himself from his yoga position with a crack of his knees. He stood up, squeezed his hip with a small grimace, and went to the kitchen, where he helped himself to a Sierra Nevada ale. He waved a second bottle in Frost's direction with a silent question.

"Definitely," Frost replied.

Herb brought two bottles to the living room and sank down onto the floor next to Frost. They drank their beers and sat in silence for several minutes. Neither one of them felt the need to fill empty spaces with small talk.

"So, Denny Clark," Herb said finally. "That was a surprise."

"It sure was."

"He showed up completely out of the blue?"

"Completely."

"I was never much of a fan of Mr. Clark," Herb admitted.

"I know."

"Still, it's a tragedy. I'm sorry."

"I am, too," Frost agreed. "I don't like unfinished business. I always assumed that one day Denny and I would find a way to put the past behind us. We didn't leave things on good terms."

"That was hardly your fault," Herb pointed out.

Frost shrugged. Herb was right, but it didn't change anything.

He'd known Herb since his college days at SF State, and Herb had been his friend throughout the beginning, middle, and end of his relationship with Denny and Carla. Frost didn't open up to others easily, but he shared everything with Herb. The only other person in his life with whom he'd been that honest was his sister, Katie. After Katie was killed, he'd been lucky to have Herb as a confidant.

"Do you know what happened to Denny?" Herb went on.

"Not yet," Frost said. "All I know is that this case keeps getting stranger and stranger."

"Including snakes?"

"Including snakes." Frost took out his phone and showed Herb the picture of the graffiti near Coolbrith Park. "Have you ever seen something like this around town?"

Herb squinted through his black glasses. "I don't think so."

"Could you put out the word to your network?" Frost asked. "If someone has seen a snake like this, I'd like to know about it."

"Of course."

Among his many activities in the city, Herb had launched a program to put smartphones in the hands of the homeless to give them a link to jobs and shelters. It had grown into an online network with the nickname Street Twitter, and when Frost needed information, it was the fastest community of spies in San Francisco. The people on the street trusted Herb.

"Can you tell me what this is all about?" Herb asked.

"I met a private detective named Dick Coyle. He has this theory that a serial killer has been at work in the city for years, and no one has figured it out. The snakes are this guy's talisman. When he kills somebody, he leaves a snake behind. Coyle just found another snake in Berkeley this afternoon."

Herb's eyebrows rose. "That sounds like a rather wild idea. Do you believe him?"

"Normally, I wouldn't, but Denny gave me a message before he died that makes me think Coyle isn't crazy. It was the only thing he said to me. Just one word. *Lombard.*"

Herb studied the photo of the snake again and spotted the significance immediately. "I see what you mean. The resemblance to the street can't be an accident."

"No."

"All right, I'll see if the name Lombard rings any bells with my network, too," Herb said with a slight frown on his face, as if something had flitted in and out of his memory. He paused and then added, "It's hard to believe this could be happening without the police having some knowledge of it."

Frost took a swallow of Torpedo ale. "You're right. That is hard to believe. What bothers me is that I have the sense there are people at headquarters who already know all about this. And they're not saying anything."

Herb smoothed his colorful robe. "Well, you know I love your mysteries, Frost. Anyway, thank you for the meditation space and the feline assistance. I'm having dinner at Cha Cha Cha with some of the students at the gallery. Do you want to join me?"

"I would if I could," Frost said, "but Duane asked me to come to the food truck tonight."

Herb gave him a pointed stare. "And?"

"And yes, Tabby will be there, too."

Herb shook his head. He was the only one who knew the truth about Frost's feelings for Tabby. "I'm trying to think of a way this ends well, Frost, but I can't see it."

"Neither can I."

"You know I love you, my friend, but you're going to have to find a way to get past your feelings for this girl. Or else the situation is going to explode for all of you."

"I know that."

Frost had been telling himself the same thing for months, but he'd found no answers.

Herb pushed himself to his feet, and Frost did the same. Outside, through the bay window, it was almost dark. The city lights were coming on down the hillside. Shack spotted a white moth that had crept in through the open door, and he galloped to the glass to bat at it.

"I'll keep you posted on my herpetological research," Herb said. "If there are snakes to be found in the city, I'll locate them."

"Thanks. Oh, I have one other question, too." Frost took his phone and called up the photo of Denny Clark and Greg Howell on the *Roughing It*, with the mystery blond woman between them. "Have you ever seen this woman before? Do you know who she is?"

Herb shoved his glasses to the end of his nose and bent closer to the phone screen. "Ah, you're playing in the big leagues with this one, Frost."

"You know her?" he asked.

"Oh yes. She runs her own public relations company. It's really more like an executive matchmaker service. When one powerful person needs to connect with another, she's the intermediary who makes it happen."

Frost tapped the photo. "Powerful people like Greg Howell?"

"Definitely."

"What's her name?" Frost asked.

"Belinda Drake."

"How do I find her?"

Herb shook his head. "That's a problem. Typically, you don't find her. If you have something she needs, she finds you."

"Has she ever found *you* for anything?" Frost asked.

"Once, yes. It was when my three-dimensional paintings were starting to make the news. She arranged to fly me on a private jet to an estate somewhere in the South Pacific. I have no idea exactly where or whose estate it was. My job was to paint a mural, and I did. I spent two weeks there, alone, with no one else around except a butler and a cook. When I was done, I was flown home. And the commission is what enabled me to buy my gallery in the Haight. It was very lucrative."

"I can't believe you never told me about this," Frost said.

"I was under a nondisclosure agreement, which is actually still in force. We should keep this discussion between us."

"I still need to talk to her," Frost said.

Herb nodded. "I'll make a couple of calls. I'll put the word out that you want to talk to Ms. Drake. After that, it's up to her. But be careful, Frost. If you're looking for poisonous snakes, there's no better place to start than the world of public relations."

# 9

The gathering of food trucks in the SoMa street park on Saturday night always turned into a party. Bluegrass music twanged from the stage. The aromas in the air mixed into a multiethnic blend of Tex-Mex, sweet Asian, Caribbean jerk spices, and wood-fired pizza. Hundreds of city dwellers crowded together for date nights, most of them young enough to make Frost feel strangely old. He'd brought Shack with him in a carrier, which meant that he had to stop for girls to crouch down and giggle as Shack licked their fingers.

As he crossed the park, he heard a shout rise above the raucous crowd. "Bro! Over here!"

His older brother, Duane, waved from a picnic table near his food truck. Seating was always at a premium in SoMa, but Duane's table had a sign that read: *Reserved for Chef Duane on Penalty of Death and/or Garlic Breath.* Everyone respected the rule. It helped that Duane often handed out free samples of whatever he was cooking.

Frost put Shack's carrier on top of the picnic table and slid onto the bench across from his brother. Duane had his arm around Tabby Blaine. His brother wore a contented smile that Frost had never thought he would see on Duane's face. For years, Duane's life had been his work, and his only relationships had been an endless series of flings with each new sous chef. Tabby had changed that. Duane was in love, and Frost was happy to see it.

"Hey, guys," he said over the din of the people and the music.

"Glad you could make it, bro!" Duane greeted him with his usual zest.

"Hello, Frost," Tabby murmured, looking at him with a slow blink of her green eyes and then looking away. His stare lingered on her longer than was healthy, and he had to force himself to stop.

Duane poked his finger into the carrier. "Shackster! Shack Attack! You want some poutine there, buddy?"

His brother dipped a French fry into gravy that had a sweet-spicy aroma and then stuck the end into the carrier for Shack to have a little taste. The cat didn't always approve of everything Duane made, but pad thai poutine was apparently a hit. Shack licked it up and put out a paw for more.

It was Canada Day in March. Duane wore a red hockey jersey from the Montreal Canadiens. The picnic table and the truck were decorated with Canadian flags, and somehow Duane had managed to procure a life-sized cardboard cutout of Justin Trudeau.

"Is it going well?" Frost asked.

"Terrific. Raymonde made Montreal smoked meat sandwiches. They're incredible. You have to try them."

"I don't see a Mountie," Frost pointed out.

"Yeah, the street-park people gave me a hard time about the horse," Duane replied, "and without the horse, what's the point?"

Duane eyed the long line at his food truck, but it wasn't long enough for his taste. He climbed onto the bench of the picnic table and waved one of the miniature Canadian flags. "Pouuuuuuuutine!" he bellowed into the night. "We've got the best poutine south of Hudson Bay! Smooooooked meat that melts in your mouth! Right over here, get it over here!"

Then he began singing "O Canada" in a surprisingly impressive baritone. The drunk crowd around him applauded, and a few of them joined the chorus.

Frost smiled at the performance. This was peak Duane. If there was one thing Frost admired about his brother, it was his relentless, caffeinated energy. He rarely slept. He never seemed to sit down or stop talking. Like their father, Duane was an extrovert who thrived on people, which made him very different from Frost.

Someone called out Duane's name from the rear door of the food truck. Frost caught a glimpse of a pale, carrot-topped sous chef who didn't look any older than nineteen. His voice had barely changed, and his accent sounded French. "Duane, we need you over here!"

Duane waved back in reply. He hopped down from the bench and kissed Tabby on the cheek. "Be right back!"

Frost's brother shoved through the crowd, shaking hands and passing around samples of poutine as he went. Duane was several inches shorter than Frost, and he had long black hair tied behind his head in a ponytail. The hockey jersey he wore was a couple of sizes too big, and his pants were a couple of sizes too small. He jogged up the rear steps of the food truck and disappeared inside. The tenor of his voice changed immediately, and Frost could hear him bellowing complaints at the sous chefs. When it came to preparing the food, Duane lived up to his nickname, which was the Beast. He even had a name tag that read "Duane Beaston."

With his brother gone, Frost was alone with Tabby on the bench. Her profile was lit up in the multicolored glow of neon. She had no smile on her lips, and her green eyes stared blankly into the crowd. She sat straight up, like someone trying to hold strong against a stiff wind. There was something both fearless and fragile about her.

"Are you okay?" he asked.

She looked back, startled, as if she'd forgotten that he was there.

"Oh, sorry, Frost. I'm not myself tonight." Tabby pushed her red hair away from her face. She reached over to tickle Shack's chin inside the carrier, and Shack nudged forward for more attention. The cat was in love with her and didn't try to hide it.

"What's going on?" Frost asked.

"It's just been a crappy day. I don't want to bother you with it."

"Bother me," he told her.

Tabby shrugged. "Up is down, down is up. That's my life these days."

"Is it your niece?" he asked. Tabby's only sister had a four-year-old who was battling a rare form of cancer. "You've been pretty quiet about her lately. How is she?"

"Hanging on. She's a brave little kid."

"And is the insurance company finally playing ball?"

Tabby gave him a smile that came and went like a flickering candle. "It's under control."

He could feel her distance tonight. She obviously didn't want to talk, but having her pull away made him want to chase her.

"Can I help?" he asked.

She shook her head. "Oh no. Thanks."

"Is there anything else going on?"

"Like I said, it's just a bad day. I've got problems of my own. I have an important catering job scheduled, and the chef I wanted bailed on me. Now I'm scrambling to get a replacement. I'm not used to relying on other people, you know? I miss being the one in the kitchen myself."

Frost didn't say anything, but he felt a stab of guilt that he tried to keep off his face. It didn't work. Tabby took a moment to catch up to what she'd said, and then her eyes widened with regret as she saw his expression. "Oh my God, Frost, why did I say that? Please don't think I blame you. It's not your fault."

He waved off her comment as nothing, but he still blamed himself for her situation. When he'd met Tabby, she had not only been Duane's girlfriend but also an up-and-coming chef at one of the city's top restaurants. Then Frost had faced down a killer who'd been holding a knife to Tabby's throat, and the only way to rescue her had been to fire a shot that hit both of them. Tabby survived, but the price was permanent nerve damage to two of the fingers on her right hand. She was never going to cook in a professional kitchen again.

"Really, I'm sorry," she went on. "I didn't mean anything by it."

"I know that."

"I owe you my life."

"You don't owe me anything at all," he replied.

She looked away again, obviously upset with herself. He felt as if he'd made her bad day worse. It drove him crazy that when she was sad, all he wanted to do was comfort her. He knew Herb was right. He needed to find a way to shut down his feelings for this girl, or it wouldn't end well for any of them.

Duane returned from the food truck with a mountainous plate of smoked meat sliders. He put the plate in the middle of the picnic table and pulled off a small piece of meat from one of the sandwiches to slip inside the cage for Shack. He took a seat again next to Tabby and put his hand over hers. Frost was surprised to see a small flinch from Tabby as he did so.

"Crisis averted," Duane announced. "I told Raymonde to add cilantro like it's a disco song. More, more, more."

Frost bit into one of the sliders. "Well, you can tell Raymonde this is delicious."

"I will."

"By the way, are pigs flying?" Frost added with a wink. "Is this a first? Did Duane Easton really hire a *male* sous chef?"

"Hey, I only hire the best," his brother protested. "Raymonde is the best. Man or woman, it doesn't matter to me."

Duane followed up that outrageous lie with a look that said, Why are you torturing me?

Frost grinned. No matter how good a chef Raymonde was, Frost was pretty sure that Duane was trying to keep temptation far away from the Easton kitchen. Everyone knew his brother's sexual history, including Tabby. He expected her to deliver a smart comeback at Duane's expense, but instead, she let it go and said nothing, which was unusual for her. She separated her hand from Duane's and took one of the sliders, but she put it down without eating.

Then her phone rang. She glanced at the screen and said softly, "I better get this."

"Work?" Duane asked.

"Yes, I'm trying to nail down another chef for the catering job next weekend, so I could be a while. I'll see you later, okay?"

"Sure," Duane replied. "You staying at my place tonight?"

"If you like."

"I could be late getting home."

"Then I'll see you when I see you," Tabby replied. She waved at Frost and Shack and headed for the gates of the food truck park with her phone pressed to her ear. Duane's eyes followed her as she disappeared.

"I am a lucky guy," he said.

"Yes, you are."

"Did you ever think you'd see Duane Easton settling down?"

"I didn't," Frost admitted.

"Me neither. Miracles really do happen."

Frost finished the smoked meat slider. "Everything okay with you two? Tabby seemed a little off tonight."

"Did she?" Duane shrugged, as if he hadn't noticed a thing. "You don't look so good yourself, bro. Did you find out what happened to Denny?"

"No, not yet."

Duane shook his head. "Pretty strange, though, huh? Him and Carla?"

Frost's eyes narrowed in confusion. "What do you mean? What about Carla?"

His brother looked angry with himself for bringing it up. "Oh, crap, you don't know? I got a call from her brother in Houston. He and I knew each other in high school, remember? We reconnected on

Facebook a while back. Nice guy. He and his wife just had another baby."

"Duane, what about Carla?" Frost repeated.

"I'm really sorry, bro. Carla's dead. She killed herself."

Frost felt the news like a blow to the head. He had to dig down in his chest and find a breath. "Are you kidding me?"

"No. It's awful, but come on, not a complete surprise, right? I mean, she tried once before. That girl was never all there."

All Frost heard was a roaring that drowned out the bluegrass music and the laughter around him. He thought he was going to be sick. "When?" he asked.

"Well, that's what's so weird. I mean, what are the odds of her and Denny dying on the same day?"

"Carla killed herself *yesterday*?" Frost asked.

"Yeah. I'm sorry, Frost. I figured you already knew about it."

"I didn't know anything about Carla. What happened?"

"Her brother didn't give me details. He said she killed herself, that's all. Does it matter? You weren't there to save her this time. Her brother got a call from the Berkeley police to break the news."

Frost's head snapped up. "Berkeley?"

"Yeah, that's where she was living," Duane told him, but Frost was already on his feet. He grabbed the carrier with Shack and pushed away through the crowd.

# 10

Frost was so consumed with the news about Carla that he didn't notice someone waiting for him near the driver's door of his Suburban. He was parked in the shadows, and he was practically at his rear bumper before he saw a silhouette move away from the SUV in the darkness.

It was Tabby.

Her shoulder-length red hair had a deep shine. She wore black leggings shoved into knee-high leather boots and a dark-green knit sweater. She was half a foot shorter than Frost, but the heels on her boots made her tall enough to stare at him eye to eye. In the space between them, he breathed in her floral perfume. Tabby had a gift for looking at ease wherever she was, and any awkwardness she'd shown in the food park was gone now. She cocked her head and gave him a casual smile and a little wave.

"I thought you left," he said.

"Well, I wanted to tell you again that I'm sorry. I was stupid to say what I did in there."

"You're entitled to feel angry at losing a big part of your life."

"Maybe so, but I'm not angry at you," Tabby said.

"Forget it. You don't need to worry about me. Did you solve your catering problem? Did you find another chef?"

"Oh, I did," she replied with an annoyed roll of her eyes. "At a ridiculous price, of course. But the guests want dim sum, and they shall have it."

Tabby squatted down in front of the cat carrier and used her slim fingers to open the door. She reached inside and pulled Shack into her arms. She hugged the black-and-white cat to her chest, and Shack stretched up his head and began licking her chin. "I miss this guy," she said.

"Obviously, he misses you, too."

"We haven't seen you in a while," Tabby pointed out. "Why is that? Is something wrong?"

"I've been busy, that's all."

"Are you heading home?" she asked. "Done for the day?"

"No, I have to go to Berkeley. I need to check into something over there."

"Oh. Do you want company?"

"You want to come with me?" Frost asked.

"If I wouldn't be in the way."

He hesitated. Saying no was the smart thing to do. Spending any time at all with Tabby was risky. He didn't know where they stood with each other, and he didn't dare find out. One time, just one time, she'd asked if the two of them had a problem, and there was no mistaking her meaning. He'd lied and said no. Since then, she'd acted as if there was nothing going on between them, and maybe for her, there wasn't. Maybe this was all in his own head.

"I wouldn't want to take you away from something," he said.

"You're not taking me away from anything at all," Tabby replied. "I'd like to forget about my own problems for a while."

"Then okay. Why not?"

Tabby looked pleased that he'd said yes. She carried Shack around to the other side of the truck and climbed inside. He got in behind the wheel. His radio was on as he started the engine, but he switched it off, leaving them in silence. The interior was cold, and he turned the vent on high to warm them.

"What's in Berkeley?" she asked.

He explained about Carla's suicide as he found the address for her apartment. He steered into the Saturday evening traffic and headed for the I-80 freeway that led toward the Bay Bridge.

"What a terrible thing," Tabby murmured. After a pause, she went on. "Duane told me a little about Carla. He called her a girl from your past."

"That's right."

"I didn't think you had a past, Frost. I thought you ran away from relationships."

"This one is complicated."

"He said Carla married your friend Denny."

"Yes, she did."

"Were you in love with her? Did she break your heart?"

Frost shook his head. "No, that wasn't the problem. I didn't love her, but she loved me."

Tabby didn't ask for more details. Not yet. A mile passed, and he merged onto the gray span of the bridge, where the dark vastness of the bay stretched out beneath them. Tabby stared out the window, which was open an inch, filling the interior with a loud, hissing wind. Shack crawled off her lap and curled into a tiny ball on the seat between them. The cat sighed as he drifted off to sleep.

"So tell me more about you and Carla," Tabby said finally.

Frost tried to decide how much to say. As he drove, the truck began to feel warm. He saw the red taillights ahead of him blur through wisps of fog. The tall bridge span, lit with white lights, loomed over their heads. He hadn't thought about Carla in a long time, but the memories felt fresh and bitter.

"She started working for me and Denny halfway through our year on the boat," he told Tabby. "Carla was the girl on the wharf, hawking customers. Most of the time she wore her bikini while she was doing it. Needless to say, she drummed up a lot of business that way. She began living on the boat with us. The three of us spent so much time together, we were practically inseparable. We were all really close."

"Close isn't always so good when three people are involved," Tabby said.

Frost kept his eyes on the road. "No. It's not. The thing is, Carla was very pretty, but she was unstable, too. You could just look at her and know there were demons rattling around in her head. Anyway, Denny began falling in love with Carla, which was fine, but for some reason Carla decided that she was in love with me."

"For some reason?" Tabby said.

"I never encouraged her."

"Well, give yourself a little credit, Frost. I can think of a lot of reasons."

He didn't know what to say to that.

"I tried to let her down gently, but she got angry and desperate about the two of us. And all the while, Denny was pissed off that Carla was interested in me, not him. Everything began to fall apart. That's when I decided to get out of the business and leave Denny on his own. Unfortunately, I was too late."

"What happened?"

Frost could see it all replaying in his head as he told her. He looked down at the black water. It had happened down there, not far away, where the currents swirled around Treasure Island. They'd taken a moonlight cruise, just the three of them. Denny had gotten drunk. So had Carla, and she'd made another wild pass at Frost right in front of Denny. Frost had rejected her again. First, she'd become enraged, screaming and throwing things at him, and then she'd gone below to cry. When too much time passed, he'd gone to check on her. He found her in the cabin, where she'd hung herself from the shower pipe. She was unconscious, but he'd managed to revive her.

"Oh, Frost," Tabby whispered.

"I felt guilty about that for a long time," he said.

"You didn't do anything wrong."

"Maybe not, but I felt like I did."

"What about Denny?" Tabby asked. "What happened between the two of you?"

"We took Carla to the hospital," Frost continued, "and then we went back to the boat. Denny was still drunk and crazy. He jumped me from behind and started whaling on me. I fought him off, but I really think he would have killed me if he'd had the chance. That was the last time I set foot on the boat. I was done. I heard that Denny and Carla got married a couple of years later, and then they split up a couple of years after that. I never saw either of them again. Not until yesterday."

Tabby blinked. "Wow."

"Yeah. Wow."

"Who else knows the whole story?"

"Duane. Herb. Katie knew about it when she was alive. That's all."

Tabby didn't say anything more. He reached the eastern shore of the bay and merged north onto the I-580 freeway, heading for the Berkeley exits. The lights of heavy traffic surrounded them, and he had to slow down. He got off the freeway at University Avenue and headed east from the water. Even on one of its main streets, Berkeley still had the feel of a small town hidden inside a city. Like San Francisco, it was young, liberal, and quirky, but Berkeley hadn't sold its soul to the tech gods the way San Francisco had. Life still revolved around the university campus and its earnest academics.

He turned into a leafy residential area and made his way to a cul-de-sac beside the green ribbon of Strawberry Creek Park. He parked and confirmed Carla's address. At the end of the street, he could make out a wooden bridge leading over the creek toward a stand of evergreens. He recognized the bridge from Coyle's photo and knew there was a snake painted on the ground in front of it.

They were in the right place.

"Do you need me to stay here?" Tabby asked.

"No, you can come with me if you'd like."

They both got out of the Suburban. Shack didn't bother waking up. Frost led them into the parking lot of a five-story apartment building that was in need of a paint job. Carla's place was on the top floor. The exterior door to the building was open, and the interior had an acrid ammonia smell. He saw no security cameras. They took the elevator, which was noisy and slow, and Frost found Carla's apartment halfway down the hallway.

A young man with bleached-white hair answered the door. He wore a flowered shirt and jean shorts, with bare feet. He had earrings through both nostrils and both ears. Behind him, Frost saw moving boxes on the apartment's beige carpet.

Frost showed him his badge. "I'm Homicide Inspector Frost Easton. This is Ms. Blaine. Did Carla Steiff live here?"

The man didn't question Frost's credentials from the other side of the bay. "Yeah, Carla was my roommate."

"Do you mind if I ask you a couple of questions?"

He shrugged. "Go for it. All I'm doing is packing up my crap. When somebody offs themselves in your bathtub, you don't feel like sticking around, you know? My name's Tony, by the way. Tony Frattalone."

Frost sat down on a sagging tweed sofa, and Tabby sat next to him. They could see the bathroom on the other side of the apartment, and Tabby kept watching it, as if a ghost might appear in the doorway. The room had the chemical smell of medical and police teams that had swarmed the place the previous day.

"Did you know Ms. Steiff well?" Frost asked.

"Not really," Tony replied, "and that was fine with me."

"Oh? Why do you say that?"

"The girl was weird, and that's saying a lot around Berkeley, you know? Believe me, if it wasn't for the cheap rent, I would have been out of here a long time ago."

"Did her suicide surprise you?" Frost asked.

"It was gruesome to find, but surprising? No. She had issues."

"Can you tell me what happened?"

"All I know is, I went to work on Friday. I got back early evening, and she was dead."

"Had anything been going on in her life that would have made her unhappy?" Frost asked.

"There was nothing specific that I knew about. She wasn't a happy person, that's for sure. Gorgeous and hot, but not happy."

"Do you know a man named Denny Clark?"

Tony nodded. "Carla's ex. He was around here a lot. If you ask me, I can't understand why someone who got dumped by that girl would keep coming back for more. Consider yourself lucky to get away, you know? But Clark kept hiring her for jobs on his boat. I think he was still hooked on her."

"What kind of jobs?"

"Hostess. Greeter. Waitress. Eye candy. She looked the part, I'll give her that."

"When did you last see Mr. Clark?" Frost asked.

"Tuesday. He picked her up midafternoon for a job on the boat."

"Did he say anything about what the job was? Or did Carla?"

Tony shook his head. "Not a word. Sounded like it was one of those 'I could tell you, but then I'd have to kill you' kind of things. All I know is, Carla showed up on Wednesday with a crap load of cash. Must have been a few thousand bucks. I can't imagine what type of job would pay like that. I asked her about it, and she just put her finger over her lips like I should shut up."

"And this job was last Tuesday?"

"Yeah."

"Did you have any reason to think that Mr. Clark was involved in any illegal activity? Or did Ms. Steiff say anything about that?"

"What, like drugs?" Tony asked.

"Anything."

"Not that I heard about, but something sure smelled funny about her coming back with that much dough."

"Did the Berkeley police take Carla's computer and phone with them?" Frost asked.

Tony stared at him as if that were a strange question. "You know, I didn't see them do it, but yeah, they must have. They're both gone now. I don't know what else could have happened to them."

Frost stood up, and Tabby did, too. "Well, thank you for your time, Mr. Frattalone."

"Sure, whatever." As Frost and Tabby headed for the door, Tony called out, "So why are the homicide cops in San Francisco so interested in Carla, anyway? I mean, she killed herself, right?"

"It's part of another case," Frost replied.

"Yeah, okay, but two cops in one day?"

Frost stopped and turned around. "I'm sorry, what?"

"One of your colleagues was already here a few hours ago. Same thing, homicide cop like you from San Francisco."

"What was his name?" Frost asked.

"I don't remember. Real tall guy, blond hair, athletic."

Frost knew who Tony was describing. It was Trent Gorham.

Gorham had traveled to Berkeley to ask questions about Carla's death. Frost couldn't understand why he would do that, or why he would even have heard about a random suicide on the other side of the bay. Unless somehow he knew there was another red snake nearby.

"We're just covering all the bases," Frost said. "Thanks again for your help."

He left Carla's apartment with Tabby, and they headed downstairs into the dark parking lot. They were both quiet until they were back at his Suburban across from the park. Then, as he opened the door for her, Tabby put a hand on his arm.

"What was that all about?" she asked.

"Honestly, I don't know," Frost replied, still thinking about Trent Gorham visiting the apartment. Then he added, "But I'm not convinced that Carla's death was really a suicide."

"You think she was killed? Like Denny? Why?"

"I don't know, but I want to find out more about this cruise on Denny's boat last Tuesday," Frost said. "Frattalone is right. That much cash changing hands smells funny."

He made sure Tabby was safely inside, and then he closed the door. As he made his way around the front of the truck, he glanced at the woods on the fringe of the neighborhood park. Under the glow of a streetlight, he saw a paved trail leading toward the wooden bridge. He could hear the gurgle of creek water beyond the fence. It was dark and peaceful.

Frost took a few steps down the sidewalk. He wanted to see the snake. But he stopped short of the bridge because he sensed the presence of someone else in the park, staring back at him. He squinted to see deeper into the night, and as he did, he saw a shadow move.

"Coyle?" he called. "Is that you?"

He waited, but he knew it wasn't Coyle. There was no answer.

Instead, very clearly, he heard the thumping footsteps of someone running away through the trees.

# 11

When the man was clear of the park and sure that Frost Easton wasn't following him, he slowed to a walk. His car was parked three blocks away on a residential street. He saw no one nearby when he reached it, but procedure said he should walk from one corner to the next to make sure there was no surveillance. He wasn't going to take any shortcuts. One contact had ignored procedure on an operation in Lincoln Park, and word had gotten back to the boss. The contact had been found shot dead the next day.

It was a lesson in following the rules.

He checked the area, then got inside his car and removed a phone from underneath the front seat. The contact number changed every week, but he had the new number memorized. He punched in the digits and waited. The process was always the same. The voice on the other end was always the same.

"Identification," the woman answered.

"Geary," he said.

"Password."

"21851."

"Status."

"Golden Gate."

He'd never had to declare a different status. Golden Gate meant all was well. If something was wrong, if he was under surveillance or being coerced, then the status was Bay Bridge. Those two words sounded the alarm.

"Report," the woman said.

Her voice had a nasal, dominating tone that broached no small talk. He had no idea who she was, or where she was, or how old she was. Even so, he found her voice oddly arousing, and he would have enjoyed being able to see her in the flesh. In his fantasies, she was young and erotically charged behind her severe ways, like a teacher who knew how to deal with naughty schoolboys. But he would never know the truth about her.

*"Report,"* she barked again when he didn't reply immediately.

"Easton visited the Berkeley location."

"Were you able to listen?"

"Yes. He's not buying the story about the suicide. He's zeroing in on Tuesday, too. I'm not sure the situation can be controlled much longer. We may need to take action."

"That's not up to you," the woman replied.

"Fine, but next time it would be helpful to know about personal connections between my targets before you order the snakes. If I'd been informed, maybe this could have been avoided."

He didn't like to be nasty with the voice—it wasn't safe—but he was the one in the field. And no one needed to lecture him about loyalty when he was taking all the risks. Geary did the dirty work.

"Have you located Mr. Jin?" she asked him, as if he hadn't said a thing.

"Not yet."

"That's priority one."

"I know that," he replied icily. "Mr. Jin disappeared before I was brought in. It's not my fault."

"Regardless, it's essential that we find him before Easton does. He's the only one left who can talk."

"I have a plan," the man said. "I'll get it done."

"See that you do."

"Anything else?"

"That's all," the woman replied.

Geary was about to hang up, but he decided to push his luck. "Make sure you tell Lombard what I said. Easton is a wild card we weren't anticipating. As long as he's alive, we have a problem."

# 12

Frost awoke to the ringing of his phone. The clock on the wall told him it was already eight o'clock on Sunday morning. He'd slept late and badly. On the way back from Berkeley, he'd dropped Tabby at her car in SoMa, and then rather than going home, he'd driven out to Ocean Beach to sit by the waves crashing in from the Pacific. Tabby was still on his mind. By the time he got back to Russian Hill and fell into a restless sleep, it was almost two.

He climbed off the sofa, dislodging Shack from the small of his back. He was still wearing yesterday's clothes. He grabbed his phone from the coffee table and saw no number on the caller ID. He tried to shake the dreams out of his head and sound conscious as he said hello.

"Inspector Easton?" a woman greeted him with a cool, professional voice.

"Yes."

"I understand you'd like to talk to me," she said.

Frost blinked. "I'm sorry, who is this?"

"My name is Belinda Drake."

He remembered now. She was the mystery woman in the photograph with Denny Clark and Greg Howell. "Ms. Drake, yes, you're right. I do want to talk to you."

"I don't typically take meetings with people I don't know, but I understand you're a friend of Herb's."

"I am."

"Well, you can have ten minutes."

"Where should we meet?"

"I'll send a car for you," Drake told him. "Be ready in half an hour."

"All right. My address is—"

"I already know the address," Drake replied, cutting him off. She hung up without another word.

Frost jogged upstairs and woke himself up with a lukewarm shower. He went into his closet to pick his wardrobe for the meeting. He couldn't remember the last time he'd worn a suit, but something told him that Belinda Drake was accustomed to dealing with lawyers and hedge-fund managers who still wore ties. He pulled the one nice suit he owned off a hanger. It was wool, navy, and very expensive. He'd bought it for a gala retirement party five years earlier for the former police chief. He put it on and matched it with an Italian silk tie that looked as lonely in his closet as his suit did.

Ms. Drake's car was prompt to the minute. Half an hour after her call, a black Lincoln arrived to pick him up at the dead end of Green Street. A cup of black Starbucks Blonde Roast was waiting for him in the back seat. So was an array of Danish and croissant muffins from his favorite bakery in the Tenderloin. The television mounted in the rear seat was tuned to the History channel, which Frost watched almost exclusively if he ever turned on the TV. The preparations all sent a message: Belinda Drake had done her homework on him.

Meanwhile, he knew almost nothing about her.

The town car cruised through the weekend morning streets, and he didn't object to the luxury ride. He drank coffee. He ate a grapefruit-ginger cruffin. The car headed south through Chinatown into the financial district, which was like a ghost town. The praying in this part of the city took place at the market's opening bell, not on church Sundays. Near the Hilton, they turned off Kearny Street into a narrow alley and then again into the underground parking lot of a high-rise apartment building. The car whisked him to a remote section of the lot where there was a lobby for a private elevator. The driver used a key card to swipe him inside.

"Someone will meet you at the top," the driver told him. He hadn't said another word since they'd left Russian Hill.

Frost took the elevator. As promised, an Asian butler met him where the elevator opened into the living room of a penthouse suite. The butler handed him more coffee and offered him another pastry, which he declined, and then the man led him through the condominium to an outside balcony thirty stories in the air, with a view immediately across the street to the pyramid of the Transamerica building. Up here, the tower appeared to float in the sky. The wind was strong, and a seagull glided on the breeze.

Belinda Drake waited for him.

"I hope you don't mind heights," she said.

Frost wandered to the balcony railing, looked straight down, and then took a seat across from her at the glass table. "I don't."

Drake wore a beret over her blond hair and a casual outfit that consisted of tight stonewashed jeans, heels, a white T-shirt decorated with a tiger, and a red leather jacket studded with zippers. She looked him up and down with an approving eye, in a way that made Frost think he'd chosen well in selecting the navy suit for the meeting. She had a ceramic teapot in front of her, a plate of multicolored macarons, and an iPad propped on an acrylic stand. She took pointed note of the time on her watch, as if making sure he knew that the clock was ticking. A ten-minute meeting with this woman lasted exactly ten minutes.

"So," she said. "Homicide Inspector Frost Easton. What can I do for you?"

"Herb says you're a matchmaker," Frost said. "You bring powerful people together."

"You could say that. Do you want to be introduced to someone?"

"Actually, I'd like to know how this man fit into your matchmaking program," Frost replied. He showed her the photograph taken aboard the *Roughing It*, and he watched her carefully as she studied the picture. With an experienced professional like Drake, he suspected that her only reaction would be in ways she couldn't hide. The widening of her pupils. The flicker of her eyelids. The tremble of her fingers. In this case, she glanced at the picture, looked away, and took a sip of tea without any change of expression.

"I assume you're talking about Denny Clark," she said.

"I am."

"I was very sorry to hear about Denny. I liked him. His death was a shock."

"Can you tell me about the cruise where this photo was taken?" Frost asked. "Who else was there? What was it about?"

"Why would that matter to you?" she asked.

"Denny Clark and Greg Howell were both on the boat. The cruise seems to be the only connection between them. Now they're both dead."

"Greg had a heart attack. That's hardly suspicious, is it?"

"I don't know. Is it?"

A puzzled little furrow came and went on Drake's forehead. "What a strange thing to say."

"Can you think of anything that happened on that cruise that could be connected to Denny's murder?"

"Of course not. It was months ago."

"I'd like to talk to the other guests who were on board. Maybe they remember something."

Drake shook her head dismissively. "I'm sorry, I don't tell anyone about the work I do or the people I work with. I'm extremely sensitive to the confidentiality of my clients. That's how I stay in business. Let's move on, shall we?"

"Okay," Frost said. "Tell me more about your relationship with Denny Clark."

"I often booked private charters on Denny's boat. In fact, I was the one who suggested the charter business to Denny and helped him arrange financing to acquire the *Roughing It*. I wanted a luxury resource at my disposal for clients. Denny understood what I needed, including my demand for absolute discretion. He knew the importance of delivering whatever I wanted for my clients without asking questions."

"Would that include anything illegal? Like drugs?"

Drake's face gave nothing away. "As I already told you, I don't answer questions about my services."

"Fair enough," Frost replied. "How did you meet Denny?"

"Finding people who can deliver what I need is my job," Drake told him. "I was looking for a yacht and a captain. I did my research, and Denny fit the bill. It was an arrangement that worked out well for both of us."

"He must have been on the boat during meetings with some very private people," Frost said.

"Yes, that's true."

"Could that be why someone wanted to kill him?"

"Unlikely. I told you, Denny was discreet. As were the people he hired. We used nondisclosure agreements, and we paid well. I don't know what happened to Denny, but I assume it was some kind of random street violence. It happens all too often in the city these days."

Frost realized he was getting nowhere with Belinda Drake. She'd built a wall around herself and sat calmly behind it, flicking away his questions without giving him any real information. He was running out of time on her ten-minute clock. His only option was to bluff.

"What about the cruise on Tuesday?" Frost asked.

Drake was good, but this time he saw just the barest tightening of her lips. If he hadn't been looking for it, he wouldn't have seen it. "Tuesday?"

"You booked a charter on Denny's boat on Tuesday," Frost said. He didn't ask it like a question. He stated it as if he already knew. "That was the last time the boat went out. Denny walked away with a lot of cash. So did Carla, the woman he used as his hostess. She's dead, too, like Denny. Did you know that?"

This time he spotted an overly long pause as Drake assessed how much he knew and figured out what to say. "I've already told you several times that I don't talk about my work," she reminded him. "That would include anything that happened on Tuesday."

"In other words, you did set up the cruise," he concluded.

Drake checked her watch and stood up impatiently. "Look at that, our time is up. I'm afraid I have to say good-bye, Inspector."

Frost got up, too. He stepped closer, deliberately invading her personal space until he was only inches from her face. He finally had her off balance, and he wanted to keep her that way.

"I can leave if you want, Ms. Drake, but you have a problem."

"Oh? And what would that be?"

He held up his phone with the screen enlarged to show a close-up of the red snake he'd found near Coolbrith Park. The empty eyes of the snake stared at Drake, and its forked tongue flicked at her. The image drew a physical reaction that she couldn't hide. She inhaled sharply, and her body tensed.

Frost leaned in and whispered right at her ear. *"Lombard."*

Drake eyed the railing of the balcony that rose thirty stories above the street. She backed away toward the door leading into the condominium. Her face was tense, as if Frost had suddenly become a threat. "You need to leave right now, Inspector."

"Tell me about Lombard. I can see that the name means something to you."

"As far as I know, Lombard is the crookedest street in the world," Drake replied with an unconvincing laugh. "That's all."

"I think it means more than that. Denny Clark warned me about Lombard while he was dying. I'd like to know why."

"Well, I'm sorry, but I have no idea what you're talking about."

"No? Denny and Carla are both dead, Ms. Drake, and two of these red snakes showed up where their bodies were found. If their deaths have anything to do with that charter cruise on Tuesday, you should probably be asking yourself if you're next. The best thing you can do is tell me everything you know and let me protect you."

Drake tugged her leather jacket around her body in the wind. Her beret slipped off her head and tumbled toward the edge of the balcony. "Protect me," she murmured so softly that he could barely hear her. "You're funny."

He showed her another photo. This one was a close-up of Denny's dead face. "You said you liked Denny. This is what they did to him. He was poisoned. As for Carla, they cut her wrists and made it look like a suicide. Whatever is going on, whatever Lombard is, I can see that you're scared and you don't like it. The only way to make it stop is to help me. Give me something. Point me in the right direction."

Drake squinted into the sky, as if she weren't even safe from prying eyes outside. He glanced over his shoulder at the Transamerica building, which aimed toward the clouds like a giant laser. Behind the dark windows, anyone could have been watching them.

"Are you under surveillance?" he asked. "Is that what you're concerned about?"

She didn't answer.

He stared at her and said, "Am I?"

Drake slid a hand into one of the pockets of her leather jacket and extracted a fresh tube of lipstick. She touched up her lips, kissed them together, and then gave him an odd, inappropriate smile. "You're right, Inspector, I liked Denny. And I wish you luck in your investigation. But I really can't give you any information that would be helpful to you. I'm sorry."

She closed the distance between them and shook his hand. Then she placed her left hand over the top of his, and he realized that the tube of lipstick was still clutched in her fingers. She scribbled something quickly on his hand and let go.

"Good-bye, Inspector. The butler will see you out."

She disappeared inside the condominium. Frost slipped his hands into his pockets, took another long look over the edge of the balcony, and then followed her inside. Drake was already gone, but the butler was there to guide him back to the elevator. He waited until he was descending in the elevator car before he took out his right hand and saw what Belinda Drake had scrawled across his skin.

It was three words, barely legible.

Not a clue, but a warning.

*Trust No One*

# 13

Two hours after his meeting with Belinda Drake, Frost was back in his Suburban on his way to meet Herb in Golden Gate Park. That was when he noticed a charcoal-gray BMW on his tail. The car's windows were smoked, so he couldn't see the driver inside. He spotted it pulling away from the curb when he turned off Green Street onto Leavenworth, as if it had been waiting for him.

At first, he felt as paranoid as Coyle. The BMW stayed with him for several blocks, but that didn't mean anything in the San Francisco traffic. Then he turned on Clay, and the BMW turned, too. When he turned again on Franklin, the car followed. They drove in tandem, but at the next stoplight, Frost timed his progress through the intersection to make sure the BMW had to stop behind him. He made several zigzag turns beyond the light to lose the other car in the maze of streets. By the time he headed south past Lafayette Park, he was sure he was alone.

That lasted two blocks.

Then the BMW appeared on his tail again. The driver behind the smoked windows wasn't following him by sight; he already knew where Frost was.

Frost didn't bother trying to lose the other car again. Instead, he headed south to Geary and turned right. He drove until he spotted a gas station on the street, where he pulled in and topped off his tank. The

BMW disappeared, but Frost knew it wouldn't be gone for long. At the pump, he purchased a drive-through car wash with an undercarriage spray, and he took the SUV through the wash, letting the jets of water hammer every inch of the chassis. If there was a GPS tracker hidden underneath the vehicle, he hoped it had been thoroughly drowned. Leaving the car wash, he made another series of quick turns with an eye on his rearview mirror.

This time, the BMW didn't reappear.

With a tight smile, Frost returned to his original route and headed for Golden Gate Park.

He grabbed the first parking spot he found, even though it was a long walk to the de Young Museum. A few clouds dotted the blue sky, but the temperature was mild. He wandered through the Shakespeare Garden, where an early spring wedding was in progress, and then made his way into the large open garden between the de Young and the science academy. It was thick with people. He didn't see Herb, but he spotted a crowd gathered near the central fountain and pushed his way to the center. Herb was there, painting on his knees as the tourists watched.

Frost stood over him, staying out of his light. Herb worked with quick, nimble brushstrokes. He was doing a reproduction of a famous painting called *Boatmen on the Missouri* that was housed in the de Young's permanent collection. One of the boatmen steered, and two others took a break, as if watching a steamboat roll by on the lazy river. They were fashionably dressed, one in a black top hat, one in a red kerchief, and they had a small tuxedo cat sprawled across a stack of firewood between them. In Herb's three-dimensional rendering, the nineteenth-century travelers on the raft seemed to rise out of the flat pavement and stare curiously at the people around them. It reminded him of what Herb said about perspective: you can trick your eyes into believing almost anything.

Herb glanced up from behind the magnifiers on his black glasses and spotted Frost. He rocked back on his knees and swigged coffee from his thermos. Frost squatted beside him. They talked under their breath.

"I was followed coming over here," Frost told him. "You might want to keep an eye out yourself. If they're interested in me, they might decide to take an interest in you, too."

"Too late," Herb replied.

"Someone followed you?"

"Yes, a red pickup was waiting outside the gallery. It stayed behind me all the way over here. I don't know who was driving, but I imagine he's watching us right now."

Frost took a casual glance at the crowd, but there were too many faces to pick out any one of them as a spy.

"Exactly what have you gotten yourself into, Frost?" Herb went on.

"I wish I knew. Did you find out anything?"

"Let's not talk here," Herb replied. "I'll meet you inside the museum in half an hour."

Frost nodded. He stood up again and studied the three-dimensional painting taking shape on the concrete. "You know, I don't remember a cat hanging out with the boatmen in the original."

A little smirk played across Herb's face as he picked up his brush. "You just never know where Shack will turn up, do you?"

Frost chuckled and headed in the direction of the de Young. He stopped periodically to glance behind him but couldn't spot a tail among the crowd. He made his way inside the cool, quiet interior of the museum. Herb had helped him become an art lover over the years, and Frost had begun to think of some of the paintings as old friends.

He was standing in front of Albert Bierstadt's *California Spring* when Herb eventually found him. Nearly an hour had passed in between. When Frost glanced at the doorway to the exhibit, he saw that a velvet rope had been placed across the entrance to the hall to give them privacy. Herb's reputation as an artist won him special treatment at most of the city museums.

"Did you talk to Belinda Drake?" Herb asked. He wore overalls and sandals, and his long face was drawn with worry.

"I did," Frost replied.

"Did she have any helpful information?"

"Information? No. But Drake is scared of something, and she doesn't seem like the kind of woman who's easily scared."

"Interesting. I've been having a similar experience with my network."

"How so?"

"I put out the word on the street," Herb said. "I asked about snakes and Lombard, but people are very reluctant to talk. The name Lombard seems to freeze them into silence. I've never encountered anything like it. There's a palpable fear out there, as if saying the name is enough to put you at risk."

"Do you have any idea who or what Lombard represents?" Frost asked.

"Well, if people know, they won't say a word about it."

"Coyle thinks it's a serial killer."

"Is that what this feels like to you?" Herb asked.

Frost shook his head. "No. This is something else."

"I agree. And something very strange is happening, too."

"What is it?"

"You'll think I'm crazy, but I have the feeling that my network is somehow being used against me. Like someone else is infiltrating it like a virus. I put out my queries and got nothing back, which is unusual in itself. Then in the aftermath, other stories started rippling through the network. I wasn't copied on the messages, but a few people told me about them."

"What did they say?"

"They were rumors. About me. It started last night, and by this morning, everyone seemed to be sharing the gossip. I've been getting calls and texts from people saying I should be careful, that stories from my past are being dredged up and spread around the city. The word is that I'm not the man people think I am. That my image is a lie."

"I can't imagine anyone believing that," Frost said. "What are they saying about you?"

"Someone is going back a long way to dig up dirt. The stories go back to the 1960s and 1970s. I'm hearing about violent outbursts during my heavier drug episodes as a young man. Fights. Even sexual abuse."

Frost laughed at the thought of it. "You? That's ridiculous."

Herb frowned. "I'd like to say none of it is true, but the fact is, I was a different man in those days."

"Different? Fine. Violent? I don't believe that for a second."

"That's kind of you to say, but I had a short fuse in my youth. I was angry all the time. Back then, many of us were angry about what was happening in the country, and I wasn't always able to bottle up that anger when it came to my personal life. It's also true that my drug use back then was extreme. There are parts of my memory that are gone. I have certain stretches of my life where I can't even tell you what I did."

"Herb, I know you," Frost insisted.

"You know me now, Frost. You know me after I had a spiritual awakening. I've lived a new life since those days, but that doesn't change or excuse my past. I'd like to deny all of these rumors, but I don't think I can. I'm sure some of the things that are being said about me are true, even if I don't remember them."

Frost turned his head to stare at his friend. He had the sense that Herb was holding back. "Is there something specific you're thinking about?"

Herb's eyes were lost in the green fields of the Bierstadt painting. "Possibly. We'll see. Rumors like this don't feel random. They feel as if they're leading up to something. If they are, then I suspect I know what it is."

"Do you want to talk about it?"

"Later. Not now. Perhaps I'm being paranoid."

"But why do you think this is coming out now?" Frost asked.

"I think we both know why."

"Lombard," Frost said.

"That's my fear. Whatever or whoever Lombard is, I'm on their radar now."

Frost shook his head. "Then drop it. Stop asking questions. This is my problem, not yours. I don't want to put you at risk."

"It's too late for that," Herb replied. "As far as these people are concerned, we're joined at the hip. Besides, if we have an invisible enemy, I'd like to know who it is that we're fighting. I've tried my street network and had no luck, so it's time to see what happens on the other end of the scale. There are a lot of people around the city council who still owe me favors. I'll see what they can tell me about Lombard."

"Well, watch your back. Belinda Drake said I shouldn't trust anyone."

Herb made sure they had the museum hall to themselves. "That sounds like good advice. You said some of your colleagues in the police department may already know what's going on. Do you still believe that?"

"I do," Frost said.

"Then listen to your gut," Herb replied. "I talked to a homeless man who haunts the Mission Bay neighborhood. He sees most of what comes and goes around there, including the cops."

"What did he tell you?"

"He wouldn't share anything on the network. He would only talk in person, and even then, he refused to give me any details about

Lombard. He simply wanted to alert me to the rumors that were going around about my past. But he told me something else, too, and he was most emphatic about it."

Frost frowned. "What did he say?"

"He said whatever I do, I shouldn't say a word about any of this to the police. Apparently, Lombard has spies at Mission Bay."

# 14

When Frost returned to police headquarters, he found that Denny Clark's bank, credit card, and cell phone records had all been delivered to his computer. He began diving into his old friend's secrets.

Denny had never been good with money, and he still wasn't. He was leveraged up to his eyeballs, including a high six-figure loan on the *Roughing It* with a spotty repayment record. Comparing his friend's debts to his modest bank accounts, Denny had a negative net worth. If someone had pushed him to do something illegal for a lucrative payoff, Denny was in no position to say no.

When Frost checked the phone records, the first thing he noticed was that Denny hadn't made any outgoing calls on his cell phone since Tuesday evening. That was unusual because Denny was otherwise on his phone multiple times a day. He also saw that none of the incoming calls had reached Denny, because he didn't see a call length longer than one minute.

After the cruise on Tuesday, Denny had stopped using his phone. Why?

Frost began using his own phone to dial the numbers in Denny's call log one by one. It was slow going and began to eat up most of the afternoon. The majority of calls involved upcoming charters; some of the customers hadn't heard about Denny's death and began peppering Frost with questions he couldn't answer. Other calls were inconsequential, involving everything from pizza deliveries to Giants season tickets.

He found several calls to Carla. When he dialed her number, he recognized her voice on the prerecorded message. There was nothing unusual about what she said—"This is Carla, tell me what you want, and maybe I'll call you back"—but he hadn't heard her deep, trauma-soaked voice in more than a decade. She sounded the same. Listening to her, he could picture everything about her again, how she looked, how she walked, how she held a cigarette, how she made you feel guilty if you didn't treat her like the center of the universe. He could picture her wild eyes that practically screamed that she had never been happy for a day of her life. Carla had always wanted what she couldn't have, and she despised what she could.

Frost was no genius about women, but he'd been smart enough to know that a relationship with Carla would have destroyed him. He would have spent his life trying to fix someone who could never be fixed.

Instead, that hopeless job went to Denny.

He shrugged off the past and kept dialing phone numbers. Among the routine calls, he found a few numbers that left him with questions. The first was a call that Denny had made to someone named Fawn. There was just one call the previous Sunday, two days before the mystery cruise. Frost dialed the number and listened to the message, and when he was done, he called back and listened to it again.

"Hi. If you want Fawn, you've got her. You can enter your code now. If you don't have a code, well, honey, hang up and don't call me back until you do."

The voice had the sultry, inviting feel of someone who made a living dealing with men. It had a hint of a foreign accent. The condescending little intonation as she said "honey" told him that she was smart and self-confident. Based on the message, he guessed that Fawn was an escort, and if so, she was one of the elite girls who charged sky-high prices. Nobody left cash on the nightstand with someone like her or quibbled about the hourly rate. The customer called a prearranged number and handled payment in advance by credit card and then got an approval code to use in scheduling an appointment.

One thing was certain. Denny couldn't afford a girl like Fawn. So why was he calling her?

Frost dialed Fawn's number a third time, and this time he left a message. "Fawn, this is Homicide Inspector Frost Easton of the San Francisco police. You're not in any trouble, but I'd like to talk to you about Denny Clark."

He didn't expect a call back.

The next phone number that he flagged for follow-up belonged to someone else from his own past. Frost had gone to high school with Chester Bagley, and Chester had always been one of Denny's close friends. A couple of times during the year that Frost and Denny had spent living on the boat, they'd used Chester as a freelance bartender, and he'd poured some of the best, strongest drinks Frost had ever tasted. He was good-looking and gay, and he probably made more money on customer tips than Frost did on his police salary.

Frost wondered if Denny was still using Chester as a bartender for his charters on the *Roughing It*. He left a message.

"Chester? Frost Easton. I'm sure you heard the bad news about Denny. I've got some questions for you. Give me a call, okay?"

He kept dialing more numbers.

Denny got and made a lot of calls, and the individual numbers in the phone records began to blur. With most of the calls, Frost got a message rather than a live person, and he rattled off his name and contact information the same way every time as he asked for a call back. He worked his way backward in the records day by day, until he was at a point three weeks prior to Denny's murder. Several hours had already gone by as he sat at his desk.

He dialed. Left a message.

Dialed. Left a message.

Dialed. Left a message.

And then a live voice answered, startling him. What made it so strange was that the voice was in stereo. He heard it over the phone, and he heard it across the busy floor of detectives around him.

"Trent Gorham."

Frost said nothing at first. He looked up from his desk and stared across the room and saw Gorham with his phone in his hand. When the dead air stretched out, the other detective said again, "Trent Gorham. Hello?"

Finally, Frost spoke softly into the phone. "Hello, Trent."

"Who is this?"

"It's Frost Easton."

Gorham's head swiveled slowly. Their eyes met from one desk to the other. Dozens of police officers passed in and out of their line of sight, but for now, they were like the only two people in the room. Frost felt tension seeping through the phone and across the floor.

"Easton," the other cop murmured in reply. "I figured you'd be calling me sooner or later."

"You want to explain?" Frost asked.

Gorham didn't even blink as he stared back. His bland, blond face was devoid of expression. He leaned back in his chair and casually propped one arm behind his head. "You mean, why I called Denny Clark?"

"That's right. And why you didn't tell me that you knew him."

"I was curious how long it would take you to find out," Gorham replied. "Everyone says you're so smart."

"Well, I'm the one who's curious now, Trent. You called my murder victim three weeks before he was killed. You came to my desk and offered to help me with the case. And you never bothered to mention that you'd been in contact with him."

"It was just one call. I'm sure you can see that in the phone records."

"What was it about?"

"You remember I used to work vice, right?"

"Yes."

"I bumped into Denny now and then back in those days."

"Why?" Frost asked.

"Why do you think? Drugs."

"Was Denny selling?"

"He was either selling or supplying his guests for free. I knew he was buying more than he'd use for himself. The product had to go somewhere."

"I don't see an arrest record," Frost said.

"That's because I used him as a snitch. He knew I could drop the hammer on him whenever I wanted, so he was more useful feeding me information than sitting behind bars. You know how it works, Easton. You keep the little fish on the hook and see who comes to eat them."

"Did you land any high-profile dealers that way? Anyone who might want revenge against Denny for ratting them out?"

"No, I didn't. I stopped leaning on him because the word came down from my lieutenant to lay off Denny Clark."

"Why?" Frost asked.

"Obviously, Denny had some powerful political friends."

"Any idea who?"

"No. My lieutenant told me to drop it, so I did. End of story."

"So why the phone call three weeks ago?"

Gorham shrugged. "I found a dead dealer in the Mission District. I wanted to know if Denny had heard anything about who took him down. He hadn't. That's all it was."

Frost tried to read Gorham's poker face across the station. "What about your friend in vice? The one who was killed. Alan Detlowe. Did he know Denny?"

"Alan? I don't think so. Why?"

"Snakes," Frost said.

"Aw, come on. That again? You said you were dropping that."

"Alan was a vice cop, and there was a red snake painted near his body. I found the same kind of snake where Denny was killed, and now you're telling me that Denny was on your radar screen at vice. That sounds like a connection."

Across the room, Gorham shrugged. "Alan didn't know Denny. Denny was my source, not his. Are we done, Easton?"

"You're still holding out on me, Trent. You were over in Berkeley yesterday asking about Carla Steiff's suicide. You want to explain that?"

Gorham took his time replying. He dug in the drawer of his desk for a stick of gum, and he unwrapped it and began chewing as he stared at Frost. Always delay when you're formulating a lie.

"Carla committed suicide on the same day as Denny's murder," Gorham said. "We both know that's suspicious. I decided to check it out for myself, but I didn't find anything."

"How did you know Carla?"

"I already told you, I was targeting Denny at vice, at least until the word came down to lay off him. If you're looking to leverage somebody, you find out everything you can about them. Carla was his ex-wife. I knew they still worked together. I interviewed her to see what she could tell me. That's all."

"How did you hear about her suicide?"

"When I found out about Denny's murder, I made a call to see if Carla knew anything about it. I talked to her roommate, and he told me what happened."

"And you didn't think it was worth mentioning this to the lead inspector on the case?" Frost asked. "I've been sitting here all afternoon, Trent. You couldn't get up and connect the dots for me?"

"We're talking about it now."

"We're only talking about it because I found out. Did you know that there was a snake painted near Carla's apartment?"

"Another snake. No kidding."

"Yeah. No kidding."

Gorham chewed his gum. "You're getting as paranoid as Coyle. I don't know anything about snakes. As far as I'm concerned, they still don't mean a thing. I knew Denny and Carla. I was trying to be helpful, but I turned up squat, so there was nothing to tell you. That's all."

They stared at each other in silence, not blinking. The rest of the room was loud with voices. Gorham began to hang up his phone, but Frost interrupted him.

"Wait. I've got another name for you."

Gorham looked impatient now. "Who?"

"Fawn," Frost said. "Denny called her last Sunday. I think she may be an escort. Do you know her from vice?"

The other detective was slow to reply again. His face was a mask of hostility. "Yeah, I know Fawn. And yeah, she's an escort. Very high-end."

"I assume Fawn is an alias. What's her real name? Where can I find her?"

"Her real name is Zara Anand. I think she shares a place with her sister in Presidio Heights."

"What's her connection to Denny Clark? Why would he call her?"

"I have no idea."

Frost clenched the phone hard. "Give me one reason I shouldn't march your ass to an interview room and interrogate you about everything you know."

Gorham deliberately angled his head toward Captain Hayden's office. Frost followed the signal and stole a casual glance in the same direction. Cyril Timko stood in the doorway, watching Frost from behind his gray eyes.

"Because neither one of us knows who to trust around here," Gorham replied.

Just like that, the other detective hung up the phone and cut him off. Gorham got up, shrugged on a coat, and disappeared toward the elevators without glancing in Frost's direction. Frost kept the phone at his ear, even though the connection was dead. He mouthed words but didn't say anything out loud. For some reason, he didn't want Cyril to realize that he'd been talking to Trent Gorham.

He remembered what he'd heard from Belinda Drake. And from Herb.

*Trust no one.*

*Don't talk to the cops.*

When Cyril went back inside Hayden's office and closed the door, Frost finally put the phone down. He went back to Denny's call list and kept dialing numbers like a robot, because that's what he'd been doing all afternoon. His mind was elsewhere. He didn't think about the numbers as he punched them into his phone and left messages one after another.

He didn't even recognize that the next number on Denny's call list was a number he'd dialed many times himself.

Instead, he simply sat there in shocked silence when he heard the voice on the other end.

"Hey, Frost, what's up?" Tabby said.

# 15

Tabby answered the door and waved Frost inside Duane's condominium, which smelled like a farmers' market spice shop. The window ledges were thick with herbs and green plants. A song by Christina Perri played softly in the background. "Jar of Hearts." That was Tabby's music, not Duane's.

The apartment was located in the Marina District a block from the bay. It wasn't big, but its prime location made it expensive even by the insane standards of San Francisco real estate. For the small number of hours Duane actually spent here, it made no sense to have such a high-priced indulgence, but a place in the Marina had been Duane's benchmark for success since he'd been a boy. Frost could trace most of Duane's life simply by glancing around the condo. He saw the street sign for Duane's first restaurant hung on the wall, lit up in neon. He saw a Pacific watercolor that Duane had purchased on a brothers vacation to Mendocino with Frost five years earlier. He saw family photographs in frames. Their parents. Duane and Frost together. Their sister, Katie, with her sunny blond hair.

"Do you want to take a walk?" Tabby asked him. "I'd love to get out of here for a while. I need some air."

"Sure. If you like."

"I had fun with you last night," she added. "I'm sorry, I know that sounds weird. I mean, you must be upset about Carla and Denny."

"I am, but I was glad for the company."

Her face brightened. "Good."

She grabbed a coat from a hook near the door. They took the stairs to the ground floor of the four-story building, and she zipped up her jacket and tucked her hands in the pockets when they emerged onto the windy sidewalk of Scott Street. Her red hair blew across her face. They didn't talk to each other as they crossed Marina Boulevard and walked beside the boats in the yacht harbor. From where they were, Frost could see the flybridge of the *Roughing It*. Clouds had swarmed the sky in the late afternoon, and fog was already slouching over the towers of the Golden Gate Bridge.

They walked in silence all the way to the bay and sat beside each other on a low stone wall that overlooked the bridge. Waves slapped against the wet sand at their feet. It was cold, but he didn't notice it. Sitting there, he saw Tabby turn her shoulders away from him and brush a tear from her cheek. She was upset, and he couldn't pretend that he didn't care about what was wrong.

"You want to talk about what's bothering you?" he asked.

She hid her sadness behind a weak smile. "It's nothing."

"Is there a problem with your niece?"

"No, it's something else."

"Well, I could tell you weren't yourself with Duane last night," Frost said.

"I know. I've been moody lately. That's very unlike me. It's a phase, and this too shall pass. But thanks for being concerned."

"Of course."

"Was Duane pissed when I left so abruptly?" she asked. "I was asleep when he got home. We haven't talked."

"No, he wasn't upset," Frost replied, trying to choose his words carefully, but Tabby saw through him. She shook her head with a little bit of disgust.

"In other words, he didn't even notice that anything was wrong," she said.

"Look, Duane is a workaholic," Frost reminded her. It wasn't the first time he'd made excuses for his brother. "He's always been that way, and he's not going to change. If you wait for him to slow down, you'll be waiting forever. I learned years ago that you have to grab Duane and make him listen if you really want him to hear you."

"You're right. I'm not blaming him. I'm busy, Duane's busy, we're just out of sync right now. It's mostly me, anyway. I'm used to feeling in control, but these days it seems like every time I know where I stand, the ground gets pulled out from under me." Then she rolled her eyes in annoyance with herself. "What the hell, will you listen to me? I can't believe what a whiner I am today."

"Cut yourself some slack," Frost said. "You've had a crazy year. You know, almost dying and all."

"I know, you shot me," she teased him with a little giggle. "We're like our very own *Dr. Phil* episode."

He laughed, and so did she. Then she wiped her cheeks with both hands and smoothed her hair.

"Anyway, I'm done complaining," she went on, shivering a little as the wind blew off the bay and tossed her hair. "You called me, and I haven't even given you a chance to say a thing. What's going on?"

"I need to talk to you about Denny Clark," Frost said.

"Your ex-friend? The one who was killed?"

"Yes."

Tabby looked puzzled. "What about him?"

"How did you know Denny?" Frost asked.

"Me? I didn't."

"Are you sure?"

"Of course. I'd never heard of him until Duane told me about you and Carla. Why? What's this about?"

"Well, when I called you earlier, I was actually in the process of going through Denny's cell phone records. The thing is, you're in them. A few weeks ago, Denny called you."

Tabby shook her head. "No way. That's crazy. Are you sure? Honestly, Frost, his name isn't familiar to me at all. I certainly don't remember talking to him. Could he have dialed the wrong number?"

"No, it was a long call. Almost fifteen minutes." He took out a copy of Denny's phone records from his pocket and showed her where he'd highlighted the call to her cell phone. She took note of the date and time and then looked off toward the bridge as she tried to remember.

"Okay. I think I know what this was about. I had no idea who the guy was. He probably told me his name at the beginning, but I didn't bother writing it down because nothing came of it."

"Came of what?" Frost asked.

"He wanted me to cater a private party. Now that I think about it, the gig was on a boat, but I never got all the details."

"When was the party?"

"I'm pretty sure it was scheduled for last Tuesday. I remember because it was the day after I was handling an anniversary party, so I would have been scrambling to juggle the two jobs." Her eyes widened. "Tuesday. Is that the charter you were worried about? The one where Denny and Carla walked away with all the cash?"

"That's it. What did he tell you about it?"

"Not much. He said it was a small party, just a handful of people. I don't think he gave me an exact number. The whole thing had to be absolutely first class. I mean, five-star food, top-shelf booze, unlimited budget, the works. He dangled a big number in front of me to make it happen."

"Sounds like a pretty good job for you," Frost said.

"It was. I was flattered that he approached me. In normal circumstances, I would have loved to take it."

"So why did you say no? Because of the conflict with the other job?"

Tabby shook her head. "No, believe me, I would have worked around it and made sure both got done. That wasn't the problem. I mean, looking back, I guess I should have sucked it up and said yes, but there was just something *off* about the whole thing."

"What do you mean?" Frost asked.

"Well, he told me that the first thing I would have to do is sign a nondisclosure agreement before he gave me any information. So would anyone I brought in to work the event. I couldn't talk about the job, who hired me, how much I got, who was there, what I saw, what I heard—and if I did, I'd be subject to a penalty equal to *twenty times* the amount of my fee. That made me nervous right away. If I brought in a bartender who happened to tell a friend, 'Hey, you'll never guess who I mixed a margarita for last night,' I'd be on the hook for a lawsuit that could bankrupt me. I didn't like that. And I don't know, it just felt weird. I've dealt with clients who are over the top about privacy, but this was more than that. Somehow it made me think there was going to be stuff going on that would make me uncomfortable, or that would put me and my team at risk."

"What kind of stuff?"

"It could be anything. Sex, drugs, who knows. I've been to catering conventions, and you wouldn't believe the stories I hear. I don't want to have anything to do with that scene."

"So what did you do?" Frost asked.

"I said thanks but no thanks."

"How did Denny take it?"

"He was disappointed. He said I had a great reputation. I liked hearing that. Although now that I think about it, I can't help but wonder if he called me because of you, Frost."

"Why do you say that?"

"Because he knew about me and my injury. He said he'd read the stories in the newspaper about me getting abducted and shot. That's how he knew about my business. You were in all of those stories, too, Frost. Denny would have seen your name."

Frost thought about it, and he suspected that she was right. Denny hadn't chosen Tabby by accident. He'd chosen her in part because of her connection to his old friend. It made him wonder again if Denny had been looking for a way to erase some of the sins of the past.

"Do you remember anything else?" he asked.

"He wanted a recommendation from me," Tabby replied. "He said if I wasn't available, who would I suggest? He was looking to bring in the best chef in the city for this job."

"Did you give him a name?"

"I did. He wanted Asian, and for me, there was only one name. Mr. Jin."

"Should I know who that is?" Frost asked.

Tabby smiled. "Not unless you're in the culinary world. Mr. Jin owns a hole-in-the-wall restaurant in Chinatown, but as far as everyone in the business is concerned, he's the best in the city. He mostly does private parties, and he doesn't even offer a fixed menu. Clients just trust him to pick things they'll like. He's that good."

"How do I find him?" Frost asked.

"I can give you his address," Tabby replied, "but I don't think he's there. You remember I told you I had a chef who canceled on a big gig for me? That was Mr. Jin. He called me last Wednesday and left a message. He said he was leaving town for a while. I haven't been able to reach him since then. I called his restaurant, and they gave me the same story. Nobody knows where he is."

# 16

The aromas of the street-level Chinese restaurant permeated the hallway in Mr. Jin's building. Frost had a takeaway container of spicy Singapore noodles in one hand, and he ate them with wooden chopsticks as he made his way down the corridor. The carpet under his feet was worn and stained. Noise pummeled him through the thin apartment doors. He heard a birdlike serenade from a bamboo flute in one room and the sick beat of a Taylor Swift song across the hall. Through an open door, he saw four Chinese teenage boys playing liar's dice as they lay sprawled on the floor.

Everyone in the hallway stared at him. They knew he was a stranger and probably guessed that he was a cop. A cluster of young girls giggled and whispered as he passed them. An old woman in a wheelchair gave him a toothless scowl. Two men in suits, talking at a rapid clip, clammed up and let him squeeze by in silence. He could feel their eyes on his back all the way to the end of the corridor.

Mr. Jin lived in the last apartment on the left. Frost stood outside the door and finished his noodles, and then he leaned in close and listened. There was no movement inside. He knocked sharply and called out Mr. Jin's name, but no one answered.

Frost twisted the doorknob. The door was unlocked. He glanced down the hallway at the neighbors, gave them a flash of his badge, and then crept into Mr. Jin's apartment and closed the door behind him.

The air was cold and fresh, tinged by remnants of incense. He found a light switch that turned on a floor lamp. The window was open, with a white curtain dancing like a ghost as the wind blew. He went to the window and looked outside at the green balcony. The apartment was at the corner of the building, with busy traffic in the street five stories below him.

He studied the rest of the living area. If Mr. Jin had money, his lifestyle didn't show it. The small room was clean, but the mismatched furniture was old and sparse. Even the kitchen appliances were dated, and the countertops were made of an ugly cream laminate. Obviously, Mr. Jin did his cooking elsewhere. It was a bare-bones place to live, mostly without luxury or ornament. The only personal touch in the apartment was half a dozen oversized posters of Niagara Falls hung in cheap brass frames on the white walls.

There was a round end table beside an old recliner. Frost spotted a white porcelain teacup with dried grounds in the bottom and a sandalwood candle beside it. The saucer underneath the cup was painted with hummingbirds. Next to the half-burnt candle, he saw several imported magazines, some in Chinese, some in English. When he picked up the magazines, he found a notepad of ruled green paper beneath them. The most recent page had been torn off, leaving scraps caught in the spiral wire.

Frost held the blank page of the notepad up to the light and could see faint indentations of Mr. Jin's scribbling. Most of the characters were in Chinese, but at the bottom of the page, he could make out a single name that had been written in large letters:

*FAWN*

That was the alias of the high-priced escort on Denny's call list. Frost frowned. Nothing in the rest of Mr. Jin's life suggested that he was the kind of man who patronized high-end hookers.

He ripped off the page from the notepad and slipped it into his pocket.

Then he continued searching the apartment. In the kitchen, there was a cordless phone next to an answering machine that probably dated to the 1990s. A red light flashed, indicating that Mr. Jin had messages. Frost pushed the button, and the first voice he heard belonged to Tabby. Her message had been left on Wednesday morning.

"Mr. Jin, this is Tabby Blaine. I'm so disappointed about the event on the twenty-eighth. I know you're out of town right now, but I'd love to see if we can work this out. We still have time, and I'm happy to make arrangements for supplies while you're away. Can you call me when you get this?"

There were other messages in a similar vein. Mr. Jin was in demand, but the messages rolled on, date stamped on each of the days since the Tuesday-night party, and there was no indication that he'd received or responded to any of them. He'd obviously canceled multiple jobs on his way out of town.

When Frost listened to the next message, he heard another familiar voice, and he pressed pause on the playback.

He'd literally heard only one word from that voice in ten years, but he recognized it immediately. It was Denny. He played the whole message, and then he played it over again.

"Mr. Jin, we have a problem. I need to talk to you right away. I'm coming over, but if you're there and you get this, get out of your apartment immediately. Go to your restaurant and wait for me there."

The date stamp was on Friday night. Denny must have left the message not even two hours before he arrived on Frost's doorstep. He'd obviously used a different phone, because there was no record of the call on his mobile number.

*We have a problem.*

That meant Denny had known something was wrong before he was killed. He'd already realized that he was being hunted.

And so was Mr. Jin.

Frost heard a noise behind him and spun around. He saw one door, mostly closed, leading toward what he assumed was Mr. Jin's bedroom. He tried to remember if the angle on the door was the same as when he'd entered the apartment, but he couldn't be sure. He crossed the room and nudged the door with his shoe. The only light was from the side window overlooking the roof of the next building, which was enough for him to make out a platform bed barely a foot high. The bed was neatly made with white linen. He felt for a light switch on the wall, but when he flicked it up, nothing happened. The bedroom stayed dark.

He took two more steps into the center of the room.

Without warning, a hard kick from behind him swept both of his feet off the ground. He dropped like a stone, landing on his back. He was dizzied for only a second, but that was enough for someone to land on top of him and put the steel point of a knife to his throat.

Frost squinted. In the shadows, he recognized the face looming over him. It was the Asian teenager he'd met on the *Roughing It*. The boy who'd been looking for his father and who'd dumped him in the bay.

"You," the boy exclaimed, recognizing him, too.

"It's Fox, right?" Frost said.

"Yeah, that's me, so what? What are you doing here?"

"I'm a cop, remember?"

"You think I trust you because you're a cop? Think again. The last people I'm going to trust are cops."

"Okay, but I'm not going to hurt you."

Fox pushed the knife until it was almost breaking skin. "No, you bet you're not. One move and I cut you bad."

"Is Mr. Jin your father?" Frost asked from the floor. Fox's knee leaned into his chest and made it hard to breathe. "Because I'm looking for him, too, just like you. How about the two of us work together?"

"How about you tell me what you want with my father?" Fox asked.

"I want to keep him safe," Frost said, "and I want to keep you safe, too."

"I do fine on my own," the boy replied.

"I can see that, but I'm not the enemy, Fox. Let me up, and let's talk, okay?"

Fox shrugged. He pulled away the knife, rolled off Frost, and was back on his feet with an effortless, graceful jump. Frost rubbed the skin on his throat and got up more slowly. His head hurt, the way it had the last time he'd met this boy. Fox prodded him toward the living room with the knife, and Frost backed up into the light.

The boy was dressed as he had been the last time, all in black, including a tight long-sleeved T-shirt. His face still had a made-up plastic glow that was more like a girl than a boy. His wild hair sprouted like a shaggy black mane from his head. He had full, feminine lips that bent into a sly smile as he stared at Frost, who was twisting his neck to work out the spasms of pain.

"Last time we met, you were all wet," Fox joked.

"I remember."

"You flopped around in the water like a fish on the line," the boy added with a laugh.

"Yes, I did."

Fox secured the knife in a long zippered pocket on his calf. "So what do you want, anyway? What are you doing here?"

"I told you, I'm trying to find Mr. Jin," Frost said. "When did you last see him?"

"Tuesday. He headed off on a job for Denny Clark. He must have come back to the apartment sometime after that because his old suitcase is gone now. But he hasn't been back since then."

"Is that unusual?"

"Him not telling me where he's going? No, he does that a lot. He's busy. There's always a catering job somewhere. He lives his life, I live mine, and that's okay for both of us. But him being away so long and not coming home? Yeah, that's odd."

"Did he tell you anything about the job on Tuesday?"

"No."

Frost slipped the page of green notepaper out of his pocket. "Mr. Jin wrote down a name on his notepad. Fawn. Did he mention her to you?"

"No. Who is she?"

"It doesn't matter. Does Mr. Jin have a cell phone? Do you have any way to reach him?"

Fox shook his head. "He's old school. He doesn't believe in things like that. He doesn't use credit cards, either. Everything in cash."

"What about your mother? Is she in the picture?"

"She lives in Hong Kong."

"So where have you been staying since Mr. Jin left?" Frost asked. "Here?"

"I come and go. I sleep here mostly." Fox gestured at the window. "I use the roof next door to get to the balcony. I don't want anyone to see me. People are watching the building. I think they're looking for Mr. Jin, too."

Frost went to the apartment door and poked his head outside. The hallway was empty now. He turned back to Fox. "Why don't you come with me? You can stay at my place if you'd like."

"No way." The boy planted his feet stubbornly on the floor. "I need to be here when Mr. Jin gets back."

"It's not safe," Frost insisted. "For you or for him. If there are people who are after your father, they may get it in their heads that you know where he is. Or they may figure they can put pressure on him by abducting you and using you as leverage. Either way, you're in danger staying here."

"You think I can't protect myself? You're wrong."

"I'm the last guy who's going to underestimate you, Fox. But right now, I'm more concerned with the best way to keep your father safe. And that's for you to be nowhere near this apartment."

Fox seemed to acquiesce, but Frost remembered what had happened the last time he misjudged this boy. Another smile came and went on Fox's face, as if he remembered, too. He put his hands up in surrender. Frost led the boy out of the apartment, and they headed back down the hallway. All the people, all the noise, all the activity had disappeared, which made Frost nervous. It was now cemetery quiet. At the end of the corridor, he led them down the empty stairwell toward the ground floor. At the bottom, he held up a hand to make the boy wait as he checked the street.

"My car's at the other end of the alley on Jackson," Frost said.

They went outside. It was dark and midevening. He kept a hand on Fox's shoulder as they walked past Mr. Jin's restaurant. People pushed and shoved on the sidewalk, jostling them. They turned into the alley, where the brick walls rose on both sides. On either end of the narrow passageway were bright lights, but in between, the closed, barred doorways of the shops were dark. On the ground, a homeless man banged a copper cup. Legs dangled from the fire escapes overhead, and cigarette smoke drifted in the air. In the doorway of a ginseng store, an old man shot himself up with heroin.

There were faces looking out from all the shadows.

"You feel the eyes?" Fox said.

"I do."

"Around here, everybody sees everything," the boy told him.

They emerged from the alley into a chaos of music and neon. He heard the pound of drums—thump, thump, thump—and the chant of songs. The sweet smells of a bakery leached onto the street. His Suburban was steps away. He kept his head down and guided the boy to the passenger door and put him inside. As he went around to the other side, he spotted a charcoal-gray BMW parked outside a shuttered Chinese theater. He locked the doors as he got inside the SUV and kept an eye on his side mirror as he started up the Suburban and merged into the traffic.

Behind them, the BMW eased away from the curb and followed.

It was the same vehicle that had tailed him earlier. The headlights were bright in the mirror. Fox watched Frost's eyes, and then the boy lowered the passenger window and craned his body outside like a dog to spy on the car behind them.

"Get back inside!" Frost snapped, grabbing Fox by the belt and dragging him back from the window.

The boy slid onto the seat again, but he left the window open. "I've seen that car before," Fox said.

"Do you know who it is?"

"Lombard's people," the boy replied.

Frost swung his head sharply. "You know about Lombard?"

"I know you keep your mouth shut about him if you want to stay alive," Fox said. "Everybody knows, but nobody talks about him, unless you want to find a snake on your wall."

"You've seen the snakes?"

"Sure. The snakes follow the bodies. It's a warning. Don't mess with Lombard's business, or you're next."

"Is Lombard a group? A person? Fox, you need to tell me everything you know."

The boy shook his head. "If you're going after Lombard, forget it, man. I don't want any part of it."

"I think Lombard's looking for your father," Frost told him. "That's who's watching the building. That's why I need to find him before anyone else does. Something happened on Tuesday night, and Mr. Jin knows what it is. They want to make sure he doesn't tell anybody."

Fox said nothing, but the boy was agitated now, and he squirmed like a caged animal.

"Do you have *any idea* at all where Mr. Jin might be?" Frost asked again. "Any favorite hangouts? Any place I can look?"

"He never goes anywhere. He's either cooking or he's in the apartment."

Frost frowned in frustration. He glanced back and saw the BMW hugging the bumper of his SUV. He turned on Kearny, and the other car followed. He accelerated through two lights but didn't lose it. The next red light stopped him at Broadway, and the BMW's headlights taunted him in the mirror.

Frost was tired of the game. He threw the SUV into park. He slid his gun out of its holster and opened the door of the Suburban. As he got out, tires screeched behind him. The driver of the BMW reversed wildly and spun into a three-point turn, denting a car parked on the street. Frost ran after it, but the BMW sped off in the opposite direction, fishtailing as it escaped. He watched the car turn three blocks away and vanish in the darkness.

He went back to his truck. The light was green. He accelerated through the intersection into a left turn where Kearny dead-ended up the hill in front of him.

"Stop," Fox said.

Frost pulled over to the curb. "What is it?"

"Don't you see, man? You can't protect me. They pegged us as soon as we left the building. If I'm with you, they'll find me."

"It's too dangerous for you to be alone."

"I'm better off on my own," the boy insisted. "I know how to hide."

"Fox, wait," Frost protested, but he was too late.

The boy reached a hand through the open window to the roof of the truck. With the speed of a snake, he slithered through the small opening until his feet were on the door frame. He launched himself into a gymnastic backflip and landed smoothly on the sidewalk in the halo of the streetlight.

Fox's mouth broke into a little smirk at Frost's shocked expression.

"If you find Mr. Jin, call me," the boy told him, rattling off the number of a cell phone. "Got it? Don't try to track me down. I'm never in the same place for long."

He sprinted up the steps of Kearny Street. Frost shouted after him and bolted from the SUV, leaving the driver's door open. He began to lay chase, but the boy was a cheetah, whipping up the hill and disappearing around the next corner. Frost didn't have any hope of catching him.

He returned to the SUV, got inside, and slammed the door. He didn't go anywhere. He sat there, alone, and his frustration seethed. Every lead was slipping away. He was in a race, and Lombard was winning.

# 17

The escort who called herself Fawn lived in Presidio Heights, two blocks from the red dome of the Jewish synagogue. The area was like a quiet suburb inside the city, with neatly maintained homes and a lineup of mature trees dotting the sidewalk. San Francisco was too pricey for most young families, but if you could afford it, this was a neighborhood for toddlers and golden retrievers. Fawn's house was a two-story Victorian with a fresh coat of yellow paint and neat window boxes filled with pink flowers on the terraced wall beside the front steps.

Frost wondered if the yuppie neighbors knew what she did for a living.

He rang the front doorbell in the darkness and waited. There was a security camera mounted above the door frame, and as he watched it, the lights of the camera came to life and illuminated him. A woman's cool voice crackled through an intercom speaker.

"Yes? May I help you?"

Frost held up his badge toward the camera. "My name is Frost Easton with the San Francisco police. I'd like to ask you a few questions."

"About what?"

"About Fawn," he said. After a pause, he added, "And no, I'm not from vice."

"I don't have anything to say," the woman replied.

"Are you Zara Anand?"

"No, I'm her sister. I still don't have anything to say."

Frost sighed. "Look, I can run my questions past your neighbors, but I don't think you or your sister want me doing that."

There was a long stretch of silence from inside. Then the front door opened in front of him. A small and attractive Indian woman with thick, long black hair studied him from behind the chain on the door. Her dark eyes were smart and suspicious.

"Let me see that badge again," she said.

Frost held it up, and she reviewed it carefully. When she was satisfied, she undid the chain and let him come inside. The house had a faintly sweet smell of honey. She led him from the foyer into a living room that faced the street, and she sat in a comfortable armchair with a glass of white wine and an open laptop beside her. Her hand, with slim fingers and long gold-painted nails, waved him to a sofa by the window. Their furniture was ornate and made of cherrywood, and the sofa had a geometric design on brown fabric. The wallpaper was a deep burgundy color.

"My name is Prisha Anand," she said. "Now, what can I do for you?"

"Your sister is Zara, is that right?" Frost asked. "But in her work, she uses the name Fawn?"

Prisha took a sip of wine. Her movements were slow and precise, as if she thought through everything in advance before she did anything. She had arching eyebrows that were carefully plucked, a sloping nose, and a jaw that tapered to a sharp V. She wore a scoop-neck yellow blouse that emphasized her long neck, loose black slacks, and open sandals. Her toes matched her gold fingernails.

"Yes. Zara calls herself Fawn."

"The two of you live here together?"

"That's right."

"It's a beautiful place," Frost said.

"In other words, how do two young women in their twenties afford it? Is that what you really want to know? I'm an in-house lawyer at Zelyx, and I was there for the IPO. But Zara is an equal breadwinner in the household, and if you know her as Fawn, then I'm sure you know why."

"I don't know her at all," Frost replied, "but her name has come up in one of my investigations."

"You said you don't work in vice. So where do you work?"

"Homicide," Frost said.

Worry fell like a curtain across Prisha's face. "Is Zara all right?"

"I don't know. I was hoping you could tell me where to find her."

"I have no idea. She left for one of her—engagements—last Tuesday, and I haven't seen or heard from her since then. Doing what she does, she's often gone for days or weeks at a time. Men fly her around the world. Africa. The Middle East. South America. It's a glamorous lifestyle in its way, although it's not what I would choose for her."

"Have you tried to contact her?" Frost asked. "I've left messages on her cell phone, but I haven't gotten a reply."

"That's not unusual. Her phone is often turned off for long periods of time. I wish you'd tell me what's going on."

Frost didn't answer. "Do you know anything about this most recent engagement on Tuesday?"

Prisha shook her head. "No. If you think tech companies are stringent about confidentiality, you should see my sister's business. I never know who she's meeting or where or how long she'll be gone. If I had to guess, though, she was heading off on a boat."

"Why do you say that?"

"She made a joke about bringing Dramamine along. She's very susceptible to seasickness." Prisha studied his face and added, "Judging from your expression, I gather that comports with what you think she was doing."

Frost nodded. "Did she say anything else?"

"No, as I told you, she doesn't give me details about her work. But I could tell she wasn't happy about this job. She was nervous and anxious before she left. I didn't bother asking why. I knew I wouldn't get anything out of her. It usually means she's meeting someone who makes her uncomfortable. There are always men like that."

"How does she find her clients?" Frost asked.

"I'm better off not knowing the specifics," Prisha replied. "Zara walls off that part of her world. Given that what she's doing is technically illegal, I think she wants to protect me, since I'm a lawyer. But rich men have networks, especially in Silicon Valley. They know how to find what they want."

"Have you ever met a man named Denny Clark?" Frost asked. "Or did your sister ever mention that name?"

"I don't think so."

"What about an Asian chef named Mr. Jin?"

Prisha looked puzzled. "Mr. Jin? Well, yes, we both know him, although I don't know why that's important. Zara and I are rather fanatical about dim sum. We've eaten at his restaurant in Chinatown many times. He's catered a few Zelyx parties, too, where I brought my sister along as my guest."

"So Mr. Jin knows her personally?"

"Oh yes. Needless to say, Zara and I aren't shy. If we like what someone does, we make a point of introducing ourselves. We've chatted with Mr. Jin on several occasions."

"Would he also know Zara as Fawn?" Frost asked.

Prisha frowned. The question unsettled her. "I don't see how. He doesn't strike me as the kind of man to have those habits. Anyway, as successful as he is, Mr. Jin wouldn't be in the financial league necessary to afford my sister. So he would have no occasion to meet her outside the restaurant unless he—"

She stopped.

"Unless he catered a party where she was working?" Frost finished the sentence for her.

"Yes. I suppose that's possible, although Zara never mentioned it to me if he did. Not that she would."

Frost tried to connect the dots in his mind and see where they led him. There was a cruise on the *Roughing It* on Tuesday evening. Small group. Expensive, first-class tastes. Mr. Jin prepared the food. Frost imagined him meeting a beautiful young woman among the guests whom he already knows as Zara Anand. But before he can say anything, she introduces herself as Fawn and probably gives him a look with her eyes that asks him to remain silent.

Later he writes the name in his notepad: *Fawn.*

"What does your sister look like?" Frost asked.

"Zara? She's very distinctive. That's the most memorable kind of beauty. You can find many pretty faces, but there aren't many that would linger in your memory the way hers does."

"Do you have a photograph of her?"

"I do."

Prisha leaned over and tapped a few keys on her laptop. She turned the screen so that Frost could see it, and he found himself staring at a young woman who was every bit as royal as her sister suggested. She could have fit in anywhere, from palaces to boardrooms. It was easy to see the family resemblance. Zara looked a lot like Prisha, with the same thick dark hair, but she also had a unique quality that would make a man stop and stare. Her long nose was slightly too long; her big brown eyes were slightly too big for her face; her angled cheekbones were so sharp they looked severe. And yet when it all came together in one package, she was like Helen of Troy launching a thousand ships.

"See what I mean?" Prisha said with a smile.

"I do. It's also obvious that she's your sister. You two look very much alike."

"That's flattering, but I know the difference. Billionaires don't pay to have me with them, but they do with Zara."

"Can you text me that photo?" Frost asked. "It may help me locate her."

"I can, but only if you stop keeping me in the dark. We're talking about my sister. I have a right to know what's going on."

Frost chose his words carefully. "Two of the people who were part of that cruise on Tuesday are dead. Mr. Jin is missing. And I can't reach your sister, which worries me."

Prisha's brown eyes opened wide. "Oh no."

"That's why it's important that I find Zara right away. I need to know what happened on Tuesday, and frankly, I need to make sure she's safe. Do you have any way of contacting her?"

Prisha got up and paced. She rubbed her hands nervously together. "Only if she turns her phone on. Depending on where she is and what she's doing, she stays off the grid. It's part of the job."

"Is there anyone else she might reach out to? What about your parents?"

"They died years ago."

"A boyfriend?" Frost asked.

Prisha stopped. "Yes, she has a boyfriend. They've been together a few years."

"Who is he?"

"I don't know. I've never met him. Zara has never invited him to our house. She lives her life in compartments, Inspector. When you do what she does, you learn to be careful. I don't know whether her boyfriend even knows about her 'career.' Very few people know anything about her life as Fawn. When she needs to be picked up for an engagement, she goes elsewhere. The limo doesn't come here."

"Would you be able to figure out who her boyfriend is?"

"I can try, but I can't promise anything. Zara may have something in her room that would help me identify him. I'll see what I can find."

"I'd appreciate it."

"You have me very scared now, Inspector," Prisha admitted.

"I understand. I apologize for alarming you further, but I need to ask you something else. Have you had any unusual experiences here at the house since Tuesday night?"

"What do you mean?"

"Have you noticed any strange cars on the street? Have you spotted anyone following you? Do you have any reason to think someone might have broken into your house while you were away?"

Prisha thought about it. She wandered to the window and looked outside. "No, there hasn't been anything like that. When you're a single woman, you usually have radar for that kind of thing. I haven't felt unsafe."

"Okay."

Frost didn't tell her what he was thinking. If no one was looking for Fawn, that was probably because they knew she wasn't a threat. She was one more loose end from the cruise on Tuesday that had already been tied off, like Denny and Carla.

"This may seem like an odd question," he said, "but do you ever recall Zara mentioning the name Lombard?"

"You mean, like the street?"

"Yes."

"I don't think so. Why?"

"It's just something I'm following up on," Frost said. He stood up from the sofa. "I appreciate your time, Ms. Anand. If you hear from your sister, I hope you'll let me know right away. And please tell her to call me immediately. I don't know whether she's in danger, but I don't want to take any chances."

Prisha nodded. "I will."

"By the way, you said that Zara looked nervous and upset before she left on Tuesday. You thought she was meeting a client who made her uncomfortable. What exactly did you mean? Has she ever felt in physical danger with any of her clients?"

She looked as if she didn't know how to answer. "You'd have to understand her world, Inspector."

"Explain it to me anyway," Frost replied.

Prisha stood close enough to him that he was in the cloud of her perfume. "The men who can afford a woman like Zara—Fawn—aren't simply buying sex. That's part of it, but they're really buying an experience. And the experience needs to be perfect. When you pay that kind of money, you feel as if you *own* whoever is with you. They're your slave. If a girl puts a foot wrong—even accidentally—terrible things can happen. I don't know that Zara has ever felt in danger herself, but she knows girls who have. A few years ago, a girl was killed, in fact. It was someone Zara knew well. It affected her deeply."

"Who was this girl?" Frost asked.

"I don't know her real name. They only deal in aliases. Zara called her Naomi, that's all I know. I only found out as much as I did because I found Zara crying in her room one evening. She was very upset about what had happened."

"When was this?"

"A few years ago. Two, three, I'm not sure."

"How did Naomi die?"

"The police said she overdosed, but Zara said that was a lie. She told me Naomi was clean. The fact is, most of the high-end escorts never do drugs. In Zara's business, you have to be on your game all the time. Physically, socially, mentally, everything. Drugs don't mix with that."

"So what did Zara think really happened to Naomi?" Frost asked.

"She said Naomi was going to expose a client who was abusing her, and the client somehow arranged the overdose to prevent her from talking. Zara was devastated. And angry, too. I tried to talk her out of saying anything—I didn't want her getting killed, too—but she swore she was going to do something about it. She wanted revenge."

◆ ◆ ◆

Frost sat in his Suburban outside Fawn's house. With his laptop open on the dashboard, it didn't take him long to find Naomi.

More than three years earlier, a twenty-one-year-old woman named LaHonda Duke had been found near the BART tracks in Balboa Park. She'd died of a heroin overdose. The investigation showed no evidence of foul play. There was nothing in the police file to indicate that LaHonda had led a separate life as a high-priced escort and nothing to confirm that her street name was Naomi.

Even so, Frost knew he had the right victim. One hundred yards away from where her body had been found, Coyle had discovered a red snake on a concrete wall bordering the 280 freeway. LaHonda Duke was on his list.

He dialed Coyle's number.

"It's me," he said when he heard the private detective's voice. "Do you remember the LaHonda Duke case? It was an OD near Balboa Park. She's one of the snake victims."

"Sure," Coyle replied. "Accidental death, my ass. Someone shot her up."

"Did you look into LaHonda's background? Did you find out anything else about her?"

Coyle sounded as if he were gulping down a late dinner. "Like what?"

"Like her being a high-end hooker."

"No. If she was, I never found it, but those girls are usually pretty good at keeping the secret."

"Do you remember anything else about her case that would connect her to what's going on now? Anything that might tie her to Denny or Greg Howell or any of the other victims?"

"I'll have to pull my file," Coyle replied, "but I don't think so."

Frost sat in the truck and was silent for a moment. He was sure he was on to something. "I'm going to send you a photo. It's a girl with the street name Fawn. She's another upscale escort. I want to know if she came up in your research on any of the other snake cases."

"Sure thing."

Frost hung up the phone and sent the photo of Zara Anand to Coyle. Then he started up the SUV's engine and was about to pull into traffic when his phone rang again. The private detective was already calling him back.

"You better get over here," Coyle told him. "We need to talk right away."

"Oh?"

"Yeah, I got the photo, and I don't need to check my files on this one."

"What do you mean? You know Fawn?"

"I do. Remember I'd been following that vice cop for a couple weeks before he was murdered? I spotted him having dinner in Pacific Heights with a really stunning Indian brunette. Got some photos of her, too. She wasn't the kind of girl you'll ever forget once you lay eyes on her."

"Let me guess," Frost said.

"Yeah. The girl was Fawn. She was meeting with Alan Detlowe."

# 18

The man in the charcoal-gray BMW watched Frost Easton drive away. He didn't follow the Suburban. Instead, he opened the glove compartment of the car and pushed a button that released a false bottom. Inside was a cell phone. He powered it up and used the latest contact number to call in his report.

"Identification," the woman answered with her usual clipped, assured voice.

"Sutter," he said.

"Password."

"87126."

"Status."

"Golden Gate."

"Report," the woman said.

She always wanted a clean update. Quick, focused, no unnecessary details, no speculation. His job was to say what happened. After that, the information got passed along, and it was up to Lombard to make the decision.

"Easton went from Mr. Jin's place to the girl's house. Fawn. He met with her sister."

"Did you have ears on the conversation?"

"Yes."

"What did the sister tell him?"

"Most of the conversation was harmless, but she mentioned Fawn's interest in an earlier victim. Easton tied the reference back to LaHonda Duke. He knows she was one of the snakes."

"That's unfortunate," the woman said.

"There's more. Easton just talked to Coyle, and Coyle made a connection between Fawn and Alan Detlowe."

"Let me hear the conversation."

The man took his voice recorder out of his coat pocket. He held the machine up to the phone and played the most recent digital recording.

When it was over, there was a long pause from the other end.

"Hang on," the woman told him.

He waited. At least five minutes of silence passed. He knew not to hang up. The silence meant the woman was passing the information directly to Lombard and soliciting instructions.

Finally, she came back on the line.

"That's all for now," the woman said.

"Do you want me to follow Easton again? He's obviously heading to Coyle's."

"No, you're done for the night, so you can stand down," the woman told him. "We need to keep the field clear for Geary. He'll be delivering two snakes tonight."

# 19

Coyle lived and worked on the upper floor of a two-story office building tucked among the industrial warehouses of Toland Street. His neighbors were electrical supply companies and food storage facilities. It was nearly midnight when Frost arrived, and the area was a ghost town of overhead electrical wires, corrugated metal walls, and empty loading docks. The only noise was the thunder of traffic on the elevated lanes of the 280 freeway a few blocks away.

The building entrance was locked. He squinted to see a stairwell inside. Tall glass windows stretched along the offices on the first floor, but there were no lights. He pounded on the door, and not long after, he saw Coyle's doughy frame as the detective hustled downstairs and let him into the building.

"This is an interesting location," Frost said.

"Yeah, a buddy of mine owns the place. He was having trouble leasing the upstairs space after the last tenant went belly up. He lets me have it cheap, at least until he finds somebody else."

Coyle trotted up the stairs, and Frost followed. The first door in the drab corridor had a sign announcing **Coyle Investigations**. The detective showed him into a small anteroom. Coyle's PI license was framed and hung above a tweed sofa. It looked like an office for someone who'd watched too many detective movies.

"It's not much to look at, but clients don't usually come here," Coyle told him. "I usually go to them."

He opened another door and led Frost into a larger room where Coyle obviously worked and slept. All the walls were covered in cheap wood paneling. Frost saw a messy twin bed shoved in one corner, a refrigerator, and a bathroom not much bigger than a phone booth. Two rectangular card tables were pushed together in the middle of the floor and covered with papers and books. There was a desk against the wall with an old Gateway computer and an electronic setup that included three monitors. On the screens, Frost could see video surveillance feeds of the street and parking lot surrounding the building. The windows in the office were covered over with plywood, making the space claustrophobic.

Coyle popped open the refrigerator door. "You want a beer? I've got Coors. I'm not into all the IPAs and microbrews."

"No, thanks." Frost nodded at the wooden barriers over the windows. "You're taking some pretty serious precautions against spies."

"I suppose you think I'm paranoid."

Frost took a seat on a fold-up chair. "Well, I'm not sure you're wrong to be cautious. I've already been followed myself."

Coyle straddled one of the other chairs and smoothed down his thinning hair. "I knew I wasn't crazy. Somebody's been watching me, too."

"Do you know who?"

"I don't, but I think there's more than one. Like a network." Coyle leaned forward, and his heavy face was flushed. "I was wrong, wasn't I? We're not talking about a serial killer."

"No."

"Then what the hell is this, Inspector?"

"I don't know yet, but I'm pretty sure you've latched on to something big."

Coyle looked pleased with the compliment. "So what do you think it means that I saw this girl Fawn talking to Alan Detlowe?"

"It could explain why Detlowe was killed," Frost replied. "According to her sister, Fawn was upset about the death of her friend Naomi and wanted to do something about it. Then you saw Fawn talking to Detlowe and he wound up with his throat cut. I checked the dates. All of this happened within a one-week span. The timing can't be coincidental."

Coyle rubbed the whiskers on his chin. "You think Fawn asked Detlowe to look into Naomi's death?"

"Could be. Then he started asking questions that made somebody nervous. The thing is, you were watching Detlowe that whole time. You were following him after he met with Fawn. So maybe you saw him checking out whatever she told him. That might give us a clue about what he found out."

Coyle hopped up from the chair. "Okay, let's grab my Detlowe file. I keep all my cases on flash drives in the library. Notes, photos, videos, everything."

"Your library? Where's your library?"

Coyle's eyebrows danced, and he gave Frost a little smirk. The detective went to the wood-paneled wall and tapped the base of one of the panels with the toe of his shoe. The panel clicked open and moved aside like an accordion, revealing a door built into the wall.

"Come on, Coyle," Frost laughed. "A hidden door? Really?"

"Hey, I have to have some fun."

Coyle opened the next door and flicked on the overhead fluorescent lights in the adjacent room. Frost followed him inside and saw that the next room was at least three times larger than Coyle's office. The space stretched to the far wall of the building. As in the office, the windows were nailed shut with heavy plywood, so the only light was from overhead. The room was a combination of library and gaming space. Built-in bookshelves lined three of the walls, stocked with hundreds of mystery and science fiction novels dating back decades. There was a huge array of collectible Hot Wheels cars on some of the shelves, too. The fourth wall featured a large flat-screen television with virtual-reality goggles slung over the screen. Frost saw a set of golf clubs, a putting green, and a treadmill that was being used to store boxes of DVDs and VHS tapes.

"You realize you're the ultimate nerd, don't you?" Frost asked.

"Guilty," Coyle admitted.

He crossed the concrete floor of the large library to a shelf that contained shoeboxes labeled by year. He opened a box marked three years earlier and dug inside it until he came out with a thumb drive labeled with black marker.

"This is what I gathered on Detlowe," he said. "Let's check it out."

They returned to the office. Coyle still had the thumb drive in his hand.

That was when the computer monitors and the office lights all went out simultaneously with an electrical pop. The machines sighed as they switched off. With the windows shuttered by plywood, they were in total darkness. There was absolutely no light at all.

"Power's out," Coyle announced, his voice oddly disconnected from his body.

"Does that happen a lot?" Frost asked.

"No, it's weird. I can't remember when it last happened."

Frost dug in a pocket for his phone and switched it to flashlight mode, throwing a beam of light between the two of them. Coyle's round face was a worried mess of shadows.

"Do you think it's them?" Coyle asked.

"We better find out."

Frost used the glowing screen to guide them to the anteroom, which was brighter because the outside window was uncovered. He switched off the phone to avoid highlighting their location and crept to the side of the window. The streetlights up and down the block were still on.

"It's just us," he said. "The power's on everywhere else."

Coyle came up beside him and stood directly in front of the glass, and Frost grabbed his arm and yanked him away.

"Don't stand where anyone can see you," Frost warned him.

"What do we do?" Coyle murmured, his voice cracking with anxiety. The game was over. This was real.

"Stay here. I'll go downstairs and check it out."

Frost went to the office door and shined a light up and down the hallway. It was empty. He crept to the stairwell. The glass door on the first floor let in enough light from the street to confirm that no one was waiting in the lobby below him. He went down the steps and slipped through the outer door and used an empty soda cup to keep the door from locking.

He followed the walkway to the curb. His Suburban was the only vehicle in sight. The overhead streetlights made a glowing white trail down the block. He checked the driveway next to the building, but it was fenced off by a gate topped with barbed wire. He was alone. The city felt like a ghost town here.

The midnight air had turned colder. The wind blew down the lonely street with a growl. Frost retraced his steps to the front of the building, and that was when he saw that one of the downstairs windows had been shattered, leaving broken fragments around the frame. Someone was already inside. He dashed back through the front door and took the stairs two at a time.

*"Coyle?"* Frost hissed from the hallway.

The detective didn't reply.

Frost stopped where he was. He reached inside his jacket for his gun. He pressed against the wall and moved sideways toward the open doorway of the anteroom. Faint light from the window spilled into the corridor. He squatted and snapped around the corner. No one was there.

The door to Coyle's inner office was open. He called Coyle's name again, but the detective still didn't answer.

Frost approached the doorway step by step with his gun leading the way. When he was almost there, he took shelter behind the wall and switched the light of his phone quickly on and off. The glow of white light attracted no attention. He spun past the door frame and used his phone to survey the room. The small office was empty. Coyle wasn't there, but he noticed that the wooden panel concealing the hidden door into the library wasn't fully latched.

He put his phone back in his pocket.

Frost slid back the accordion panel silently. The inner door was closed. He stood clear of the doorway and reached around to twist the knob with one hand and push the door open several inches.

*"Coyle?"* he called again.

No answer.

The interior of the library was blacker than night. So was the office where Frost was standing. He couldn't see inside, and if anyone was waiting for him in the library, they couldn't see out. He held his breath, not wanting to make a sound. He listened to his senses for any noise, any smell, that would tell him that the room wasn't empty. He heard only one thing, faintly.

It was a slow, terrible, intermittent drip splattering on the floor. He remembered the layout of the room and could think of only one thing that would be dripping inside the library.

Blood.

Frost got down on his hands and knees. He crawled with agonizing slowness through the doorway, avoiding every noise. He was utterly blind. The room was a coffin, devoid of light. He reached out with his hands, feeling his way into the larger space of the library. With each movement, he stopped. If someone was here with him, they were frozen, too. Waiting.

He crawled and reached out, crawled and reached out.

Something dripped again. Very close by. The sheer silence around him made it sound loud.

His hand bumped against the warmth of skin. There was a body on the floor. He traced the fingers of a hand and followed the arm until he reached the face. His knuckles scratched against the stubble of a weak beard. It was Coyle, lying on his back, head turned sideways. Frost went to check the detective's pulse, but when he did, his fingers sank into a sea of blood. He recoiled, clamping his mouth shut. Coyle's neck had been cut, viciously and deeply, nearly decapitating him. His arteries had already bled out. Frost bent to the man's chest to listen for a heartbeat and heard none.

Coyle was dead.

Frost didn't have time to feel regret. He knew he wasn't alone in the room. Coyle's murderer was here with him, too. Silent and deadly, hidden somewhere, invisible in the darkness.

Frost eased himself to his feet and backed away from the body. It didn't matter whether his eyes were open or closed; he couldn't see anything. He backed up until he felt bookshelves pressing into his back. At least he knew no one was behind him now. He extended his gun in one hand and slid out his phone, but before he could turn on the screen, the folds of his jacket snagged on something on the shelf behind him. A small object rolled and fell. Even as it slipped off the bookshelf, Frost knew what it was. One of Coyle's Hot Wheels cars.

The toy clanged to the ground, giving him away. Instantly, he felt a whip of air from his left side. He turned, pointing his gun, but he wasn't fast enough. Someone crashed into him, taking him to the floor and knocking away his gun and phone. A wildly aimed knife sliced through the air and cut into his jeans and skin. Frost gasped with pain and rolled. The knife came down again, but it missed this time and struck against the concrete floor with a metallic clatter.

Frost kicked hard. He got lucky. The blow landed, yielding a grunt of breath, but by the time he threw himself toward the sound, the killer had already moved. Frost pushed himself up. The cut on his leg stung. Blood pulsed down his skin. He tried not to breathe, but the exertion made his chest demand oxygen. He had to inhale. As soon as he did, the noise brought his assailant charging through the darkness and landing against his torso like a battering ram. Frost staggered backward. He heard the swish of the knife again and ran blindly, coughing as he tried to suck air back into his lungs. He zigzagged, hearing footsteps chasing him, and collided with the wall. Boxes flew, and books tumbled around him.

Another assault barely missed him as he dove free. The entire bookshelf toppled with a crash.

Frost skidded across the floor and stopped. So did the other person. He could hear breathing in the room, but the noise came from everywhere and nowhere in the darkness. His senses began to play tricks on him. He was seeing things when he couldn't see anything at all. Shapes moved. False lights fooled his eyes. Frost stretched out his arms and felt nothing at the end of his reach. He took a few silent steps and reached out again.

Nothing.

And again.

Then he felt something cool and leathery under his hands and realized it was Coyle's golf bag. It toppled away from his grasp and fell with an obscene noise. He ducked away from the sound, but as he did, he slipped on something under his feet and hit the ground. Golf balls rolled wildly around the floor. When he crawled, he came upon the clubs that had spilled from the leather bag.

Frost grabbed a golf club and stood up. He swung it through the darkness like a baseball bat, causing a ripple of air. He moved and swung it again. He kept swinging over and over, making fast, vicious circles.

There he was.

The club slammed hard against the other person in the room and produced a howl of pain. Frost dropped the club and landed a blow with his fist. And another. Then a foot shot into Frost's stomach with the impact of a brick and threw him off his feet. His skull hit the concrete. Even in blackness, the room spun; he could feel his brain doing somersaults. Nausea rose in his throat.

He didn't have much time. The man was coming for him. He skittered backward along the floor, and as his hands scraped across the concrete, a miracle happened.

His fingers closed over his gun.

Frost scrambled to his feet. With no hesitation, he rammed back the slide and fired. He couldn't see anything but a kaleidoscope in the orange flash. He fired again. And again. The noise of running footsteps banged on the floor. And again. And again. The man was getting away. He fired wildly as the door opened somewhere in the spinning darkness. He fired twice more, causing blows of thunder in his ears, but he was alone with the echoes now. He'd missed; the killer was gone. He stood there, breathing hard, as sweat poured down his face.

# 20

Frost stared at the snake.

The paint was still wet, dripping from its jaws like blood. He'd found it two blocks from Coyle's building on a concrete pillar underneath the 280 freeway. This one looked rushed, as if the killer had been in a hurry to get away. Frost wondered if the plan had been to have a second snake painted under the first one. If he hadn't stumbled across his gun, he'd be dead, too.

He reached around to the back of his head and felt sticky blood in his hair. The cut on his leg throbbed. When a speeding truck above him made the freeway shudder, the vibration shot like spasms up his neck and made his headache worse. He closed his eyes and squeezed his forehead.

"You look like crap, Easton."

Frost turned around. Trent Gorham stood a few feet away, his shoulders slightly slumped on his tall frame. Behind him, at the end of the block, the whirling lights of emergency vehicles clustered near Coyle's building. Frost leaned against the highway column, feeling dizzy.

"I'm fine," Frost told him.

"That's not what I hear. The EMTs want you in the ambulance to tape up your leg, and then they want you at the hospital for a CT scan. You could be dealing with a concussion."

"I'll worry about that later."

"Not later. Now. You need to get checked out. I'll put you in cuffs if I need to."

Frost didn't protest. "Fine. Whatever."

"Listen, I'm sorry about Coyle," Gorham added. "The guy was a wacko, but I have to admit, I liked him."

"I liked him, too." Frost nodded his head at the graffiti on the freeway column. "Another murder, another snake. Do you still think this is just a crazy conspiracy?"

Gorham's pale blond face gave nothing away. He shoved his hands in his pockets and looked over his shoulder at the police officers standing nearby. They were out of earshot, but he lowered his voice anyway.

"A snake doesn't *prove* anything, Easton. Half the people on the street probably knew about Coyle and his serial-killer-snake theory. If it was me going to knock him off, I'd paint a snake nearby, too, just to throw us off the scent."

"You don't believe that," Frost said.

Gorham shrugged. "All I'm saying is that Coyle was a private detective. When you dig into people's dirty laundry for a living, you make enemies. The suspect list is going to be a mile long. Don't be surprised if this one goes unsolved."

"It seems like that happens a lot with you, Trent. Whenever there's a snake involved, the case goes nowhere."

The taller inspector took a step into Frost's space. The man's sheer size made him intimidating. "You don't know what you're talking about, Easton. You have absolutely no idea."

"Then why don't you fill me in? Because I'm pretty sure you know more than you're telling me."

Gorham snapped his mouth shut without saying anything more. He stepped away and grimaced as he watched the lights of the freeway traffic overhead. He pinched his big nose between his fingers with a snuffling noise.

"I'll have one of the uniforms drive you to the hospital," he went on, ignoring Frost's question. "You'll need to write up a full statement tomorrow about what happened to Coyle. Hayden and Cyril want a debrief about Denny Clark, too, so think hard about what you're going to tell them. My advice is to steer clear of snakes if you don't want to look like a fool."

Gorham turned away, but Frost grabbed his arm.

"Hold on, Trent. Coyle had a flash drive with him before he was killed. The drive contained all of his surveillance notes from when he was following Alan Detlowe. I want a copy. I want to dig through whatever Coyle found."

"The Detlowe murder is my case," Gorham snapped.

"Yeah, but now there's a link between Detlowe's murder and what happened to Denny Clark. And Denny's death is *my* case."

"What's the link?" Gorham demanded. "What are you talking about?"

"Fawn. The escort. Denny called her, remember? Coyle also saw Fawn talking to Detlowe the week before he was killed."

Gorham's face reddened. His voice got louder. "So what? Alan was a vice cop. He was on a first-name basis with half the hookers in the city. It doesn't mean a damn thing."

"I don't think this was an ordinary meeting," Frost told him. "Fawn was upset about the death of one of her friends—another escort who went by the alias Naomi. I think Fawn asked Detlowe for help, and he started digging into Naomi's clients. That may be what got him killed. Coyle's notes might tell us who Detlowe was going after."

"And how will that help you with Denny Clark's murder?" Gorham asked.

"Because there's a good chance that whoever killed Naomi and Detlowe killed Denny, too."

Gorham shook his head. "I think you're out in left field on this, but it doesn't matter. There was no flash drive."

"What?"

"We didn't find a flash drive on Coyle's body. There was nothing in his outer office. Whoever killed him must have taken it."

Frost scowled with frustration. Another lead had been stripped away. But it also meant he was knocking on the right doors. Denny. Detlowe. Fawn. Lombard. They were all connected.

"I need to get back to the crime scene," Gorham went on when Frost was silent. "We're done here. Go get somebody to look at your head."

The other detective began to walk away toward the warehouses of Toland Street, but then he stopped and retraced his steps.

"Hey, Easton," Gorham leaned in and whispered. "I'm not saying you're right about the snakes, but if you are, that means you were lucky to walk away alive. Whoever took out Coyle missed you. Maybe next time you won't be so lucky, huh? You should think about that."

The sun through the bay window in his Russian Hill house finally woke Frost up. He lay on his back on the sofa in the living room, with his right arm draped to the floor. He blinked and saw two pairs of eyes watching him. One pair belonged to Shack, who was in a sphinx position on his chest. The other pair belonged to Tabby, who sat on the carpet next to the sofa with her legs crossed.

"You're alive," she said. "Are you okay? I was worried about you."

Frost saw that her pretty mouth was pressed into a frown. "Thanks, but I'll be fine. There's no concussion, just a monster headache and a nasty cut on my leg. What are you doing here?"

"The hospital called Duane. Duane called and asked if I would check on you. He's busy with the food truck."

"What time is it?" Frost asked. "I didn't get home until dawn."

"Noon."

He groaned and sat up, dislodging Shack. He was late. The sudden shift sent little knives up his neck, making him wince. Tabby got off the floor and took a seat next to him on the sofa. Her eyes noted the blood on his jeans.

"Are you really okay?" she asked.

"Some coffee, some Advil, I'll be good to go."

"What happened? They didn't give Duane any details."

"I came out on the losing end of a fight. It's nothing to worry about."

Tabby's forehead crinkled with displeasure. Her voice rose. "Don't lie to me, Frost. I heard on the news that somebody got killed. Tell me the truth. Did you almost get killed, too?"

"Yeah, I was lucky," Frost admitted.

Tabby closed her eyes and inhaled loudly. "I don't know how the spouses of cops do it. If I had to live with that fear every day—"

"Hey, I'm here. That's the main thing."

"Don't you wonder whether it's really worth it? I wish you would just give it up and do something else."

"Yeah, I think about that sometimes myself. Then I think, what if I hadn't been out on that pier with you last fall? Bad things will always happen. At least I have a chance to do something about it."

Tabby picked up Shack from the floor and stroked him in her lap. "I know. You're right. I'm being selfish. And I'm sorry about raising my voice. I think you're getting some of the firepower I was aiming at Duane."

"Are you guys having problems?" Frost asked.

"We had a huge fight last night. The worst I can remember."

"Sorry."

"Oh, I didn't handle it well. There was a lot of yelling. I told him he wasn't listening to me and that he didn't care what was going on with my life. And then he started asking how come I didn't want to set a date for the wedding, and I was in his face about him not realizing what I've been through and how I needed more time. It was all real mature."

"Duane likes to fight," Frost said. "It's how he communicates. Duane Beaston, remember? Then he always makes up."

"Well, I don't like to fight. I hate it. But I also know he's right."

"About what?"

"I've been putting him off about the wedding. I'm not ready to take that step." She grabbed Shack from her lap and hugged the cat to her chest. "The truth is, I'm not sure I'll ever be ready. Not with him."

"Tabby," Frost murmured. "Come on. You said yourself this is just a phase. Duane loves you. You love Duane."

Her green eyes shone with tears. "Do I? I don't know anymore. Lately I don't know what I feel."

He was shocked to hear her say that. "Why the change?"

"I wish I could tell you. I'm trying to figure everything out myself. Life is just so complicated right now. I'm sorry, Frost. Here I am putting you in the middle, and that's not fair of me. Duane's your brother. I know you have to put him first. Really, I'm sorry. Please don't say anything to him."

Tabby put Shack down. She wiped her eyes and looked embarrassed. Then she changed the subject. "Did you find Mr. Jin?"

"No."

"Do you think he's okay?" she asked.

"I don't know. I hope so."

Tabby twisted her fingers together. She still looked uncomfortable. "This other man who was killed last night, did you know him?"

"Not well, but yeah, I knew him. He was a decent guy."

"Why was he killed?" Tabby asked.

"He knew things that somebody didn't want exposed. The irony is that he'd been talking about it for years, and nobody listened to him. Me taking him seriously is probably what got him killed. As it is, I still don't understand how they—"

Frost stopped in midsentence.

"What?" Tabby asked.

He didn't answer. He sat there, frozen to silence, thinking through the chain of events from the previous night. The meeting with Fawn's sister. His phone calls to Coyle. The attack on Coyle's office. He realized it couldn't possibly be an accident that Lombard had targeted them just minutes after Coyle told Frost about the connection between Fawn and Detlowe.

"They *knew*," he murmured to himself, barely aloud.

"Knew what?" Tabby asked in a normal voice.

Frost put a finger over his lips to warn her to stay quiet.

"Nothing," he said. "I'm just thinking aloud. Hey, would you mind making me a cup of coffee? I need some caffeine today."

Tabby gave him a puzzled look. "Sure. Okay."

She headed for the kitchen, and Shack followed her. Frost got up from the sofa with a wince and retrieved his black sport jacket from the chair where he'd thrown it when he returned from the hospital. He held the jacket up in his hand and rifled through the pockets. Left side, right side, breast, inside. He found nothing. Maybe he was wrong.

Tabby came back into the living room with coffee from his Keurig machine in a Mark Twain mug. He took a sip and put the mug down. She waited for him with her arms crossed and a curious, expectant expression on her face. He studied the sport jacket in his hand again, and this time he flipped both of the lapels back. Still nothing. Then he turned the jacket around and flipped up the collar.

There it was.

The square electronic device was smaller than a postage stamp. It clung to the inside fabric of the jacket with little metal teeth. He tried to remember who'd bumped into him and where it might have happened, but it could have been anywhere.

Tabby saw the bug and opened her mouth in horror to say something, but he quickly held up his hand to stop her. She shut her mouth without saying a word. He put the jacket back on the chair and walked up to her. Without even thinking about what he was doing, he put his arms around her waist and put his face next to her cheek and whispered in her ear.

"It's a listening device."

She murmured back. "Well, don't you want to destroy it?"

"Not yet. I don't want them to know I've found it."

"How long has it been there?"

"I'm not sure."

"That's so creepy. Who would do that?"

"That's what I want to find out."

There was nothing else to say. At that moment, they had no reason to be as close as they were. And yet they didn't move. His hands were on her waist, they were face-to-face, but he didn't let go right away. She was warm and soft and close. The sun through the bay window turned her hair to fire.

Frost stepped back and let his arms fall to his sides. He bent down and retrieved his coffee. "I have to go," he said. "I'm late."

"Me too." Tabby's voice was hushed. Her eyes blinked with confusion.

"Thanks for checking on me."

"Of course. Do you want me to come back tonight? I mean, if you want me to cook dinner for you, I can—"

"You don't have to do that."

"I know. I just thought—"

She didn't go on. Her words hung there, unspoken, and they both left them there. Without saying anything more to him, she turned and walked away. He heard the quick tap of her shoes in the foyer, then the opening and closing of the front door. She was gone.

He was alone.

Then he looked at his jacket and remembered that he wasn't alone at all. It was time to figure out who was behind this.

# 21

When Frost drove toward the headquarters building in Mission Bay, the charcoal BMW showed up on his tail again, as he'd expected. The driver played it smarter this time, leaving several cars between them. Frost had to keep a careful eye on his mirror to see the BMW come and go in traffic. The car was far enough away to disappear if necessary, but close enough to listen in on the bug.

When he reached Mission Bay, Frost didn't stop. He headed past the police headquarters building and continued south on Third Street. His wary follower stayed a couple of blocks behind him.

Frost tapped a button on the steering wheel and used the voice commands to dial his brother.

"Bro!" Duane answered, and Frost could hear a crowd of voices in the background. "I'm wrapping up the lunch rush. You okay?"

"I'll live."

"I asked Tabs to check on you. Did she show up?"

"She did."

He heard a metallic bang as Duane put down the phone, and his brother's irritated voice grew muffled in the background. "Raymonde, you call this al dente on the linguine? Are you kidding me? Dump it, start over, hand this crap out to the kids as shoelaces."

Frost smiled to himself. In the kitchen, Duane was still the Beast. But his smile faded as he thought about his conversation with Tabby.

His brother came back on the line. "Sorry. Usual craziness. What's up?"

"I have a question. Tabby mentioned an Asian chef named Mr. Jin. Do you know him?"

"Sure. Man's a genius. First time I had his xiaolongbao, I swear I cried. Why, what's up?"

"He's missing, and I'm trying to find him," Frost explained, and then he shifted into a lie for whoever was listening in the BMW behind him. "I got a text from a guy who claims he's a sous chef for Mr. Jin and might know where he is. I'm meeting him down at Candlestick Point. I thought maybe you knew some of the chefs on Mr. Jin's team."

"Sorry, bro. I don't." Duane's voice became muffled again. "There's too much ginger beer in the marinade, damn it! You're not making a fricking Moscow Mule!"

"I'll let you go," Frost said.

"Yeah, sorry to rush you off. Glad you're okay."

"Thanks," Frost said, but then he continued before his brother could hang up, "How about you, Duane? Are you okay?"

"Me? Great, never better. Why?"

"It's just something Tabby said."

"She told you about our fight, huh? Don't sweat it. The harder we fight, the hotter it is when we make up. We're fine."

Frost knew that wasn't true, but he didn't know how to tell his brother. He wanted to say something more, but he didn't want to say it this way, and he didn't want to say it with someone listening to every word. "Well, good."

"I'm glad she talks to you, you know," Duane went on. "You need somebody to talk to, Frost. Nobody's ever going to replace Katie, but I like that you and Tabby are already like brother and sister."

"Yeah," Frost replied, his voice clipped. "I like that, too. Later, Duane."

"Later."

He clicked on the wheel to end the call.

He cleared his head and checked the mirror again. The BMW lagged behind him, but it was still there. The trap was laid, and now it was a question of who walked into it. He turned off Third Street as he approached the waterside trails near the old site of the Candlestick Park stadium. This was an area that had a lot of memories for him. As a teenager in the 1990s, he'd gone to dozens of Giants and 49ers games at Candlestick, huddled under thick blankets against the frigid night winds off the bay. Sometimes it was the whole family. Sometimes it was just him and Katie. She'd always been the rabid sports fan between the two of them, yelling herself hoarse at every game.

Driving past the land where the stadium had been, he could picture Katie with her Giants cap tugged low over her blond hair and mustard on her face as she ate a foot-long hot dog. Duane was right. He missed Katie; he missed having a sister he could talk to.

Duane was also wrong. Frost didn't see Tabby as a sister at all, and the guilt behind his feelings was eating away at him.

He pulled into a parking area practically across the street from the old stadium site. He was alone for now. He took his sport jacket and slipped it on as he got out. The wind blew in from the water not even a hundred yards away. The sun was high, but the air was cold. He followed a paved trail past flat marshland that was emerald green after a winter of rains. He didn't look back to see if anyone had shown up behind him. When he reached the water's edge, he tramped off the trail into the shelter of a thick stand of fir trees, where he was invisible.

He didn't have to wait long.

Another man appeared on the walkway that led to the bay. Frost peered through the branches at him. He was young, probably not more than twenty-five years old, with tanned Hispanic skin, glasses, and a trimmed businessman's haircut. He wore a suit, which was unusual in San Francisco, but he also wore athletic shoes that muffled his footsteps. He wasn't tall or muscled; he was the kind of unmemorable man who would blend in with just about any surroundings. The cords of his earphones wound from his suit pocket to his ears, as if he were listening to music on his phone, but Frost knew he was listening to something else.

Him.

He could see a flash of puzzlement in the man's eyes as he studied the trail ahead of him. He was wondering where Frost had gone.

In the trees, Frost murmured aloud, "That's far enough. Stop right there."

The man was good. He covered his shocked reaction so quickly that Frost would have missed it if he hadn't been watching carefully. The man stopped dead on the trail. He removed his phone from inside his suit pocket and fiddled with the buttons as if he were simply switching songs on his playlist. But his eyes were moving, and he glanced sharply in every direction around him.

Frost took out his gun and badge and emerged from the trees.

"Looking for me?" he asked.

The man slid his earphones out of his ears. His gaze shifted to the badge and the gun in turn, and he demonstrated just the right amount of surprise and fear. He let the earphone wires hang down his suitcoat and raised both arms in the air with his fingers spread wide. "I'm sorry, Officer, is there a problem?"

Frost pushed through the brush to the paved trail. He kept his gun pointed at the ground. "I know you've been following me," he said. "Let's not pretend, okay? I found the bug."

The man acted his part. His eyes widened. "I think there's been some kind of mistake. I'm just here taking a walk."

"What's your name?" Frost asked.

"Luis Moreno."

"What kind of car do you drive, Mr. Moreno?"

"A gray BMW."

"And where were you coming from?"

"Nowhere, really. I mean, my last job was in South Beach, so I thought I'd come down here and take a hike on my lunch hour."

"What do you do?"

"I'm a city inspector," Moreno replied. "I can show you identification."

Frost nodded. "Slowly, please."

"Oh yeah. Of course."

Moreno did as he was told. He peeled back the flap of his suit coat and carefully removed his wallet using two fingers. Awkwardly, he flipped it open and held out his driver's license and city identification for Frost to see. He was telling the truth. Luis Moreno worked in code enforcement for the city's Department of Building Inspection.

"Hand me the earphones," Frost told him.

"What?"

"I want to hear what you're listening to."

Moreno's brow wrinkled with confusion, but he held the purple earbuds out to Frost, who held one of them close enough to hear the beat of loud music. He recognized a song by Pitbull, rather than an echo of their own conversation. Moreno had already switched away from the listening device as soon as he knew Frost had spotted him. Frost was sure that the man had also deleted the app on his phone that controlled the electronic surveillance.

These people were professionals.

Professional spies. Professional assassins.

"Are you armed, Mr. Moreno?" Frost asked.

"What, like a gun? No, of course not."

"Gun, knife, any kind of weapon," Frost said.

"Well, I carry pepper spray. It's for self-defense. I deal with a lot of people who aren't too happy to see me, and I'm often inside abandoned buildings where criminal activity goes on."

The man had an answer for everything. His cover story was perfect. He was also a liar, but Frost knew he was never going to prove it.

"Let me see your fingernails," Frost said.

"What?"

"You heard me."

Moreno held out his hands, and Frost checked the nails carefully. There were no traces of blood. If Moreno had been the man to kill Coyle, he'd cleaned up well, but Frost didn't think this was the same man. Even so, there was one way to be certain.

"Untuck your shirt, lift it up. Let me see your stomach."

"Look, Officer, I've been very patient—"

"We can do this here, or we can do it at our central processing facility, Mr. Moreno."

The man nodded quickly. He yanked the flaps of his dress shirt out of his belt and bunched the fabric so that his midriff was revealed. Frost checked his stomach and sides and saw no bruises. He'd landed a solid blow on the body of the man last night, and there would have been evidence of where the golf club had hit him. Moreno wasn't the killer.

Frost reached behind his collar and slid the small listening device into his hand. He dropped it on the concrete trail and crushed it under his shoe. Then he waved his hand toward the marshland on the other side of the trees.

"Get the hell out of here, Mr. Moreno. I better not see your car behind me again, okay?"

"Um, sure, yes," the man replied.

Moreno stuffed part of his shirt into his pants again and backed up awkwardly, just like an innocent man who'd been accosted by the police.

But he wasn't innocent. Frost knew that. When he was a few yards away, Moreno turned and half walked, half ran toward the parking area.

"Hey, Moreno," Frost called after him.

The man looked over his shoulder. At that distance, Frost could see a glint of the truth in the man's eyes. The I-know-nothing expression on his face had disappeared, and his mouth had hardened into an arrogant smirk. Moreno knew he'd won.

"I've got a message for you," Frost said.

"What kind of message?"

"I'm coming for Lombard," Frost told him. "Pass it along."

# 22

Captain Hayden looked up over his reading glasses as Frost came into his office. The captain filled the high-backed chair, all bulk and muscle. His hand-carved walnut desk was as big and imposing as he was. Cyril stood behind him in crisp dress blues, and the angle made Hayden's assistant look like a vulture perched on the captain's shoulder. Trent Gorham was in the office, too, leaning against the wall near the large window that looked north toward AT&T Park.

"Close the door, will you, Easton?" Hayden said.

Frost did, and then he sat in a chair across from the captain. He felt surrounded by the other men, as if the setup had been designed to intimidate him.

"Nasty business last night," Hayden continued, shaking his head. "You wrote up your statement? You gave Trent the information he needs?"

"I did."

Hayden's mottled black-and-tan brow wrinkled like a topographical map of the world. "I'm not happy that the killer got the better of you, Easton. You had a murderer in the room with you, and you let him get away. Now we're starting from scratch to catch whoever it was."

"You're right. I'm sorry, sir."

"I don't like it when the criminals are better fighters than the people on my team."

"This man was well trained, that's for sure," Frost said.

"Military?"

"Possibly."

"Did you get any kind of description?" Hayden asked.

"No, the room was pitch-black," Frost explained. "I never saw him."

Hayden's breath rumbled loudly, like an engine in need of tuning. "Well, this business with Coyle is unfortunate, but it's also a distraction. If you're a private dick, you better develop eyes in the back of your head. Trent will go over the man's case files and see what he can find."

"I'd like to help with that," Frost said. "I knew Coyle. I want to put his killer away."

Hayden shot him down with a wave of his big hand. "No, leave this to Trent. I want you focused on the Denny Clark homicide. I'm getting a lot of pressure to put that one to bed quickly."

"Pressure?" Frost asked. "From who?"

"The chief. The mayor. The city council. Apparently, a lot of rich people set foot on Clark's boat at one time or another, and they don't like the attention. The longer this case sits open, the more questions are going to get asked. Khristeen Smith over at the *Chronicle* will be camping outside my door to do an exposé. Nobody wants that, so wrap it up fast, Easton."

"I'm trying to do that, sir—" Frost began, but Hayden interrupted him impatiently.

"Cyril tells me you found cocaine hidden on Denny Clark's boat."

"That's right."

"So we're looking at a drug-related murder? That's what I said from the beginning. Talk to some of Trent's friends in vice. They can probably tell you whose pool Clark was pissing in."

"I'll do that, sir." Frost shot a glance at Gorham, who was studying his own fingernails and not looking up.

"Ask them to canvass the dealers working the marina," Hayden went on. "Somebody knows something. Even if we can't make an arrest,

I want to have something I can tell people when they call. Get me more information by tomorrow. If you need extra support in the investigation, run it by Cyril. He'll get you what you need."

Hayden slapped a file folder shut on his desk. He was literally trying to close the book on Denny. Frost knew he'd been dismissed, but he waited out the silence until Hayden looked up again and picked at his multiple chins as if he were plucking a bass guitar.

"Is there something else, Easton?" the captain mumbled.

"I think there's more going on in this case than just a drug hit," Frost replied. "I've got three other people from Denny's boat who are missing or dead."

"Excuse me?" The captain twisted around and growled at Cyril. "Why am I only hearing about this now?"

Cyril's face was cool as he stared past Hayden at Frost. "Because I'm only hearing about it myself, sir."

Hayden studied Frost with marble-black eyes. "Well, you better fill us in, Easton. What's going on?"

"Denny Clark took out his boat on a charter cruise last Tuesday," Frost told them. "I haven't been able to get details about the guest list, but it sounds like it was small and very exclusive. Denny walked away with a lot of cash, and so did his ex-wife, Carla. Same with the catering chef, Mr. Jin. The thing is, now Denny's dead, and Carla is, too. The Berkeley police say she committed suicide, but it was the same day as Denny's murder, so I'm suspicious about the timing. Mr. Jin disappeared on Wednesday morning, and no one has seen him since."

Hayden frowned. "That's two. You said there were three others. Who else?"

"Denny was in contact with a high-priced escort who uses the name Fawn. She's been missing since Tuesday night, too. I've left messages, but she hasn't checked in. If an escort was on the boat that night, then somebody on the guest list probably hired her. Fawn doesn't come cheap."

"What do you know about this cruise?" Hayden asked.

"Not a lot. I talked to a woman named Belinda Drake who uses the *Roughing It* as an entertainment venue for her clients. I think she's the one who set up the Tuesday charter, but she won't say anything about it. For now, I don't have any leverage to make her talk."

"I'm familiar with Belinda Drake. She's close to the mayor. Tread carefully with her, Easton." Hayden's fingers drummed the desk. "Do you have a theory about all of this?"

"My theory is that something happened on that cruise last Tuesday that somebody wants to cover up," Frost said. "All of the witnesses are disappearing."

"But you have no idea what actually happened?" Hayden asked.

"No."

"Or who was on the boat?"

"No."

"So how do you propose to find out?"

"I have one more lead to follow up," Frost told him. "Denny had a friend named Chester Bagley. I think he used him as a bartender on his charters. I'm going to try to find Chester and see if he knows anything about Tuesday."

"Is that all you have?" Hayden asked.

Frost took a look at Trent Gorham, who almost imperceptibly shook his head.

"No, that's not all," Frost went on, ignoring Gorham. "I'm also following up on a theory that started with the PI. Coyle. He was convinced that several unsolved homicides in the past few years are connected."

"Connected how?" Hayden asked.

Frost showed the captain a photograph of the red snake he'd found on the column of the 280 freeway the previous night. Behind Hayden, Cyril leaned forward to study it, too. He couldn't read their faces to decide if they'd seen the graffiti before.

"This snake symbol has appeared near the scene of at least thirteen unexplained deaths in the last five years," Frost said. "Actually, fourteen now that Coyle is dead. That includes Denny Clark and Carla Steiff, too."

"I'm sorry, did you say fourteen deaths?" Hayden asked.

"Yes, sir. Including one of ours. A vice cop named Alan Detlowe."

"Alan?" Hayden said sharply. "I knew Alan. Trent, that was your case, wasn't it? I never heard about anything like this in conjunction with Alan's murder. How is it possible this didn't hit our radar earlier?"

Frost intervened as Gorham stammered for a response. "If I was in Trent's shoes, I wouldn't have taken Coyle seriously, either, sir. I was pretty dubious about the theory myself, but now it's hard to ignore."

"So what do you think this is about?" Cyril inquired from behind the captain's shoulder. "Is it a gang related symbol? Or part of an organized-crime syndicate?"

"It could be either," Frost said. "Whoever is behind this, I've got their attention. They've been following me for two days. Someone planted a bug on me, too. They've been listening in on my conversations."

Frost deposited a plastic bag with the disabled listening device on the desk in front of Hayden and Cyril. This time, even Gorham came off the wall and looked concerned.

"Who the hell has the balls to bug a police detective?" Hayden demanded.

"I identified one of the people who was following me," Frost replied. "I tracked him down at Candlestick Point a couple of hours ago. He's a city employee named Luis Moreno. When I got back to my desk, I called the department where he works. Moreno never checked in after lunch. His cover was blown. I think he's gone."

"Do you have anything else?" Hayden asked.

Frost hesitated.

*Trust no one. Don't talk to the cops.*

"I have a name," he said, ignoring his own hesitation.

Frost saw Gorham shake his head again and mouth a single word at him: *No.*

But Frost had come too far to stop.

"Lombard," he said. "The name Lombard keeps coming up in my investigation."

Hayden cocked his head in surprise. Then he did something Frost would never have expected. He laughed. The captain reclined in his chair at a dangerous angle and exchanged a grin with Cyril. "Lombard," he chuckled. "Seriously? That's what you heard?"

"Yes, sir. The name Lombard is all over the street, but no one will talk about what it means."

"I bet."

Frost was puzzled. "I'm sorry, have I missed something?"

"I think you've fallen for a myth, Easton."

"What do you mean?"

Hayden's shoulders shook as he laughed again. "The story of Lombard has been around as long as I can remember. Hell, one of the captains teased me about it when I was a rookie, and that was a very, very long time ago."

"The 'story' of Lombard?" Frost asked.

"That's right. Nobody knows who originally came up with it, but any time we had a case that went cold, the gag line among the cops was 'Lombard did it.' Like there was some kind of supercriminal out there we could blame. It was an inside joke for years. Unfortunately, a reporter got hold of it and actually wrote a story about this mystery killer named Lombard. How come the police were keeping him secret? How come nobody could catch him? The chief was furious. He had to explain that Lombard didn't really exist, but the conspiracy had already taken hold around the city. I thought the joke died out years ago, but I guess it's back."

Frost didn't know what to say.

He felt like a fool.

"The snake graffiti isn't a myth," he protested, but as soon as he said it, he knew he was making the situation worse. Hayden and Cyril studied the image again and recognized for the first time how the twists of the snake's body resembled the San Francisco street. The captain laughed again. He thrust his enormous bulk out of his chair and came around the desk and slapped Frost cheerfully on the back.

"Lombard," Hayden said. "Yeah, I see it. Oh, this is good. Don't feel bad, Easton. Somebody out there is playing an elaborate joke on us, and you're just the one who got tagged with it."

"Coyle's dead," Frost replied. "So is Denny Clark. That's not a joke."

"You're right, but I think you better reexamine what's real and what's not in this case. It's easy to get sucked into a conspiracy, particularly with somebody like Coyle. These nuts can be pretty persuasive. Go back over the evidence in the Denny Clark case and stop worrying about snakes, okay? Odds are, you're going to find that this was a drug murder, just like I said. This Luis Moreno who was following you is probably on the payroll for a local dealer."

Frost stood up. He felt heat on his face.

"I'll do that," he said. "I'm sorry to bother you with this, sir."

"Don't worry about it, Easton. Believe me, you're not the first cop to get played."

The laughter of the three men followed him as he left the captain's office and made his way back to his own desk. He sat down, his head spinning. Hayden was right about one thing. Frost no longer had any idea what was real and what was not.

This had all started with Denny's last word as he was dying. *Lombard.*

That was no myth. Denny believed in Lombard. And yet maybe Denny had been fooled, too. Maybe none of it was real.

A story that had been around for years.

An answer for every cold case.

A joke. *Lombard did it.*

Frost shook his head and thought about Herb's street network being turned against him. He thought about the fear on Belinda Drake's face. He thought about Fox: *Don't mess with Lombard's business, or you're next.*

What if Captain Hayden was wrong?

What if someone had turned the Lombard myth into reality?

Frost felt a shadow cross his desk. Trent Gorham stood over him. The other detective bent down with one big hand on Frost's desk and the other on Frost's shoulder. Gorham's face was split by a huge smile, and his blond eyebrows danced with amusement. In the doorway of Hayden's office, Cyril Timko watched the two of them. Cyril grinned, too.

"Don't worry, Easton," Gorham told him in a loud voice so that everyone in the department could hear. "For what it's worth, you almost had me convinced about those damn snakes."

He straightened up with a laugh and headed for the elevators.

That was when Frost noticed that Gorham had left a scrap of paper on his desk. With a casual glance around the office, Frost turned the paper over and saw that Gorham had scribbled a message for him on the back.

*We need to talk.*

*10 p.m. Pier 45.*

# 23

Frost went through the door of Zingari into a room filled with live jazz and the aromas of mushroom and basil floating by on white plates. He'd been here once before, almost a year earlier, to confront a psychiatrist who specialized in manipulating the traumatic memories of her patients. Back then, Francesca Stein had been a regular here. He looked around curiously but didn't see her at any of the tables. He wasn't even sure if she'd stayed in San Francisco after the investigation ended.

He made his way to the bar. There was one stool open at the end, near where the band was playing. The bartender was busy, and while Frost waited for her, he exchanged smiles with a young African American woman who was singing and playing guitar. Being here among the Monday crowd reminded him that life as a loner wasn't always a good thing. On those rare occasions when he had an evening free, he usually spent it at home with Shack, eating dinner from one of Duane's care packages and digging into a history book set years before he was born.

"What'll you have?" the bartender asked him.

She leaned both elbows on the bar in front of him. She was tall enough that she had to have played basketball at some time in her youth, but now she was at least forty, with shaggy brown hair shot through with blue highlights. She wore a sleeveless black blouse with a high neck, and her skinny bare arms were canvases for multicolored tattoos.

"Anchor Steam," Frost replied. "And some information. I'm looking for an old friend. His name's Chester Bagley. Does he still work here?"

"Chester? No, sorry, he quit."

"When was that?"

The woman shrugged. "Last week, I guess. His loss is my gain. I'm the new Chester."

"So you never met him?" Frost asked.

The woman popped the top on his amber beer and poured it out. The glass was ice cold. "No, but I think one of the waiters, Virgil, was a buddy of his. You could try talking to him."

"Is he around?"

"Yeah, I'll send him your way. You want anything to eat?"

Frost eyed an empty bar table that overlooked the windows near Post Street. He realized he was hungry. "How about some crab cakes?"

"You got it."

Frost took his beer and snapped up the table before anyone else could get to it. The guitarist in the band had a raspy, cigarette-soaked voice that was perfect for sad songs, and he sipped his beer as he listened to her. She made love to the microphone and flirted with him with her dark eyes. He realized that he hadn't had sex in months, and this was the kind of evening where a one-night stand matched his mood. But Frost had never done casual well. That was Duane's specialty.

He was halfway through his beer when a twenty-something waiter with wavy shock-white hair dropped into the chair across from him. The man had a cocky smirk and the build of someone who worked out a lot. He stretched out his long legs and slumped sideways at the table with his chin balanced on one hand.

"Are you Virgil?" Frost asked.

"In the flesh," the waiter replied. His voice was extravagantly gay. "I remember you."

"Oh?"

"You're Frankie's cop, right?"

"You have a good memory," Frost told him.

"I do for some people, and you've got that Justin T vibe going on. Very nice." Virgil primped the gel in his hair and grinned. His dark eyes were accented by lavender eye shadow.

"Speaking of Dr. Stein, does she still come in here?" Frost asked.

"Frankie? Oh, sure, she's in here a lot. Always alone, like you. Sad, sad, sad, you people. She's not doing the memory thing anymore, did you know that?"

"I didn't."

"Would you believe she's doing *psychic* research now? She's on the hunt for what she calls sensitives. The people who can bend forks and do remote visualization and wild things like that. It's very creepy."

Frost smiled. "Well, her memory practice was pretty creepy, too."

"Ain't that the truth. Of course, there are some nights in my teens that I wouldn't mind forgetting if you gave me a choice." Virgil waved at a waiter who was carrying a plate of crab cakes and pointed at Frost. The plate arrived at the table. "So Lydia the Tattooed Lady says you were asking about Chester."

"That's right."

"Are you a friend, or is this police business?"

"A little of both. I knew Chester back in high school, but mostly, I have some questions for him. I want to make sure he knows that a mutual friend of ours was killed. Chester and Denny were pretty close."

Virgil's eyebrows cocked. "Denny? Denny Clark? He's dead?"

Frost leaned across the table. "He is. You knew Denny?"

"Oh yeah. He was a regular at the bar whenever Chester was here. Nice enough guy. One hell of a boat, too. I could get used to living like that."

"You spent time on the *Roughing It*?"

"A million-dollar yacht on the bay? Are you kidding? I was all over that. Chester brought me along sometimes when Denny needed an extra hand for one of his gigs."

Frost realized that he hadn't met anyone yet who'd actually worked on one of Denny's charters. "What were the gigs like? Who was there? How did it work?"

"Well, technically I'm not supposed to say anything," Virgil replied with a roll of his eyes. "Can you believe they made us sign confidentiality agreements? Please, what kind of nonsense is that? But hey, I get it. Some of the guys looked like billionaires, and these were tripped-out parties. Plenty of eye candy. Plenty of nose candy, too. Denny was a generous host."

"When was the last time you were on the boat?"

"Last summer. There was an overnighter in August. Super crowded, really glam. When Chester and I took a break, we had to squeeze into a bunk down with the engines. Not that I ever got much sleep with Chester around. Just a little recreation for an hour and then we were back at it. Most of the guests were up all night, too."

"August," Frost murmured. He dug out his phone and found the photograph taken on the *Roughing It* of Denny Clark, Belinda Drake, and Greg Howell. "Do you remember seeing these people on the boat? The ones with Denny?"

Virgil nodded. "Yeah, I've seen the lady a few times, but I don't know who she is. Stick-up-her-ass type. She never remembered me from cruise to cruise, and I'm pretty memorable, if I do say so myself."

"What about the guy?"

"The silver fox? Greg Howell? Yeah, he was on the August cruise. Tipped me a hundred bucks with each drink and told me to split it with Chester. I got the feeling he wouldn't have minded a little party with the two of us, but it never happened. His mind was elsewhere. He wasn't exactly having a good time."

"Oh? How so?"

"He kept getting into it with one of the other guests."

"You mean like fighting?" Frost asked.

"No, it wasn't physical. The two of them were just arguing, but it was pretty hot. I wouldn't have been surprised to see one of them take a swing at the other."

"What were they arguing about?"

Virgil shook his head. "No idea. I wasn't being paid to listen, and I wouldn't have cared anyway."

"Did you recognize the guy that Howell was arguing with?" Frost asked. "Do you know who he was?"

"No idea. I'd never seen him before."

"What did he look like?"

"I couldn't tell you," Virgil said. "He wasn't anything special to look at, but I guess it doesn't matter when you've got that kind of money, right? I was more impressed with the girl he had with him. She was high class. If I had to guess, she was a pro."

"A hooker?"

"Oh, honey, not just a hooker. She was the kind of girl who gets the big bucks to *not* look like a hooker. Chester and I sussed her out right away, but we were probably the only ones who knew."

Frost scrolled to the picture of Fawn on his phone. "Is this the girl?"

Virgil leaned forward and whistled. "Definitely, that's her. Don't you love Indian women? They manage to look haughty and horny at the same time."

"Did you talk to her?"

"Oh no. She wasn't there to talk to the help."

"Is there anything else you can tell me about the guy she was with? The one who was arguing with Howell?"

"No, sorry. I might recognize him if you had a picture, though."

Frost eased back in his chair. He took a bite of one of the crab cakes and then followed it with a swallow of Anchor Steam. "So why did Chester quit? The new bartender made it sound sudden."

"Yeah, it was very sudden. And weird, too. Like I told Denny, Chester didn't even come into the restaurant. He texted the manager on

Thursday morning and said he was moving to Idaho. I mean, seriously? Are you kidding me? He said he wanted to be closer to his parents. I guess some people voluntarily choose to be in the same time zone as their parents, but not me."

"Whoa, whoa," Frost interrupted him. "You talked to Denny Clark? When?"

"Friday night. He called looking for Chester. I told him he was too late, that Chester had given us the heave-ho. I figured Denny had another gig that he needed help with. I was going to volunteer my services, but he got off the phone before I could say anything. I can't believe he's dead. That sucks. No more cocktails on the bay, I guess."

"What time did he call?"

"Middle of the evening, I guess. Ten o'clock, maybe? It all runs together."

"Did Denny say anything else?"

"Nope. He just said he needed to talk to Chester and that it was important."

Frost was silent. The voice of the singer wrapped itself around his brain while he gathered his thoughts. Denny had called Mr. Jin on Friday night and left a message telling him to get out of his apartment. He'd called Chester, probably to give him a similar warning. Denny knew that something bad was happening. He knew the witnesses to the cruise were being eliminated and that he was next.

"When did you last see Chester?" Frost asked Virgil.

"Wednesday night. He did his shift at the bar like usual, and the two of us left together."

"Did he mention anything about a gig on Denny's boat on Tuesday?" Frost asked.

"Yeah, he told me about it last weekend. I asked if he could get me in, but he said it was a small party. Too bad. When I saw him on Wednesday, he flashed me the cash in his pocket. Must have been five thousand dollars. I mean, that's crazy. I joked about it with him. I asked him how many bananas he had to peel to wind up with that kind of dough."

"What did he say?" Frost asked.

"He didn't laugh. Actually, he was kind of jumpy and nervous. When I pushed him about the cash, he called it hush money. And then he clammed up and wouldn't say a word."

Hush money.

Denny, Carla, Mr. Jin, Chester all walked away from the Tuesday cruise with wads of cash to make sure they didn't tell anyone what they'd witnessed on the boat.

First they got paid off. Then they got killed.

But what did they see?

"You said you left with Chester on Wednesday night?" Frost asked.

"Yeah. After midnight. Chester shared an apartment on Hyde with six other guys. Sometimes I'd crash there, too, but I had a late date on Wednesday. We walked together for a couple blocks; then he went his way and I went mine. That was it. I haven't heard from him since. It's not like he and I were boyfriends, but I would have expected something more after hanging out together for a couple of years. He didn't say a word to me about this Idaho crap."

"Have you talked to any of his roommates?"

Virgil nodded. "I called. I was a little pissed at him, you know? They said they didn't even see him before he split. He must have been up and out before dawn, left a month's rent behind in cash. Some movers showed up to get his stuff. Totally weird."

Frost didn't think it was weird at all. It was Lombard.

Behind them, the jazz singer finished her latest song. Frost applauded and won another smile from her. Virgil whistled, and then he waved at a manager who was standing on the other side of the bar, tapping his watch. The waiter checked his fingernails and fixed his white hair again.

"I have to go, man."

"Sure. Thanks for the information, Virgil. One last thing, did Chester say anything else about the Tuesday cruise when you guys were walking home? Even the smallest detail?"

Virgil got up from the table and smoothed his skintight black outfit. "No, like I said, he was jumpy all evening. He didn't want to talk. He was paranoid, too, like somebody was out to get him. He swore someone was following us on the street. It had him freaked out."

"Following you?" Frost asked.

"Yeah. There was this car behind us going real slow. But come on, it's the Tenderloin. It was just some guy cruising and checking us out."

"What kind of car?"

Virgil shrugged. "A BMW, I think. Dark, like charcoal."

# 24

Neon lit up the Embarcadero near the bay at Fisherman's Wharf. It was late evening and cold. The restaurants and fish shacks were closed, the street performers were long gone, but the sidewalk was still crowded with tourists. Frost walked quickly beside the water, which glowed with hazy reflections. He was surrounded by silhouettes and drunken laughter. He passed between the bright lights of the Franciscan restaurant and the Boudin bakery and headed toward the deserted warehouse buildings of Pier 45. No one followed him.

At the pier, seagulls huddled near the concrete walls, and the pavement was dotted with dried guano. A salty, fishy smell blew in with the wind. The alley between the warehouses was empty. He didn't see Trent Gorham among the loading docks, and he glanced at his watch. It was exactly ten o'clock.

Frost waited for the other detective by a wooden railing that bordered the inner harbor. The sand-colored warehouse buildings were behind him. Beyond the wharf, high-rises climbed the city hills like dominoes. He leaned on the railing and watched the spars of the fishing boats sway in their slips. This was where he and Denny had berthed the *Jumping Frog*. They'd lived on the boat, eating, drinking, and playing poker until the early hours. Sometimes they'd been alone; sometimes tourist girls had joined them for the night. He could remember the sweet taste of Dungeness crab claws fresh out of the pot, dripping butter and garlic. They'd played their music loud. They'd slept in their clothes. For a few months, he'd never been happier in his life.

He recognized their old boat in the harbor. It was still there, still in the same berth, years after Denny had sold it. The new owners had fixed it up with fresh paint and rechristened it. The *Jumping Frog* was now *Daze Gone By*, which seemed appropriate. The boat was dark; no one was sleeping on it now.

When he checked his watch again, he saw that it was ten fifteen. Gorham was late. He wondered if the other detective was coming at all, and the worry crept into his mind that the meeting might be a trap. He thought about leaving, but then his phone buzzed with an incoming text.

It was from Gorham.

Keep going.

Frost continued along the harbor past the warehouse building. Where the road ended, a narrow driveway led between the warehouse wall and the green waters of the inlet that led out to the bay. He saw Gorham standing twenty feet away. The other cop wore a tan windbreaker zipped to his neck and black khakis. The yellow lights made his blond hair look snow white.

As Frost came closer, Gorham took one hand out of his jacket pocket and pointed a gun at Frost's chest.

Frost stopped dead and raised his hands slowly. He'd been certain all along that Gorham was hiding things from him, but he hadn't expected this. "Are you going to shoot me, Trent? Is that the plan?"

"I'm just being cautious. Take your gun out of your holster and put it on the ground."

"Okay."

"No sudden moves, Easton."

"Whatever you say."

Frost used one hand to open the flap of his jacket, and he carefully withdrew his gun with two fingers. He bent his knees, not taking his eyes off Gorham, and put the gun on the ground.

"Back up," the other detective instructed.

Frost did. Gorham walked closer until he was standing beside Frost's gun. He hadn't lowered his own weapon yet; it was still pointed at Frost's heart at a range from which the other cop couldn't miss. Gorham's long arm was stretched straight out and as solid as an arrow.

"Identification," Gorham barked.

"What?"

*"Identification,"* Gorham repeated sharply.

"What the hell are you talking about, Trent?"

Gorham's pale eyes narrowed. His finger was bent around the trigger. Frost felt sweat gathering on his neck, and his heartbeat accelerated. The silence between them stretched out, long and dangerous. Then Gorham's head tilted slightly back, and the cop's face softened. His elbow dipped, and he secured his gun and slipped it inside his jacket again. He squatted and retrieved Frost's gun and passed it to him by the handle.

"Sorry," Gorham told him, "but I've learned the hard way not to trust anyone."

"I don't trust people, either," Frost replied, "especially not cops who pull their weapons on me."

"I'll explain, but I needed to make sure you weren't playing me. I've been watching you for twenty minutes. If you had someone with you or if you'd been followed, I would have spotted it. But I still didn't know if you were one of Lombard's operatives. They all have special ID codes to identify themselves. I had to find out if you were clean."

"And I passed the test?" Frost asked.

"So far. I hope I'm right about you, because I'm betting my life on it."

The two men wandered to the edge of the water. There was no railing here. Debris floated below them.

"You're pretty paranoid over a myth," Frost said.

"Lombard's not a myth. He's as real and as lethal as it gets."

"He? Lombard is one person?"

"That's what I've been told," Gorham said. He turned to face Frost. "I've never met anyone who has actually seen him or knows who he is. His network is blind. No one knows who's in and who's not. There's a central admin who manages them by phone, but she's as anonymous as Lombard is."

"How do you know all this?" Frost asked.

"I stumbled onto one person who was part of the network, and she told me how it worked. She said every operative has a unique identification code based on the names of San Francisco streets. This woman's ID was Folsom. They also use a numeric password and a separate code to indicate whether they're safe or under pressure when they make a report."

"What happened to this woman?"

"I tried to use her as a mole to penetrate the network. Lombard found out and killed her."

"So if I'd said a street name like Market or Stockton when you asked for my identification?"

"You'd be dead down there in the bay right now," Gorham replied.

Frost stared into the water. "You better tell me what this is all about. How did it start? How did you get involved?"

"You know how," Gorham said. "Coyle."

"He told you about the snakes after Alan Detlowe was murdered?"

"That's right. Alan's wife, Marjorie, told me about hiring Coyle, and I wanted to see his surveillance notes. That was when he sprang the snake thing on me. I didn't believe him at first, but when I looked into it, I felt like you did. It was too strange to be just a coincidence. Not that I was going to tell him that. Coyle was a loose cannon, and the safest thing was for him to chase his crackpot theories by himself. But I began looking into the backgrounds of the victims to see if I could figure out why they were targeted."

"Did you find anything about Detlowe?" Frost asked.

"No, I never figured out why Alan was killed. He was a cop. Too many people had beefs with him."

"What about Fawn? Did you talk to her?"

"Sure I did. She said her conversation with Alan was routine. He was trolling for contacts in the escort world, who the big players were, how the technology works. She didn't say anything about him looking into the death of her friend Naomi."

"So how did you find out about Lombard?" Frost asked.

"I got lucky. I was digging into the murder of a plumber in Mission Terrace. It was a stabbing death, looked like a home invasion, but there was a snake painted nearby. I couldn't figure out why anyone would want this guy dead. I was actually starting to think Coyle might be right about a serial killer picking victims at random. Then I found out the guy had been on a jury in a political corruption trial a few months earlier. Remember the guy on the city council accused of taking bribes? The jury hung, and the councilman walked. That was the only thing in this guy's life that didn't revolve around toilets and leaky faucets, so I decided to talk to one of the staff attorneys in the prosecutor's office. I didn't really suspect anything. I just wanted to see if this plumber could have been influenced."

"What did you find?"

"Like I said, I got lucky. The staff attorney cracked like an egg. I talked to her at home, and she thought I was there to kill her. She asked if Lombard had sent me, and she was crying and said she'd done everything they'd asked. By the time she realized she'd screwed up, she'd already dug a hole for herself. I got her to spill everything she knew."

Frost waited. Gorham checked the pier again to make sure they were still alone.

"She was an operative. She'd been recruited by someone she called Lombard to provide information from the prosecutor's office on certain cases. Strategies, witnesses, juror personal data. It had been going on for two years. She claimed she had no choice but to do what he asked. Lombard had leverage over her."

"What kind of leverage?" Frost asked.

"Her son. He'd been the driver in a hit-and-run a couple of years earlier and never went to the cops to confess. Somehow, Lombard knew about it. If she didn't cooperate, her son was headed to prison for a long time."

"This sounds like the way the mafia operates," Frost said. "Or the Russians."

"That was my thought, too, but if it's organized crime, it's not any of the usual suspects. This lawyer only knew the name Lombard. She didn't think it was a group; she said it seemed to be one person who made all the decisions. All she knew was her protocol. Burner phones, coded identifications, reports and instructions. I could have brought her in, but I decided to use her as a double agent to see if she could unearth more details about Lombard. Instead, a week later, she washed up out of the bay in San Mateo."

"How did Lombard know she'd been turned?" Frost asked.

"That's the problem. I only told one person what I was doing."

"Who?"

"Captain Hayden. I told him I was looking at a staff attorney in the prosecutor's office who might be able to lead us to a crime ring involving corruption and murder."

"You think Hayden's connected to Lombard?" Frost asked.

"I don't know, but I'm not taking any chances. If he's not, then he passed along the information to someone who is. Nobody else knew. From that point forward, I didn't trust *anybody*, and I didn't tell anyone what I was doing. My investigation was completely off the books. I figured if Lombard saw me as a threat, I'd be the next one with a snake painted on the wall. So publicly, I treated the whole thing as a dead-end conspiracy."

"And what have you found out behind the scenes?" Frost asked.

"Not much. That's the frustrating thing. I can't find anybody in the network to lead the way in and help me find out who Lombard really is and what he's doing. The only thing that makes sense to me is that Lombard is some kind of fixer. In one way or another, all of the victims have been problems for prominent people in the city. Lombard solved them. Mostly with murder."

Frost frowned. "What about Denny Clark? How does he fit in?"

"You said it yourself. Something happened on his boat on Tuesday night. Denny became a problem to be solved. So did the others who were there. Lombard has been tying up the loose ends ever since."

Frost studied Gorham's face in the evening lights. "That's not what I mean, Trent. You *called* Denny. Why? That wasn't a follow-up on a drug homicide. You were looking for something else."

Gorham walked into the middle of the alley and shoved his hands in his pockets. Frost called to the man's back. "If you expect me to trust *you*, then you need to tell me what's really going on."

"All right," Gorham replied impatiently. "All right, yeah, I called Denny. I asked him to be on the lookout for Lombard. I wanted him to call me if he heard anyone using Lombard's name. I knew Denny's business. I knew a lot of movers and shakers in the city used his boat. I wanted him to work as my spy. I gave him a burner phone so we could communicate securely. And yeah, I put pressure on him. He was vulnerable on drug charges, and he knew I could get him busted whenever I wanted. I didn't give him a choice."

"Is that all? What happened next?"

"What do you mean?"

"I mean, did Denny reach out to you after the cruise on Tuesday? He knew people were after him. He went to find Mr. Jin, and he called

Chester Bagley. I'm sure he knew Carla was dead, too. Are you saying he never talked to you about any of this?"

Gorham turned around. "Okay, you're right. He called me."

"When?"

"Friday evening. He was in Chinatown. He was terrified. He said they were killing everyone."

Frost shook his head. "Why keep that back? Why didn't you tell me about it?"

"I already told you that I didn't trust anyone. That includes you. And what the hell difference does it make? I was too late."

"You weren't too late on Friday. Denny called you and needed help. He was still alive."

"I know, and I offered to come get him and protect him, but he wouldn't listen to me. He thought I was part of it, that they were tracking him through the phone I'd given him."

Frost stared at him. "Were they?"

"Of course not. I'm *not* a spy, Frost. I want to catch this guy even more than you do, believe me."

"Did Denny tell you why they wanted him dead? Did he tell you about the cruise?"

"No, he hung up without giving me any details."

"Denny knew about Lombard. That was his last word."

"That's because I *told* him about Lombard," Gorham said. "He must have guessed that there was a connection when people started going missing. Or maybe he heard someone talking about it on the boat. I don't know. He didn't tell me."

"So you don't know what happened on Tuesday night?"

"The only thing I know for sure is that Lombard is *active*," Gorham retorted. "We're closer to him than we ever have been before. Denny's murder can lead us straight to Lombard. You and I need to work together to find him and stop him."

Frost's phone rang before he could reply. It was as if he were still being watched, as if Lombard somehow knew everything he was doing and everyone he talked to. He checked the caller ID.

"Who is it?" Gorham asked with suspicion in his voice.

"Cyril Timko," Frost told him.

"Did you tell him we were meeting?"

"No. Nobody knows." Frost answered the phone and put it on speaker so they could both hear the call. "Cyril, it's Frost Easton. What's up?"

The raspy voice of the captain's aide crackled through the phone. "I need you in Dolores Heights right away. We've got a dead drug dealer up here. I'm pretty sure he's the one who killed Denny Clark."

# 25

Nobody had moved the body yet. It still lay sprawled across the train tracks where the MUNI J line came down the hill into Mission Dolores Park. Dr. Finder from the medical examiner's office, who had studied the body of Denny Clark in Frost's foyer, was crouched over this body, too. The remains were gruesome. The man on the ground had no face, just an unrecognizable jam of blood, bone, and cartilage. One arm had been scissored from his body and lay with its shirt sleeve still intact on the redbrick sidewalk leading into the park.

"Heart attack?" Frost asked.

Dr. Finder chuckled behind his mask. A plastic cap struggled to contain the halo of hair sprouting like wheatgrass from his head. "Well, I guess his heart might have stopped in the second or so before he got run over. But let's assume not. Tonight MUNI stands for man underneath it. He was hit as the trolley came down the hill and then dragged here before the undercarriage spit him loose. Or most of him, anyway."

"Was this an accident? Was he playing chicken with the train?"

The pathologist shook his head. "Not according to the MUNI driver. He says there were two men struggling near the tracks, and one pushed the other. There was no way to stop. I believe Officer Timko has the man who did the pushing in a squad car over there. Apparently, the man claims it was self-defense. He's the one who called the cops after it happened."

"What about the pushee?" Frost asked. "Who is he?"

"According to his driver's license, our deceased's name was Diego Casal. Twenty-three years old. He's well known to our friends in vice."

"Why does Cyril think Diego was involved in Denny Clark's murder?" Frost asked.

"Probably because of what I found in Mr. Casal's pocket. Namely a long-barreled pellet pistol that would have worked very nicely to fire the kind of gel round that poisoned Mr. Clark. And if that weren't enough, there was a dissolving pellet left in the chamber. I won't know until I test it in the lab, of course, but I won't be at all surprised if we find a matching poison."

"Hmm," Frost said dubiously.

"You don't sound pleased, Inspector."

"When I was a kid and Santa got me exactly what I wanted for Christmas, I always wondered how he knew."

"What a suspicious boy you were," the pathologist chided him. "Me, I'm pleased to have a corpse with no mystery for once. And if it wraps up the saga of Mr. Clark, that's an added bonus."

"Yes, all neatly tied up with a bow," Frost said. "Ho, ho, ho."

He left Dr. Finder to continue his work with the body, and he headed across the green grass of Mission Dolores Park to find Cyril Timko. The park overlooked the glowing city skyline. Around him, the J line was shut down, and half a dozen squad cars surrounded the intersection at Twentieth Street. Gawkers ringed the area with cameras that flashed like lightning. He suspected that pictures of Casal's mangled body had already made their way onto social media.

Captain Hayden's aide stood alone in the middle of the park, sucking on his e-cigarette. The streetlights made his badge glow like a gold star on the breast of his uniform. He had perfect posture, as always. His face was bony and white, except for the dark stubble at his beard line. The widow's peak in the middle of his forehead looked sharp enough to cut glass.

"Looks like you've been busy doing my job, Cyril," Frost said.

The man's eyebrow cocked as he tried to decide if Frost was annoyed. "I called you as soon as we realized there was a connection to Denny Clark. When the report first came in, we had no idea."

"So what do we know?"

"I assume Dr. Finder already told you about the pellet gun and the gel cartridge?"

"He did."

Cyril blew out a cloud of vapor. "Well, there's a lot more. I checked Casal's phone. Denny Clark is among his contacts. There's a record of calls between them going back for months. According to vice, Casal is a known dealer, so if you found cocaine on Denny's boat, it's a good bet it came from him. He has a reputation for violence, too. He's a suspect in at least two drug-related homicides in the past year."

"Did either of those killings involve poison?" Frost asked. "Poison's an odd weapon of choice for a dealer. If it was Casal, why not just shoot Denny and be done with it?"

"I don't know, but the poison was slow and nasty, right? Bitch of a way to die. Maybe Casal wanted to send a message. The word is that the guy ran on a short fuse. It could have been a fight over pricing. It could be that Casal thought Denny was freelancing and moving in on his turf."

"In other words, Captain Hayden was right all along about the drug angle," Frost said.

"That's what it looks like."

Frost frowned. "What about my three other missing persons? Why would this Diego Casal want them dead?"

"I think we can explain that, too." Cyril nodded his head toward one of the squad cars parked on Church Street. "We've got the guy who pushed Casal in front of the train. He calls himself Romeo Laredo. Hell of a name, huh? He's a hotshot IT guy with an apartment in the Presidio."

"What's Romeo's connection to Diego Casal?" Frost asked.

"He says he doesn't have one. Romeo was at a party in the Castro a few blocks away, and when he left, he noticed this guy following him. He figured he was being stalked for a mugging. Romeo's a big guy, so he stopped and confronted him. Casal tried to pull out the pellet gun, and it turned into a struggle. That's how Casal wound up eating the train."

Frost shook his head. "What does that have to do with my missing persons?"

"Romeo says he doesn't know Diego Casal," Cyril continued, "but he *recognized* him."

"From where?"

"The guy's a jogger. He does an early morning run from his apartment down along the Golden Gate Promenade. That includes running past the yacht harbor on most days. He says last Wednesday morning, somewhere around five thirty, he was doing his usual run when a limousine with its lights off nearly clipped him. He got steamed. He chased down the limo where it pulled in to park and started laying into the driver. It was pretty hot between them. Then a few tough guys in suits arrived from one of the boats tied up in the harbor. The leader of the pack suggested that Romeo move along, and he backed up the suggestion with a knife in his hand."

"Casal?" Frost said.

"That's right. Romeo swears it was Diego Casal, says he wasn't likely to forget a guy who made a threat like that. That puts Casal down near Denny's boat on the morning after this mystery cruise. Casal must have started taking out the witnesses, probably including your missing persons. Then he came to get Romeo, but ended up on the losing end of the fight."

Frost thought again, *All neatly tied up with a bow.*

"Do you believe this guy?" he asked.

"I don't think he has any reason to lie," Cyril replied. "The guy's not a gangbanger. He's a fricking coder who makes more than the two of us combined. And it all fits, doesn't it? We've got Casal, the boat, the witnesses, the drugs, the phone contacts, the poison."

"Yes, it all fits," Frost agreed. "Do you mind if I talk to this Romeo for a couple of minutes?"

Cyril shrugged. "Knock yourself out. We'll do a full interview at the station. Assuming that checks out, we'll cut him loose. We don't have any witnesses, but so far, what we've got adds up to self-defense."

Frost felt like Coyle, obsessed with paranoid conspiracies. Yes, everything fit, but it fit too well. It fit like loose ends being tied up. He said nothing more to Cyril. He walked through the wet grass of the park and across the MUNI tracks. He climbed a shallow slope to Church Street, where a squad car was parked at the curb. The uniformed officer outside unlocked the rear door. Frost got inside with Romeo Laredo.

Romeo didn't look like an IT nerd. He looked like Chris Hemsworth. He was bulky and big, with messy blond hair and blue eyes. He was probably in his late twenties. He wore a snug pale-blue T-shirt and jeans, and he had the muscled physique of a weightlifter. Diego Casal would have been crazy to take him on in a fight.

"Hey, how are you?" the man said politely, extending his hand with a winning smile. "I'm Romeo Laredo."

Frost made no effort to shake the man's hand. He waited until Romeo pulled his arm back with a puzzled expression on his face. The man was obviously used to disarming people with his earnest charm, and he didn't know what to do when it failed him.

Then Frost said, "Identification."

Romeo's eyes widened with surprise. It was obvious that he'd heard that demand before, but not in this context, and he wasn't sure what to believe.

*"Identification!"* Frost snapped again, broaching no hesitation.

The man's whole body stiffened. He became a soldier, obeying orders. "Guerrero."

Frost nodded slowly without saying anything more, and Romeo realized that he'd tipped his hand with the wrong person. The eager mask disappeared from his face. He was a big, strong man who was suddenly scared.

"So," Frost said. "You work for Lombard."

"Who? I don't know who that is."

"Come on, Romeo. Don't play games with me. You screwed up, but you're in too deep now. You might as well talk to me. Lombard came up with the whole cover story, right? He told you what to say about Wednesday morning. You never saw Diego Casal at the harbor, did you? That was a lie."

"No, I did. The guy threatened me, and then tonight he came after me."

"Really? See, I think it was the other way around. You came after *him*, Romeo. Lombard told you where to find Diego Casal, and then you followed him here and pushed him in front of the train. Did Lombard give you the pellet gun to plant on him, too?"

Romeo held up both hands. "Whoa, dude, you are freaking me out. I'm the victim here. This Casal guy was going to kill me."

"Then what's Guerrero? Most people would pull out their driver's license when a cop asks for identification. Instead, you said Guerrero. Why?"

The man grasped furiously for a lie. "I wasn't thinking straight. It's been a hell of a night, okay? Some dude tried to kill me, and then I watched his brains get squirted out by the train. I said the first thing that popped into my head. I spotted this guy following me over on Guerrero. That's where I identified him. It was a brain fart, man, that's all."

Frost shook his head. "That's the best story you've got?"

"What can I tell you? It's the truth."

"So you won't mind if I put the word out on the street that Guerrero is talking to the police? That won't mean anything? That won't make you nervous?"

Romeo rubbed his fingers. He was sweating. "Say whatever you like. I'm innocent, man. I just want to go home and have a beer and forget about this whole night."

Frost shrugged. He wasn't going to get anything more out of Romeo Laredo. He was sure the man's biography would check out. He was sure they wouldn't find anything to disprove his story. Lombard didn't leave things like that to chance. The pieces of the puzzle that was Denny Clark's death were falling into place one after another.

They had a killer—Diego Casal—and the killer wasn't around to say he was innocent.

They had a motive. Drugs.

They had evidence and a witness tying the killer to Denny and the boat. Everything was in a pretty package. And it was all a lie.

He opened the back door of the squad car again.

"Watch your back, *Guerrero*," he told the man as he got out. "You made a mistake by opening your mouth tonight. We both know that Lombard doesn't like mistakes."

# 26

"They're closing the case right out from under me," Frost told Herb the next morning.

They sat at an outdoor table at a café on Cole Street. Herb nursed a large mug of chai tea that wafted cardamom into the chilly air. Frost had black coffee and a plate of eggs. It was barely past dawn, and the neighborhood around them was slow to wake up. Victorian homes made a side-by-side checkerboard down the street. Near the intersection at Haight, the walls of the shop buildings were painted with murals of rainbows and a guitar-playing Jerry Garcia.

"Captain Hayden thinks Denny's murder is connected to drugs," Frost went on, "and right on schedule, a dead drug dealer drops into our laps. As far as headquarters is concerned, it's time for me to let it go."

Herb didn't say anything in response. His attention was focused on a two-story Victorian home almost directly across from the café. A black wrought-iron gate blocked the front steps. The lights behind the curtains were on, and children's paintings were taped to the bay window. Herb's mouth was pinched into a frown. He played with the beads that were strung into his long strands of gray hair.

"Herb?" Frost said. "Everything okay?"

His friend awakened as if from a trance. Herb adjusted his black glasses on his face. "Yes, yes, sorry. I'm somewhere else today. I understand your frustration, Frost, but isn't it possible that Mr. Clark's death is exactly what it appears to be? The result of his unfortunate dealings with a violent cocaine dealer?"

"You mean, instead of a cover-up contrived by a mysterious criminal mastermind with a network of operatives around the city?" Frost asked with a little smile. "I know, I sound as crazy as Coyle."

"Well, Occam's razor and all. The obvious answer is usually the right one."

Frost shrugged. "Do you think I'm nuts? Should I forget about it?"

"Even if I thought you were wrong, Frost, you've earned the benefit of the doubt from me many times over. Besides, in this case, I think you're correct. Lombard certainly seems to be real."

"Unfortunately, I have no way to prove it," Frost said. "Technically, I have nothing left to investigate with regard to Denny's murder. I could keep trying to find witnesses who are probably dead, but even if I find their bodies, Romeo Laredo has already pinned the blame on Diego Casal. I could try to break Romeo's story about the cruise, but that means interrogating Casal's associates, most of whom are drug dealers themselves. Their word isn't going to carry much weight if they tell me Casal wasn't on that boat."

"What about Inspector Gorham?"

"He has no proof about Lombard, either. His only contact was a dirty lawyer in the prosecutor's office, and she's dead. For all I know, she was being played by a defense attorney who knew about the Lombard myth and decided to use it as cover for a jury-tampering scheme."

Herb stretched out his legs and his knees popped, making him grimace. His eyes drifted across the street again to the same Victorian home. He took another taste of chai and licked his lips.

"I remember the original Lombard story," Herb said. "Honestly, I'd forgotten all about it, but after we talked last time, I recalled the exposé that hit the *Chronicle*. It must have been thirty years ago. It was the kind of story that made people run wild with conspiracies. Murder, corruption, political influence, all guided by an unseen hand. An invisible syndicate shaping the future of the city. Then the chief had to stand up and say, no, it was really just an inside joke that got out of control. The city council wasn't amused. The chief took early retirement and said it was for health reasons, but in truth, it was the Lombard myth that brought him down."

"Speaking of the city council, you said you were going to approach some of your contacts at city hall. Did you?"

Herb nodded. "I did, but I'm not sure what I found will help you. Most of the younger people in the building said they know nothing about it, and the original Lombard story was long before their time."

"But?"

"But I did talk to one old codger like me. He goes back to my time, and he remembered the story. He's been a true believer all these years. He described Lombard the way Inspector Gorham did, as a problem solver for the rich and powerful. As far as this man is concerned, it's not clear whether the people who run the city are using Lombard to stay in power—or whether Lombard is using them for his own ends."

"Do you trust this man?" Frost asked.

Herb's eyes twinkled behind his black glasses. "Well, I recall an impassioned conversation with him in the 1970s about the authenticity of the moon landings. He was dubious."

Frost shook his head. "Great."

Herb chuckled as he finished his chai. "So what's your next step?"

"I need to find out more about Alan Detlowe's murder," Frost said. "Even after three years, there's something about that case that seems to make Lombard nervous. As soon as I found out that Fawn had met with Detlowe, they came after us and made sure Coyle's surveillance notes disappeared. Plus, Fawn was in contact with Denny, and I don't think that's a coincidence. There's some kind of link between these cases."

"If you don't have Coyle's notes, how do you proceed?" Herb asked.

"I'm going to talk to Detlowe's wife. She hired Coyle, so maybe she has copies of what he found."

Herb began to reply, but then he stopped in midsentence. Across the street, there was activity in the Victorian house he'd been watching. A woman came through the door with a young boy in tow, and she unlocked the gate at the bottom of the steps and headed for a blue Volkswagen parked up the street. Herb's eyes followed mother and son until they got in the car and did a U-turn. Even after they were gone, Herb sat in silence, lost in another world, as if Frost weren't there at all.

"Friends of yours?" Frost asked.

"What?" Herb looked startled by the question.

"You seemed very interested in that woman and her son."

"Oh no, no," Herb went on. "I don't know who they are at all."

"Well, you've hardly taken your eyes off their house since we got here," Frost said.

Herb studied the house again. It was nothing special, just one of thousands of Victorian row homes dotting the city. Pea-green paint, beige trim, white columns on either side of the steps. And yet every time Herb looked at the house, something about it seemed to draw him into a tunnel where the opposite end was far away.

"Once upon a time, I lived there," Herb murmured. "The upstairs apartment was mine."

"When was this?" Frost asked.

"From 1967 to 1969."

"That was your Summer of Love pad? Right there?"

Herb nodded. "Yes."

"How come I didn't know that?"

"Oh, I don't remember a lot of that time," Herb replied, "and much of what I do remember, I'd like to forget."

That wasn't entirely true. Frost had heard many stories over the years of Herb's youth in the drug-crazed, free-love world of San Francisco in the 1960s. Herb had known everyone back then. The rockers. The politicians. The protesters. However, there was always a shadow surrounding Herb when he talked about those days. A reluctance, a sadness, a regret.

"So why are we here?" Frost asked.

Herb took off his black glasses. He wiped his eyes, which seemed to be tearing up. "I've told you about Silvia, haven't I?"

"Yes, you have."

Silvia had been Herb's girlfriend for a sex-soaked summer of music, LSD, and protest in 1968. He'd described her as his one true love. She was the reason he'd never married anyone else. They'd been together for two months, but then she'd vanished without a word, a note, or an apology. He'd never seen her again.

"You remember the circumstances of her departure?"

"She disappeared," Frost said.

"That's right." Herb was wearing a rust-colored button-down wool sweater, and he reached into one of the pockets and drew out a folded letter on heavy watermarked stationery. "This was delivered to me by courier yesterday. It's from a lawyer in Houston. Apparently, Silvia's brother hired him to look into the circumstances of her disappearance. The brother has cancer, you see, and is looking for some kind of closure about his sister before he dies. The lawyer wants to meet with me to talk about what happened to her. We lived together, and as far as I know, I was the last person to see her alive."

Frost frowned. "Okay. That makes sense."

"Yes, it does."

"I assume you talked to the police back then."

"Naturally," Herb said, "but in those days, it wasn't unusual for young people to pick up and disappear. If you wanted to vanish, it wasn't particularly hard. There was no Internet watching our every breath. The police thought Silvia had gotten bored and moved on, but I never could bring myself to believe that she'd done that. We were in love."

"What do you think happened to her?" Frost asked.

Herb's eyes were dark and hooded. "I think someone killed her."

"Do you have any suspects?"

"No, but this lawyer obviously does."

Frost took the letter from Herb's hand and read it. He was a lawyer himself, although he'd graduated from law school with no interest in working as an attorney. However, his legal background meant that he knew exactly how lawyers layered their true meaning behind the bland words of their correspondence. Herb was right. The backstory to the letter practically screamed from the page. Silvia's brother and his lawyer were both convinced that Herb had murdered Silvia.

"This is what you meant the other day, isn't it?" Frost asked. "You were concerned about rumors. You thought they were leading up to some kind of specific accusation."

Herb nodded. "The rumors soften people up to believe the worst about me. They'll say I killed Silvia and hid her body."

"But you're innocent," Frost said.

"Of murder? Yes, of course. But I already told you that I was a different man back then. After so much time, innocence becomes a slippery thing. Mark my words, Frost. They're coming for me."

Frost's fingers tightened around the coffee mug. He took a sip, but it had turned cold in the morning air. "It can't be a coincidence that this is happening right now."

"Oh no. This had to have been planned for some time, but for them to pull the trigger now? In the midst of your investigation? That's not an accident. It's a shot across the bow. Someone is painting a target on me, Frost. Which also suggests they're painting a target on you."

"They want me to stop going after Lombard," Frost said.

"Yes, I suspect that's the message."

"I walk away, and the lawyer goes away, too. The rumors about you stop."

"Precisely."

Frost studied the ordinary little Victorian house on the other side of the street. In his eyes, fifty years washed away. He could imagine it painted in wild colors, windows open in the summer, scratchy vinyl records playing Jefferson Airplane. He could see the young people on the hot streets, long haired, topless. And in the midst of it was Herb, when his hair wasn't gray and his knees were good and there were no lines of wisdom and age on his skin.

"Do you want me to stop?" Frost asked. "Say the word, and I will. Headquarters thinks Diego Casal killed Denny. No one wants me to dig further. Lombard can stay a myth for all I care."

Herb reached across the small table and took hold of Frost's wrist. His grip was fiercely strong, and his gravelly voice was like a needle getting to the end of an old LP. "Absolutely, unequivocally, *no*."

"You're my best friend, Herb," Frost told him. "I will not let these people destroy you."

"Oh, I'm an old man. There's very little they can do to me now. If I know one thing about you, Frost, it's that you have a moral code. Remember what your old boss, Ms. Salceda, used to say? You're a Boy Scout. You won't compromise yourself. I certainly won't have you do it for me."

"If I talk to Detlowe's wife," Frost said, "they'll know I haven't given up. At that point, there's no going back."

"Then talk to her. Find the truth. We both know Lombard is real. You need to expose him."

They sat in silence as the day brightened, and more people arrived at the café, and traffic began to fill the streets. Frost finished his cold coffee. He knew further argument was wasted with Herb, and in the end, his friend was right. Frost couldn't stop. That wasn't who he was.

He began to get up from the table, but as he did, Herb motioned him back.

"One more thing," Herb murmured so that only the two of them could hear. "If Lombard is everything we suspect, then he's a resourceful and violent enemy. You need to be extremely careful. He's your Moriarty, Frost. Taking him down will be the most dangerous thing you've ever done."

# 27

Marjorie Detlowe lived in a small row house south of the fog-swept trails of Lincoln Park. The rocky overlook at the Pacific coast was only two blocks away, and the damp chill of the ocean was always in the air. It was an old neighborhood, but the house looked new, with fresh blue paint, bright-white Tudor crossbeams, and a single steep gable. A red MINI Cooper was parked in the driveway.

The forty-something woman who answered the door had fluffy hair that was more silver than blond. She wore a white crocheted sweater and pleated slacks that were loose enough to hide a couple of extra pounds on her frame. At her feet, a gray terrier barked excitedly until she bent down and scooped him into her arms.

"Ms. Detlowe?" Frost said. "I'm Inspector Frost Easton. I was hoping to ask you a few questions about Alan."

Her smile was friendly, but her head cocked in surprise. "I'm sorry, isn't Trent Gorham still with the police? I thought he was in charge of Alan's investigation."

"He is, but Alan's name came up in the context of a different case. I'm following up."

"Oh, all right. You better come in."

She waved him through the doorway and put down the dog, which scampered ahead of them to the living room. Frost took a seat on the sofa, and the dog jumped up and sniffed around him, as if immediately suspicious that Frost was a cat person. Marjorie sat on the adjacent love seat and patted the cushion beside her, and the dog quickly relocated to her lap.

"Let me say first how sorry I am for your loss," Frost said.

"Thank you. Three years probably seems like a long time, but it may as well have been yesterday. You learn to live with it, but you never get over it. And please, call me Marjorie. I'm a police widow. We're all part of the same team. You said your name was Frost?"

"That's right."

"What an unusual name. I like it. Well, what can I tell you, Frost?"

He hesitated because he wasn't sure if the cordial rapport between them would evaporate with his first question. "This is actually a little awkward."

"Oh, please don't worry about that. Charge ahead. What do you want to know?"

"I believe you're familiar with a private detective named Richard Coyle," Frost said.

Marjorie turned her eyes down to her lap. She stroked her fingers idly through her dog's curly fur. "Ah. Now I see."

"Mr. Coyle told me that you hired him to follow your husband not long before he was murdered."

"Yes, I did. I feel stupid about it now. I hope Alan never found out. I would feel awful to think that he knew I didn't trust him, given what happened."

"If you don't mind my asking—why didn't you trust him?"

Marjorie shook her head and looked embarrassed. "Oh, it was as much me as him. It was a time of my life where I wasn't feeling good about myself. I'd gone through cancer treatment and had major surgery done. It took an emotional toll, not just a physical toll. I had trouble seeing myself as an attractive woman after that. I became obsessed with the idea that Alan was going to look elsewhere, that he would never be satisfied with me again. Part of it was his job, of course. He dealt with all these women whose lives revolved around sex. It had never bothered me before, but at that particular juncture, I questioned everything."

"I'm sorry," Frost said.

"That was the worst year of my life. First the cancer, then Alan's murder. Afterward, I felt guilty about having him followed, because Mr. Coyle never found any evidence that he was unfaithful. You'd think that would have made me feel better, but it only made me feel worse about what I'd done. I was caught up in this awful cycle of jealousy and self-hatred. Of course, it didn't help that Alan was such a handsome man. Have you seen pictures of him?"

Frost shook his head. "I haven't."

Marjorie reached into a pocket for her phone. "All I have left of him are a few digital photos."

She handed him the phone, and Frost saw a picture of Alan Detlowe with his wife at what was obviously a Christmas party. He could see mistletoe above them, and Alan wore a big smile as his wife kissed his cheek. Alan was tall and broad shouldered, with trimmed salt-and-pepper hair and a discreet mustache. His chin was chiseled and square. Marjorie was right. He was a good-looking man.

Frost swiped to the next photograph, which showed two men mugging for the camera at the same party, with their hands wrapped playfully around each other's necks.

One was Alan Detlowe. The other was Trent Gorham.

"Were Alan and Trent good friends?" Frost asked.

"Oh, best friends. Alan was about ten years older than Trent, but the two of them were practically brothers. They worked together for years at vice, you know. Trent was devastated by Alan's death."

"I'm sure."

"Trent was very sweet to me afterward. He was always checking in on me to make sure I had everything I needed. I know he feels bad that he hasn't been able to bring Alan's killer to justice, but I understand how hard it is. The badge on your shirt makes you a target. If you're good at your job, you make a lot of enemies."

"Did Trent know that you'd hired Coyle?" Frost asked.

"Yes, eventually, I admitted it to him. I was ashamed of myself, but I realized he needed to know everything. Trent and Coyle talked, but unfortunately, Trent told me there was nothing helpful in what Coyle had discovered. That made me sad. At least if hiring Coyle had helped identify Alan's killer, I would have felt better about losing faith. I suppose that sounds foolish."

"No, it doesn't," Frost said. "In fact, I'm hoping that there might still be useful information in what Coyle found."

"I don't see how," Marjorie replied.

"As I mentioned, another case has come up, and it's possible Alan was looking into it in the days before he disappeared. Unfortunately, Coyle's surveillance notes aren't available. I was hoping you might have copies of the reports he sent to you about Alan."

Marjorie shook her head. "No, I don't. I'm sorry."

"Did you destroy them?" Frost asked.

"I intended to, but honestly, I couldn't bear to take them out of my desk and look at them. They were a bad reminder to me. However, as it happens, the reports were destroyed anyway. God works in mysterious ways."

Frost looked at her, puzzled. "What do you mean?"

"About six months after Alan's death, this house burned down. I lost everything. All of the memorabilia from our marriage was gone. It was like losing Alan all over again. And of course, the reports Coyle had given me were destroyed, too."

"You rebuilt in the same spot?"

"Yes, I did. I didn't want to move anywhere else."

Frost leaned forward with curiosity. "How did the fire start?"

"The fire department says I left an old electric space heater plugged in, and it must have been sparked by a power surge. I don't remember doing it, but I wasn't exactly myself that year. It's just lucky that I was away with my sister that weekend."

Frost didn't think that luck had anything to do with it.

He also didn't think that Marjorie Detlowe had left her space heater plugged in. The fire was Lombard's doing, making sure there was no evidence left behind of what Alan Detlowe had been investigating in his final days.

"I'm sorry I can't be more help," Marjorie added. "Did you talk to Mr. Coyle? He may have kept his notes."

Frost looked at her. "Dick Coyle was murdered two nights ago."

"Oh, how awful! He was such a nice young man." Marjorie's face flushed with concern. "You don't think there's a connection to Alan, do you? After all this time?"

"I don't know, but that's why I'm trying to trace Alan's movements before he was killed." Frost pulled out his own phone and showed her a photograph of Fawn. "Do you recognize this woman?"

Marjorie studied it. "She's lovely, but no, I don't know her."

"Did Alan ever mention the name Fawn to you? Or the name Zara Anand?"

"Not that I recall," Marjorie said.

He showed her another photograph. This one was of LaHonda Duke, who went by the street name Naomi. "What about this woman?"

Marjorie shook her head. "No. I'm sorry. Who are these women?"

"They're professional escorts," Frost said.

"Ah. Well, Alan was certainly familiar with that world. It's possible he knew them, but I can't tell you for sure."

"Before Alan was killed, did he tell you anything about what he was working on? Did he share information about his cases?"

"No, he rarely did that. The last thing I wanted to hear about was his work with hookers and drug dealers. All the violence scared me. Of course, sometimes he needed to let it out. Some of the stories he told me about what these women went through, well, it was just terrible. Alan always dealt with them kindly, even when he had to arrest them. He was a rare breed as a cop. He helped them put their lives back together whenever he could. I hate to say it, but that was one of the reasons I found it difficult to trust him. I knew how easily he got emotionally involved with the people he dealt with."

"Was there anything like that in those last days?" Frost asked.

"Not that he mentioned. However, I wasn't being particularly receptive at that point, so I'm not sure he would have opened up to me anyway."

"Do you remember anything unusual happening during that time?"

Marjorie hesitated. A wrinkle appeared in her forehead and then went away. "No."

"Are you sure? You looked like you remembered something."

"Oh, it wasn't anything unusual. Not really. But it did cause a big fight between us. I wish I could take it back."

"What happened?" Frost asked.

"Well, two days before Alan was killed was our wedding anniversary. We'd made dinner plans. He was going to take me to the Top of the Mark. And then at the last minute, he had to cancel. I was upset about it, and I told him so."

"Why did he cancel?"

"That's the thing. His reason wasn't very convincing. He said Billy Chee at the Moscone Center hired him to do private security for an event that evening. Do you know Billy? Or was he before your time?"

Frost nodded. "I know him. We overlapped on the force for a couple of years before he left."

"Well, those kind of private corporate jobs are lucrative, as I'm sure you know. Alan made a lot of extra money for us that way. But on our anniversary? I wasn't happy about it. Honestly, I thought he was making up the whole thing, but Mr. Coyle told me that Alan really did go to the Moscone Center that evening. So I assume it was legitimate."

"Did Alan tell you anything else about it?"

Marjorie settled back in the sofa cushions, looking smaller. She stared at the ceiling as she tried to remember. "I asked him why this job was so important that he had to miss our big day."

"What did he say?"

"He said it wasn't just the security detail. He needed to talk to someone who was going to be at the event."

"Did he say who? Or why he needed to talk to this person?"

"No."

"Did Coyle see him with anyone?" Frost asked.

Marjorie shook her head. "No, it was a private event of some kind. Coyle wasn't able to get inside. He simply told me that Alan did go to the Moscone Center. That was all he knew."

"And Alan didn't tell you anything more afterward?"

"No, at that point we weren't talking," Marjorie said sadly. "I was angry, and he knew it. I have to live with that. But now that I think about it, I do remember one other thing. I asked Alan how come he couldn't talk to this person some other time. Why did it have to be on our anniversary? And he said the convention was almost over, and this person was from out of town. He was going to be leaving San Francisco the next day."

# 28

Frost walked through the cavernous halls of the north building of the Moscone Center, surrounded by thousands of men and women with convention badges slung around their necks. The lobby signs told him that the annual meeting of a national dental society was in town, along with an army of salespeople hawking digital-imaging systems and ultrasonic scalers for the high-tech dentist's office. Sooner or later, every major trade group in the world made their way to Moscone Center.

He took the escalators down to the sprawling lower level. The dental trade show was in full swing, and he could see hundreds of vendor kiosks beyond the ballroom doors. Even his police badge didn't get him past the security personnel with their bar-code scanners, checking the credentials of every participant. Instead, he asked them to call their boss, and he waited in the huge lobby for Billy Chee along with crowds of dentists glued to their phones.

Billy arrived in less than ten minutes. He was a slim Asian man in a gray suit, with a headset and microphone covering one ear. He was almost fifty, and his thinning black hair left him with a high forehead. He had a tablet computer nestled under his right arm.

"Billy," Frost said, shaking his hand. "Look at you, running the world."

"Just a couple square blocks of it," Billy replied with a smile. "Sorry about the cold reception at the door. We tell them nobody gets in without a convention pass, and they're afraid they'll get their ass handed to them if they make a mistake."

"No problem. You miss the old days?"

"Not even for a minute," Billy said. "I don't have time."

Billy Chee had been a popular captain inside the police department until he'd been lured away with three times his police salary to run the security department at Moscone Center. The convention halls were ground zero for threats of corporate espionage, political protests, sexual assault, and mass shootings, and every major event was a potential target for terrorism. It was a big job, and Billy routinely recruited cops as temporary help to bolster the security team.

"How's your father?" Billy asked. "This place isn't the same without him."

"He misses the city, but my mom loves Arizona," Frost replied. His dad had been a convention planner for Moscone Center for most of his career and had led the search team that hired Billy five years earlier. "I'll tell him you said hi."

"Do that. What brings you over here, Frost? I'm sorry to rush you, but I only have a couple of minutes."

"That's all I need. Do you remember Alan Detlowe from vice?"

"Alan? Of course. Terrific guy, terrific cop. It was horrible what happened to him. It must be two years ago now."

"Three."

"It's been that long? Unbelievable. Alan and I were friends on the force, and he used to help me out on some of the larger gigs around here."

"That's what I wanted to talk to you about, actually. His wife tells me that Alan worked security on an event just a couple days before he was murdered. I'd like more details."

Billy nodded. "I remember that. Trent Gorham talked to me about it after Alan was killed. He was wondering if the event raised any red flags for me with regard to Alan's death."

"Did it?" Frost asked.

"Oh no, nothing like that. There were no major security issues."

"What was the event?"

"As I recall, it was the closing ceremony for a big week-long tech convention," Billy replied. "Digi-Con or Data-Con or some other Con. They all run together after a while."

"Do you remember what Alan's role was?"

"Not specifically. Alan was experienced, so I usually kept him with the VIPs. Plus, he was vice, so he knew to alert me if he spotted any working girls crashing the parties. That's always an issue."

"What about that particular night? Did he report any prostitution problems?"

Billy shrugged. "If he did, it doesn't ring a bell with me, but it would have been low on my priority list."

"Alan told Marjorie that he needed to talk to someone who was attending the event. An out-of-towner. Did he mention anything about that?"

"Sorry, no. I doubt Alan would have told me if he had a secondary motive in doing the gig. He knows I don't like it when cops use my events as cover to talk to people who don't want to talk to them. That makes everyone around here unhappy, and I get angry phone calls. If Alan was looking to question somebody, he would have kept it to himself."

"So you don't know who it could have been?"

Billy shook his head. "We're talking about an event with a few thousand people in attendance."

"And do you have a way of looking up exactly what the event was?" Frost asked.

"I could do it tonight when I'm back at my desk," Billy told him.

"Any chance you could do it now?" Frost asked with a smile.

Billy glanced over his shoulder at the doors to the trade show. Frost could hear a stream of alerts crackling through the man's earpiece. Billy sighed and unlocked the screen on his tablet. "Okay, but only because I miss your dad. Hang on, let me check my database."

"I really appreciate it."

Billy's fingers buzzed around the screen. When he was done, he slapped the vinyl cover shut, and Frost felt his own phone vibrate a few seconds later.

"I just texted you the info," Billy told him. "The convention was one of our largest annual tech shows. Net-Con. Alan worked the gala dinner to wrap it all up. It was a who's who of top execs from Amazon, Google, Facebook, all the big names. Security was tight. We had a lot of protesters outside, and there were a couple arrests for disturbing the peace. Inside, everything came off without a hitch. My data log doesn't show any significant incidents. A few medical alerts and that's all. Alan made no reports of any problems."

"Do you have an attendee list?" Frost asked.

"Even if I did, I couldn't share it with you. You know that."

Frost nodded. He wasn't even sure the list would help in an event filled with thousands of people. Alan Detlowe could have been meeting anyone inside the convention hall.

"Well, I need to run, Frost," Billy told him. "Sorry I couldn't be more help."

"No, I'm grateful. Thanks."

Billy turned toward the convention doors, but then he retraced his steps. "Listen, if you want more dirt about that event, check in with Khristeen Smith over at the *Chronicle*. You know Khristeen. She's never afraid of a quid pro quo with the police when it comes to handing out information."

"Khristeen was there?" Frost asked.

"I'm sure she was. Hell, half the media in town was there, plus most of the national and cable networks, too. It was a huge night. That was when the mayor announced that Zelyx was relocating its headquarters from Chicago to the new high-rise in Mission Bay. You're talking about a hundred-billion-dollar public company coming to town and bringing along thousands of new jobs. Everyone was covering it."

"Zelyx," Frost murmured. "That was a big deal for the mayor, right?"

"Big deal?" Billy laughed. "Are you kidding? A new hospital or a new school is a big deal. This was an earthquake. Denver, Los Angeles, Dallas, Phoenix, all the big cities wanted to land Zelyx. And we got it. Believe me, politicians *kill* for that kind of deal."

*Zelyx.*

Frost sat in his Suburban on Howard Street near the convention center and let the name roll around his tongue.

He had no idea what the company actually did. He looked them up on his phone, but the website buzzwords didn't make their technology any easier to understand. Zelyx built security software for corporate customers, which left them in the shadows for the rest of the public. They'd started in a Northwestern University dorm room, launched an IPO within three years, and grown into one of the largest technology companies in the country.

Their CEO, who was five years younger than Frost, had gotten into a public feud with the Illinois legislature over tax policy. He'd threatened to relocate the company if he didn't get his way, and the state's politicians had called his bluff and lost. Zelyx was on its way to San Francisco, and their shiny new building was already rising above the Mission Bay neighborhood just a few blocks from police headquarters.

Zelyx.

Frost realized that the name kept coming up wherever he went.

Fawn's sister, Prisha, worked as an in-house counsel for Zelyx. Mr. Jin had catered Zelyx parties, including parties that Fawn had attended.

Greg Howell had a Zelyx connection, too, through his real estate holdings. According to the newspaper articles Frost had found, Howell had been involved in an eminent domain dispute over the land on which the Zelyx headquarters was being built.

And now Frost knew that Alan Detlowe had sought out a security job at an event where Zelyx and its CEO were the heroes of the night. Two days later, Detlowe was dead with his throat cut.

Maybe it all meant nothing.

Or maybe Lombard had played a behind-the-scenes role in San Francisco's corporate coup.

Frost grabbed his phone and dialed Prisha Anand's cell phone number. He recognized her silky voice when she answered.

"Ms. Anand? It's Frost Easton with the police."

The woman hesitated when she heard his name. "Inspector Easton. I'm afraid to ask, do you have news? Have you located my sister?"

"I haven't. Have you heard from her?"

"No. I've left messages, but nothing. I'm very worried."

"As soon as I know anything more, I'll tell you. Right now, I have a few more questions, but I need to ask first, are you at work?"

"Excuse me?"

"I was wondering if you were at home or whether you were in one of the Zelyx offices."

"I'm working from home," she told him, "but what difference does that make?"

"I don't want you answering these questions where anyone else could hear you."

She took a long pause before saying anything more. "And why would that be?"

"My questions involve Zelyx."

"I see. Well, you can ask whatever you want, but the odds are that I won't be able to answer. You have to remember my position at the company. I'm one of their lawyers."

"Yes, I know that. I don't believe this involves any privileged information. You told me that your sister was upset about the death of a woman she called Naomi. You also mentioned that you and Zara had attended several Zelyx parties together. I was wondering about the timeline. Did any of those parties happen around the time that Zara told you about the death of her friend?"

Prisha let the silence stretch out. Frost wasn't sure she was going to say anything at all. "Yes, now that I think about it, we were at a Zelyx party a couple of days before that happened," she finally replied.

"Did Zara talk to anyone at the party?" Frost asked.

"I don't remember. It was three years ago."

"Why was the party going on?" Frost asked.

"Our founder and CEO, Martin Filko, was in town. This was the week before the big Net-Con trade show. Martin was going to be announcing our corporate relocation to San Francisco. The party was an early celebration."

"Were there any pictures taken?"

"No. No pictures. Martin has a rule about that. It's one of his little quirks. Why? What do you want to know?"

"Is it possible your sister saw her friend Naomi at that party?" he asked.

"Naomi? An escort? Why would she—" Prisha stopped before she finished her question. She knew what Frost was driving at. "You think Naomi was at the Zelyx party with her client, don't you? The one who was abusing her. The one she told Zara she wanted to expose."

"I think it's possible," Frost replied.

"Anything's possible, Inspector, but I have no proof that Naomi was there. And frankly, I don't think it would be appropriate for me to tell you even if I did."

"Well, I appreciate the information, Ms. Anand."

Frost hung up.

He had a timeline of events now, and he didn't like what it suggested. Fawn had been at a Zelyx party with her sister shortly before the death of her friend Naomi. Then Fawn had lunch with Alan Detlowe from vice, and Detlowe canceled his anniversary plans in order to work the Zelyx event at Moscone Center. Two days later, Detlowe was dead, too.

There was plenty of smoke in the air about this tech company.

But did the smoke mean there was a fire?

Frost decided to play a hunch. Zelyx had made a lot of money for a lot of people, but there was one man who had profited more than anyone else. He used his phone to search for the name Martin Filko. The Zelyx CEO might not like pictures, but it was impossible for an executive at a public company to avoid them altogether. He found the best photograph he could, and he saved it from the web to his camera roll.

Then he called the Zingari restaurant and asked for Virgil. The sleek gay waiter picked up the call less than a minute later.

"Inspector," Virgil breathed into the phone. "Apparently you can't stay away from me."

"I need your phone number, Virgil," Frost said.

"Gladly. I was hoping you'd ask."

"I'm going to send you a photograph. I want to know if you've seen this man before."

"Text away, but feel free to use the number whenever you like. You'd be surprised how many straight men change teams when they get to know me."

Frost laughed. "Just the picture, Virgil."

He hung up and forwarded the photograph of Martin Filko. Virgil took less than a minute to call back.

"Oh yes. That's him."

Frost didn't want to coach the man at all. "And by *him*' you mean . . . ?"

"The guy on the boat last August. The one who kept arguing with Greg Howell. He had that amazing woman with him."

"You're absolutely sure?"

"Definitely. Guy was a first-class dick, and not in a good way."

"Thanks, Virgil."

Frost ended the call.

Smoke, meet fire.

If the way to get to Lombard was through his clients, Frost was pretty sure he'd found one. Martin Filko, the billionaire CEO of Zelyx, was leaving a trail of red snakes wherever he went.

# 29

The building that housed the *San Francisco Chronicle* was only a block away from Moscone Center, so Frost walked over there to find the investigative reporter named Khristeen Smith. The receptionist told him that she was expected back at the paper within the hour. It was late afternoon, and Frost hadn't eaten anything since breakfast with Herb, so he left a message for Khristeen to meet him at the restaurant near the Pickwick Hotel across the street.

While he waited over a Greek meze platter, he booted up his MacBook and searched the newspaper's online archives. He had to go back twenty-eight years to find what he wanted. It was an article by a *Chronicle* reporter named Stephen Post, and it was the story that had launched the Lombard myth.

Rumors of a Supercriminal Trouble Police

By Stephen Post

Exclusive to the *Chronicle*

They call him Lombard.

No one knows if that's his real name. In fact, no one knows if Lombard is a man or woman, one person or many people. But among police investigators, Lombard has become a legend. They will tell you that Lombard is the prime suspect in a string of unsolved murders related to bribery and corruption cases inside and outside government.

That includes the case of Tim Holley. Last year, Holley stepped off the curb on California Street across from Tadich Grill and was struck and killed by a hit-and-run driver. Holley was a stockbroker and whistleblower who had been planning to testify about insider trading schemes at three of the city's largest banks. Now the SEC investigation has stalled.

An ordinary traffic accident? The police don't think so. In fact, sources inside the police are sure they know who was behind the hit-and-run. "Lombard did it," says one of the department's homicide inspectors with knowledge of the case.

No one in the police or city hall would speak on the record about Lombard, but the picture they paint is of a ruthless criminal who operates at the behest of the powerful . . .

Frost read the entire article, and the description of Lombard from nearly three decades earlier tracked precisely with everything that he'd discovered in the past several days. The only thing missing was a reference to red snakes marking each murder site. Stephen Post's article clearly had stirred up a firestorm in the city, because the follow-up articles in the succeeding days reflected panicked attempts by the police chief to put the genie back in the bottle.

He read the headlines in the archives:

Police Chief Calls Lombard "Fiction," "Myth"

City Council Launches Review of Lombard Claims

Chief Steps Down Following Lombard Controversy

Mayor Says "No Evidence" That Lombard Exists

Months After Lombard Story, Doubts Linger

After that last article, Frost didn't find another reference to the Lombard myth anywhere in the newspaper archives. It simply went away. Even so, the tone of Stephen Post's final story suggested that he wasn't convinced by the official denials. To the reporter, Lombard was real, and the myth was a cover-up.

Frost looked up from the computer as he heard a tapping on the window next to him. Khristeen Smith was on the street outside. He waved her in, and she hustled through the restaurant, dumped her backpack on one of the empty chairs at his table, and slid into a chair across from him. She downed a full glass of water and flagged a waiter for more.

"Hey, Frost, how are you?" Khristeen said, her words tumbling together. "I was surprised to get your message. You don't usually knock on my door. Normally it's the other way around."

"This time I'm the one looking for information," Frost told her.

"Well, color me intrigued. Where's Shack? He's not with you?"

"No, he's at home today. I'm sure he'll complain about it when I get back."

"I love that cat," she said. "One of these days I'm going to write a story about him, you know."

Khristeen grabbed a menu and called out an order to a waiter passing the table. Her silver glasses slipped to the end of her nose, and she pushed them back. Her face had a sheen of sweat, as if she'd been running. She had limp dark hair parted in the middle without any particular style, and her face had no makeup. She wore a black nylon jacket zipped to her neck, blue jeans, and old sneakers.

She wasn't even thirty years old, but in seven years with the *Chronicle*, she'd earned a reputation as the paper's hardest-working reporter. Khristeen seemed to be everywhere in the city on every story. Frost didn't know her well, but she'd written the front-page profile of him after the incident with Tabby the previous fall. He knew that she always did her research and had a good eye for details. Sometimes too good. As she asked him about Tabby, she'd seen something in his face that made her start digging into his relationship with her to a point that made him uncomfortable. He'd explained it away as a close friendship with his brother's fiancée, but there was something in her smirk that made him think she didn't entirely believe him.

Khristeen leaned across the table and lowered her voice. She had a fast, breathless way of talking that made her sound in a perpetual hurry. "So what's going on, Frost? When the police come to me, it makes me think I must be missing something. Spill the beans, I want to know what you're up to."

"This whole conversation has to be off the record," Frost said.

Khristeen stuck out her tongue at him. "Killjoy. Fine. But if you want something from me, I'm going to want something from you, too."

"We can negotiate."

"Yeah, yeah, go ahead. Off the record. What's up?"

"What do you know about Zelyx Corporation?" Frost asked.

Khristeen's eyebrows danced, and she rubbed her hands together. "Ooooh, I like this already. Well, I know pretty much everything there is to know about Zelyx. And about their CEO and founder, Martin Filko. I've been following this one for years. That's my kind of story, baby."

"Tell me about Filko," he said.

The waiter brought a plate of falafel, and Khristeen dove in as if she hadn't eaten for days. "Like what? He's another wunderkind like Zuckerberg. Came up with some groundbreaking security protocol during a kegger at Northwestern. He's like a year older than me, which is annoying. I haul my clothes to the laundromat, and this guy is the sultan of Brunei."

"What about his personal life?"

"Oh, that's a big yuck. Filko's a frat boy. So are the execs around him. Zelyx gets a terrible rap for its culture. Their lawyers are constantly swatting down sexual harassment claims. You never see Filko out and about without some Victoria's-Secret-model wannabe on his arm. It's like the fantasy of every fourteen-year-old boy come true."

"Have you heard any stories about the women he hangs out with?" Frost asked.

Khristeen studied him with squinted eyes across the table and clucked her tongue loudly against the roof of her mouth. "You realize this is the kind of conversation that gets a reporter horny, right? What the heck are you trying to find out?"

"I can't tell you that. Not yet. Have you seen Filko with women at any of his public events?"

"Some."

Frost found a photo of LaHonda Duke. "What about her?"

"She looks like Filko's type, but I don't remember her specifically."

He showed her Fawn's picture next. "And this woman?"

"I'm pretty sure she's been on his arm at least once. Who is she?"

Frost smiled and didn't answer, but Khristeen got the message.

"She's a *pro*? Come on, Frost, just a hint. Do you think Filko hangs out with escorts?"

"No comment. What do you know about his reputation in Illinois? Has he had any run-ins with the police?"

"Run-ins over what?" Khristeen asked. "Narrow it down for me."

"Assault. Abuse."

"Sexual assault?"

"Possibly," Frost said.

"Well, I haven't heard anything, but that doesn't necessarily mean there's nothing there. Filko has the money to fix things. I'm sure he knows how to make problems go away."

"What was Filko's relationship with Greg Howell?" Frost asked.

Khristeen looked disappointed that they weren't talking about sex anymore. "Bad. Those two hated each other. Howell controlled the Mission Bay land that Filko and the mayor wanted for the Zelyx headquarters. Howell was trying to drag it out with litigation and jack up the price. Frankly, I think Howell just wanted to screw Filko, too. Howell was a classy guy, and he thought Filko was a turd."

"What happened after Howell had his heart attack?"

"Howell's sons settled. It was all quick and quiet. Filko got his building site."

Frost tried to make his next question sound casual. "So when was Filko last in San Francisco? Do you know?"

Khristeen's lips puckered into a self-satisfied smirk. "Yes, I do know."

"And?"

"And this one is going to cost you, Frost. I think you have something very specific in mind about what Filko was doing, and you need me to confirm it for you."

"Why do you say that?" Frost asked.

"One, I know how to read people, and I can read you. Two, do you think I somehow missed the story about a guy dying on your front doorstep last Friday? I smell a connection. If Martin Filko, CEO of Zelyx Corporation, has anything to do with a poisoned guy on Russian Hill, then I sure as hell want to know about it. I'm not saying another word until you give me something more."

"You're not the only reporter in town, Khristeen," Frost said. "I can go elsewhere with my questions."

"But you won't, because you know I have the information you need."

Frost frowned. "We're still off the record."

"For now."

"The man who died at my house was named Denny Clark. He ran VIP charter tours on a yacht out of the marina. I want to know if Martin Filko was on his boat on Tuesday night."

"Because?" Khristeen asked.

"No. That's all you get for now."

Khristeen took a large bite of falafel. "Okay. I don't know anything about the boat, but yes, Martin Filko was in San Francisco on Tuesday."

"What was he doing?" Frost asked.

"He toured the HQ building site, and then he spent the rest of the day with the mayor and his staff. Economic development, affordable housing, that kind of stuff. The relocation is a big deal, you know."

"And in the evening?"

Khristeen winked. "Well, that is an excellent question, and I wish I knew the answer to it. But I don't."

"Why is that?"

"Because Filko and the mayor pulled a bait and switch on the press. The schedule said that the two of them were going to have dinner at the Fairmont. However, that turned out not to be true. They never showed. And they did a fake-out with the limo at city hall so no one was able to follow them. I have no idea where they went or who they were with or what they did."

Frost felt the unmistakable electricity of getting closer to the truth. It shot up his spine with a combination of fear and excitement. "But Martin Filko was definitely with the mayor on Tuesday evening?" he asked.

"Definitely."

He stood up, dug cash out of his wallet, and slapped it on the table. "This should cover everything. In fact, order something else if you want. Thank you, Khristeen. This was very helpful."

"You're welcome. And remember, Frost, I expect you to be very helpful to me in the near future."

"Count on it," he said. He picked up his laptop, and as he did, he thought about the archived articles he'd found about Lombard. "Oh, one other thing. Have you ever heard of a reporter named Stephen Post who used to work at the *Chronicle*? This would have been about three decades ago, so he was long before your time. I was just wondering if you'd heard the name."

A strange, suspicious expression came over Khristeen's face. "Stephen Post? Why are you interested in him?"

Frost shrugged. "He wrote some articles a long time ago that I just came across. If he was still in the Bay Area, I thought I might talk to him. You know me. I'm interested in history."

Khristeen didn't look convinced by his explanation. "Well, I do know about Stephen Post. All of us at the paper do. He's a hero to journalists. Actually, there's a portrait of him in the lobby with a special plaque underneath it."

Frost stared at her, confused. "Why is that?"

"It's a memorial," she told him. "Stephen Post was shot and killed while on assignment. The police never found out who did it, but everyone believes it was because of one of his stories."

# 30

Frost arrived home after dark. The only thing he could see inside the Russian Hill house were the lights of the city through the rear windows. A low, intermittent rumbling rose out of the silence, and that was Shack, snoring on the living room sofa. Frost didn't turn on any lights. Instead, he went to the refrigerator and got himself a bottle of Torpedo ale, and he went out to the cool patio, leaving the glass door open behind him.

He leaned on the railing. This place felt like an oasis on top of the world, with the glowing neighborhoods below him and the black mass of the bay in the distance. Trees clung to the hillside, making a jungle on the steep slope. He drank his beer, listened to the wind, and wasn't even aware of time passing. Throughout the day, he'd barely thought about the fight two nights earlier, but now that he was alone and his adrenaline had seeped away, the pain caught up with him again. The wound on his leg where the knife had slashed him throbbed. His neck stabbed him when he turned his head. He was tired, and all he wanted to do was tumble onto the sofa and sleep.

A tiny noise like the chiming of a bell rose from the darkness at his feet. He looked down. Shack was awake and had joined him on the patio through the open door. The cat bumped his head against Frost's leg, but with every step he took, a metallic music followed him.

"You're jingling, buddy," Frost said. "What's up with that?"

Frost bent down and scooped up the small cat with a hand under his stomach. He lifted Shack up until they were nose to nose. The cat licked his face. Shack normally wore a black collar, and although he was microchipped, Frost had also attached a badge to the collar with his cell phone number on it, just in case Shack decided to go exploring.

Except there was something else on his collar now.

A small charm, the kind that would hang from a teenager's bracelet, jangled against the ID badge. Frost had no idea how it had gotten there. He couldn't make it out, and he had to open up his phone to shine a light on the collar to see what it was.

When he did, his heart stopped.

His whole body shook with a wave of rage and fear.

The charm hanging on Shack's collar was a snake. Its coils glinted in red. Its jaws were open, its teeth bared, as if it were hissing and laughing at him all at the same time.

Lombard.

Lombard had been here. In his house.

The naked cruelty of the threat overwhelmed him. He put Shack calmly down on the patio floor and stroked his black-and-white fur from head to tail as the cat purred. Then Frost grabbed the railing tightly with both hands and tried to drag breath out of his chest. He closed his eyes and opened them, and he felt a sting where he'd bitten down hard on his tongue.

He had no idea if he was alone or if anyone was on the wooded hillside to hear him. He shouted anyway.

"*Don't . . . you . . . dare!* Don't you try it, you sons of bitches! I will rain down hell on all of you! Do you hear me? Are you listening to me?"

The exhaustion, the ache, the loss, the confusion, the sleeplessness of the days since Friday night cascaded over him. He pounded both fists on the iron railing until he thought his bones had broken. Everything in his life felt brittle, like glass riddled with cracks, about to split open.

"Frost?"

He heard a voice behind him, and his reaction was instantaneous. His gun was in his hand. In a single fluid motion, it was cocked. He spun, ready to fire. His arm stretched out; his finger went to the trigger. Halfway through the turn, his mind caught up with him, and he realized that the shadow in the doorway was Tabby. He froze, but he couldn't seem to let go of the gun. She saw it, too, and the starlight showed the panic in her face.

"Frost, it's me!"

He breathed hard and came to his senses. He secured the gun and returned it to his holster and squatted next to Shack on the patio. When he did, he found he couldn't even stand up again. He ran one hand back through his hair and left it awry. Tabby came and bent down beside him and put an arm around his shoulder.

"Are you okay?"

Frost shook his head. "No."

He said it again in a whisper. "No."

She helped him inside. Shack followed, and Tabby locked the patio door behind them. She eased him onto the sofa, and when she started to get up, he pulled her down beside him. She didn't protest. She sat next to him in silence and stroked his hair, until he winced when her fingers neared the bruise at the back of his head. They sat like that for a long time. Neither of them said a word.

Eventually, she got up and went to the kitchen to get him another Torpedo. She brought back one for herself, too. They sat and drank, but they didn't talk. When those bottles were empty, she got them two more. And two more after that. And again. By the time he was able to say anything, they were both drunk. Being drunk only made her more beautiful to him.

"I'm sorry," he said.

It was probably an hour later.

Tabby gave him one of her incandescent smiles. "Well, it's not like it's the first time you've pointed a gun at me."

He couldn't help but laugh.

"Do you want to tell me what's going on?" she asked.

He didn't want to, but he did. It was wrong, but he did. He told her everything. He told her about Denny and Lombard and Coyle and Gorham and Mr. Jin and Filko and the snakes and Herb. He told her about the invisible fight in the darkness, Coyle with his throat cut, his fear of dying. He told her about Shack and the charm. When he did, Tabby simply undid the cat's collar, removed the snake, and went out onto the patio. She threw the charm into the thick of the trees below the house, where it would be buried forever under mud and leaves.

She came back inside and sat next to him again. She looked calm. Brave. That was just one thing he loved about her.

"So what are you going to do?" Tabby asked him.

"I have to get him," he said. "I have to get Lombard."

"Frost, maybe you should stop," she replied. "This is too dangerous."

"I wish I could, but I can't do that."

Tabby didn't look surprised to hear him say that. "How can I help?"

"You can't. What you can do is stay a thousand miles away from this. And a thousand miles away from me."

"Well, maybe you didn't hear me. How can I help?"

"*You. Can't. Help.* Do you understand me?"

Tabby sighed in annoyance and rolled her eyes. She didn't like being put off, and she didn't give up easily. "So what are you going to do next?"

Frost leaned his head back against the sofa. "I need to prove that Martin Filko and the mayor were really on Denny's boat on Tuesday, and then I need to figure out why they called in Lombard. Obviously, something bad happened that they couldn't let go public."

"But how do you prove they were on the boat if no one saw them?" Tabby asked. "At least, no one who's still alive."

He shrugged. "I don't know yet."

Tabby sat next to him with her hands on her knees. She reached over to the coffee table where she'd put her phone. He watched her run a search, and then she glanced over and asked, "What's the code for blocking your number?"

"What?"

"If you don't want your name or number showing up when you call," she said.

"It's star six seven. Why?"

Tabby tapped the keys and dialed a number. She put the call on speakerphone and put a finger over her lips to keep him silent. He had no idea what she was doing.

Then a voice answered. "City hall answering service."

"I need the after-hours contact for the mayor's office, please," Tabby said brightly.

Frost began to protest, but Tabby reached over and put her fingers against his mouth.

Another voice picked up the call. "Mayor's office, this is Justine."

"Oh, hey, Justine," Tabby announced, as if they'd been friends their whole lives. A strange little Southern accent popped into her voice. "I just knew someone would be there to help me in the evening. You all are so efficient out there. This is Lizzy in Martin Filko's office. Martin's got a friend coming into San Fran tomorrow who needs a good limo service. He was pretty impressed with the driver last Tuesday and was wondering if you had a contact number for the limo company. It would be a big help, hon."

There was a long, tentative pause on the line.

And then, "Sure, Lizzy, hang on a minute."

The minute turned out to be no more than a few seconds before Justine came back on the line. "Lizzy, are you there? It was DiMatteo Limousine. Oh, and the driver's name was Jeffrey, if that helps."

"It sure does, hon. You're the best."

Tabby hung up.

Frost stared at her. "I can't begin to tell you how crazy that was."

She winked. "Uh-huh. You can thank me later. Right now, how about I make dinner for the two of us? That was the whole reason I came over here, you know. Duane promised a care package, but he wasn't sure he could leave the truck, so I volunteered. How does shrimp risotto sound?"

"It sounds great," Frost said.

Tabby picked up Shack from the floor with one hand. "Yes, you get some, too," she said.

She wandered unsteadily toward the kitchen, and he pushed himself off the sofa to join her. They were both feeling the effects of the alcohol. He turned on the downstairs lights, and the house looked warmer and brighter. Like the professional chef she was, despite the lack of mobility in one hand, she began to assemble ingredients from the brown grocery bags she'd brought and to manipulate everything into her *mise en place*. As she was heating a pan, she said, "How about some music? I like to rock when I cook."

"Sure. Anything you want."

Frost hooked up his speakers. He shuffled the songs on his phone, and the first song that boomed into the room was Parachute's "Can't Help."

"Oh!" Tabby exclaimed happily as she recognized the beat. "Oh, I love this song!"

Her head tilted back and forth with the music. Her hips swayed, and her red hair flew. Drinking with him for an hour had erased her inhibitions. She left the stove and strutted from the kitchen into the middle of the living room. He'd never seen her dance before, and he admired the utterly natural flow of her limbs, the ease she had inside her own skin.

At the moment the words began, she surprised him by spinning around with her arms outstretched and both index fingers pointed at him. She lip-synched the song, which she knew by heart, and the lyrics crushed him. They just crushed him. Like the song said, he couldn't help himself from falling in love with her. He found himself frozen with a smile that told her everything that he needed to hide. His emotions were like Mr. Jin's posters of Niagara Falls, a torrent that threatened to drown him.

He tried to walk away because watching her was torture, but she grabbed his hands and made him dance with her. He couldn't find any rhythm; he simply circled the room, nodding to the song, while she followed him and teased him. He mouthed the words to her, too, but he wasn't pretending. He meant it. He couldn't help it. The only thing he could think about was wrapping her up in his arms right there.

When the music finally stopped, they were inches apart. Tabby was breathless, and her flushed face beamed. They were out of control. They were drunk, they had no idea what they were doing, and they didn't care. She slung her arms around his neck and kissed his cheek. He was falling, falling, falling, and there was no way she didn't know it, no way she couldn't see the truth in his eyes. He wanted to kiss her back hard. On the lips. He wanted to show her what he'd been feeling for months. Something in her face said she wanted it, too.

"Girl can dance, can't she?"

The voice from the foyer stunned them like the blaring wake-up call of an alarm. It was Duane. He'd been watching the whole thing.

Tabby disentangled herself from Frost as if she were running from a burning building. She put her hands on her pink, blushing cheeks. "Oh," she said to Duane. "Oh, hi."

"Hi."

"I didn't think you could make it."

"I got out of the truck early," Duane replied.

Her voice stuttered. "Well, good. Great. That's great. I was starting risotto. Can you stick around?"

"Sure I can." Duane stared at the two of them with a strange coolness in his eyes. "Assuming that's okay with you guys?"

"More than okay," Frost said.

Tabby turned and disappeared into the kitchen with an embarrassed sideways glance at Frost. Duane didn't join her. Not right away. He let her get to work. The clatter of pans sounded extra loud and extra fast, as if she were throwing a wound-up ball of nervous energy into the sizzle of shrimp. His brother simply stood in the foyer with his hands on his hips. He watched Frost, and Frost watched him back. Neither one of them said a word.

"So," his brother said finally, when the silence had gone on for too long. "I guess I should go help my fiancée."

Frost didn't miss the little emphasis Duane put on that last word.

"I guess so."

"What can I get for you, bro? Is there something you want?"

"Nothing."

"Really? Because it sure looks to me like you want something. How about another beer?"

Frost heard the innuendo in Duane's voice and tried to ignore it. The room spun as he collapsed onto the sofa. His headache was back, like a spike burrowing into his neck. He couldn't remember another time in his life where he'd felt as if the walls were closing in on him the way they were now.

"No," he said. "I've had too much already."

# 31

Shack went along for the ride the next morning. Frost wasn't about to let him out of his sight.

He called DiMatteo Limousine and found out that their driver Jeffrey was on assignment at the airport. He headed south out of the city and immediately got locked up in the traffic on 101. It was the same slog every morning as tech commuters crawled toward Silicon Valley. Bay Area traffic had always been bad, but since the dot-com boom had taken over the area, it was near-constant gridlock on all the freeways and bridges.

He was hungover and angry with himself. He felt like a fool for coming so close to making an irreversible mistake with Tabby, and he felt like a traitor because his brother had seen it all happen. The dinner among the three of them had been a long, uncomfortable hour of silence, and then Tabby and Duane had both left with barely a word to him or to each other. Duane's face was a blank mask, showing nothing. Tabby looked as if she were standing on the edge of a cliff.

Frost wasn't sure what would happen next. He felt as if lines had been crossed everywhere, and there was no going back.

His one comfort was that Shack seemed no worse for his brush with Lombard. The cat slept through the traffic jam at first, then got up and went from window to window to examine the other drivers stuck around them. His tail swished. He put a paw on the glass, as if handing out high fives. Young women cooed and waved back. Everywhere they went, Shack was the star.

His SUV inched past the calm bay waters. The Pacifica hills loomed to the west, still tipped with morning fog off the ocean. The sun was low. It took him nearly an hour to reach the airport, but he finally left the freeway at San Bruno Avenue near the huge United maintenance facility and found the private parking lot where taxis and limos waited for their fares. His badge got him past the gate, and he drove to the lineup of town cars parked near the barbed wire fence. Several of the drivers were hanging out together, laughing and smoking cigarettes.

Frost pulled into an open spot near them. He saw no signage to identify the cars for DiMatteo Limousine, but that didn't surprise him. Their clientele preferred anonymity. When he asked the drivers about Jeffrey, they pointed him toward a young Filipino man in a black suit hanging out by himself on the other side of the lot.

He walked through the rows of cars, and the eyes of the other drivers followed him. Jeffrey sat in a fold-up canvas chair next to a sleek navy-blue Lincoln. The tall, skinny driver was eating slices of mango from a plastic bag and reading a well-thumbed paperback copy of David McCullough's biography of the Wright brothers. Frost had already read the book himself. Before he could say anything, he had to wait for the thunder of a departing 767 to clear overhead.

When it was quiet again, Frost said, "Long way from then to now."

Jeffrey looked up at him. Unlike his wary colleagues, the young man's face was curious and open. He was probably no more than twenty years old. "I'm sorry, what?"

Frost nodded at the jumbo jet vanishing north toward the city. "We've come a long way since the Wright brothers."

"Oh yeah."

"'No bird soars in a calm,'" Frost quoted. "Isn't that what Wilbur's wrote?"

"Yes! You've read the book?"

"I have."

"I don't meet many people with an interest in history," Jeffrey said. "Me, I can't get enough of it."

"Same here." Frost extended a hand, and the man took it. "Are you Jeffrey? Do you work for DiMatteo Limousine?"

Jeffrey finished his last slice of mango and shoved the empty bag in his pocket. "Yeah, that's right. It pays the bills. I go to SF State in the evenings."

"My alma mater," Frost said. "Are you studying history?"

A smile creased the young man's face. "Oh no. My parents wouldn't like that. College has to be practical. I'm studying business."

"My parents told me the same thing," Frost said. "Not that I listened."

Jeffrey grinned. "So what do you do?"

Frost took out his badge. "Mostly, I ask people questions. Mind if I ask you some?"

"About what?"

"A limo charter you drove last Tuesday night," Frost said.

Jeffrey looked nervous. "The boss doesn't like it when I talk about the rides. We're pretty high end. We get a lot of people who are really concerned about privacy. Celebrities and such."

"I understand. The thing is, I'm investigating a murder that might be connected to the people who were in your limo. It would help a lot to know what happened on Tuesday night. I won't tell your boss."

The young man glanced at the cluster of drivers on the other side of the lot. They were still watching the two of them. "There are other DiMatteo guys over there. They're going to tell my boss that they saw me talking to you. I'll get in trouble, and I can't afford that. This job pays my tuition."

Frost reached into his pocket and let one of his cards drop to the greasy pavement at his feet. "Tell you what. I'm going to walk away, and I'm going to make sure those other guys see that I look unhappy. Like you didn't tell me anything. Then I'm going to drive away, but I'd appreciate it if you'd call me after I'm gone. Five minutes. That's all I need."

Jeffrey glanced at the card on the ground near the car door. "Yeah, okay. What the hell. 'No bird soars in a calm,' right?"

"Right."

Frost walked away. He made a show of looking frustrated and angry, which prompted an undercurrent of conversation in another language as he passed the drivers near his Suburban. He climbed inside and drove out of the parking lot, and he wondered whether Jeffrey would follow through on his promise. He didn't have to wait long to find out. He wasn't even back to the on-ramp at 101 when his phone rang.

"Inspector?"

"Thanks, Jeffrey. I'm glad you called."

"Well, there isn't a lot I can tell you about Tuesday, because I don't know much. Yeah, I had a limo pickup, and the boss told me it was a big deal and everything had to be perfect. No mistakes. I made sure the car was washed, bottled water, champagne, special hors d'oeuvres from some bakery, all the perks."

"Who got in the car?" Frost asked.

"I don't know, because I never saw them. My instructions were *not* to get out to open the doors. That's pretty weird."

"Where did you do the pickup?" Frost asked.

"That was weird, too. It was in a parking garage on Larkin. I went in and waited, and I saw the headlights of another car pulling up. A few people got out and climbed in the back, and after they did, I got a thump on the screen to tell me to go. I don't know who they were. I'm paid not to be curious. When my boss says to be deaf, dumb, and blind, that's what I am."

"Where did you take them?"

"The marina. I let them out near one of the expensive yachts down there. Someone was at the dock to escort them onto the boat, but I didn't look at any of the faces. Plus, it was dark, so I wouldn't have been able to see much anyway."

"Do you have any idea how many people were there?" Frost asked.

"Maybe three or four. It was a small group. I heard a couple different male voices and at least one woman. But I don't know how many it was. I was trying not to listen, you know?"

Frost shook his head in frustration because Jeffrey had told him everything and nothing. If the people in the limo included the mayor and Martin Filko, they'd been careful. No pickup at city hall. No interaction with the driver. Their tracks were covered. He had no way of proving they'd been on the *Roughing It* at all.

"Did you see the person who met the limo?" he asked. "The one who took them on board the boat?"

"It was a woman. That's all I can say for sure."

"Then what?" Frost asked.

"Then I left. The job was done."

"What about the pickup on the other end? Did another driver meet them when they came back from the cruise?"

Jeffrey sounded uncomfortable. "Look, Inspector, I really don't want to get into trouble."

"I know that, but this is important. If you know something, I need you to be honest with me."

"Except if I tell you, then everybody knows it was me."

Frost was on the freeway again, and the traffic went nowhere heading back into the city. "Whatever you say is just between us. I'll leave your name out of my notes. But I need to know what happened."

"Well," Jeffrey said, drawing out the word. "Here's the thing. I was supposed to get them on Wednesday morning. The pickup time was eight o'clock. I got there early because I live over in San Ramon, and I didn't want to take any chances with the traffic. Believe me, if you're late for a ride, you're done. It was still dark when I arrived, like six thirty in the morning. I had a long time to wait, but I didn't care. I figured, coffee, doughnuts, Wright brothers, know what I mean?"

"Okay."

"Except when I arrived at the marina," Jeffrey continued, "the boat was already there."

"What?"

"The boat was in its slip in the harbor again. They weren't supposed to get in for another hour and a half, but there they were. For a minute, I panicked. I thought I'd gotten the time wrong, you know? But I hadn't. They were early."

"Did you see anybody getting on or off?" Frost asked.

"I did, but not passengers."

"What do you mean?"

"There were two black SUVs parked at the dock, and maybe half a dozen guys were on the boat. I could just barely make them out. They looked like a cleaning crew. They were scrubbing everything down. And I saw two guys bring out a couple boxes from the boat and put them in the back of one of the SUVs. Looked like electronic equipment. The whole thing was strange. I mean, these guys looked like serious dudes."

"Did you see anything else?" Frost asked.

"That was all."

"What did you do next?"

"I didn't know what to do. I thought about leaving and coming back at eight o'clock because that's what the itinerary said. But it looked pretty obvious to me that I wasn't going to be picking anybody up. They were already gone. So I called my boss, and he said, what the hell was I doing there so early? He told me to stay put and wait for instructions."

"What happened next?" Frost asked.

"About five minutes later, a woman came off the boat. She walked right up to my driver's window and tapped on it. I rolled it down, and she told me the pickup was canceled. She said somebody else had already picked up the passengers, and she told me to get the hell out of there. And she gave me a thousand bucks in cash. She said it was a bonus. She told me to forget I was ever here, forget I'd seen anything or anybody. I told her that was easy because I didn't see anything at all."

Frost frowned. "Who was this woman? Did you get her name?"

"No way. I wasn't going to ask."

"What did she look like?"

"Blond. Hard-ass attitude, not somebody I was going to mess with. Hard to say how old. She wore big sunglasses even though it was dark out. I remember she wore a cool jacket, though. Red leather with lots of zippers."

That was the tip-off. Frost knew who it was.

She'd been wearing the same jacket when he met her on the balcony of her condo across from the Transamerica pyramid.

Belinda Drake.

She was a direct link to Lombard. She had all the answers he needed about the cruise on Tuesday. If he could get her to talk.

# 32

Belinda Drake met him at the elevator inside her penthouse condominium. There was no butler this time. They had the apartment to themselves. She greeted him coolly and led him outside to the balcony where they'd talked before. It was noon, and the sun cast a maze of shadows among the skyscrapers. The wind was cold, but she didn't seem affected by it. Drake wore a white button-down blouse untucked over skinny jeans, and black high heels. Her hair was loose, and the thirtieth-floor gales played with it like a toy. She went to the railing, where the building wall went straight down below them. He stood next to her and leaned over the edge.

"That's the best way to go, you know," she told him.

"What's that?"

"Jump. You get one last exhilarating ride, and then you're dead before you even feel the pain."

"No, thanks," Frost said.

"Well, that's the plan when my time comes," Drake told him. She turned her back on the view and stared at the city's reflections in the mirrored windows of her condominium. "What do you want, Inspector?"

"You were at the yacht harbor on Wednesday morning," Frost replied. "The *Roughing It* wasn't due until eight in the morning, but at six thirty, the boat was already back in the marina and everyone was gone. Passengers and crew. Thanks to you."

Strands of wheat-colored hair practically covered her eyes, but she made no attempt to brush it away. "Yes, I was at the marina. So what?"

"What happened on the boat Tuesday night?" Frost asked.

She shrugged. "I have nothing to say about that."

"You brought a cleanup crew with you. There were two black SUVs at the marina and people carrying equipment off the boat. What were you trying to hide?"

"You're way too fond of conspiracy theories, Inspector," Drake replied. "Did I have people cleaning up the yacht? Of course I did. It's SOP after every charter. You wouldn't believe the lengths that people go to when money and fame are involved. I'm not kidding, I've had celebrities whose DNA showed up for sale on the dark net. You blow your nose in a hotel bathroom, and the next thing you know, some Saudi sheik is paying a couple million dollars to buy a used Kleenex and clone you. The world is a bizarre place."

"Who was on the boat on Tuesday night?" Frost asked. "Who were you trying to protect?"

She hesitated, as if she were rehearsing the lines in her head. "His name was Diego Casal. The cruise was some kind of party for him and a few of his associates. Based on the news, I think the police already know this, so I'm not sure what you hope to accomplish by talking to me."

Frost shook his head. He should have seen it coming. "Diego Casal?"

"That's right."

"Do you routinely take on drug dealers as clients?"

"Casal knew Denny, not me. My only involvement was when Denny called to arrange for an early pickup and cleanup at the harbor."

"Didn't you find that suspicious?"

"I didn't ask questions. Denny and the *Roughing It* were both assets of mine. If there was a problem, it would affect my business. So I agreed to help."

"Did the cleanup suggest what happened on the boat?"

"Like what?"

"Did you find any blood?"

"No, nothing like that. There was no evidence of violence."

"What about the equipment you removed? Do you still have it? Do you have an inventory of what you took?"

"Anything we removed was destroyed. That's how it works."

"And you didn't bother mentioning any of this to me when we first talked?" Frost asked. "After Denny was murdered?"

"Pointing the finger at drug dealers isn't a recipe for a long life," Drake replied, "but with Mr. Casal dead, you can put your conspiracy theories to rest."

Frost looked over the edge of the balcony again. Not even a hundred yards away, the Transamerica building tapered to a point in the sky. He was silent for a while. There were holes in her story, but she had the upper hand, and they both knew it. No one in the police department wanted him to poke and prod to get to the truth, and even if he did, he would never be able to prove it. The case was already closed.

"So Denny had a problem, and you fixed it?" he asked.

"That's what I do."

"Well, you're very good at it. For a minute, it made me wonder if *you* were Lombard. Everyone says he's a problem solver, too. But the first time I mentioned Lombard, you were afraid of the name. You couldn't hide that. You take orders like all the others. Right? You're just a pawn."

Her face was frozen. "Don't talk to me like that."

"Why not? That's what you are. He controls you."

"You don't know anything about me," she snapped at him. "Now, I want you to leave and not contact me again."

Frost didn't move. "What's your identification? Sansome? Fillmore? You all use a different San Francisco street name, right? Just like your boss. Look, Belinda, let's not play games. The Diego Casal story is a lie. I know who was on that boat last Tuesday. The mayor of San Francisco and Martin Filko of Zelyx. You set it all up for them, and then something happened that they needed to cover up. So you called Lombard."

Drake hissed under her breath. "Do you have a death wish?"

"Maybe I do, but if I go down, so do you. If I leave without you telling me the truth, my next call is to Martin Filko. I'm going to make sure he knows that *you* gave me his name. I'm going to tell him you're cooperating with the police. What do you think happens then, Ms. Drake?"

"You wouldn't dare do that."

"Try me," Frost said.

"Do you think I'm a fool? I know who you are, Frost Easton. You're a Boy Scout. You'd never lie. You'd never compromise yourself or anyone else. This is a game of poker and nothing more. Well, you're holding a pair of deuces, so why don't you fold and go on home?"

"Are you willing to take that risk? I don't want to do it, but you're not giving me any choice. I want to know what happened on that boat. If you hold out on me, I'll make sure no one in Lombard's world ever trusts you again. And I think we both know what happens to people he can't trust."

Even in the cool outside air atop the building, he could smell her sweat and fear. He came closer to her, and he spoke softly.

"Belinda, I don't believe you're a willing participant in any of this. That's why you warned me last time. Lombard has you under his thumb, and I think you'd like to get out. So help me take him down."

"You'll never do it."

"If I fail, that's on me. But I need information. No one will ever know we talked."

She bit her lip. Her breaths came faster.

"I must be crazy," she murmured.

She took him by the hand and led him back inside the condominium. As they walked through the glass doors, she put her finger over her lips for silence, and then she pointed to her ears. He understood. People were listening. The place was bugged. She went to the private elevator and pushed the call button, which sounded with a distinctive bell.

"I don't know what else to tell you, Inspector," she said, as if the previous five minutes of their conversation had been erased. "Whatever happened between Denny and Diego Casal was between the two of them. I'm just glad that the man who killed Denny has paid a price for it."

Frost frowned in confusion. "Yes, it looks that way."

"I hate to rush you off, but I have a lunch to go to, and I have to get in the shower."

"Of course."

The elevator bell sounded again as the door opened.

"Good-bye, Inspector," Drake said, but she put a hand in front of his chest to prevent him from getting into the elevator car. The doors closed, and the empty elevator descended. She put a finger over her lips again and guided him silently down the condominium hallway to the oversized master bathroom, which was like a spa. The air was perfumed, the walls and floor were tiled in pink ceramic, and the huge walk-in shower had dual heads and body sprays. Drake turned on the shower and stood just outside the cascading water, where the noise was loudest. She crooked a finger and beckoned him closer. He walked up to her, and she took him by the collar of his shirt with both hands and pulled him until they were face-to-face just inches apart.

She began to unbutton her blouse. He didn't understand what she was doing, because this didn't feel like a seduction. Her brightly colored nails glistened as she undid every button, and then she separated the silken flaps, revealing her bare torso underneath. Where her breasts rose in half-moons above the lace cups of her bra, he saw dozens of tiny, circular scars, mottled in gray against her peach skin. They continued down to her stomach like insect bites.

"Cigarette burns," she whispered. The pound of the water drowned her voice. "That's what Lombard does to people who resist."

"You resisted?"

"Initially. He knew things about my clients and my deals. He was willing to expose them to destroy my business. I didn't care. I told him I wouldn't help him, that I wanted nothing to do with him. So he decided to have his people use other methods to get what he wanted. That's when I became his *pawn*."

"I'm sorry."

"It wasn't just the pain. It was a symbol. Lombard was branding me. Making me his." She slipped her right breast out of its cup. It wasn't a sensual act; she was just revealing her truth. Next to her rose-colored nipple, a garish red snake had been tattooed across the full curve of her flesh.

She covered herself again. Hot steam from the shower made her face damp.

"Who is Lombard?" Frost asked.

"I don't know. I've never met him in person. But he knows everything about me."

"Tell me how it works."

"Anything I tell you will put both of us in danger. I just want you to understand the reality of the threat. He is cruel and ruthless. And his spies are everywhere. You won't win."

"I was lying before, Belinda," Frost told her. "I wouldn't have tried to expose you."

"Believe me, I know that. My whole life has been reading people, and I can read you. It doesn't matter. I think you're a fool trying to destroy Lombard, but if you're willing to sacrifice yourself, go ahead. Someone needs to take him down. I'll help if I can, but I'll never say a word of this in court or in public. If anyone asks me, I'll deny it."

"Understood."

"You're right about the cruise. It was the mayor and Filko. I arranged the whole thing. I helped the mayor win him over from the beginning. I knew exactly who Filko was when I first met him. The Marquis de Sade with an unlimited bank account. Regardless, the mayor was willing to do whatever was necessary to get the Zelyx HQ to San Francisco, and my job was to make sure Filko got whatever he wanted."

"And Lombard?" Frost asked.

"I kept him informed. That's all. I didn't want to know the details."

"But he's been part of it?"

She nodded. "Yes, he solved some problems."

"Three years ago, did you set up Filko with an escort named Naomi? Was she one of the problems?"

Drake's face twitched. "Yes. For all his money, Filko can't get a normal woman to last five minutes with him. The only ones who will put up with him are the ones who get paid for it."

"What happened to Naomi?" Frost asked.

"She told me that Filko would tie her up, choke her until she was unconscious. He would use—devices—on her. She said she wasn't going to let any other girls go through that. I told Lombard about it in my reports."

"You told him that Naomi planned to expose Filko?"

Drake bowed her head. "I did, but I swear, I never thought anything would happen to her. I thought Lombard would pay her off to keep her quiet. And then I heard about her death. I knew she hadn't OD'd."

"And Greg Howell? His heart attack? Was that Lombard, too?"

"I wasn't in the loop on that one, but I think so. Howell was being a pain in the ass. He was getting in the way of the land deal for the new headquarters with his lawsuit. Having him die like that to clear the legal path for the project was awfully convenient."

"Tell me about the cruise on Tuesday," Frost said.

"It was supposed to be a social thing. Filko's been difficult about some of the tax and environmental issues, so the mayor wanted to schmooze him with a fancy overnight on the *Roughing It.* It was all going to be hush-hush, very private, nothing in the press. The mayor actually likes Filko. I don't know why. I think they're cut from the same cloth. The thing is, Filko wanted companionship for the trip. So I arranged an escort. One of the best I know."

"Fawn," Frost said.

Her eyes widened. "You know about her?"

"I know she was on the boat. I know she's missing."

"She's not missing," Drake said. "She's dead."

Frost took a heavy breath. He was thinking about giving Prisha Anand the news about her sister. "Go on."

"I got a call in the middle of the night."

"Denny?" Frost asked.

"No, the mayor. He was in a panic. Everything went okay, great food, lots of drinks, Filko was happy. But the mayor turned in around two in the morning, and that's when things went to hell."

"What happened?"

"Fawn went overboard," Drake said.

"She went off the boat? How?"

"Supposedly, she fell. They were cruising offshore in the Pacific. Denny spun the boat around, but he couldn't find her in the water. She must have gone straight down. That's when the mayor called me."

Frost shook his head in disbelief. "She fell? Or she got an assist from Filko?"

"I don't know. The mayor didn't see it happen. Filko claimed he was asleep, and Denny backed him up. Denny thought Fawn was too drunk or stoned to know what she was doing."

"Fawn? According to her sister, Fawn was always clean. No drinking. No drugs."

"You're right. I thought that, too."

"Fawn *knew* all about the problems between Filko and Naomi," Frost went on. "She *hated* him. The only reason she would have agreed to go on that boat was to confront him. What do you think would have happened when she did that?"

"I swear, I don't know anything more," Drake said. "All I know is, I got the call."

"And you called Lombard," Frost concluded.

"Yes. You have to understand what a catastrophe this would have been. The mayor and the CEO of Zelyx go out on the water with a hooker and she goes off the boat and drowns? It would have been a media feeding frenzy. There would have been criminal charges, jail time. The deal for the Zelyx headquarters would have died in a wave of litigation. This needed to be fixed. No one could know. That's what Lombard does. He sent the cleanup crew and arranged to get everyone off the boat. He provided a ton of cash so I could pay off Denny and the others."

"Don't be naive, Belinda. Giving them cash simply shut them up for a few days. It bought Lombard some time. He was never going to let them live."

She folded her arms tightly across her chest. The shower drummed behind her shoulder. "Yes, I suppose I knew that."

"And now it's done," Frost said. "Everyone who could talk about what happened on that boat is dead."

Drake got even closer to him. Her breath was on his lips. "*No.* Not everyone. That's why they're panicking."

"What are you talking about?" Frost asked.

"*They can't find Mr. Jin.* He got paid off, and then he disappeared on Wednesday morning. Lombard didn't do it. They don't know where he is, and they're desperate to find him. Mr. Jin is the key, Frost. He's alive. You need to get to him first."

# 33

Frost met Trent Gorham at a bench across from the palm trees of the Embarcadero near Pier 14. Out on the water, the four silver towers of the Bay Bridge swept majestically toward Yerba Buena Island, and white sails dotted the waves. It was midafternoon. Gorham had a cup of coffee from the Ferry Building on the bench next to him, and he ate kernels of popcorn one at a time from a takeaway box. His pale eyes were hidden behind sunglasses. A pink bloom spread across his cheeks and large nose.

"So you talked to Marjorie Detlowe," Gorham said as he digested the update from Frost. "How's she doing?"

"She's still grieving."

Gorham nodded. "I should go see her. It's been a while."

"I didn't realize you and Alan were so close," Frost said. "She said the two of you were best friends."

"Oh yeah. Alan was a great guy. If you're right about Martin Filko, it pisses me off to think of Alan getting killed because of a rich little punk like that."

Frost heard the bells of a trolley clanging its way north toward Fisherman's Wharf, and he glanced over his shoulder to keep an eye on the people around them.

"I'm surprised Alan didn't tell you about Filko and Naomi before he was killed," Frost said. "You were in homicide. He wasn't."

Gorham shrugged. "It doesn't surprise me. That's the kind of cop he was. Cautious. Alan always played things close to the vest. He wouldn't have come to me without some real evidence to prove that Filko was involved in Naomi's death. Rumors don't count."

"Do you think he confronted Filko at Net-Con?" Frost asked.

"Knowing Alan, I'm sure he did. A sleazebag like Filko wouldn't have intimidated him, no matter how much money the guy had. Alan probably made some veiled threats to see how he reacted. Obviously, Filko freaked out and used Lombard to eliminate him."

Frost studied the sailboats on the water. "And Fawn?"

"She saw what happened to Alan. I'm sure she was scared that she'd be next. That's a good incentive to keep your mouth shut." Gorham's head swiveled, and he stared at Frost from behind his sunglasses. His sandy hair was windswept. "So we know what really happened on the boat, and we can't prove any of it. What do we do now?"

"We find Mr. Jin," Frost replied. "He's the last witness. If Lombard gets to him first, he'll disappear permanently."

Gorham worked his tongue around his jaw to get a piece of popcorn that was stuck in a tooth. "Okay, I'll start canvassing Chinatown. I've got a lot of contacts over there from my vice days. If Mr. Jin is hiding out in the community, someone will know where he is."

"I'll check at his restaurant," Frost added. "Maybe they can point me to family and friends. Plus, I want to find his son, Fox, again. He shouldn't be on the streets. If Lombard is desperate, he wouldn't hesitate to snatch the boy."

Gorham stood up from the bench. "If I hear anything, I'll let you know."

"I'll do the same," Frost replied. "I'm going to talk to Prisha Anand, too. Fawn's sister."

Gorham looked down at him with a frown on his face. "Is that such a good idea?"

"Fawn's dead. She should know."

"Yeah, but what can you tell her? The story in the media is that Diego Casal killed Denny. If you mention the mayor or Filko, you're putting her in jeopardy."

"I don't have to tell her anything about that. Not yet."

"You don't think she'll start asking questions? You already mentioned Zelyx, didn't you? She's going to connect the dots and wonder what's going on. The safest thing is to say nothing at all."

"Maybe so, but I'd rather not leave her in the dark," Frost said.

Gorham ate more popcorn and watched the pedestrians on the sidewalk. His face was unhappy. "Look, it's just a matter of time before she finds out the truth. The odds are that Fawn's body will wash up along Ocean Beach sooner or later. It's harsh, but why not wait?"

Frost nodded but made no promises. "I still want to talk to her."

"Do what you have you do," Gorham said. "I think you're making a mistake."

He wandered away with his big shoulders slightly hunched. When he passed a wastebasket, he dumped the remains of his popcorn box inside. Frost stayed on the bench, watching as the other detective disappeared in the crowd. The next time he spotted the man's profile, Gorham was on the other side of the Embarcadero, passing between the palm trees in front of the Hyatt Regency.

He thought about what Gorham had said about Fawn's body washing up on Ocean Beach. Gorham was right. The ocean usually gave up its dead eventually, even if the body was nothing but bones when it rolled up on the sand. His remark was an offhanded comment, a meaningless detail that probably meant nothing.

Even so, it nagged at Frost's mind like a loose thread.

Ocean Beach was an oddly specific location for Gorham to mention. Frost had never told him that the *Roughing It* was out on the Pacific when Fawn went over the side.

Prisha Anand answered the door at her home in Presidio Heights. When she saw Frost, the expression on her face was eloquent in its horror. She only expected one thing from him, and that was to hear that her sister was dead.

She led him silently into the same heavy Victorian living room in which they'd met before. A fire roared in the fireplace, making the room warm and smoky. She waved him to the sofa, but she could hardly even look at him as she sat down herself. Her fingers kept moving nervously, as if she didn't know how to calm them.

"So?" Prisha asked.

He was genuinely undecided about how much to tell her. "I don't know anything for certain," he said finally.

"But you know something. Yes?"

"Well, it looks increasingly likely that Zara was on a boat on Tuesday evening and that she didn't make it back alive. Without a body being found, of course, we can't be absolutely certain."

Prisha didn't cry. Her face didn't move. Her only reaction was in the shallowness of her breathing. She got out of the chair and turned her back on him and stood like a statue in front of the fire. She didn't say anything, and she didn't move for a long time. Frost waited for her.

Eventually, she turned back, and her face was flushed. She straightened her hair with delicate movements and arched her back as if she were summoning her courage.

"I studied the news after you came here the last time. I know about this man you mentioned, Denny Clark, and how he died. Now they're saying he was on a cruise with drug dealers and that one of those men killed him. Is that the cruise Zara was on? Did this same man kill her?"

Frost hesitated. "That's possible."

"So was this drug dealer her client?" she asked.

"Again, that's—"

"Possible, yes, everything in the world is possible. Except I don't think you believe that, and I don't believe you're telling me the truth,

Inspector. Do you think I've forgotten the questions you asked me? About Fawn and her friend Naomi? About the Zelyx party where *I* brought my sister? Those questions don't seem to have much to do with a dispute over drugs."

He wanted to tell her more, but he couldn't. Gorham was right. It would have been better to say nothing at all. As it was, his silence enraged her. Prisha stalked across the room, and her voice rose like the violins at a symphony.

"Did someone at Zelyx murder my sister?"

Frost shook his head with regret. "I can't answer that question. I'm sorry."

Her hand flew across the space between them and slapped his face with an audible crack. He took the blow with no reaction, but when he touched the tender spot on his cheek, his fingers came away with blood where the metal of her ring had cut him. The sight of it shocked her. She spun away and sat down and buried her face in her hands. Frost found his way to the small powder room in the front hallway.

He ran cold water from the sink and washed away the blood, but it bled again when he stopped. His face throbbed. He found a tissue and pushed it against his cheekbone and held it there, staring at his own eyes in the mirror, until the flow of blood diminished.

When he left the bathroom, Prisha was in the doorway of the living room. She stared at her feet to avoid meeting his gaze.

"I apologize," she said. "That was unforgivable of me."

"I understand how upset you are. I wish I had more information to share with you." When she still didn't look up, he added, "Do you mind if I look at Zara's bedroom?"

She spoke in a hushed voice. "It's upstairs on the left."

He took the varnished wooden steps to the second floor. Zara's door was closed, and he opened it and turned on a light. The windows faced the street. It wasn't a particularly large room, but it was furnished with expensive antiques and dark, heavy wallpaper. Zara had money and good taste. He saw Bulgari face and hand cream on the nightstand, along with a copy of Zafón's *The Shadow of the Wind*. A mirror with an ornate, slightly tarnished brass frame was hung over her redwood dresser. He opened some of the drawers and found neatly folded lingerie. In her closet, which was almost as big as the bedroom itself, he saw the wardrobe of someone who could dress perfectly for any occasion. She could be intellectual, erotic, businesslike, fun, demure, anything that the situation demanded.

This was Zara's and Fawn's room all in one, but he had no idea who either woman was. She was more than her possessions, but her possessions were all she'd left behind. There were no photographs, no diaries, no computer, no phone, nothing to give a clue about any of the other compartments of her life.

"I hurt you. You're still bleeding."

Frost looked up. Prisha stood inside the room, looking uncomfortable. Her hands were knit together in front of her. He touched his cheek and realized she was right.

"It's nothing," he said. He waved a hand around the room. "There's no real person here. All I see is the disguise of a woman."

"Well, yes, that's Zara," Prisha said. "She kept secrets even from me. There's a lot I don't know about her life."

"You said she had a boyfriend. You saw pictures of Denny Clark on the news, didn't you? Had you ever seen him before? Is it possible he could have been involved with Zara?"

She shook her head. "I didn't recognize him, but that doesn't mean anything."

Frost took another look at Zara's bedroom. Where Prisha was standing, he saw the corner of a wooden picture frame on the wall behind the open door. He went over to look at it and saw a charcoal sketch of Zara's face and bare shoulders. The painting was signed only with the artist's initials, but it was dated with the current year, so it had been done in the past three months. It was all black and white, except for a few streaks of deep red color sketched into Zara's lush black hair. This portrait of her was very different from the photograph he'd seen. She was unforgettably beautiful, but she wasn't acting or putting on a role for a client in this sketch. She was being herself. Her dark eyes had a fierce intelligence. Her mouth was turned upward in a *Mona Lisa* smile, inscrutable but happy.

"Do you know where she had this done?" Frost asked.

"The Cannery, I think. One of the street artists down there did it for her."

"Was her hair really tinted like this? With red highlights?"

Prisha nodded. "That was a recent thing. It was lovely."

The painting didn't tell him anything, but he used his phone's camera to take a picture of it anyway. He found it hard to look away from Zara's face. There was a strange magnetism about it.

"I should go," he said.

"Yes, of course," Prisha replied. "Again, forgive me for striking you like that. I've always been very protective of my sister. I would do absolutely anything to save her."

"I know how that feels," he told her.

He didn't mention that he'd failed to save his own sister.

Frost took one last long look at the portrait of Zara Anand on the wall. Her beauty was in her bare skin; her courage was in her eyes. When he stared at her enigmatic smile again, he knew that Prisha was right. Zara was a woman who kept secrets, but whatever she'd been hiding was buried now under the unforgiving ocean waters.

The only one who knew what really happened was Mr. Jin.

# 34

Darkness caught up with Frost as he headed across the city toward Chinatown. Traffic crawled from red light to red light. Up and down the hills, the neighborhoods changed. First there were painted ladies among the houses, and then there were painted ladies on the streets. Neon lit up the storefronts, glowing on leather and fishnets on the sidewalks. He passed Fillmore, which was young and hip and rocking with music. He rolled on through Nob Hill, where the rose window of Grace Cathedral glowed like a blue star and the smell of money oozed from the Mark Hopkins, the Stanford Court, and the Fairmont hotels.

At Stockton, he turned north and crossed into Mr. Jin's world.

His favorite Chinatown restaurant was on Washington Street only two blocks from Mr. Jin's apartment. He pulled his Suburban into the tow-away zone outside the brightly lit door. The owner was a tiny Chinese woman who knew him well. She could have been anywhere from fifty to four hundred years old. She saw him and waved, and five minutes later, one of her daughters brought a brown paper bag out to his truck. He paid and gave the girl a large tip, and then he divvied up the order between himself and Shack. Frost ate stir-fried beef and baby bok choy with an order of barbecued pork. Shack ate shrimp fried rice and a fortune cookie.

The paper fortune that Frost took out of the cookie felt ominous. *Someone close to you is not your friend.*

He tried calling the number that Fox had given him, but the boy's cell phone was turned off, so the call went straight to voice mail. He left a message. When he was done with dinner, he hiked uphill. The street was lined with gift shops, dragon murals, pagoda facades, and second-floor acupuncture clinics. Paper lanterns glowed like cherries under the awnings, and car headlights swept the walls. Every other doorway was a bakery or restaurant, and he found Mr. Jin's hole-in-the-wall dim-sum house on the ground floor of the building adjacent to the chef's apartment.

The restaurant itself was simply called Jin. It was nothing to look at outside, but inside, the handful of tables were covered with white tablecloths and surrounded by black lacquered chairs carved with Chinese characters. The clientele was all Asian, and there wasn't an empty seat anywhere. Waiters in starched white uniforms pushed dim-sum carts from table to table Hong Kong style, and he saw steaming bamboo pots of *har gow* and *shu mei*. He noticed that the framed posters decorating the wall were not Chinese cityscapes from Kowloon or Shanghai but were all pictures of Niagara Falls, just like in Mr. Jin's apartment.

He asked to see the manager, who was younger than Frost expected. He didn't look old enough to drink. He was dressed in a tuxedo, and his black hair was oiled and lay flat on his head. He bowed when Frost showed him his badge.

"How may I help you?" he asked politely.

"I need to find Mr. Jin," Frost replied. "Has he been in here lately?"

"Mr. Jin? Oh no, he rarely comes here. He hires me to run his restaurant. Best dim sum in Chinatown. You want a table? I always find a table for a police officer. You keep us safe."

"Thank you, but no. It's very important that I find Mr. Jin quickly. He isn't in his apartment, and he's not in his restaurant. Where should I look for him?"

The young man's face wrinkled unhappily. "I'm very sorry. If Mr. Jin is not at home, then he must be cooking somewhere. I have never known him to do anything else."

"How does he get around? Does he have a car?"

"No, mostly he walks," the manager told him.

"He *walks*?"

"Oh yes. Mr. Jin does not believe in modern things. Sometimes he will take the bus, but more often than not, he walks."

"What about friends or family? Is there anyone local he might stay with?"

"His only family is his son. The rest of his family is in China. As for friends, I don't know of any. Mr. Jin is a very private person. When he is not working, I believe he is usually by himself."

Frost couldn't help but think that he and Mr. Jin had been cut from the same cloth. If the chef had a cat, it would have been uncanny. The good and the bad of Mr. Jin being an elusive loner was that he was hard to find. If Frost didn't know how to track him down, neither did Lombard.

"Has his son been in here recently?" Frost asked. "Do you know where he is?"

"No, I haven't seen Fox in nearly a week."

Frost handed the man his card. "If you see or hear from Mr. Jin, tell him to call me immediately. It's extremely important. Understand? No delay."

"Immediately," the man repeated.

Frost headed out of the dining room. He stopped in the foyer to examine several framed magazine reviews that were hung on the wall. Most of the articles included photographs of Mr. Jin, and Frost realized he'd never seen a picture of the man before. The photos had all been taken at different times, but Mr. Jin's expression was identical in each one. He wore no smile or frown, just seriousness on his face. He wasn't old, probably no more than forty, and he was lean, which made sense for someone who spent his days hiking the San Francisco hills. His eyes were dark, and his black hair was shaved to stubble on his skull. Despite reviews calling him one of the city's top chefs, he looked unimpressed by all the fuss.

Outside, the sidewalk was busy, and the night air was fragrant with flowers. Cars jammed the street like a backed-up pipe, and pedestrians jaywalked between the bumpers. He headed downhill toward his Suburban but stopped when he felt the buzz of a text arriving on his phone. He checked it and saw a single-line message from a blocked number:

Meet me in the alley.

Frost turned around. He studied the Chinese faces coming and going on the street. No one in the crowd seemed interested in him. He turned the corner into the alley and waited for his eyes to adjust. The lone streetlight was broken, making the walkway darker than the bright neon of Washington Street. It smelled of burnt oil from the restaurant kitchens. The same homeless man who'd haunted the alley three nights earlier was still there, eyeing him from under his wool blanket. People came and went like ghosts in the wisps of fog. Overhead, clotheslines stretched between the windows and the fire escapes.

Not far away, a silhouette in black stood with one foot propped against the redbrick wall. It was Fox, grinning at him.

"Hey, Copper. You find Lombard yet?"

Frost didn't like hearing Lombard's name shouted out loud. He checked the alley in both directions and then walked up to Fox. The boy was a foot shorter than he was, and half his weight, but Frost had learned the hard way not to treat him as harmless. "Hello, Fox."

"I got your message. Here I am."

"I'm glad you came, but you should stay away from this area," Frost warned him. "Don't go back to your father's apartment. If people aren't looking for you right now, they will be soon."

Fox shrugged. "If they see me, they have to catch me. Nobody catches Fox."

"Don't underestimate these people," Frost said. "Have you heard anything from Mr. Jin?"

"Not a word. You know where he is yet?"

"No, but the good news is, he's alive."

"Yeah? How can you be sure?"

"Because Lombard's still looking for him," Frost said. "That's also the bad news. Your father's not safe."

"Is this about Denny and the boat?"

"Yes."

Fox frowned. "Word on the street is that the guy who killed Denny ate a train. So why is Lombard still after Mr. Jin?"

"There's a lot we don't know about that cruise last Tuesday," Frost said. "Mr. Jin may be the only one who has the answers. That's why Lombard wants to keep him quiet. If you see your father or he contacts you, make sure he does *not* go home. Got it? Call me, and I'll meet the two of you wherever you are."

"Yeah, okay."

"I wish you'd let me find you a safe place to stay until we locate him," Frost said. "I can protect you."

Fox laughed at the suggestion. "Protect me? You seen a mirror lately? You don't look so good. Maybe I should be protecting you."

Frost laughed, too. "Well, I could do a lot worse than you for a bodyguard, that's for sure. But you said yourself that everybody sees everything around here. If you hang out in Chinatown, Lombard will know it, and sooner or later your luck is going to run out."

The boy winked. "It's not luck, man."

"Don't get cocky, Fox. You're good, but Lombard has a lot of people working for him."

"So do I. Around here, people have my back."

"Oh?"

"See for yourself," Fox said.

The boy snapped his fingers.

A moment later, a sharp crack like the explosion of a bullet erupted behind Frost. He ducked and spun around and yanked his gun into his hand. The acrid smell of black powder filled his nose. He looked for a shooter but saw no one, and then he focused on the homeless man crouched against the opposite wall. The old man's eyes glittered with amusement in the reflections from the street. He flicked something from his fingers, sending a ribbon of sparks through the air. A firecracker hit the ground, sizzled, and then exploded with a bang.

The homeless man laughed so hard he began to hack into his blanket.

Frost turned around again. Fox was already gone. No more than a few seconds had passed; there simply hadn't been time for him to disappear entirely. He squinted down the alley, but the boy wasn't there. Then he heard more laughter, directly over his head this time. Frost looked up.

Fox stood six feet over the alley, balanced on a metal strip of pipe bracketed to the brick wall. He had barely an inch on which to stand. As Frost watched, the boy sidestepped along the pipe like a ballet dancer and launched himself across the open space to the nearest fire escape, which seemed like an impossibly long jump. He grabbed it, dangled, and then swung his leg over his head in a way that made it look as if he had no bones in his body.

In the next second, he was standing on the platform of the fire escape.

"Don't you worry about Fox," he called as he began to climb the building with the grace of Spider-Man. "You just find Mr. Jin for me."

# 35

When Frost got back to his Suburban in front of the Chinese restaurant, his phone rang as he climbed inside the truck.

"I've been looking for you, Inspector," Cyril Timko told him. "The captain wants a face-to-face right away."

Frost didn't bother asking what the meeting was about. "Okay, I'll get back to headquarters now."

"Don't bother. Hayden wants to do this outside the office."

"Where?"

"Follow me," Cyril said. "And turn off your phone."

Frost spotted a flash in his rearview mirror as the high beams of the car behind him switched on and off. The car pulled from the curb onto Washington, and as it passed Frost's SUV, Cyril waved through the open window of a black Accord. Frost clicked off his phone, then got into traffic and stayed on the sedan's bumper. Cyril headed west through Chinatown but soon made a series of turns to dodge the one-way streets and cable car tracks. Eventually, he took Hyde south to Market, where he crossed into the SoMa neighborhood.

Even at night, traffic made it a slow crawl. The farther Cyril went, the closer he got to the street park where Duane had his food truck, and Frost began to wonder if the captain planned to meet him there. But no. Two blocks from the park, Cyril turned onto a one-way street that led under an elevated off-ramp from 101. There, he bumped onto the sidewalk next to a barbed wire fence and stopped. Frost parked behind him.

They both got out.

Frost took a wary look at the area below the overpass, which was an urban jungle of homeless tents and graffiti.

"This is where Hayden wants to meet?" Frost asked.

"The captain wants this under the radar," Cyril replied.

They walked under the freeway's rusting I beams, and Cyril flicked his finger toward the black loading door of a warehouse. Someone had spray-painted a caricature of the 1970s stripper Carol Doda on the outside. At the steel door, Cyril pulled out a key and unlocked it and slid the door up on tracks. The inside was cool and pitch-black. Cyril waved Frost ahead of him and then followed him inside and shut the door again. Frost was blind in the darkness, and his unease made him slip his hand inside his jacket close to the butt of his gun.

Then Cyril turned on bright overhead fluorescents.

"Hayden will be here soon," Cyril told him. He fired up his e-cigarette and added with a smirk, "Don't worry, you won't need your gun."

Frost studied the loading dock. There were two white panel vans parked inside. The floor was concrete. He saw import crates stacked in ten-foot columns, smelling as if they'd come directly from container ships at the harbor. The space was quiet except for the occasional hiss as Cyril inhaled his vape pen. The other cop leaned against the crates, watching Frost but making no attempt to engage in conversation.

Fifteen slow minutes passed with the two of them alone. Frost began to get impatient, but finally, he heard the bang of an interior door and the click of leather shoes on the stone floor. The captain emerged from behind one of the vans, walking with a slight limp. He wore a business suit, which was a surprise. Frost couldn't remember seeing him out of his dress blues. Hayden's bulk tested the seams of the fabric.

"Hello, Easton," the captain's foghorn voice rumbled.

"Good evening, sir."

Hayden shot a glance at Cyril. "Anyone follow you two?"

"No, sir. We're good."

Hayden nodded, satisfied. "Sorry for the cloak-and-dagger," he told Frost, "but I didn't want anyone in the department to see us talking. I own this building, and I keep an office here."

Frost didn't ask how the captain could afford seven-figure San Francisco commercial real estate. The city ran on sweetheart deals for people in power. "What did you want to talk about, sir?"

"I'm sure you can guess. Lombard."

"I thought Lombard was a myth," Frost replied evenly.

"Yes, I know that's what I said, and if anyone asks, that's still the story. The official word is that Lombard doesn't exist and never has. That's what we tell anyone from the press, too. Is that understood? I don't want to read otherwise in the papers."

Frost got the message. Hayden knew he'd met with the reporter from the *Chronicle*, and that meant he was being watched.

"Of course," he said.

"I don't imagine you're surprised to learn that Lombard is real," Hayden went on.

"I'm not surprised at all, but why keep it a secret?"

"Two reasons. First, the best way to catch Lombard is to lull him into thinking we still don't believe he exists at all. If he gets complacent, maybe he'll make a mistake."

"And the other reason?" Frost asked.

"I'm fairly sure that Lombard has spies in the department. That's why I'm careful what I say inside Mission Bay. For the time being, the only people who know about this are the three of us in this room."

Frost's eyes went to Cyril and then back to Hayden. "Not that I'm complaining, but why do you trust *me*? You and I haven't exactly been allies over the years."

Hayden's face broke into a smile. "You're direct, Easton, I'll give you that. Whatever you may think, I've always liked that about you. The fact is, no, I didn't know if I could trust you. That's why I've been cautious. But you've convinced me that you're not in Lombard's pocket."

"How did I do that?"

"You didn't buy the Diego Casal story. You kept pushing. Look, the Denny Clark murder smelled of Lombard's involvement from the beginning. That's why I was there as soon as it happened. I told you that I thought this might be a drug-related homicide because I wanted to see if Lombard took the bait. Which he did. If you were working for him, you would have dropped the case as soon as we had a witness who claimed that Casal was on Denny's boat. You didn't. You're still investigating. So it's time to bring you into the loop so we can work together."

"Off the books?" Frost asked.

"Exactly."

"In other words, I disobey your official orders by going after Lombard, and if I screw up, you burn me?"

This time, Hayden and Cyril both smiled. "Yes, that's about the size of it," the captain admitted. "I could lie and tell you otherwise, but you wouldn't believe me. The fact is, you're already disobeying my orders about Lombard, right? You're still going after him. At least this way, we'll have an understanding, which is more than you have now."

"What do you have in mind?"

"First, bring me up to date on what you've found out. Who was really on Denny Clark's boat last Tuesday? I know it wasn't Diego Casal. What happened that brought Lombard into play?"

Hayden made his inquiry sound smooth and casual. He was simply a captain looking for an update on a sensitive homicide investigation.

Maybe. Or maybe he was using this entire conversation as a ruse to find out whether Frost had uncovered the truth. If Frost mentioned the mayor or Zelyx or Martin Filko, then it was still possible he wouldn't leave the loading dock alive. And Lombard would know that Belinda Drake had betrayed him.

Frost thought about what Gorham had said. *I only told one person what I was doing. Captain Hayden. No one else knew.*

He thought about Belinda. *Trust no one.*

And Herb. *Don't talk to the cops.*

"Is there a problem, Easton?" Hayden asked when Frost was silent.

"You said you like that I'm direct. Well, I'll be direct, sir. I'm in a deserted loading dock. My phone is off. No one knows where I am. A suspicious man might be concerned."

"Secrecy protects all of us," Hayden replied. "I explained that."

"You also said there were spies inside the department, and there's no way to know who."

Hayden nodded his huge head slowly. "In other words, how do you know that I'm *not* on that list? Or Cyril?"

"That's right."

"Let me guess. Trent Gorham told you not to trust me."

Frost didn't say anything.

"You don't have to pretend," Hayden went on. "I know you and Gorham have been meeting. That's why I wanted to see you right away. You need to be very careful with Gorham. The more you tell him, the more you put yourself at risk."

"Are you suggesting that *Gorham* is a Lombard operative?" Frost asked.

"Is that such an outrageous idea? Don't you find it strange that Gorham has managed to take the lead on so many cases that seem to be connected to Lombard? And that most of those cases have gone unsolved?"

Frost frowned. The captain knew how to play on his doubts. "Gorham told me about finding a Lombard spy a couple of years ago. He tried to use her as a mole, and she was killed. Do you remember that?"

"I do. She was a staff attorney in the prosecutor's office."

"Gorham says you were the only one who knew about it. He didn't tell anyone else. So how did Lombard find out?"

"I wish I could tell you. However, I wasn't the only one who knew. I shared the details with a handful of senior people inside and outside the department. The idea of prosecutions being compromised is politically sensitive. I couldn't keep it to myself."

"Do you mind if I ask who you told?"

"The chief. A couple of other captains. The mayor. Two people on the city council. It wasn't a large group."

Frost kept his reaction off his face, but he'd heard what he expected. *The mayor.*

"Anyway, someone obviously leaked it," the captain went on. "Probably a staffer in one of their offices. That's why I'm very cautious now about spies."

"Okay."

Hayden clapped one of his big paws on Frost's shoulder. "Look, Easton, if you still don't trust me, I get it. It pays to be careful. But do you trust Gorham? Do you think he's been straight with you?"

"Not necessarily."

Hayden nodded. "Then your instincts are good. Gorham knows a hell of a lot more about the Denny Clark case than he's told either of us."

"How do you know that?" Frost asked.

Cyril interrupted from where he was standing near the shipping crates. "Because I've been tracking him. I know where he's been."

The captain gestured for Cyril to join them. "Obviously, this is off the record, Easton. If anyone knew about this, it would put my position in the department at risk. A few months ago, I asked Cyril to investigate Gorham. That included putting a GPS tracker on his personal vehicle. I didn't get a warrant. I just did it. I needed to know whether I was right about him."

"What did you find out?"

"Well, for one thing, Gorham keeps a place across the bay and lives well beyond his means. That's suspicious in itself. But we didn't find anything that we could specifically tie to Lombard, not until this week."

Cyril dug in his pocket and extracted a computer-printed map that showed a close-up of the beachfront parking area near the San Francisco Bay Trail. The parking lot was circled with red marker. He handed it to Frost. "You know where this is?"

"Sure. It's the trail that leads along the water to the Golden Gate Bridge."

"That's right," Cyril said. "Lots of people go jogging down there. I didn't think anything of it when it showed up on Gorham's GPS record. Then you started talking about Denny Clark and his boat."

Frost's eyes narrowed. "Why is that important?"

"Because Gorham parked there last Wednesday at six o'clock in the morning. That lot is only a couple hundred yards from the yacht harbor. Gorham was down there when Denny Clark's boat was coming in from its mystery cruise."

"Did he tell you that?" Hayden asked.

"No," Frost murmured. "He didn't."

"That's why you need to be careful. Trent Gorham is not who you think."

Frost stared at the map. He was afraid that he'd made a serious mistake. "It may be too late, sir. I briefed Gorham a few hours ago."

"What did you tell him?" Hayden asked.

"Among other things, I told him that I know Lombard hasn't found one of the witnesses from the cruise last Tuesday. Mr. Jin is still alive."

The captain shook his head. "Well, in that case, you better find Mr. Jin before Gorham does, or he won't be alive for long. You asked me whether Gorham was a Lombard operative. Originally, I thought so, but based on everything Cyril has uncovered, I've come to a different conclusion."

"What's that?" Frost asked.

"I think there's a real possibility that Trent Gorham may *be* Lombard," Hayden told him.

# 36

Frost sat alone in his SUV for nearly half an hour after the meeting was over and Hayden and Cyril had both left. There were few signs of life in the homeless city underneath the freeway. He watched a stray dog nose among the tents, and every now and then a hand poked out with food. When the dog barked at a rat scurrying under the barbed wire fence, Shack stirred from his nap on the dashboard and peered through the windshield. Then he curled back into a tight ball and fell asleep again.

*Trent Gorham may* be *Lombard.*

The idea sounded crazy.

And yet it was impossible to ignore the fact that Gorham had been hiding his role in the Denny Clark case from the very beginning.

As the cold seeped inside the truck, Frost finally drove away under the freeway. Car engines roared from the lanes overhead, and headlights splashed across the pavement. At the end of the block, he debated which way to turn. He was tired, but he was so close to Duane's food truck that he knew he should stop and see his brother. There were things he needed to say. It was late, and the food park was closed, but Duane would still be there. He always was.

Frost drove two blocks until he saw the kaleidoscope of painted food trucks under the streetlights. Most of the cars outside had left, so he parked near the gate and strolled inside. A few customers lingered with drinks on the benches, but the serving windows on the trucks were closed and locked. He headed for the rear fence, where Duane's truck had a permanent location. He had to step aside as one of the large vans rumbled past him toward the exit. Muffled Spanish music played from inside a paella truck. The inviting aromas of dinner hung in the air.

Near Duane's truck, a chalk sign still advertised the evening menu. Short ribs braised in mirin and soy. Edamame tortilla salad. Monterey chicken egg rolls. Raymonde's waka waka guacamole, whatever that was.

He went around to the back and then stopped short.

Duane sat on the rear steps outside the truck door. His white chef's coat was unbuttoned, revealing a black T-shirt underneath, and he wore only cargo shorts. His feet were bare. His long black hair was loose. He clutched the neck of an expensive bottle of tequila and swigged it, letting some of the alcohol spill onto his coat.

His brother, who almost never drank, was drunk.

"Duane?" Frost asked. "Are you okay?"

"Hello, *bro*!" Duane told him in a loud voice. "Sorry, you just missed Tabby. She left half an hour ago."

There was something in the way Duane said Tabby's name that made Frost stiffen with concern. "What's going on?"

"What's going on?" Duane took another extended swallow of Patrón. "Tabby ended it with me, that's what's going on. She and I are over. Done."

*"What?"* Frost felt as if a snake had wrapped itself around his chest and begun to squeeze. "What are you talking about?"

"I'm talking about the fact that the one woman I have ever loved in my entire life just told me she was really sorry, but she doesn't love me anymore, and she doesn't want to lead me on or prolong the pain or pretend to feel something that she doesn't. So that's it. Engagement off. Thanks for the memories."

"Oh my God," Frost said. "Duane, I am so sorry. I can't believe it."

"Well, you'll be pleased to know it's not me. It's her. It's all her. I'm a great guy, and she hates the idea of hurting me. I shouldn't blame myself. That made me feel so much better."

Frost struggled with what to say. He'd expected bad things after the previous night, but he hadn't expected this. "Give her some time, Duane. I'm sure she'll come around. She's just confused. This isn't about you and her, it's about everything else that's going on in her life. I'm telling you, this is *not* the end for you two."

Duane blinked at him through drunken eyes. His jaw hardened with anger. "Well, at least she has a shoulder to cry on."

"What's that supposed to mean?"

"You know *exactly* what it means. If Duane's too busy and doesn't have time, she can always run to Frost. My brother is always right there for her."

He felt heat on his face. "Duane, come on."

"Come on nothing. Do you think I'm blind? Do you think I haven't noticed how the two of you are together?"

"There is nothing between us," Frost insisted, but his denial felt limp and false even as he said it.

"Oh, who are you trying to kid? I saw it all over your face last night. And hers, too."

"Look, I'm sorry. Last night was awkward, I know that. She and I both drank way too much. That's all it was. Nothing happened, and nothing was going to happen."

"You were about to kiss her! You call that nothing? Are you saying the two of you wouldn't have ended up on the floor after that?"

"No way," Frost told him. "No way in hell. I would never do that to you."

"So it's just a coincidence that I catch the two of you together last night, and today Tabby breaks up with me?"

Frost shook his head. His mouth felt dry, and his stomach was sick. He couldn't deny the truth of what Duane said. This was no coincidence. This was his own fault. "I swear I did not see this coming, Duane. I knew Tabby was unhappy, that's all she told me."

"And you didn't play a role in any of this? Is that your story? Come on, Frost, you can do better than that. I know you have feelings for Tabby. Was this your plan all along? Break us up so you can have her for yourself?"

"If you think I would ever deliberately come between you and your fiancée, then you don't know me at all."

"Oh, I know you too damn well, Frost. Nobody knows you better than me."

Duane leaped off the steps of the food truck and shoved both hands hard against Frost's chest, forcing him backward. Frost regained his footing and had to stop himself from responding in kind.

"Knock it off, Duane. You're upset, I get it. You're hurting. I'm hurting for you, too. I can't believe this is happening to the two of you, and I'm sorry."

"Sorry?" his brother yelled. "That's all you have to say? This is your fault! Everything was great between me and Tabby, and then suddenly, she was moody and distant and upset, and I didn't understand what she was going through and I was pushing her too hard. You know when that happened, Frost? You know when Tabby started pulling away from me? When I introduced her to *you*."

"Duane, listen to me," Frost began, but his brother interrupted him.

"Screw that! I don't want any more excuses from you. You never answered my question. Tell me the truth. Are you in love with Tabby?"

Frost lowered his voice. "Whatever's going on here is between you and her. This has nothing to do with how I feel."

"In other words, yes."

"In other words, I'm done. I'm leaving. You need to cool down."

He began to turn away, and he took his eyes off Duane for a second. He heard the swish of his brother's sleeve and a rush of air as Duane's arm swung toward his face. Frost dodged but not fast enough, and Duane's fist collided with his chin. The impact snapped Frost's head back, and he staggered as pain shot through his jaw. Duane swore as his hand stung with the blow.

Frost felt his own fists open and close. He took a slow, deep breath and tried not to listen to the roaring in his head. He had to go now, or he'd regret what happened next.

"I'm not fighting with you, Duane," he warned him, but his own anger rose out of his chest. As he spoke, he tasted the copper of blood in his mouth.

He headed for the gate, but Duane bellowed after him and charged. His brother threw himself into Frost's back, and Frost stumbled forward and nearly fell. When he got his balance back, he tried to walk away again, but Duane jumped across the distance between them and grabbed Frost's shoulder. This time, Frost lost it. As Duane spun him back, Frost unleashed his left fist on his brother's face. The impact hammered Duane's nose, which broke with a spray of blood. Duane crashed down. He looked up from the ground, blood smeared across his face and pouring from his nostrils, his eyes wide with shock.

Frost stood over him. They were both breathing hard.

"Okay, Duane. You want me to say it? I'll say it. You're right. I do have feelings for Tabby. I didn't want it to happen. I wish it weren't true. But I have *never* told her that I felt that way, and I would never let anything happen between us. The only thing I ever wanted was to see the two of you happily married. That's the truth."

His brother swore at him from the ground, long and loud. Over and over.

"See you, Duane," Frost muttered, rubbing his swollen jaw.

He walked away, but Duane's curses chased him out of the food park and onto the street, getting softer and more distant, like an echo slowly sinking into a deep canyon.

# 37

Frost sat at the counter of a twenty-four-hour pizza café a block from the street food park. He ordered a beer and a slice of pizza for himself and Shack, who was in a carrier on the bar stool next to him. The kid behind the counter noticed the blood on Frost's knuckles and the purplish bruise on one side of his face. When he brought a tap glass of Fat Tire and a slice of sausage pizza on a paper plate, he also brought along a plastic zipper bag filled with crushed ice.

"For your chin," he said.

"Good man," Frost replied.

He took a ball of sausage from the pizza slice and pushed it through the door of the carrier. Shack began to play hockey with it. Frost took a bite of the pizza itself and realized that he wasn't hungry. Instead, he drank his beer and held the bag of ice against his face, where it numbed his jaw.

There were a couple of teenagers at a corner table in the café, but Frost was the only person sitting at the counter. Everyone else was in the nightclub next door. Live rock music blasted through the wall, and the thump of the bass made Frost's beer glass vibrate. He grimaced at the noise. His head spun.

Silently, he swore at himself for fighting back. Duane had touched a raw nerve, mostly because all his accusations were true. Frost had tried to walk the safe side of the line with Tabby for months, but he'd been kidding himself. All along, he'd been playing with fire.

Now the fire had burned them down.

He wondered what his sister, Katie, would have said. He could almost hear her voice in his ear as if this were the most delicious gossip in the world.

*You and Duane? In love with the same girl? Oh, Frost, that is too funny.*

It wasn't funny at all, but Katie would have laughed.

Frost shook his head. He knew his parents wouldn't laugh. Sooner or later, and probably sooner, his mother would be on the phone to ask him what on earth he was thinking by getting in the middle of his brother's relationship. And by breaking his brother's nose. It didn't matter that Duane had thrown the first punch and kept going when Frost tried to stop the fight. Frost was the younger brother, but he was supposed to be the adult between the two of them.

"You want another?"

Frost looked at his beer glass. It was empty. "Sure, why not?"

"So who got in the way of your fist?" the kid asked as he brought Frost his beer. The name tag on his apron read "Lido."

"My brother, actually."

"Ouch. That's biblical. So what happened between you guys? A girl, right? It's always a girl."

"It's a girl," Frost said.

"Who won?"

"I'm pretty sure we both lost."

"I hear you," Lido replied. "Sorry, man."

He left Frost to return to the pizza oven as two gay men came into the café hand in hand and began perusing the menu that was posted behind the counter. While they mulled their order, Frost drank his beer and listened to the rock music roaring through the wall. The volume made it hard to think about anything else, which was fine.

He studied the indie rock band posters crowded on the café wall and recognized almost none of them. Pinned among the band posters, oddly, were half a dozen postcards featuring the ruins of Machu Picchu among the green Peruvian mountains. For some reason, he found himself unable to take his eyes off the postcards. They made him think about going somewhere far away.

His phone rang. There was no one he wanted to talk to right now, but he checked the caller ID anyway. It was Trent Gorham. Frost frowned, and then he answered the call.

"Trent," he said.

"Just checking in. Any word on Mr. Jin?"

"Not a thing."

"You find his kid? You talk to him?"

Frost decided it was safer to lie. "No."

"Too bad. Anything else I should know about?"

"I can't think of a thing," Frost replied.

"Well, let me know if you catch a break. I've been all over Chinatown. If anyone spots Mr. Jin, I'm their first call."

"Keep me posted," Frost said.

He hung up and finished his beer. It was time to go. He took a last look around the restaurant, then flagged down Lido and pushed a couple of bills across the counter. "Will that cover it?"

"Definitely. You want change?"

"No, keep it."

Frost grabbed Shack's carrier and headed for the door. He was halfway outside when he stopped. He wasn't even sure why he stopped or why the question popped into his head, but he turned around and went back to the bar stool where Lido was wiping down the counter. The kid looked up.

"I'm curious," Frost said, pointing at the postcards on the bulletin board. "What's up with Machu Picchu?"

Lido shrugged. "It's the coolest place in the world. You been there?"

"No."

"Yeah, me neither," Lido said.

"Then how do you know it's the coolest place in the world?"

"Well, just look at it. The stone walls. The mountains up in the clouds. Imagine the Incas building something like that hundreds of years ago. It's my spirit place."

"Your what?"

"My spirit place," Lido repeated. "Hey, we all have one of those. Some place that really speaks to you, you know, that follows you wherever you go. Like maybe you lived there in a past life, know what I mean? Don't you have a place like that?"

Frost smiled. "San Francisco."

"Then you're lucky, man. Not many of us get to live where we're supposed to live. For me, it's Machu Picchu. I don't even know if I'll ever get there, but I just know it's out there, and that makes me happy. I'll tell you, though, if somebody ever drops a few thousand bucks in my lap, I'm out the door the next day and on my way to Peru."

"Your spirit place," Frost said.

Lido nodded. "Damn straight."

Frost took another twenty dollars out of his wallet. "Put this toward Peru," he said.

Then he practically ran for the door. He knew where Mr. Jin was.

No one at the dozens of Niagara Falls motels appreciated the call from the San Francisco policeman in the middle of the night. It was almost midnight as Frost dialed, which meant it was three in the morning in upstate New York. Some of the larger chain hotels had overnight staff, but many were mom-and-pop proprietors who bit his head off when he woke them up to ask about Mr. Jin. For the ones that didn't answer, he left messages asking them to call back.

Over the course of two hours, he made more than sixty calls, but he still had nearly two hundred hotels left to reach on his TripAdvisor list. No one recognized or remembered Mr. Jin, and Frost began to wonder if he'd been wrong about where the chef had gone with his sudden influx of cash. Maybe Niagara Falls wasn't his spirit place after all.

He decided to take a shower to wake himself up before going on with the calls. He spent a long time letting the hot water pour over his head and attack his sore muscles, and then he went back downstairs to the sofa where Shack was already asleep. He picked up the phone and grabbed the list, but his eyes blinked shut before he made another call, and he was gone.

He slept heavily. It was still dark outside when something started him awake. He had to shake off his bad dreams before he realized that his phone was ringing. He grabbed it from the coffee table and saw that it was six thirty in the morning. He'd slept for nearly five hours.

"Frost Easton," he said groggily.

"Inspector Easton, good morning! This is Weazie Palmer at the Summer Mist Motel in beautiful Niagara Falls, New York. You left a message on my machine overnight. My goodness, you were up late!"

His first conscious thought was that Weazie should drink decaf.

"Thanks for calling me back, Ms. Palmer. I was wondering if you had a guest staying with you from San Francisco named Mr. Jin. J-I-N."

"Call me Weazie! I don't picture Californians as the formal type, for heaven's sake. Do you have a first name for this Mr. Jin?"

Frost thought about it. "Honestly, no, I don't. I'm sorry."

"Oh, well, no matter. I'm sure we're talking about the same man. I spent a whole lot of time chatting with him about the Golden Gate Bridge and Alcatraz and those seals at Pier 39. I love San Francisco. My guests come here to honeymoon, but I went out there to honeymoon, isn't that ironic? Very nice man, Mr. Jin. A chef, he said. When I found that out, I tried to pepper him for recipes, but he wouldn't give up any secrets."

"Is Mr. Jin still there? Can you connect me with his room?"

"Well, I would, Inspector, but he checked out three days ago."

"Three days?" Frost asked.

"Yes, he didn't stay with us long. Paid cash, too, which is unusual."

Frost closed his eyes. He didn't understand. If Mr. Jin had left Niagara Falls three days ago, he should have been back in the city by now. "Did Mr. Jin tell you anything about his itinerary?" he asked. "Did he say where he was heading next?"

"Home is what he told me."

Frost shook his head. "Do you happen to know what airline he took?"

"Airline?" Weazie said. "No, no planes for Mr. Jin. He said he'd never flown in his life and wasn't about to start. He took the bus here, and he took the bus back. I can understand being afraid of flying, but he must have spent practically his whole vacation sitting in a Greyhound seat."

A bus.

Greyhound.

Frost thanked Weazie Palmer and quickly hung up the phone. The next thing he did was pull up the Greyhound website and check the routes between Niagara Falls and San Francisco for departures three days earlier. The time and distance explained Mr. Jin's long absence. It was a sixty-nine-hour cross-country journey with four transfers along the way in Buffalo, Columbus, Las Vegas, and Los Angeles.

When Frost checked his watch, he saw that the last leg of the journey would be bringing Mr. Jin into the Greyhound bus station on Folsom Street at 7:05 a.m.

That was in twenty minutes.

# 38

Frost made good time through the dark, early morning city, but so did the Greyhound on its way into San Francisco from its last stop in Oakland. By the time he reached the block-long stretch of parking stalls where the buses dropped off passengers, the incoming Greyhound was empty. A handful of riders lingered in the terminal with maps and luggage, but most had already vanished into the city. He checked with a customer service agent who pointed him to a bus driver sitting on a nearby bench with a cup of coffee and a doughnut.

When Frost showed him a photograph, the driver recognized Mr. Jin.

"Oh, sure, he was on the bus when I took over in LA," the man told him. "Quiet guy, sat in the very back row."

"Did you talk to him at all?" Frost asked.

The man took a bite of doughnut, wiped sprinkles from his beard, and shook his head. "No, nobody likes to chat on the red-eyes. We keep the lights off, and most people try to sleep."

"When did you get in?"

The driver checked his watch. "About fifteen minutes ago. I'm still on my first cuppa joe."

Frost did the math in his head as he ran back to his Suburban. If Mr. Jin was heading home on foot, he had a half-hour's walk ahead of him from the bus terminal into the heart of Chinatown. There was still time to catch him and stop him, but not much time. Frost had assumed all along that Mr. Jin was running from the danger when he left town, but now he wasn't so sure. This trip felt like a vacation, not an escape. If Mr. Jin had simply decided to make a once-in-a-lifetime visit to Niagara Falls, then he might have no idea he was coming home to a trap.

Outside the bus station, dark clouds made a canopy in the sky, blocking out the sunrise among the canyons of the downtown skyscrapers. He could smell rain in the air, and when he sped away from the curb, the first drops of a storm spat across his windshield. He drove fast, but rush-hour traffic was already gathering around him, and time ticked by as he closed in on Chinatown.

Two texts arrived at his phone almost simultaneously as he weaved through the zigzag streets.

The first was from Gorham. Mr. Jin spotted at Dragon's Gate.

The next was from Cyril. Gorham is on the move. I'm heading in.

The other cops both knew. They were both ahead of him.

Frost shot northward on Grant toward the jade-colored gate that marked the entrance to Chinatown. He drove into a different world where English was a second language and pagoda roofs topped the buildings and streetlights. The lanes narrowed from curb to curb. Ahead of him, brake lights flashed. The driver of a delivery truck double-parked in the middle of the block and created a parade of cars behind him, with their horns going wild. Frost was stuck in place. There was no going forward or back.

He swung his SUV out of the lineup of cars and got out at the curb. He spotted a fruit merchant stacking crates of berries under the awning of his store, and he showed the man a photograph of Mr. Jin. The shop owner, with baskets of huge red strawberries in both hands, nodded his head and said something in Chinese that Frost didn't understand. When Frost made arrows with his fingers in both directions, the man gestured up the Grant Avenue hill.

"How long?" Frost asked.

The man put down the strawberries and held up both hands with all his fingers outstretched. Ten minutes.

Frost left his Suburban where it was. Over his head, the clouds suddenly opened up, and rain swept down, making it hard to see. He hiked into the misty rain, and the day around him was still dark as night. He hadn't gone half a block when his phone started ringing in his pocket. The number was blocked, but he could guess who it was.

Fox.

"Where you at?" the boy said when Frost answered.

"Grant and Sacramento. Have you talked to your father?"

"No, but my spies called. Mr. Jin just got home. I'm on my way there now."

*"Don't do that!"* Frost barked into the phone. "Fox, stay away, don't go anywhere near that apartment. It's not safe. I'm heading to the building right now, and I'll get him out of there."

"You? No way. This is my turf, not yours."

*"Fox."*

But the phone was dead.

Frost sprinted up the street with the rain beating his face. The sidewalk was slick under his shoes. He could feel time running short as everyone converged on the same Chinatown building with its dragon roof and green wrought-iron balconies. Himself. Fox. Mr. Jin. Gorham. Cyril.

And Lombard, whoever he was.

He spun around the corner onto Washington Street. The building was a block away; he could see it from where he was. He dodged around the morning shopkeepers and veered across the street when there was a gap between the cars. At the building doorway, he dove inside and grabbed his gun from its holster. He took five seconds to catch his breath. Rain dripped from his clothes onto the floor. When he looked down, he saw wet tracks leading up the stairs, leaving puddles behind.

Someone was already here.

Frost ran up the steps toward the top floor. Where the stairs ended, the wooden door to the hallway had swelled in the humid morning, and he had to pry it open. The hallway was empty, leading past rows of apartment doors that were all closed except one.

One door at the very end was open, letting out a pale triangle of light.

Mr. Jin's door.

He crept toward the far wall of the building. The floor groaned, announcing his presence. Beside him, one of the other doors opened, and a huge young man in a bathrobe filled the doorway. Frost held up his hand to stop the man from coming out to the hallway and waved him back inside with a flick of his fingers. The young man saw his gun and complied, and then his voice erupted in loud Chinese as soon as the door was closed.

Frost stopped near the end of the hallway. From where he was, he could see that Mr. Jin's door had been kicked off its frame. It lay flat on the apartment floor, and splintered wood hung from the hinges. He pressed against the wall and heard the slap of wet curtains inside, blown by wind and rain. The noise of traffic on the street sounded loud. The window to the balcony was open.

He slipped around the doorway into the apartment. The first thing he saw, sprawled right in front of him, was a body.

It was Mr. Jin. He was wearing a Niagara Falls T-shirt.

Frost bent down next to him, but he was too late. The chef lay on his back, his limbs making an X. His eyes were wide open and fixed, his head twisted at an unnatural sideways angle. His neck had been broken with a swift, ruthless snap. Frost felt the man's skin, which was as warm as life. He'd been dead for only minutes, maybe seconds. But dead was dead.

Lombard had won.

Frost pounded the floor with a fist. He got up and checked the rest of the apartment. It was empty, and there was no sign of who had been here. He made a quick call to report the homicide, and then he went to the open window that led out to the balcony and stared down at the lights of the street below. Rain poured over him in a silver sheet. The fire escape ladders led down one floor at a time, but he didn't see anyone escaping to the street.

Instead, over his head, he heard the muffled crack of a gunshot.

Frost scrambled outside. A ten-foot mesh fence jutted from the building wall. He pushed his fingers and feet into the holes and began to climb. The metal was wet and slippery from the rain, and the rusted bolts joining the fence to the wall were loose enough to make it shudder. He climbed to the top and grabbed the pagoda-style overhang jutting from the roof, but his fingers struggled to get a grip. His shoes balanced precariously on the top rail of the fence. When he pulled himself up, one hand slipped, leaving him dangling, and he looked straight down at the five-story drop to the street. The rain mixed with sweat on his hands.

He grabbed the overhang again and pulled himself up. He leveraged one foot against a dragon sculpture that curved outward like the figurehead of an old warship. Creeks of water spilled toward him over clay shingles. His body flat, he scuttled upward along the overhang and then tumbled over the mortared edge of the roof and landed on the concrete floor at the top of the building. It was dark and empty.

Another gunshot cracked above the noise of the rain.

Frost ran to the eastern edge of the building. The neighboring roof was ten feet below him. He swung his body over the wall, letting his legs hang down, then let go and dropped to the next roof. The impact rippled through his body. No one was in sight, but the roof was an obstacle course of air conditioning units and ductwork. A throbbing mechanical roar battled with the noise of the rain, deafening him. His view was blocked by a rusted metal shed that led to the interior of the building. He squinted into the darkness and wiped rain from his eyes. Awkwardly, he weaved among the steel units and crept to the door of the shed. It was locked. No one had gone that way. He moved sideways to the corner and glanced around the far side.

Cyril Timko stood twenty feet away. His back was to Frost, his arms outstretched with a gun in his hands.

Then everything happened at once.

Someone shouted. It was muffled by the roar on the roof.

Cyril fired. Once, twice, three times, four times, in almost instant succession, with a flash of light each time. Smoke burned the air. Frost wheeled around the corner and aimed his own gun at the other cop.

*"Cyril!"* he shouted, his voice barely audible.

The captain's aide turned his head and saw him, and his gun hand went slack. "It's okay," he called. "It's over. We're clear."

Frost hurried toward him as Cyril calmly holstered his gun. On the other side of the shed, ten feet away, Frost saw Trent Gorham stretched across the ground, motionless, leaching blood into the puddles. Gorham's own gun was next to his hand. Beyond Gorham, trapped against one of the air conditioning units with nowhere to run or escape, was Fox.

"Gorham was going to kill the kid," Cyril said. "I had to take him out."

Frost studied the man's face, which was expressionless. Cyril had just killed another cop, but the incident seemed to have taken no emotional toll on him. Frost went to Gorham and checked his condition, but Cyril's aim had been precise. Three bullet holes made a tight circle around Gorham's heart. One was in the center of his forehead, bright red below his wet sandy hair. He'd died instantly.

They could hear sirens on the street below.

"The cavalry is here," Cyril said. "I'll let them know where to find us."

Frost didn't say anything in response. He stared at Fox, who was frozen in place, his back against the metal panel, his hands clenched into fists. The boy was dressed in black, as he always was, but his teenage James Dean bravado was gone. His eyes were frightened and wide, shifting back and forth from Frost to Cyril to the dead body on the roof.

"Is that what happened, Fox?" Frost asked the boy, his voice low enough that Cyril couldn't hear him. "Was the cop on the ground going to shoot you?"

Fox's eyes darted nervously to Cyril, and Frost took a step sideways to block him from the boy's view. He repeated the question. "You can tell me the truth. Was he going to shoot you?"

"I guess he was," the boy murmured.

"You guess?"

"He had a gun," Fox said, "and he killed Mr. Jin."

"Are you sure? Did you see him do it?"

"He was standing over the body when I came in the window," Fox said. "Who else could have done it?"

Frost stood up in the rain and shook his head. When he looked over at Cyril, their eyes met across the dim light of the roof. The other cop had already pulled out his e-cigarette again and was sucking on it calmly.

"Yeah," Frost said. "Who else?"

# 39

It was midafternoon by the time Frost had wrapped up several hours of questioning inside police headquarters in Mission Bay. When he was done, Captain Hayden called him into his office. The captain closed the door behind them and settled into the oversized chair that he filled completely. The smell of a cigar wafted from his uniform.

"How's Fox?" Frost asked.

The captain cocked his large head. "Fox? Who's that?"

"The boy. Mr. Jin's son."

"Oh, of course. The psychiatrist says he's not dealing well with his father's death, but that's to be expected. He's in the hands of Human Services now. They'll look after him until we can find other relatives."

"Is that safe?" Frost asked.

"Given the way things turned out, he shouldn't be in any further danger," Hayden replied. "With Gorham dead, the boy doesn't know anything that would put him at risk from Lombard."

Frost frowned. "I hope you're right."

"Meaning what?"

"Meaning the boy may be too scared to tell us everything he knows."

Hayden shook his head dismissively. "What are you saying, that Gorham was innocent? If Gorham didn't kill Mr. Jin, who else could have done it? You said yourself that the apartment was empty. Cyril didn't meet anyone coming down the stairs, and neither did you. There's no way anyone else made it out of the building."

"Yes, that's true." Frost waited a moment and then added, "I'm curious, sir. Why did Cyril move in on Gorham so quickly?"

"You know exactly why," Hayden said. "We talked about it last night."

"Yes, but we had no actual proof that Gorham was connected to Lombard."

"Maybe not, but Gorham was on the move, so I felt we couldn't take any chances. It was my call to have Cyril go into that building. And now we know we were right about Gorham. Whether he was Lombard himself or just an operative, he was definitely part of the network. He killed Mr. Jin, and he would have shot the boy if Cyril hadn't been there to stop him. He took two shots at him up on the roof. What more do you want, Easton?"

Frost had been asking himself the same thing. What more did he want?

The truth was, he wanted to know what Fox had seen from the balcony window. And he wanted to know who Gorham was really shooting at on the roof.

"I'd like to talk to Fox myself," Frost said. "If he knows more than he's telling us, I may be able to get it out of him."

Hayden shook his head. "That's not how it works. You know that. We're talking about a cop shooting a cop. I don't want anyone coming up with the idea that we're coaching witnesses."

"So what are you going to tell the press about Gorham?" Frost asked.

"I'll tell the truth. Gorham was dirty. He was involved in eliminating witnesses, including Mr. Jin and possibly several others. Given that he was formerly on the drug beat in vice, the obvious conclusion will be that he was recruited by Diego Casal or one of Casal's competitors."

"In other words, Denny and the others were casualties in a drug war," Frost concluded. "That's exactly what Lombard wants everyone to believe."

Hayden shrugged. "Look, you know how it works, Easton. Sometimes we have to accept the cover story because we don't have a choice."

"In other words, Lombard wins?" Frost said.

"Maybe. For now. Or maybe Lombard died on that roof."

"I'd like to share your optimism about that, sir," Frost replied, "but I'm cynical. Lombard gets everything he wants and then gets shot just as he eliminates the last witness? I have a hard time believing that."

"You may be right," Hayden agreed. "That may be wishful thinking on my part. It's possible Gorham was just one more Lombard pawn. But if you take enough pawns, eventually you get the king."

Frost studied the captain behind his desk. He knew he had to make a decision about whom to trust. He thought about his former lieutenant Jess Salceda, who'd been killed the previous year. Frost and Jess had been colleagues. Friends. One-time lovers. Jess had also been Captain Hayden's ex-wife. It made for an uncomfortable triangle, and Frost was sure it was part of the reason that Hayden had never liked him.

But he also remembered what Jess had told him about Hayden. She hated him as much as she loved him, but as a cop, he always had her back. He was ambitious and political, but he was one of the good guys.

He was willing to put his faith in what Jess believed.

"Do you mind if I ask you a question, sir?" Frost said. "You won't like it."

Hayden offered him a curious smile. "Go ahead."

"How well do you know Cyril?"

The captain was silent. Frost expected anger, but there was no sign of it on Hayden's face. He leaned back dangerously far in his chair and stared at the office ceiling. "In other words, could the spy be in my own house?"

"I'm just asking if it's possible," Frost said.

Again the captain took a long time to reply. "I'm aware that Cyril doesn't always play well with others. That's because he doesn't care what people think. It's one of the reasons I chose him. He's loyal to me and no one else."

Frost's voice was quiet. "Are you sure?"

"I am sure," the captain replied, "but then again, I've been wrong about people before. It's your job to find out the truth. I told you last night I want you in the loop, and here you are. You're working directly for me now, Easton, and this is where you start. Dig into Trent Gorham's life. Find out if there was anything about him that would help us crack Lombard's network. And if you conclude he's innocent, well, that tells us something about Cyril, doesn't it?"

Frost nodded. "Thank you, sir. And Denny Clark's murder?"

Hayden leaned across the desk with a sigh. "For now, that's a dead end, Easton. The book is closed on Denny Clark and that cruise last Tuesday. You're going to have to move on."

When Frost got back to his Suburban, he called Human Services to check on Fox. He wasn't surprised to learn that they'd already lost him. The boy had gone out a bathroom window, climbed over a fence, and disappeared.

He sat in his truck with an intense sense of failure about the entire investigation. Fawn was dead somewhere in the ocean, and anyone who knew how it had happened was dead, too. Lombard was still a mystery, and the mayor and Martin Filko were untouchable. Every loose end had been tied; every door had been locked. He'd been outplayed.

His phone rang and broke him out of his thoughts.

The caller ID on his screen told him it was Tabby. He stared with conflicted emotions at the phone and then tapped the button to ignore the call. Instinctively, he nursed his jaw, which was still tender where Duane had hit him. He wasn't ready to talk to Tabby about any of this yet. He wasn't sure he ever would be.

Instead, he called Belinda Drake. She answered in a clipped voice, and he could hear the rush of wind in the background. She was outside on her balcony again, high above the city.

"You heard about Mr. Jin?" he asked.

"Yes. I warned you what would happen if you didn't get to him first."

"So what do I do next?"

"You forget about Lombard. That's what you do."

"That's not an option," Frost replied. "I need your help."

"I've already told you more than I should. There's nothing I can do."

"I have a name for you."

"What is it?"

"Trent Gorham."

"What about him? According to the news, he's the one who killed Mr. Jin."

"That's my question. Was Gorham part of Lombard?"

"I have no idea," she replied.

"Gorham was at the yacht harbor on Wednesday morning when the boat came in. Did you call him? Was he part of the cleanup crew?"

"No, he wasn't with me, but that doesn't mean anything. Sometimes Lombard sends observers to make sure things go according to plan. Now I really have to go, Frost."

"Wait, I'm not done. What about Cyril Timko? He's the personal aide to Captain Hayden. Could he be part of Lombard?"

"I'm telling you, I don't know," she replied impatiently. "Do you think the left hand knows anything about the right hand? We don't. We're all separate tentacles. That's why it's so easy to cut one of us off if we cause any problems."

"I want to meet. We need to talk."

"About what?"

"Anything else you can tell me," Frost said.

"I can't give you anything more than I already have."

"I still have questions, Belinda. Right now, you're the only one with answers. Please."

In the silence, he heard the wind whistling around her. He could picture her alone on the balcony, debating with herself. He knew he was asking her to take a risk. Then she said softly, "Fine. Be here in one hour."

He hung up.

He didn't have time to go home before their meeting. He got out of his SUV and walked past police headquarters toward China Basin. He didn't really think about where he was going, but three blocks later, he found himself across the street from the Zelyx construction site. It was a multimillion-dollar building project for a multibillion-dollar company. Thousands of new jobs would keep the city's tech economy humming along, and it was happening here, not in Austin, not in Denver, not in Charleston. All because of Martin Filko and the mayor. And Lombard.

If you got in the way, you were expendable.

Frost watched the construction activity for several minutes, and then he turned around and went back to his truck and headed uptown. While he drove, Tabby called again. This time, she left a message, and he played it over the speakerphone as he sat in traffic.

"I need to see you, Frost. Call me as soon as you get this."

But he didn't know what to say to her.

Ten minutes later, he crossed into the Financial Center, where the pyramid top of the Transamerica building peeked above the other skyscrapers. It was almost the thick of rush hour, and the streets and sidewalks were dense with people. The rain had stopped, but dark clouds still blotted out the sun and made the afternoon look like dusk.

He'd nearly reached the alley behind Belinda's building when he realized that something was wrong.

On the sidewalks near the pyramid, he saw people running.

Through his open window, he heard the wail of sirens. Ahead of him, on the cross street, a police vehicle screamed through the intersection. Only seconds later, an ambulance followed.

Frost drove up onto the sidewalk. He bolted from the car and followed the crowd. He sprinted through the plaza at the base of the Transamerica building. The white high-rise climbed above him against the black sky.

Across the street, people swarmed around an Acura sedan, its car alarm blaring. Police and EMTs tried to hold a perimeter around the car. Frost shoved his way in and yanked out his badge when a uniformed officer tried to hold him back. He pushed to the front and saw the damage to the car up close, its roof flattened, its windows shattered. Glass littered the street.

Belinda Drake lay atop the sedan.

She was on her back where she'd fallen thirty stories from the balcony above the street. Her limbs were spread. Her head was turned, her eyes wide open and staring at him. Blood made a lake underneath her, but her face was untouched, without even a scratch. Her lips were bent into the tiniest smile.

He remembered what she'd told him about going off the building.

*You get one last exhilarating ride, and then you're dead before you feel the pain.*

# 40

Frost crossed the Golden Gate Bridge to find Trent Gorham's house in the hills of Tamalpais Valley, tucked among tall trees that towered over the roof. It was small and old, but the neighborhood alone meant it was worth more than a million dollars. Cyril and Hayden were both right about one thing. Gorham, who was single and on a cop's salary, should never have been able to afford it.

He parked in the driveway. There were no streetlights nearby, and the neighborhood was dark. The first thing he noticed when he approached the house was that the window next to the front door had been smashed, and the door was ajar. He took out his gun and cautiously went inside, but the house itself was empty. Whoever had broken in had already come and gone.

This wasn't a robbery. Gorham had a seventy-inch Ultra HD television in the living room—also unusual for a cop—and it hadn't been touched. The intruders had ignored other expensive items, too. He saw a high-end Blu-ray player, vintage rock albums, a cherrywood humidor, and several bottles of single-malt scotch on a mirrored bar. Gorham had lived well. Too well.

As Frost searched the house, he kept seeing Belinda Drake's face in his memory. She'd looked alive enough to open her mouth and talk to him. He could hear her voice in his head. An hour earlier, they'd been on the phone; now she was dead. He felt responsible. It was sharing secrets with Frost that had led to her death.

Another loose end tied up by Lombard.

He checked Gorham's office. This was where the intruders had done their work. His computer and printer were gone. There were charging cables on the desk but no devices. The drawers of two steel file cabinets were open and empty. A section of the hardwood floor had been pried up, leaving an empty hole that Gorham had obviously used to hide things he didn't want found. It didn't work. The intruders had taken whatever was inside.

Gorham's life had been sanitized, much like Denny's boat. The thoroughness of the job—and the evidence of Gorham living beyond his means—led Frost to think that Gorham was dirty, just as the captain believed. If so, he wondered how far back the corruption extended into Gorham's past.

What if Alan Detlowe really had gone to Gorham with his suspicions about Martin Filko?

What if that was what got Detlowe killed?

Frost shook his head. *Trust no one.*

He checked the kitchen. Gorham was surprisingly neat. There wasn't a dirty dish anywhere, the stainless steel appliances gleamed, and the refrigerator was perfectly organized. Frost studied the contents and had a hard time imagining a high school jock like Gorham drinking soy milk and eating takeaway vegan meals from Trader Joe's, but this was California. Anything was possible.

The last room to search was Gorham's bedroom.

Most of the memorabilia inside was sports related. He saw photographs and trophies from Gorham's days on the college track team. There were also pictures of him and Alan Detlowe drinking beer at a Giants game, which didn't make sense. Frost couldn't imagine Gorham killing Detlowe and still keeping pictures of the two of them on his dresser. He was missing something.

He studied the other items, which included a beer stein filled with loose change, a baseball signed by Madison Bumgarner, and two objects that felt out of place among Gorham's possessions. One was a Middle Eastern music box, obviously expensive, inlaid with colored gems. The other was a wood carving of an African elephant.

Frost picked up both of the items as if they could speak to him, and then he put them down. He felt an odd, cresting wave of adrenaline that he couldn't explain. The clues in this room were pointing him to something, but he didn't know what.

He noted two nightstands on either side of the king-sized Tempur-Pedic bed. The one closest to him was obviously used by Gorham and included a man's dress watch and diamond cuff links. On the other nightstand, he saw a bottle of hand cream and Jean Patou Joy perfume.

That was the missing link.

A woman.

Gorham didn't live alone in this house. He was unmarried, but a woman obviously spent time here, too. Frost went to the closet and opened the doors, and among the clothes that Gorham would wear, he also saw a lineup of sexy, elegant dresses. He opened the built-in drawers and found lace lingerie.

Soy milk. Vegan dinners.

Not Gorham. Gorham's girlfriend.

Frost took another long look at the bedroom, and the truth came to him in a rush. It wasn't just hand cream on the nightstand next to the perfume. It was *Bulgari* hand cream. He stared at the Middle Eastern music box and the African elephant, and he could hear the voice of Prisha Anand in his head.

Men fly her around the world. Africa. The Middle East. South America.

He thought about the indications of money in the house. The expensive toys. Even the house itself. It wasn't Trent's money. It wasn't a payoff for his work for Lombard. It came from somewhere else. *Someone* else. A woman with highbrow tastes and the means to pay for it.

Fawn.

Gorham's bedroom door was wide open, but behind it, Frost could see the wooden edge of a picture frame. He went over and pushed the door aside, and there on the wall was a sketch of Trent Gorham, black-and-white except for his sky-blue eyes. The style, the picture, the pose were all a match for another picture he'd seen two days earlier. In Fawn's bedroom.

Trent Gorham. Zara Anand.

They were in love. He could see that in the eyes of each sketch, as if they were looking at each other across the miles. It was a relationship they'd kept secret, the escort and the cop. She'd kept her own portrait, and he kept his, the opposite of what couples would usually do.

Trent and Fawn.

This changed everything.

Yes, Gorham had been waiting at the yacht harbor on Wednesday morning, but not because he was in league with Lombard. He'd been waiting for his girlfriend to return from the Tuesday-night cruise. And knowing that secret led Frost to a cascade of other questions.

Why did Fawn agree to go on a cruise with Martin Filko, a man she hated and feared?

Why did Gorham call Denny before the cruise?

Why were there hidden cameras on the boat?

He began to realize that he'd been wrong, wrong, wrong. Wrong about Trent. Wrong about Fawn. And all wrong about the cruise on Tuesday. He could only think of one explanation that tied everything together. One answer to solve the mysteries.

The cruise had been a sting.

A setup.

It was Trent Gorham's plan to trap Martin Filko and lure Lombard out of hiding.

◆ ◆ ◆

The night was dark on the *Roughing It.*

The only lights were from the city on the other side of the harbor. There was no moon and no stars overhead. The bay was angry, slapping against the breakwater with gusts of wind and surging across the pier into clouds of spray. When Frost climbed onto the yacht, he tried the lights, but the power was off. All he had was his flashlight to guide him.

The windswept sway of the boat took him back to his own past. He could remember being out in the open water with Denny, where the ocean would come to life without warning and toss you around like a cork. He remembered the loneliness out there with no other crafts around, out of sight of land. He wondered if Denny had thought about those days, too, when he took the *Roughing It* under the Golden Gate Bridge that night and out to sea.

Frost cast his light around the luxury interior. He knew there would be nothing to find on the upper decks. Lombard's team had been here to remove the evidence, and they'd been thorough. He descended to the bowels of the boat, following the beam of his flashlight. He passed the crew quarters and could imagine Chester there, playing cards with Carla and Mr. Jin. He wondered if the awful noise from upstairs would have carried to the lower deck for the others to hear. Martin Filko, alone with Fawn. The sex. The drugs. The abuse.

All with cameras secretly rolling in a panel on the wall.

Fawn had been on the boat for a reason. There was no way Trent Gorham would have let his girlfriend walk into harm's way without some other motive. There was no way Fawn would have agreed if she didn't think that the night would end in revenge against Martin Filko and justice for Naomi.

But how had it all gone wrong?

Sooner or later, the people on the boat would have gone to sleep. Except for Denny. He was the captain, and the captain was always awake. The *Roughing It* would have been dead silent, the way it was now, riding the swells of the Pacific. Denny would have been on the flybridge, keyed up and nervous, alone with the ocean and the night.

And then what?

What happened next?

Frost made his way to Denny's office at the rear of the boat. There wasn't much to find. Denny's bunk. A filing cabinet. His desk. Pictures on the wall. Behind the desk, tightly locked, was a narrow door that led to the mechanical areas of the ship. No one went there without the captain opening the door. It was the one place on the ship that Denny always kept private and secure.

Frost could have picked the lock, but he knew Denny. Some things never changed. He opened the desk drawer and located the blue gift box that housed Denny's silver Waterman pen. He opened the box top and lifted out the cardboard platform where the fountain pen was nestled among velvet.

Underneath the velvet layer was a Schlage key. Same old Denny.

He put the key in the engine room door and unlocked it. It was cold on the other side. Iron steps took him down below the waterline. He was surrounded by gleaming silver ductwork reflecting his flashlight, propulsion engines, heat exchangers, and electrical generators. Everything was squeezed together. The corridor among the machinery was narrow, and he had to turn sideways. When the boat was operating, the throbbing noise would be deafening down here, but now it was silent, and he could hear every one of his footsteps.

He followed his flashlight.

He wasn't sure what he expected to find. Maybe Denny had been able to grab the cameras before Lombard's team arrived. Maybe the evidence was still here. Or maybe there was nothing left and the plan had ended in failure.

But no.

This was something completely different.

At the very end of the engine room, where the ceiling narrowed with the shape of the boat, was a makeshift cot. It had a four-inch foam mattress and a single pillow. He examined every inch of the cot, looking for clues to who had been hiding here. At first, he came up empty, but when he yanked the mattress off the frame, he saw a few strands of long hair caught in the coils of the spring. Most were jet-black, her natural color, but one was tinted red.

Just as it had been in the portrait on her bedroom wall.

Fawn.

Frost took out his phone in the silent darkness of the boat. He dialed the number and got her message. The same message he'd heard every time he called her all week. This time he knew what to say.

"Fawn, this is Frost Easton again," he said. "You're in danger, and you have to call me right now. I know about you and Trent. I know about the cruise on Tuesday. And I know you're alive."

# 41

Frost didn't know when or if Fawn would call him back. His phone was dead quiet as he drove home from the yacht harbor. The rain had started again. The next wave of the storm was stronger and harder than the morning showers. A deluge poured across his windshield. He climbed the sharp peaks of Russian Hill and watched rivers flooding back down the asphalt. It wasn't even safe to stop at the uphill intersections; all he could do was slow down and keep driving upward with his foot on the gas. By the time he arrived home, it was almost eleven o'clock. He opened his truck door and ran for the stairs, and in the few fast paces it took him to get there, he was drenched.

Someone was waiting for him.

She sat in the pouring rain at the top of the steps. Her red hair was pasted to her face and neck. She stood up as he climbed to his front door.

Tabby.

"I'm sorry to ambush you," she said.

Frost shrugged. "It's fine."

"We need to talk."

"I know. Come on in."

He let them both inside, where it was warm. She wasn't dressed for the downpour. All she wore was a simple blue dress with spaghetti straps. She shivered, and water dripped from her skin in the foyer.

"Do you want some dry clothes?" he asked. "I probably have something upstairs you could put on."

"No. Not right now." Her voice sounded low and distressed. She kicked off her heels; her feet were bare. She was nothing like the girl who'd danced and sung with him two days earlier.

"Well, wrap yourself in a blanket," he said. "I have to go rescue Shack."

"Where is he?"

"I made a little nest for him in the attic. I couldn't take him with me today, and I wanted him out of the way in case I had visitors."

Tabby made no effort to move from the foyer, and he went to the living room and grabbed a fleece blanket and came back and wrapped it around her. He led her to the sofa, where she sat down and made a cocoon around herself. He got a towel from the kitchen, and she used it to dry her face.

"I'll be right back," he said.

Frost ran upstairs. There was a drop-down ladder in the walk-in closet that led to the attic, and he lowered it to the floor, leaving a rectangular hole above him. Shack's unhappy face peered over the edge. Frost climbed to the top of the ladder and let the cat hop onto his shoulder.

"Sorry about that, buddy," he said. "This was for your own good."

He descended to the closet floor, and Shack jumped down and began to review the house to make sure nothing had changed while he was locked away. Frost didn't bother changing his own wet clothes. He went downstairs and poured two glasses of brandy at the bar for himself and Tabby.

When he handed it to her, he watched her silently close her eyes as she took a sip. He did, too, feeling a river of warmth in his chest. Shack walked along the top edge of the sofa and shoved his nose into Tabby's wet hair. It was enough to bring a fleeting smile to her lips.

Finally, her emerald eyes opened, and she stared at Frost. "You know, right? About me and Duane?"

"Yes. I know."

"I'm sorry," Tabby said. "I've been trying to call you. I wanted you to hear it from me. I wanted to explain."

"You don't owe me any explanations," he said.

"Did you see Duane?" she asked.

"I did."

"How is he?"

"He's devastated. He loves you, Tabby."

"I know he does." Just as the rain had dried on her face, she began to cry in front of him. Her shoulders shook, and she talked through her tears. "Believe me, I didn't want it to go like this. I wanted to still be in love with him. I wanted to feel the way I did last summer. The thing is, I just don't. I realized that the other night. Those feelings are gone. They've been gone for a while, and I couldn't pretend anymore. That's not fair to him or me."

"I have to ask," Frost said. "Are you really sure? You told me it was a phase. I don't want to see you throw something away and then find out you wish you still had it."

Tabby shook her head. "I've been lying to myself. I kept thinking things would change long after I knew they wouldn't. He's a wonderful person, but we're not right for each other. I can't make it into something it's not. And I'm sure he hates me for it, and I'm sure you hate me now, too. I broke your brother's heart."

"I feel terrible for both of you," Frost said. "But I don't hate you."

She finished the rest of the brandy and held out her glass so he could pour her another. He went to the bar and got her a double. He'd finished his own and he wanted more, but the last thing he could afford to do was get drunk with her again.

"Here you go," he said, handing her the glass. "Drink it slowly."

Instead, she drank all of it in one burning swallow. Her hands were trembling as she returned the empty glass to him. As she did, she looked at his face and reached out and grazed her fingertips across the bruise on his cheek. When he grimaced, she pulled her hand away.

"What happened?" she asked.

He shrugged. "Nothing."

"Frost, come on. Tell me."

"Duane and I got into it. He took a swing at me. I took a swing back. I lost my cool. It wasn't good."

"Why did Duane hit you?"

Frost didn't answer her. It didn't matter, because he could see that Tabby already knew the truth. Her wide-open green eyes held him in their grasp, and he was powerless to look away.

"Duane said some things to me when I told him it was over," she murmured.

"What things?"

"He accused me of being in love with you," Tabby said. "He said I was breaking up with him because of you."

"Duane was upset. I'm sure he said things he didn't mean."

"Oh, he meant what he said," Tabby replied. "I wanted to deny it. The thing is, the other night—with you and me—"

"The other night we were very, very drunk."

"We were going to kiss," she murmured. "Weren't we?"

"Tabby, it didn't mean anything."

Her eyes widened. "It didn't mean anything? Really? Because it meant something to me. It made me realize I couldn't marry Duane when I felt the way I did being with you."

"Tabby, don't do this."

"Duane says you're in love with me, too," she murmured. "Is he right?"

"Maybe you should go," he said.

"Do you *want* me to go?"

Frost shook his head. "No, but you should."

"He told me it was never just him and me in our relationship. You were always there between us."

"And what did you say?"

"I didn't say anything. Just like you're not saying anything. It seems like we're both afraid of something, Frost. What are we afraid of?"

She undid the cocoon of the blanket around herself. Her clothes were still wet. She nudged closer to him on the sofa until their thighs brushed together. Behind the dampness, he could smell her perfume. Her lips parted, ready to be kissed. Her eyes were full of wonder about what would happen next.

"Do you want to take me upstairs?" she asked quietly.

"I can't do that."

"But you want to. I know you want to. Right? It's not just me."

"Don't ask me that, Tabby."

"I'm putting myself out there for you, Frost. I'm tired of lying about what I feel. I'm tired of *both* of us lying. Last fall, I came to your door and asked if we had a big problem. You knew exactly what I meant, but you said no. Ever since then, I've assumed it was just me, that I was the only one feeling something. But that's not true, is it?"

Frost stood up from the sofa. He ran his hand back through his wet hair and stared at the ceiling. "Tabby, stop. Just stop. It can't be like this between us. What I feel or don't feel doesn't matter. Duane is my brother. There couldn't be anything between you and me before, and there can't be anything between us now."

She stared at him in horror. "Oh, hell, what have I done?"

"You haven't done anything."

Tabby put down her glass and got up and pushed past him. She marched across the carpet to the foyer and began shoving her feet back into her heels. "No, you're right, I should go. It was wrong of me to put you in this position. I'm sorry for coming here, Frost. What the hell was I thinking? Please forgive me. I can't do this to you, I can't, I can't, I won't."

"Tabby, wait."

But she was gone. She rushed out through the front door and left him alone. Frost followed her onto the porch, where the rain blew in across his body and soaked him all over again. He saw the taillights of her car as she drove away. He was in love with her, and she was leaving him behind, just as he'd asked her to do. He was mad at her for making him choose. He was mad at Duane for giving him only one choice. Most of all, he was mad at himself for walking into a disaster he'd seen coming a mile away.

His silent grief was broken by the ringing of his phone.

He almost didn't answer it, because he assumed that Tabby was calling from her car. But he checked, and it wasn't her.

Instead, he recognized the number he'd been calling all week.

"Inspector Easton," an intoxicating Indian voice said when he answered. "This is Fawn. We need to meet."

# 42

The giant lobby of the Hyatt Regency across from the Ferry Building was mostly empty. It was nearly midnight. A few businessmen lingered over cocktails in the bar, but their loud voices sounded far away. The white floors of the hotel rose over Frost's head on all sides like the ivory keys of a piano, and ribbons of green foliage dripped from the railings. A three-story sculpted metal globe called *Eclipse* loomed over the lobby floor and gave the space a purple glow.

He walked the entire length of the atrium, which was the equivalent of walking a full city block. A glass elevator took him to the fifteenth floor near the top of the building. He emerged to a deserted hallway and a tomb-like quiet. He walked along the corridor beside the closed hotel room doors, looking down at the lobby far below him. He found Fawn's room near the end of the hallway, and he knocked.

She answered the door with a gun pointed at his face.

"Identification," she snapped.

Frost shook his head. "Trent tried that with me, too. I'm not part of Lombard. You're just going to have to trust me on that."

Fawn breathed slowly, but she didn't lower the gun. "Move back," she told him.

Frost raised his arms and backed up until he stood against the railing. "This is as far as I can go."

She looked both ways down the corridor to confirm that Frost hadn't brought anyone with him. Then she opened the door wider, but she kept the gun pointed at his chest. "Okay, come in."

He did. It was an elegant hotel suite. The television was on, with the sound muted. The bed was perfectly made. He saw the balcony beyond a set of glass doors, and the nighttime view overlooked the Ferry Building and the bay. The room smelled of perfume drifting from her skin, and he'd smelled that aroma twice before. Once in her bedroom in Pacific Heights. Once in Trent Gorham's house.

"Do you prefer Fawn or Zara?" he asked her.

"For now, let's stick with Fawn. I can't exactly go back to my life as Zara now, can I? And I guess soon I may need a third identity."

"Well, Fawn, why don't you put the gun down, and let's talk."

She hesitated and then pointed the small revolver at the floor. With her defenses down, her emotions welled to the surface. She wasn't a rock. Her dark eyes filled with tears. "Is it really true about Trent?" she asked.

"Yes, it is. I'm sorry."

Her foot tapped the carpet in a nervous tic as she dealt with the reality of losing him. "I thought—I hoped—maybe it was another trick. I'm supposed to be dead, too."

"It isn't a trick," Frost said.

Her breath caught in her chest. She couldn't speak for a while. He waited, giving her time, and he felt the aura of her presence. She looked a lot like her sister, with sweeping black hair, a honey-colored angular face, and hooked, wicked eyebrows. She was a small woman but lithe and athletic. She wore tight-fitting blue jeans, an off-the-shoulders black knit sweater, and high-top red sneakers. Like Prisha, she was attractive, but she also had something undefinable that lifted her into a rarefied world. If she looked right at you, you remembered the experience.

"I loved Trent," Fawn murmured. "I suppose that must strike you as funny."

"Not at all."

"It's not like we could tell anyone. I never even told Prisha."

"How long were you two together?" Frost asked.

"Three years. Practically from the day we met. There was an instant chemistry between us. Most men look at me like fine china, like something fragile that you need to keep behind glass. Even the ones that buy me sometimes can't even talk to me. But Trent was different. He saw me as a person. He didn't care what I did. Most guys would never be able to handle it. The jealousy would eat them up. Trent never gave me grief, never told me to quit. It was my job, that was all. I was able to be normal with him, and trust me, that's a rare thing in my life."

"I'm sure."

She shook her head. "That bastard Filko."

"Lombard, too," Frost said.

"I don't care about Lombard. That was Trent. For me, it was all about taking down Martin Filko. I meet some sleazy characters in my line of work, but Filko is in a category by himself. The bro culture in San Francisco and Silicon Valley is so disgusting. People have no idea. But I'm going to make Filko pay. Count on it. I'm bringing him down whatever it takes."

Her anger was like a fire shooting sparks from her small body. She had an intensity about her that was both attractive and a little unstable. Where her sister was cool, Fawn was hot.

"Maybe you should go back to the beginning," Frost said. "Tell me what happened."

Fawn sat on the bed. She stared at the silent television and then switched it off. She looked at Frost. "Do you know about Naomi?"

"She was an escort who was killed."

Fawn nodded. "Naomi and I were close. She was a couple years older than me, and she'd been in the business longer than I had. Her advice saved me more than once when I was starting out. Three years ago, I was at a Zelyx party with Prisha, and I bumped into Naomi there.

She was working. And by working, I mean she was with Filko. I knew something was wrong. I could see it in her face. We had a few minutes alone while he was making his remarks to the team, and she told me what was going on. The things he did to her. She'd had enough, and she was going to expose him. That was big. Believe me, if you're in my business, you don't come to that decision lightly. For Naomi, it meant she'd never work again, but she was willing to go that far to make sure people knew the kind of man Filko is. Only she never got the chance."

"The overdose," Frost said.

Fawn's lip curled with contempt. "It was murder, pure and simple. Naomi never took drugs. Never. I knew what had happened. Filko found out she was planning to expose him, and he had her killed."

"So what did you do?" Frost asked, although he knew exactly what she'd done.

"I talked to a vice cop I knew. Alan Detlowe. Alan was a good guy. I mean, no offense, but some cops are pigs and want a quid pro quo for keeping quiet, if you know what I mean. Alan was more concerned with us being safe and whether we were being treated right. He kept an eye on the escort scene to make sure organized crime wasn't moving in, but otherwise, he didn't hassle us. I told Alan what was going on and what I suspected about Naomi and Filko. He said he'd look into it, and he obviously did, because the next week, they killed him, too."

Frost nodded. "That's how you met Trent?"

"Yes. He found out that I'd been talking to Alan, and he wanted to know what it was about."

"You told him?"

"Oh yeah. I told him everything."

"Trent kept it quiet," Frost said. "Nothing went into his reports."

"That's because we already knew there was something between the two of us. We liked each other. We began dating. It wasn't quite the Montagues and Capulets, but it was close. Cops don't date hookers, and hookers don't date cops. We had to be really careful. And we were worried about what might happen to us. Naomi and Alan both got killed. So Trent kept his whole investigation under wraps. He told me what he'd found out about Lombard and the snakes, but I was the only person he trusted with it. He didn't want anyone else to know."

"Keeping it quiet meant you couldn't do anything about Filko."

"I know. I hated it, but I was falling in love with Trent, and that was more important. I was willing to put Filko on the back burner for him."

"So what changed?" Frost asked.

"Last summer, I met Filko myself," Fawn said, and he could hear the contempt in her voice.

"Was that on the cruise with Greg Howell?"

"Yes." She looked surprised that he knew that. "Belinda Drake set it up for me. I didn't know who the client was going to be. She just said he was 'difficult' and she needed someone who could handle him. I don't intimidate easily. Then it turned out to be Filko. Being with him, knowing what he'd done, brought it all back for me. Every second I was with him, I kept thinking about Naomi. When I got back, I told Trent that we had to do something. We had to get him, no matter what the risks were. And that was when he came up with the plan."

"A sting," Frost said.

Fawn nodded fiercely. "Yes, exactly. Trent said if we found the right opportunity, we could set a trap to get both of them. Filko and Lombard. So I told Belinda Drake that I was willing to see Filko again when he was in town. Believe me, most girls were one-and-out when it came to him. I knew she'd call me in, and she did. It was going to be on Denny Clark's boat again. Late night. Small party. Trent put the screws on Denny to install cameras so we'd have proof of what the son of a bitch did to me. And he came up with the idea of faking my death. He figured if Filko was face-to-face with a disaster like that, he'd have to call in Lombard to fix it like he did with Alan. And then Trent would be able to expose the whole operation."

"So what really happened on Tuesday?" Frost asked.

"At first, it went off just like we planned. When I saw the mayor with Filko, I couldn't believe our luck. This was big. There was no way they wouldn't call for Lombard's help when I disappeared. So I did my thing with the two of them all evening, and when Filko and I were alone, I knew the cameras were getting everything. It would ruin him when it came out."

"How bad was it?"

"Bad. I deal with my share of freaks, but I knew why Naomi was so desperate to take him down. Even so, I didn't care. When Filko finally passed out, I slipped up top to find Denny on the bridge, and he took me below deck. We'd arranged it all in advance. Everyone else was asleep. He hid me in the engine room, and after that, he sounded the alarm that I'd gone overboard. As far as the others were concerned, I was dead in the ocean."

"And when the boat came back in?" Frost asked.

"Trent was in the harbor waiting for us. He'd given me and Denny special phones. As soon as the trouble was starting, we could speed-dial Trent and get him in there with the whole damn cavalry. We could nail Lombard. We could nail Filko. But it didn't work that way. Nobody got hurt. Belinda handed out cash to keep everyone quiet. And the cleanup crew found the cameras, so that meant we had nothing on Filko. The whole thing was a bust. We couldn't prove a thing."

"Except Lombard wasn't done," Frost said.

"Yeah. Trent was afraid of that. That's why he hid me here for a few days while we waited to see what happened next."

"Why didn't he watch the witnesses? He had to know they were in danger."

"He didn't want to scare off Lombard. They didn't know Trent, they knew Denny. He was their contact. Trent told Denny to make sure everybody kept their eyes open and to call if they noticed anything weird. Nobody did. Except once Lombard went into action, he moved as fast as a snake. Trent didn't know anything was going on until Denny called him on Friday night, and by then, it was too late to stop it. I've been lying low ever since, until Trent could figure out what to do. As long as I was still dead, I was safe."

Frost shook his head. "Trent should have told me the truth."

"He wasn't sure if he could trust you."

"And I didn't trust him, because I knew he was keeping things from me," Frost said. "Instead, we all got played by Lombard."

Fawn got up from the bed and came over to him. "It's time for me to come back to life. I can blow the lid off the whole thing. I can tell everyone what happened on the boat, and we can tie it to Trent, Denny, Chester, Carla, Mr. Jin, all of them. The only way for Lombard to fix it was to eliminate every witness. Well, he missed one. Me."

"It might be safer for you to stay dead," Frost told her.

"I know, but I can't do that. I won't hide from these people anymore." She brushed her hair from her face and then went on. "Besides, it's too late. There's no going back now."

Frost looked at her sharply. "What do you mean by that?"

"I called Martin Filko. He knows I'm alive."

"*What?* Fawn, why did you do that?"

Her mouth hardened into a scowl that was a defiant mix of guilt and pride. She knew she'd been foolish, but she didn't care. "Don't you get it? Trent's dead! The man I loved is gone because of Martin Filko. I wanted him to know I was coming for him."

"Did you actually talk to him? What did you say?"

"I asked if he was afraid of ghosts," she said with a smirk, "and believe me, he was. It scared the crap out of him to hear my voice."

Frost shook his head. The hotel had just become a trap, and he wondered how much time they had before it sprang shut. "When did you call him?"

"Tonight before I talked to you," Fawn said. "But I didn't tell him where I was."

Frost hurried to the hotel room door, checked the peephole, and put his ear to the door to listen to the hallway. He heard nothing on the other side. "That doesn't matter. They'll be able to pinpoint your cell location. They're probably on their way."

A crack broke through Fawn's studied composure. Her eyes blinked rapidly. She bit down nervously on her lower lip and joined him by the door, where her face was in shadow. "So what do we do?"

He slid his gun out of his holster, and he took Fawn's hand. "We need to get you out of here. Right now."

# 43

Frost checked the hallway. No one was there.

The carpet hushed their footsteps as they hurried toward the glowing bank of capsule-shaped elevators. He kept his gun in the pocket of his jacket with his fingers curled around the butt. As they walked, he looked over the railing at the nearby floors. He didn't like what he saw.

Six floors down, a twenty-something man lingered in the corridor on the far side of the hotel with a phone pressed to his ear. The man acted casual, as if he were simply on a late-night conference call, but his eyes moved pointedly, studying each floor. Frost tried to back out of sight, but he was too late. The man spotted him, and his stare fixed on Frost and Fawn long enough to make it clear that they were targets.

"Lombard's here," Frost murmured.

"Should we go back to my room?"

"No, it's too late for that. They know where we are."

He guided them to where an empty elevator was waiting. He went first and pulled Fawn in behind him, but he kept them far from the floor-to-ceiling window. Instead of going to the street level, he pushed the button for the atrium lobby, which was actually the third floor of the hotel. The elevator descended swiftly, and he watched the huge *Eclipse* sculpture looming closer.

His gun was in his hand as the lobby doors opened. He tensed, expecting a welcoming committee, but they were alone. He tucked the gun into his pocket again and led Fawn into the vast open space of the atrium. Across from the sculpture, he saw the check-in desk, where two bored hotel employees chatted. The hotel bar was directly ahead. The drunk businessmen who'd been there when he first arrived had left, but someone else was there now, casually reading a paper copy of the *Chronicle*, with his phone on the cushion of the chair beside him.

Frost recognized him.

It was Romeo Laredo, the muscular IT guy who'd pushed Diego Casal in front of the train. The Lombard operative with the code name Guerrero. Romeo was looking across the lobby at Frost and Fawn, as if he'd been expecting them. His face broke into a friendly grin, but there was a buzz saw hiding behind his smile. Romeo had a raincoat draped across his lap, and as Frost watched, the man's right hand slipped under the coat. He was armed.

"This way," Frost whispered to Fawn, pushing her toward an escalator that led down one floor to the conference center. "Quickly."

They reached the second floor of the hotel, and he took a moment to orient himself. The solid wall in front of them rose from the downstairs ballroom, and a corridor on their left led to a series of smaller meeting rooms. When he glanced back to the top of the escalator, he saw Romeo standing there, watching them. The young man's huge smile didn't change. Romeo looked in both directions to make sure he was alone, and then he headed calmly down the escalator steps.

"Run," Frost said.

He grabbed Fawn's hand, and they sprinted along the ballroom wall toward the northeast corner of the hotel. Halfway there, the corridor turned sharply as the building narrowed to a point. Ahead of him, he could see glass doors leading outside with nothing but blackness behind them. He drew his gun into his hand, but no one was waiting for them. He shoved through the doors, and they emerged onto the top of stone steps that descended toward a cobblestone plaza on the Embarcadero.

The Ferry Building was across the street, and palm trees lined the curb. Cold rain swept like a curtain into their faces.

"My car's on Market Street," he told her.

They splashed down the steps. He could see his Suburban at the curb under the streetlights, but his truck had company. A charcoal-gray BMW was parked beside it, and he saw Luis Moreno from the Department of Building Inspection leaning against the BMW's door. Another of Lombard's twenty-something army. Moreno, like Romeo, wore a casual grin and had his hands buried in the pockets of a trench coat. When he saw Frost and Fawn, he started toward them through the pouring rain.

Meanwhile, Romeo was coming for them down the plaza steps.

Frost spun around and marched the opposite way with Fawn at his hip. When they were out of sight, they ran through the outdoor shops of Embarcadero Center toward the opposite side of the hotel. It was a long block, and before they reached the other end, he heard voices shouting behind them. He couldn't see anyone through the downpour, but he knew the two men weren't far behind.

They emerged onto Drumm Street. The rain drowned out the noise around them. The hotel was on their left, and across the street was a series of chain stores. Subway. Starbucks. 7-Eleven. Walgreens. All closed. He pointed toward the opposite side, and they ran that way, passing under a streetlight and then reaching a darker section of the block near the deserted storefronts. There were cars parked all along the curb, including a large black van with a logo for a local coffee company. He looked back at the Embarcadero Center corridor and didn't see Romeo or Moreno on the street yet. They only had a few seconds.

"Underneath the van," he said. "Hurry."

He pushed on Fawn's shoulders, and the two of them dropped to their hands and knees and slithered under the chassis of the black van. A torrent of water flooded along the curb, soaking them. Rain dripped like waterfalls around them on every side. He held his breath. He had his gun in one hand, and his other arm was draped around Fawn's shoulder. She huddled against him. In the darkness, he put a finger over his lips and made sure she stayed silent.

Footsteps closed in on them.

One man was on the street, and the other was on the sidewalk. They kicked through rainwater, searching the block, going back and forth. Frost heard one of them shout to the other in frustration, "Where the hell are they?"

Then silence.

"We've lost them!"

More running echoed through the wet street.

Then a minute later: "Call Lombard."

Frost and Fawn waited as the footsteps receded. Ten minutes passed with no other sound. The men had vanished. He checked his watch and saw that it was after twelve thirty now. The streets around them were empty. He didn't hear the men coming back.

"Let's go," he whispered.

He squeezed toward the street side of the van, then rolled free and quickly stood up. He didn't see Luis Moreno or Romeo Laredo anywhere around them. He bent down and helped Fawn out from under the van, and then he pointed to the intersection at the corner of the hotel.

"There's an entrance to the BART station there," he told her. "There should be one last train to the airport in a few minutes. We'll go there and find you another hotel until we can figure out what to do next."

Fawn nodded her agreement. Her black hair was matted, and her face and clothes were smeared with dirt and grease, but she still had an unquenchable elegance about her. She also had a determined distance in her eyes. For now, she was with him, but as soon as their interests diverged, he knew she would be gone.

Heads down, they crossed to the hotel and walked quickly toward the corner. She held his hand, making them look like a couple out for a romantic San Francisco stroll. Where the hotel ended, they were at the arrowhead where California and Market came together, immediately in front of the terminus of the cable car tracks. He saw stairs leading into the BART underground.

"Come on, let's get off the street before anyone spots us," he said.

They hurried across the cobblestones and down into Embarcadero Station. The shops around them were closed and gated. The floor was wet. Every footstep they made on the white tile floor sounded loud. He went to a kiosk and bought two tickets to the last stop at the airport. There was a BART attendant behind glass near the ticket gates, and he thought about stopping to ask him to call the police. But that would give Lombard time to find them.

Frost sent Fawn through the ticket gate, and he followed. He put an arm around her waist as they headed for the deep steps that led to the trains. At the bottom, a dozen people were spread out along the southbound side of the platform, waiting for the Oakland train to emerge from its transit under the cold waters of the bay.

The platform was narrow, the ceiling was low, and the underground air was cool. There were stairs and escalators on both ends of the station, and the train tracks ran on either side. In the middle of the platform was the shiny steel housing for an elevator.

Frost took Fawn's hand. He walked past the people waiting for the train, assessing each one. They looked innocent. He checked the electronic sign and saw that the airport train was due in fourteen minutes. He led them to a circular bench near the elevator, and they sat down next to each other to wait. Neither one of them said a word.

Five tense minutes passed that way.

More people arrived on the platform, bringing the smell of the rain and the city with them.

The train was due in nine minutes.

Eight minutes.

Seven. He began to think they were safe.

Then Frost froze. He heard boots clip-clopping on the platform steps, and they had a different, measured character compared to the noise of an ordinary passenger. He slid his hand into his jacket pocket, where his gun was. He heard a sharp intake of breath from Fawn.

It was Romeo Laredo.

The husky blond man reached the platform and spotted them. Frost and Fawn stood up. Romeo had his raincoat over his hand, but he slipped it away to reveal an automatic pistol already pointed at them across the short stretch of white tile.

The passengers around them noticed the gun. Several screamed. They began a charge toward the other end of the platform, and Frost and Fawn joined them, heading for the stairs as part of the crowd. Romeo made no motion to follow. When they neared the far steps, Frost saw why. Romeo's partner, Luis Moreno, had already taken up position on the other end of the platform. He had a gun, too.

Moreno waved everyone else past him. They weren't the ones he wanted. In less than a minute, everyone had fled. The platform was deserted, and it was just the four of them in the channel between the northbound and southbound tracks. The six minutes until the train arrived might as well have been forever. They had nowhere to go.

Frost had his gun in his hand. He stood next to Fawn on the yellow rumble strip at the edge of the southbound tracks, where they could see in both directions into the tunnel. Neither of the two men made any effort to get closer to them. They simply guarded both exits, preventing their escape.

"Half of the people on this platform probably just dialed 911," Frost called to them. "The police will be here in a couple of minutes. You better leave now."

Moreno said nothing. Neither did Romeo. Then the second man tapped a receiver in his ear and signaled to his partner. Both men got on the escalators and rode upward until they disappeared. Frost and Fawn were alone.

"What the hell's going on?" Fawn said.

Frost shook his head. "I don't know."

Then he heard the mechanical whir of the elevator descending toward them. Someone was coming. He thought about taking Fawn into the tunnel, but there was no time to get away. The elevator car was already arriving. The doors were about to open in front of them.

Somehow, when they did, Frost knew he would recognize the face emerging from the other side. His enemy was no stranger.

He was right.

The elevator doors slid open, and Fox strolled onto the platform.

# 44

"Hello, Frost," the boy said.

Except he wasn't a boy at all. Frost realized that now. Fox was dressed the way he always was, all in black. His tank top was soaking wet from the rain. A cigarette dripped from his mouth. He had no gun, but he had two heavy leather balls that he juggled gracefully in one hand without even looking at what he was doing. He looked the same with his oddly plastic skin and tousled dark hair, but he looked different, too. He'd traded his innocence for the sharp eyes of a hawk. His smile was smarter, nastier, and more arrogant. He knew he'd played Frost for a fool.

"So how old are you really?" Frost asked him. "I would have guessed fourteen."

"I'm twenty-six," Fox replied. Then his voice rose an octave. "But don't feel bad, it's easy to make people believe what they want to believe."

"Obviously, you're not Mr. Jin's son."

"Obviously."

"Where's the real boy?" Frost asked. "The real Fox."

"I didn't kill him, if that's what you're thinking. No, Fox is safe and sound. I grabbed him as soon as Mr. Jin disappeared. I kept him around in case we needed him to lure out his father. As things turned out, that wasn't a problem."

The strange leather juggling balls went up and down, slapping into Fox's palm.

"So it was you," Frost said. He wanted to make sure that Fawn, standing next to him, understood the truth. "Not Cyril. Trent broke down the door and saw *you* killing Mr. Jin. That's why he was chasing you."

"Yeah, he would have shot me, too," Fox replied. "He had me cornered. Good thing the other cop got him first."

Frost glanced at Fawn. Her dark eyes were two little dots of hatred.

"And who exactly are you?" Frost asked, eyeing the screen that counted down the minutes until the train arrived. "You may not be a kid, but I can't believe you're Lombard."

"You're right about that. I'm Geary, actually. He uses me for the dirty work. Lombard only comes out for the occasional job. When we have to take out one of our own, he likes to do that himself. It sends a message."

Fox turned his attention to the woman beside Frost.

"So you're Fawn," he went on. "You're looking good for a dead woman. That was quite the stunt you and Gorham pulled. Very impressive. None of us suspected a thing."

Fawn said nothing, but her breathing was loud, and her nostrils flared with anger.

"If it makes you feel any better," Fox told her, "Martin Filko really is a pig. I don't blame you for wanting to get rid of him. Unfortunately, you played the game, and you lost."

Frost stepped in front of Fawn. He lifted his gun and pointed it at Fox's chest. It was cocked, and his index finger was on the trigger. They were no more than twenty feet apart, close enough that he couldn't miss. Fox stood in front of the elevator doors, and Frost and Fawn were on the very edge of the platform, with their backs to the train tracks.

"Put the gun away and stop being silly, Frost," Fox said.

He grinned as he juggled the two leather balls in his hand. They were hypnotic and oddly threatening, and Frost tried to follow them with his eyes, but the constant motion was dizzying.

"I don't think so," Frost said.

"Look, I have no beef with you," Fox added. "I actually like you."

"Really? You tried to kill me when I was with Coyle. That was you, wasn't it?"

"It was," Fox acknowledged. "But things change. All I want now is the girl, so if you walk away, we'll call it no harm, no foul. You'll be perfectly safe. My boys upstairs won't touch you."

"I'm not going anywhere," Frost said.

Fox nodded without surprise. "No, of course not. Well, I gave you a chance. Everyone says you're a Boy Scout, so I didn't expect you to leave a damsel in distress. Too bad, though. I've never understood the mathematics of hero types. Only one of you has to die, but instead, you both do. It seems like a waste."

"Or maybe you die, and Fawn and I take the train that's coming in a couple minutes and get the hell out of here."

"That's brave talk, Frost, but this isn't our first rodeo, remember? Didn't you learn anything on the boat? Or in Mr. Jin's apartment? You can't beat me. I always win, you always lose."

"Your Cirque du Soleil tricks aren't as effective when I have a gun," Frost replied.

"Except you don't have a gun," Fox told him.

Frost was ready, and still he never saw it coming. As one leather juggling ball flew up in the air, Fox's wrist flashed. The ball in his hand shot across the space like a missile, striking the barrel of Frost's gun and kicking it away. The pistol spun through the air and hit the wall on the far side of the train tracks. Frost felt an intense shock of pain and realized that his index finger had been snapped backward and broken. It stuck upward from his hand as if it were pointing at heaven.

This all happened in the time it took for the second ball to rise up and drop casually back into Fox's hand.

"Lead pellets," Fox told him with a smile. "They give these things the kick of a mule."

Frost charged across the space between them. He was far bigger than Fox, but size didn't matter. As Frost leaped, Fox's foot jabbed like a piston underneath Frost's rib cage, and the air burst from his lungs. Fox's arm spun into a roundhouse and hammered the back of Frost's head, driving him face-first to the ground. The impact shuddered through his skull and bloodied his forehead. Frost rolled away just as Fox's next kick flew by his head. He staggered to his feet and backed up, gasping for breath and trying to shake off a wave of nausea.

Fox hadn't even broken a sweat. He tossed the second leather ball up and down in his hand.

"Had enough? I mean, after a while, I'm going to get bored with kicking your ass, Frost. Eventually, the cat always kills the mouse. You know that, right? You've got a cat."

Frost charged again.

Fox's left leg flew upward, and his whole body followed it around. This time, the kick landed against Frost's shoulder and threw him sideways against the elevator doors. He slammed hard and had to brace himself not to slip down to the floor of the platform. Blood dripped down his face, mixed with sweat. His broken finger throbbed like the searing burn of a cattle brand. His head spun. He could barely move his arm.

Fox still casually juggled the leather ball in his hand.

"How do you want this, Inspector? Fast or slow?"

Frost smiled and spat out the words. "You just made a mistake."

Fox cocked his head warily. "A mistake?"

"You missed something."

"Yeah? What'd I miss?"

The voice came from behind Fox. It came from Fawn.

"I have a gun, too, you son of a bitch," she told him.

And she began to fire.

Her first two bullets went wide. She wasn't a good shot. But the next blast from her revolver slammed the meat of Fox's shoulder, and the bullet exited his body with a spray of blood and ricocheted off the steel of the elevator bank near Frost's head. Fawn fired one more time, searing Fox's thigh, before he spun around and whipped the second leather ball squarely into her forehead. It landed like a hammer, and she fell straight back and hit the floor of the platform, unconscious.

Ignoring the screams of pain in his body, Frost launched himself off the elevator bank and crashed into Fox's back and took him down. He shot an elbow into Fox's face, buried a thumb in his wounded shoulder, then turned him over and rained down blow after blow with his uninjured fist. Fox took the assault without flinching, but Frost's strength quickly waned, and the killer wriggled out of his grip and clapped both sides of Frost's head sharply with his feet. It felt like a tornado in Frost's brain. He threw his head back in agony, and instantly, Fox squirmed free and was on his feet.

Frost stood up, too. They circled each other like wounded prizefighters. Fox was losing blood that soaked through his black clothes and puddled on the platform floor, but Frost could hardly keep the world in focus.

When he saw an opening, he attacked again. It was a mistake.

Fox nimbly sidestepped his charge and delivered another ferocious kick that landed in the middle of Frost's back. The impact drove him into the air and off the platform, and he landed in the dust and dirt on the far side of the train tracks. He got up but then collapsed. The same thing happened when he tried again. And then he was finally on his feet, propped against the wall of the tunnel.

Everything began to happen at once. He tried to make sense of it.

A wail sounded, muffled and distant in his ears. He stared into the blackness of the tunnel hole and saw two glowing eyes growing larger and brighter. The BART train whistled, screeched, and roared as it flew from under the bay and closed in on the Embarcadero Station.

Meanwhile, on the platform, Fox bent over Fawn, dripping blood onto her body. He reached for her head. He was going to break her neck.

Frost couldn't get to them in time. He had only seconds to leap off the tracks and escape the oncoming train. He was frozen with indecision, but then he looked down and spotted his gun where it had landed between the rails. He took two steps, picked it up in his right hand, and tried to steady his arm as he aimed at Fox, but his index finger had swelled, and he couldn't move it or fit it inside the trigger guard.

The train stormed closer. Its whistle shrieked. Its headlights bathed him in light.

Fox had his hands on either side of Fawn's skull, ready to twist. She was awake now, frozen in terror, her eyes wide.

Frost threw the gun into his left hand and fired and fired. He was a terrible shot with his other hand, but he got lucky. After missing three times, one bullet shattered Fox's elbow, and another burned through the flesh of his stomach. Fox howled and fell, writhing on the ground.

The train clattered and bore down on him with a hurricane of air exploding from the tunnel.

With his gun still in his hand, Frost took two steps and jumped for the platform. His heels barely cleared the sleek silver body of the train. He rolled, and his broken finger jammed into the floor like a shock of lightning. Before he even came to a stop, he passed out from the pain.

When Frost opened his eyes, half a dozen faces loomed over him. They were passengers from the train.

"I called 911, Officer," someone said, who'd obviously spotted the badge on his belt. "The cops and the ambulance should be here soon. Just hang tight."

He blinked, remembering where he was and what had happened. He pushed himself to his elbows, but as he did, his finger delivered another shock of pain that almost split him in half. He touched his face, which was wet with ribbons of blood. His whole body felt pummeled.

"Whoa, hang on, man," someone else said. "You probably shouldn't move."

Frost turned his head sideways, feeling the effort in his neck. He looked through the legs of the people clustered around him, and the floor of the platform was empty. Fawn was gone. He scrambled to his feet and nearly collapsed, and one of the men nearby grabbed him and propped him up.

*"The girl,"* Frost said urgently. "Where's the girl?"

The people around him looked at each other, and then a woman said, "The pretty one with the big bump on her forehead? She took off."

"Where? Where did she go?"

The passenger from the train shrugged. "I don't know. It was crazy town around here. She got up and ran for the escalator."

Frost swung his head in the other direction, and again his knees buckled.

Fox was gone, too. The blood trail led into the elevator. Frost broke free from the crowd and followed the trail. Several of the people shouted after him, but he didn't pay any attention. He limped, trying to stay upright, trying to stay conscious. He jabbed the elevator button again and again, as if that would make it come faster. When the doors finally opened, he piled inside. He crumpled against the far wall and closed his eyes as the car went upward. It only took a few seconds, but it felt like an hour.

The trail of blood continued into the lobby of the station. Romeo and Moreno were both gone. The Lombard presence had melted away as the emergency sirens got closer.

Frost tracked Fox all the way to the escalator leading up to the street, but when he climbed the steps to the sidewalk outside, the rain had washed away the blood trail. The ambulances were coming. So were the police. He couldn't wait for them. He squinted into the pounding rain, which had driven away the late-night people. The streets looked empty. At first, he thought Fox had vanished again, but then he spotted a shadow near the wall of the Hyatt hotel, staggering toward the Embarcadero.

Frost took off after Fox. It was a battle to see which one could stay on their feet longer. Frost felt thunder behind his eyes with each step, but he sprinted anyway. Fox passed under a streetlight and looked back and saw Frost gaining ground behind him. The killer tried to run, but the loss of blood had caught up to him, and all he could manage were stutter steps. He made it to the empty plaza beyond the hotel, and so did Frost, only a few yards behind him.

At the edge of the street, under the palm trees, Fox stopped. He turned on his heel to face Frost. His one arm hung limply at his side. As he bled, the rain washed it away. Frost kept a wary distance, not trusting the man's tricks, but Fox had no tricks left. Behind him, cars splashed along the southbound lane of the Embarcadero, their headlights washing over his body. The clock tower of the Ferry Building gleamed with yellow light across the street.

"You think you've won?" Fox called. "You're wrong."

Rain shined on his face, which was half in shadow. His whole body shivered as he tried to stay standing.

"This is the end," Frost told him. "It starts with you."

"I'm already dead," Fox said.

Frost shook his head. "No way. You are *not* going to die. I'm not going to let you. The surgeons are going to fix you up, and then I'm going to put you in a room, and you're going to tell me how it all works. You're going to tell me everything, Fox."

"You still don't get it, do you?" Fox shouted.

The traffic roared. The rain sheeted down, and wind rocked the palm trees. The gauzy lights made the sidewalk look like a carnival.

"Get what?"

"He's coming."

"Who?"

Fox gave him a bloody grin. "Lombard."

Frost twisted his neck to survey their surroundings. They were alone. He took a step closer to Fox. The man looked serene in the midst of his pain.

"No one's here," Frost said.

"You're wrong. He's always watching."

Over the driving rain, Frost heard the muffled ping of a text message arriving on his phone. Fox heard it, too.

"You better get that," Fox warned him.

Frost yanked the phone out of his pocket, and the screen lit up. He didn't recognize the number. The message itself was only three words.

King takes pawn.

Frost spun, looking for a ghost. He still saw nothing and no one.

"You should duck," Fox went on, making no attempt to run, "unless you want to die, too."

That was when it happened.

Among the flood of cars kicking up torrents of spray on the Embarcadero, one car squealed to a stop at the curb barely ten feet away from them. It was a Bugatti, black, low, sleek, and incredibly expensive. Its passenger-side window was already down, and Frost hurled himself to the ground, knowing what came next. Gunfire erupted from inside with bursts of fire and noise. Fox shuddered like a puppet on strings as multiple bullets riddled his back, and by the time the Bugatti sped away, the young killer twitched and crumpled sideways. It all took less than ten seconds.

Frost pushed himself out of the mud and ran to Fox, but there was no hope of saving him. Fox had taken a dozen new bullet wounds. Bile and blood bubbled from his mouth. He managed a few gasping breaths but didn't say a word, and his eyes lit up with an odd gleam of victory before they froze in place.

Then he was dead, and all the secrets died with him.

Frost slumped to the ground. The rain poured in waves over his head. His phone sang again like a taunt as he clutched it in his hand. It was another message from the same phone number as before.

He read the text as he sat next to Fox's lifeless body.

A pleasure to finally meet you, Inspector.

Lombard.

# 45

Three days passed. There was no sign of Fawn.

Frost left multiple messages on her phone, but he got no reply, and he assumed that she'd long since disposed of it. He was able to get a copy of the security video from Embarcadero Station on the night of the incident, and he spotted Fawn running for the exit along with others from the Oakland train. He saw no evidence that she'd been followed from the station by anyone from Lombard.

Even so, she was still missing.

When he couldn't reach her, he went to her sister's house. He drove to Presidio Heights at seven in the morning and found a large moving van parked outside and a "For Sale" sign in the window. He squeezed past the moving team and discovered that the house was already empty. Everything was gone. He went up to Fawn's bedroom on the second floor. It had been stripped clean.

Prisha Anand was standing in the foyer when he came back downstairs. She had her coat on and her purse over her shoulder. She was dressed down, in jeans and a simple cotton top, with her black hair tied behind her head. She didn't look surprised to see him.

"So you're leaving?" he asked.

"Yes. It's time for a new life."

"You're quitting Zelyx, too?"

"It's already done. I'm out."

"Where are you going?"

Prisha shrugged. "Somewhere else. Far away."

He could see in her face that she knew Zara was alive. She knew where her sister was hiding. The two of them were selling the house and making their escape together. They were trying to run from Lombard.

"You won't be safe no matter where you go," Frost told her. "Distance won't protect you."

"Don't worry about that," Prisha replied. "I've taken care of everything."

"How?"

"The situation is complicated, Frost. That's all I can say."

He exhaled in frustration. "You're not going to pretend with me, are you? You know that Zara's alive. You know what happened at the Embarcadero."

Prisha made sure the movers were nowhere nearby. She hooded her eyes, and then she gently reached out and touched his elbow. "Of course I do. Zara came directly to me from the station. She wants you to know—we *both* want you to know—how grateful we are. You saved her life."

"Then take me to her, and let me talk to her. The only way to keep her safe is to let her go public with what she knows. These people won't take it on faith that she'll stay quiet. As long as she's alive, she's a threat to them."

Prisha didn't say anything immediately. She took his hand and led him out of the house, and they crossed the street to where Frost's Suburban was parked. She looked up and down Clay Street, which was free of pedestrians. The red dome of the synagogue shone in the sun two blocks away. It was a calm, unusually warm morning, as if summer had jumped ahead of spring in the seasonal lineup.

"I'm sorry, Frost," Prisha said. "You can't see Zara, and I can't tell you where we're going. That's part of the deal."

"The deal?" he asked.

"I made a deal with Lombard."

"You know about him?"

"Yes. Zara told me everything. Lombard and I worked out a mutually agreeable solution to our problem."

Frost shook his head. "How did you contact a man that no one can find?"

"Actually, he called me," Prisha said.

"Lombard called *you*?"

"He figured Zara would come to me, and he was right."

"What did he want?" Frost asked.

"To put an end to this. He said that the cruise on Tuesday had gotten out of hand and put everyone in far more jeopardy than was necessary. He wanted to close the book on it once and for all. So we negotiated the terms of Zara's safety. I'm a lawyer, Frost. Negotiating is what I do, and I'm very good at it. I did a deal that keeps us safe. We all get what we want."

"You can't trust him."

"Deals aren't done on trust. They're done on parties acting in their own self-interest. That includes Lombard."

"What did he offer you for Zara's silence? Money? That's how it starts. He gives you money, and you think you're safe, but you're not."

"Zara and I don't need money," Prisha replied. "We have far more than we'd ever want. In fact, you have it backward. We purchased our safety."

"You *paid* Lombard for your freedom?" Frost said. "You're kidding yourself if you think that will work. I don't care how much you gave him. It won't be enough."

"No, this is different. I paid Lombard to solve a problem for us. That's what he does, after all. He's a fixer."

"And what did you want him to fix?"

"I told you, it's complicated."

"He'll still kill you both, Prisha," Frost insisted. "Wherever you go, he'll track you down."

"No. He won't. I'm satisfied that it's not in his interest to harm us after we leave, because he knows that it's not in *our* interest that Zara ever say another word about the cruise on Tuesday or about him. You'll never see her again. You'll never see me again. Don't bother looking for us, because you won't find us."

Frost felt a wave of concern. "What did you do, Prisha? Tell me."

"Really, Frost, it's better that you not know the details. Zara and I can live with what we've done, but I know you couldn't. You're too honorable. So it's time to drop it. Walk away. Zara and I would hate to see you come to any harm. We're both fond of you."

"This is a mistake," he said.

She gave him an uncomfortable smile. "It's sweet of you to worry about us, but there's no need. Please don't hate us when you learn the truth. I know it's not the choice you'd make, but it's the best thing for everyone. And now I'm sorry, but I have to say good-bye."

Prisha dashed across the street with quick little steps. There was a white Jaguar convertible parked in front of the moving van, and she climbed inside. She threw a little wave at Frost, and then she fired up the engine and sped away.

He was pretty sure she was never coming back.

Frost spent the rest of the day investigating Bugatti registrations. Given that it was a multimillion-dollar vehicle, he was surprised at how many there were throughout the state, but California was home to the crazy rich of both Hollywood and Silicon Valley. He pulled the license information on every owner and made a list for follow-up, but there was nothing to suggest that any of the Bugatti drivers was Lombard.

He also checked the mobile records on the phone that had been recovered from Fox's body, but they led him nowhere. The numbers that the killer had used to communicate with Lombard—which obviously changed every week—all ended at disconnected burner phones.

The operatives were gone, too. Romeo Laredo had vanished and left behind a vacant apartment. So had Luis Moreno.

By the time the clock ticked to midnight, Frost was still at his desk in police headquarters, and he was at a dead end. None of the threads in the case brought him any closer to finding Lombard.

The man was still a mystery, a ghost. He was Moriarty.

Frost rubbed his eyes, which were tired from staring at the brightness of the computer screen. He leaned back in his chair and studied the desk where Trent Gorham had sat. It had already been cleared off, leaving the surface stark and empty. Gorham had spent years conducting a shadow investigation of Lombard, and the only result was to get him killed.

"Easton?" a voice called to him. "You're still here?"

Captain Hayden filled the doorway of his office. The rest of the detective floor was quiet. The graveyard shift was mostly out on the streets. Hayden waved him inside, and Frost joined him and shut the door. Cyril was there, too, standing behind the captain the way he always did.

"Why don't you go home," Hayden told him. "You're not going to accomplish anything more today. And frankly, you still need to recover. You're not one hundred percent by a long shot."

"I'm fine," Frost replied.

"That wasn't a suggestion," Hayden told him.

Frost nodded. "All right."

"Hey, Easton," Cyril called to him from the window. His hard-edged voice sounded apologetic. "You know, I really thought Gorham was going to shoot that kid. That's why I fired. I sure as hell never thought Gorham saw the kid break the neck of that chef."

"Fox fooled me, too," Frost said. "And he wasn't a kid."

"Well, I'm not happy about how it went down," Cyril went on. "I wanted you to know that."

"Okay."

Hayden nodded at Cyril and then gestured toward the door. "Give me a minute alone with Frost. Warm up the car. I'll be leaving soon, too."

"Yes, sir," Cyril replied.

The other cop left, and the two of them were alone in the captain's expansive office.

"I told Cyril you had suspicions about him," Hayden said. "I hope that Fox's confession took care of that. We're both sorry about Gorham, but Cyril had to make a split-second call. You or I would have done the same thing. What happened on the roof was bad luck."

"You're right," Frost agreed, but he also remembered what Fox had told him in the Chinatown alley. *It's not luck, man. Around here, people have my back.*

"It's important that the three of us trust each other going forward," Hayden went on, as if he could hear the doubts in Frost's voice.

"I understand," Frost said.

"Lombard is still out there."

"That's true. Although I'm not sure where we go from here."

"You haven't found anything else?"

"No."

"So what's your next step?"

"I don't have one," Frost said.

"What are you saying, Easton? Are you done with Lombard? Are you walking away?"

"That depends, sir," Frost said. "Do you *want* me to walk away?"

Hayden took a while to say anything more. His breath smelled of coffee and chocolate, and his teeth were wine stained. He grabbed a half-smoked cigar from an ashtray and rolled it between his fingers. "I was at a political dinner tonight. I hate those things, but they're a necessary evil. The mayor was there. He asked about the incident at the Embarcadero."

"What did you tell him?" Frost asked.

"I said it was about drugs," the captain replied. "He seemed relieved to hear that."

"I'm sure he was."

"He also asked about Denny Clark. I told him the investigation was closed. He was pleased about that, too."

"No doubt," Frost said.

"What I'm saying is, nobody's pushing for the truth. I won't blame you if you want to let it go."

"I appreciate that," Frost replied, but he left the original question unanswered. He wasn't making any promises.

Hayden waited. The silence between them drew out. "You know, Easton, you've still never told me who was really on that boat."

"That's because I can't prove it. I have no witnesses."

"But you know, right?"

"Does it matter now, sir? I mean, since the case is closed."

"I guess not," Hayden said.

"Will there be anything else, sir?" Frost asked.

"No. You can go home. We can talk more tomorrow."

Frost left the office. He gathered up his things at his desk and took the elevator down to the street. Outside, in the darkness, the unusual early-season heat stubbornly refused to yield to the typical cool evening air. Between the downtown buildings, it was still warm enough to make him sweat. His Suburban was parked at the water on the east end of China Basin, and he walked that way alone past the glass windows of upscale condominiums. His pace was slow as he passed in and out of the glow of streetlights. The neighborhood was deserted. He could smell the bay as he got closer, and when he reached the water, the city skyline and the baseball stadium came into view on his left.

He stopped.

Directly in front of him on the other side of the street was a black Bugatti. Its ferocious engine idled. Its distinctive C-curve swooped along the roofline and bent below the driver's door, making the machine look like the Batmobile.

Romeo Laredo leaned against the hood. "Well, hey, Inspector, how are you? We keep running into each other, don't we? San Francisco's a small town."

"Looks that way," Frost replied. He stayed where he was and slid back the flap of his jacket like a gunslinger to reveal the holster for his weapon.

"Oh, you won't be needing that," Romeo told him. "In fact, I'd really appreciate it if you could come over here and hand it to me."

"Why should I do that?" Frost asked.

"Well, first of all, if you look around, you'll see that I'm not alone, so if you're thinking about being a hero, that's a really bad call. Second, there's somebody in the car who'd like to talk to you, and I sort of think you'd like to talk to him, too."

Frost took a quick glance in every direction and confirmed Romeo's story. Other men with guns had appeared on all sides and were closing in from the shadows. He slid his pistol slowly into his hand with two fingers and then crossed the street and deposited it in Romeo's palm. The athletic operative grinned.

"Don't worry, you'll get it back," Romeo told him.

Frost went around to the passenger side of the Bugatti. He noted that there was no license plate. The door opened on its own for him with a soft click, and he got inside. As he sank into the rich leather seat, which practically melted around him, the door closed automatically. There was almost no light inside the vehicle behind the smoked glass. The man at the wheel was very close to him, but Frost could make out few details of who he was. He wore an elegant dress fedora tilted to cover much of his face, and his eyes were hidden by owlish sunglasses. The collar of his dark raincoat was up, and his mouth and cheeks were in shadow. He was ageless and had no identity. All Frost could make out was a sheen of black hair and the outline of an unremarkable nose that he tried to capture in his memory.

"Hello, Inspector Easton," Lombard said.

He had a much softer voice than Frost was anticipating. His tone was firm but calm, like a teacher discussing the ins and outs of Plato with a student. It wasn't the kind of voice that would intimidate strangers, but this man's entire world had been built around intimidation and cruelty. Frost thought about the cigarette burns on Belinda Drake's chest and about the trail of dead bodies, and it reminded him whom he was dealing with.

"Why are we meeting?" Frost asked. "Are you planning to kill me?"

In the darkness, he saw the smallest smile creep onto Lombard's lips. "Now, why would I do that when I've already won, Inspector? You're no threat to me now."

"Then why? Or do you just want to gloat?"

"Actually, my first thought was to see if I could recruit you to join my organization," Lombard told him.

"I thought you already had spies inside Mission Bay," Frost said.

"One can never have enough information. Besides, there are many roles for someone with your talent and intelligence. I'm sure you see me as one of the bad guys, but I would argue the point with you. We're both trying to make San Francisco a better place."

"With murder?" Frost asked.

"With whatever's necessary. I hope you don't think the status quo is working here. Rampant homelessness. Unaffordable housing. Crime and street problems that your colleagues and the politicians seem unable to do anything about. This is not the city we both love, Inspector. My goal is change. I'm offering you a chance to be part of it."

"Pass," Frost said.

"Of course. I assumed that would be your answer, and I respect that. Well, then my second goal is to arrange a truce. A cessation of hostilities between you and me. We may not be friends, but there's no need for us to be enemies."

"I thought I was no threat to you," Frost said.

"Now? You're not. But you're the kind of person who doesn't give up, and who knows where that might lead? I'd rather you realize that it's in your best interest not to pursue me."

"Like you agreed not to pursue Zara and Prisha Anand?" Frost asked.

"Something like that," Lombard replied. "They're lovely women. Extremely bright and courageous. I respect that."

"And what exactly did they hire you to do?"

Lombard tapped a gloved finger on the dashboard clock, which showed that it was one in the morning. "It's in process at this very moment. The news will reach you soon enough. Who knows? You might even thank me when you find out."

"I doubt that," Frost said.

"Well, we shall see. So what do you say, Inspector? What do you think about my proposal? Can we agree to retreat to our separate corners?"

Frost shrugged. "It doesn't matter what I say, does it? Actions speak louder than words."

"How true."

"I assume you'll be watching," Frost said.

"I will indeed. I must admit, I really do like you, Frost. I wish I could persuade you to come over to my side. But for now, I'll say good night."

With another soft click and a warm, sticky burst of air, the door of the Bugatti swung open again next to Frost. He climbed out, but he blocked the door from shutting with his body, and he leaned back inside. The man behind the wheel was still little more than a ghost.

"The next time we meet, it probably won't go well for one of us," Frost told him.

"No, I suppose not," Lombard replied. "Either way, I look forward to it."

# 46

"A truce?" Herb asked.

Frost nodded. "That's what he said."

"Interesting. Do you believe him?"

"Not for a moment," Frost replied.

Herb drank coffee from his silver thermos. It was midmorning the following day, and the two of them leaned against the base of the Willie Mays statue outside AT&T Park. Herb had just completed his latest three-dimensional sidewalk painting near the stadium gate, in honor of the Giants returning home for the season opener. The portrayal of hometown baseball legends, some in black and white, some in color, was already attracting a crowd.

"So it's true," Herb said. "Lombard exists. In the flesh."

"He does."

"What were your impressions of him?"

"I still don't know anything about him at all," Frost replied. "Honestly, he could be standing right there in the crowd and I wouldn't even recognize him. But you know how you can hear intelligence in someone's voice? That's Lombard. He's brilliant."

"A brilliant sociopath," Herb said. Then he noted the braces keeping Frost's right index finger in place. "What's the report on your finger?"

"The surgeon thinks I'll get full use of it back. The break was pretty clean. Vicodin and I were pretty good friends on day one, but it's better now."

"And the rest of you?"

"Bruised but intact."

"Well, that's excellent news." Herb drank more coffee and wiped sweat from his brow on the warm morning. He smelled of paint and pot, as usual. "As it happens, I wouldn't entirely discount the idea of Lombard wanting a truce. He may be sincere."

"Oh? Why do you say that?"

"Do you remember the threat that was hanging over my head? Silvia's disappearance all those years ago and the lawyer who seemed to think I was involved? Strangely, that all went away yesterday."

Frost's eyes narrowed. "How so?"

"The lawyer sent a follow-up letter. He said Silvia's brother is no longer interested in pursuing the circumstances of her disappearance. His condition has worsened, and he has to focus on his health. So there will be no investigation, no interrogation, no more innuendos about my guilt. At least for the time being."

"That sounds like a good thing."

"It is, although I have to say, they piqued my curiosity by bringing it up again. After all these years, it would be nice to know what really happened to Silvia. Anyway, the fact that the lawyer backed off strikes me as a peace offering. This wasn't directed at me, but at you."

"Lombard is using a carrot instead of a stick," Frost said. "He gives me what I want as an incentive to let it go."

"I think that's about the size of it."

Frost glanced at the crowd around them. From now on, he had to assume he was always being watched. "I woke up to another goodwill gesture," he said.

"Oh?"

"The real Fox—Mr. Jin's teenage son—was dropped off at Human Services overnight. He's unharmed. The social workers are trying to track down his mother in China."

"I'm delighted to hear it."

"So am I."

Herb lowered his voice. "I'm curious. If the offer of a truce is real, why do you think Lombard is so anxious to keep you on the sidelines?"

"I assume he's planning something," Frost said.

"But you don't know what?" Herb asked.

"No, but given who he is, it must be something important. He wants me far away from it."

"Or perhaps he's simply baiting a trap for you," Herb suggested.

"Yes, that's possible, too."

"So what do you intend to do?"

Frost had thought about little else since the meeting in the Bugatti. He felt as if a spider's web were being spun around him, entangling him limb by limb. The more he fought it, the tighter the bonds grew. "For now, all I can do is what Trent Gorham did."

"Which is?"

"Go underground," Frost replied.

"Can you really do that? That doesn't sound like you."

Herb was right. Frost didn't like fighting in the shadows, but that was where his enemies lived. If he shined a light on them, all they would do is scatter and hide. He had to stay in the darkness.

"For now, I don't think I have a choice," Frost said. "As far as the world is concerned, Lombard can stay a myth. In the meantime, I can pursue him behind the scenes. It may take time, but sooner or later, I'll get him."

"Well, my advice remains the same. Be careful."

"Always."

"Even if you try to hide what you're doing, Lombard seems to have eyes everywhere."

"Yes, he does."

Herb gave him one of his penetrating stares. "Meanwhile, what about your personal life? How are things in that regard?"

"No change."

"Have you talked to Duane?" Herb asked.

"No."

"And Tabby?"

"No, not her, either."

His friend sighed long and hard. "I did warn you about all this, Frost."

"I know you did."

"It seems to me you've ended up with the worst of all possible worlds, haven't you? You're estranged from your brother, and you don't have the woman you love in your life."

"Yes, I'm setting new records even for myself," Frost agreed. He was reminded of his mistakes every time he went inside the house on Russian Hill. There were no messages on his phone. No care packages in his refrigerator. No perfume in the air. Even Shack looked lonely without Duane and Tabby.

"My mother called me from Arizona," he added. "She heard what happened."

"How was that conversation?"

"Loud," Frost said.

Herb chuckled.

Frost laughed, too, because there was nothing else to do.

Then he dug into his pocket when he heard the text tone on his phone. His forehead wrinkled with concern. It was another number he didn't recognize, but he suspected that it had come from the man in the Bugatti.

You're welcome.

Below the text was a link to the *San Francisco Chronicle* website.

"What's that about?" Herb asked, noting the frown on Frost's face.

"I don't know, but let's find out."

Frost clicked the link and found himself on the newspaper's home page. He spotted the breaking news article immediately, and he read the opening paragraphs of the story aloud.

Zelyx CEO Found Dead in Illinois

By Khristeen Smith

Martin Filko, the thirty-one-year-old wunderkind entrepreneur who built Zelyx Corporation into one of the most successful new tech companies of the past decade, was found dead in his car late last night in the garage of his Highland Park home. Police in the north Chicago suburb announced the cause of death as carbon monoxide poisoning.

An initial toxicology screening confirmed high levels of alcohol and opioids in Filko's system, police said, but they noted it was too early to speculate whether the death was suicide or accidental.

As CEO of Zelyx, Filko was in the process of relocating the company's headquarters to a new high-rise under construction in the Mission Bay neighborhood of San Francisco. A joint press release from the mayor's office and the Zelyx board this morning promised that Filko's death would have no impact on the relocation, which the statement called "a highly strategic move that is in the best interests of Zelyx and the people of San Francisco . . ."

Frost stopped reading.

Herb whistled in surprise. "Well, well, well. Apparently, Mr. Filko outlived his usefulness."

"Apparently so," Frost agreed, his lips pushed together in thought.

"Another gesture of goodwill?" Herb asked.

"Murder isn't exactly goodwill, no matter who the victim is."

"Well, in this case, I can't say I'm sorry. Based on everything you told me, Mr. Filko had to go. The mayor and the city still get the Zelyx jobs but none of the awful baggage of its CEO. Everybody wins."

Frost read the article again, and he could hear Prisha's voice in his head. *I know it's not the choice you'd make, but it's the best thing for everyone.*

"So this was the deal they made," Frost said.

Herb's eyebrow cocked. "What?"

"Prisha and Zara paid Lombard to get rid of Martin Filko once and for all. As you say, with Filko gone, everybody wins. Fawn gets her revenge. That's also why Prisha wasn't worried about Lombard coming after them. They have as much to lose as he does if Lombard gets caught. They'd wind up in prison for murder."

Herb frowned. "Is it brave or foolish to get in bed with the devil?"

"It never ends well," Frost replied.

"No, I can't say I approve of their methods," Herb agreed, "even if their hearts were in the right place. It's a dangerous thing to assume the ends justify the means. However, I'm not going to cry over the loss of Mr. Filko."

Frost shook his head. "Except for every Martin Filko, there's also Trent Gorham. And Mr. Jin. And Carla and Denny and who knows how many others? This man is a monster. He has to be stopped."

Frost stared at the crowd again. His eyes went from face to face, wondering if Lombard was right there, looking back at him. He'd made a promise in the Bugatti, and sooner or later, he'd keep it. It didn't matter how long it took. The two of them would meet again. He knew when they did, only one of them would walk away alive.

Herb had the look of a man who could read his mind and didn't like what he saw. "I've lived long enough to be sure of one thing, Frost, although you may not want to hear it."

"What's that?" Frost asked.

His friend took him by the shoulder. "Sometimes the road to justice is a crooked street."

# 47

When Frost got home to his house on Russian Hill after dark, he walked inside to the briny aroma of shellfish and the thump of Twenty One Pilots singing "Stressed Out" on his speakers. That could only mean one thing.

Duane.

He found his brother in the kitchen. Duane still wore his white chef's coat, with his long black hair tied up in a ridiculous man bun. Below the coat, he wore khakis and Crocs. The patio door was open, letting warm air into the downstairs. The city's spring heat wave continued with no end in sight. Shack sat on the counter, supervising the cooking process and getting the occasional nibble of crab as Duane made a stir-fry.

His brother's shoulders bobbed to the song. The volume was loud enough that Duane didn't even notice Frost until he was standing next to him. He acted as if it were no big deal to be here in Frost's house, and any other time, it wouldn't be. Duane pointed at a blender half-filled with thick orange slush.

"Carrot juice?" he asked.

"Are you kidding?" Frost replied. He went to retrieve a beer.

After he opened a bottle of Sierra Nevada, Frost examined the damage to his brother's face. The rainbow colors around Duane's eyes had begun to fade, but he still wore a bandage over most of his nose.

"What did you do to yourself?" Frost asked. "Walk into a door?"

Duane shot him a sideways glance. "Something like that."

"You should be more careful."

"Uh-huh. You look like you've seen better days, too."

"I have definitely seen better days," Frost agreed.

He sat on a stool at the kitchen island as Duane worked. They didn't say anything for a while. Shack hopped over to the island and climbed onto Frost's shoulder. A chunk of crab in an Asian marinade flew off the grill, and Frost ate it before Shack could grab it for himself. It was delicious, because everything Duane cooked was delicious.

The music shifted from Twenty One Pilots to Tove Lo.

"So did Mom call you?" Frost asked finally.

"Yup. You?"

"Oh yeah."

"She fights much better than we do," Duane said.

"She sure does."

Duane finished off the stir-fry and scooped the crab and noodles into bowls. "You hungry?"

"Not really," Frost said.

His brother shrugged. "Yeah, me neither."

Duane covered the bowls with plastic wrap and stored them in the refrigerator. He found a tulip dish in one of the cabinets and made up a bowl for Shack. Then the two brothers took their drinks and headed out to the patio. The cool fog hadn't overtaken the heat of the day, and they sat around the table in the darkness, both of them sweating. Duane sipped carrot juice. Frost played with the bottle of beer between his fingers. Shack wandered out to the patio and sprawled on the table between them.

Ten minutes later, Duane said, "So you and me, we're pretty different."

"That we are," Frost said.

"Why is that?"

"I don't know. Did Mom drop you on your head or something?"

"Weird, I was going to ask you that," Duane said.

They both chuckled. The ice broke a little between them, which it was bound to do in the heat.

"You know, I try hard not to be a bad person," Frost said, "but I guess sometimes I fall short."

"Why on earth would you say that?" Duane asked him. "You are the best person I know."

"I hit you. I hit my brother."

"Well, I hit you, too. Don't forget that. You may be better at it, but I got in the first punch."

"I should have taken it and walked away," Frost said. "After all, you were right. I broke the two of you up. I never, ever meant to do that, but I guess I did. And I am really sorry, Duane."

His brother looked away at the city below them. His lips were pinched with unhappiness, which was a rare thing for Duane. His brother was almost always happy. It was something Frost envied about him. And yet maybe he was content because, on most days, Duane lacked a capacity for self-reflection. He lived every second as it happened to him, whereas Frost spent every second thinking about the next one. They both lived in traps of their own making.

"You didn't break us up," his brother replied. "People change. Tabby changed. That's not your fault."

"No, I was in the middle. Just like you said."

"I'm trying to give you an out, bro. Work with me here."

Frost smiled. "Okay."

"I went to see her," Duane went on. "Not to get her back. I knew that wasn't going to happen. Actually, I told her she was right. I was pretending, just like her. Things weren't working between us. I wasn't putting her first. My life is in the kitchen, period. Sooner or later, if we'd stayed together, I would have screwed it up."

"You don't know that."

"Oh, sure I do, and you know it, too. I probably would have banged another sous chef."

"Not Raymonde, I hope," Frost said.

"No. I think I'm safe with him." Duane paused and then added, "She admitted it to me, you know."

"Admitted what?"

"Come on, bro. Don't be dense. Tabby's in love with you."

Frost opened his mouth to say something, but what was there to say? He shrugged and drank his beer.

"She told me she came to see you," Duane continued. "She said she told you how she felt and that you all but admitted that you were in love with her, too. Except you made it clear that you were never going to do anything about it, no matter how you felt. Because of me."

Frost stared back at his brother. "She's right about that."

Duane shook his head. "Well, that is pretty damn stupid."

"Maybe, but that doesn't change anything."

"Come on, Frost. Given that you're in love with her and she's in love with you, that makes absolutely no sense. I want you to be happy, too. Do I need to spell it out for you? I hereby free you from screwing up your life in the name of fraternal loyalty. I state now, for the record, with Shack as a witness, that I will hold no grudge if my brother chooses to date my ex-fiancée."

"That sounds like the carrot juice talking," Frost said.

"I'm serious," Duane replied.

"You? You're never serious."

"Well, at this one moment of my life, I am," his brother said. He leaned across the table next to Shack, and he and the cat both studied Frost with the same intense stare. "So are you going to go talk to her, or what?"

◆ ◆ ◆

The windows in Tabby's apartment were open, and so was the door, but there was still no air moving on the stifling night. She lived in a fourth-floor studio on Fillmore not far from the painted ladies of Alamo Square. A seafood restaurant occupied the street level, making the building smell like bouillabaisse.

Frost stood in the apartment doorway, watching her and not saying a word. Her back was to him. She had music on as she chopped vegetables for a cool salad on a hot evening. She wore white nylon shorts and a pink tank top that clung to her skin in the humid apartment.

"You really shouldn't leave your door open," Frost said after a while. "Anyone could walk in."

Tabby turned around in shock at the sound of his voice. She almost dropped the knife in her hand. He could see emotions passing across her face like fast-moving clouds. Anger. Hope. Desire. Frustration. Fear.

"Frost." Her voice was cool. "What are you doing here?"

"I needed to see you."

Tabby pushed away the preparations of her salad. She wiped her hands on a towel and walked out of the kitchen. "Why? I thought you'd said everything you needed to say already. You didn't want me in your life."

"That's not what I said at all."

"Well, that's what I heard."

Frost felt tongue-tied. He didn't know how to make it right between them. He put down Shack's carrier on the floor and opened the door. The cat wandered out into the strange place to explore. When he spotted Tabby, he padded to her immediately.

"Shack wanted to see you, too," Frost said.

Tabby picked up Shack and softly kissed his head, and then she put him down and let him rummage through her apartment. Frost hadn't moved. Her white sofa sat between them like a barrier they couldn't cross.

"So what do you want, Frost?" she asked.

"I want to stop hiding what I feel for you."

"You told me we couldn't be together. Now or ever."

"I know I did. But I can't live with that."

Tabby stared down at the floor. Her hair fell across her face. "What about Duane?"

"He said if I'm in love with you, then I'm an idiot to let you go."

"Really? He said that?"

"He did."

She walked up to the back of the sofa. "And do you? Love me?"

He came to the other side of the sofa, until only the soft cushions separated them. "Tabby, you know I do."

"Are you sure? Maybe I'm not who you think I am."

"I don't care."

"I hurt Duane. I don't want to hurt you, too. That's the last thing I would ever want to do."

"I'll take my chances."

She leaned forward over the edge of the sofa. He reached out and grabbed her by the waist and lifted her up and over until there was no barrier between them, and he set her on the floor directly in front of him. She wrapped her arms around his chest and held on and wouldn't let go. Her skin was hot; so was his. Her face was wet. She pressed herself so tightly against him that their two bodies were like one. Her lips were next to his cheek, and she leaned up and kissed the lobe of his ear and whispered no louder than a breath, "I was hoping you'd come back."

He ran his fingers through her hair, separating the strands, feeling her do the same to him. With the back of his hand, he lifted her chin. Her lips were full and ready. Her eyes were a maze of emotions, but he only focused on the want he saw there. What came next, what was coming down the road didn't matter. For that one moment of his life, there was nothing but joy in the sticky, still air of the apartment and in the dampness of their skin.

Frost finally did what he'd dreamed about doing for months.

He pulled her face to him.

He kissed her without any guilt at all and felt her kiss him back.

# 48

Tabby's eyes blinked open. The apartment around her was dark. It wasn't dawn yet, but she was already awake.

The night had finally cooled through the open window. She lay atop Frost as he slept. Their arms were wrapped around each other on her sofa. She felt the warmth of his face buried in her hair. They'd never undressed, never touched each other. They'd kissed, they'd talked, they'd kissed again, and they'd fallen asleep.

She disentangled herself without waking him. Shack snored at the foot of the sofa, and the cat didn't move, either. She slipped away to the bathroom, where she showered and stood for the longest time simply letting the hot water pour over her body. When she was done, she went back to the other room and stared down at Frost. She was naked and aroused, and she thought about waking him up so that he could make love to her for the first time. He'd asked her to wake him before she left.

But she didn't. It was easier this way.

She found clothes in her closet, and she got dressed silently. She opened the refrigerator and took out a bottle of water. She sipped it and then found a pad of paper so that she could leave Frost a note.

She wrote,

*Breakfast meeting with a client.*

After a pause, she added beneath it,

*I love you.*

Tabby collected her wallet and keys and let herself out of the apartment and closed the door softly behind her. She took the steps slowly, as if dreading that she had to go into the world again. Outside, there was a faint pinkness in the sky, like the promise of another warm day. She was alone on Fillmore. She breathed in the air and studied the other buildings around her. There were only a few lights. Everyone else was sleeping. She watched the dark cars around her, the dark windows, the dark roofs. Her eyes went from one place to the next, all around her, with a strange unease. She listened to the rare silence, as if San Francisco were holding its breath.

It was the kind of morning where you never wanted to die, but if you did, you would die happy. Except happiness was inside with Frost, and this, she remembered, was the other world.

Tabby crossed the empty street. Her car was parked on the opposite side. She unlocked it and got inside and sat in the gloom. She slid in the key, but she didn't turn on the motor or the radio. Not yet. Instead, she wrapped her arms around her chest and breathed in and out. She checked the mirror, which showed nothing behind her, and she studied her own green eyes as if they belonged to a stranger.

A minute passed.

Then two.

She couldn't wait any longer. She had to do it.

Tabby reached under the front seat, took out a cell phone from its hiding place, and dialed the number.

"Identification," the woman on the other end answered in a cool, alert voice, as if she'd been awake for hours.

"Van Ness," Tabby said.

"Password."

"35415."

"Status."

"Golden Gate."

"Report," the woman inquired.

"Tell Lombard I'm on the inside," Tabby replied.

# AUTHOR'S NOTE

Thanks for reading the latest Frost Easton novel! If you like this novel, be sure to check out all my other thrillers, too. Visit my website at www.bfreemanbooks.com to join my mailing list, get book-club discussion questions, and find out more about me and my books.

You can write to me with your feedback at brian@bfreemanbooks.com. I love to get e-mails from readers around the world, and yes, I reply personally. You can also "like" my official fan page on Facebook at www.facebook.com/bfreemanfans or follow me on Twitter or Instagram using the handle bfreemanbooks. For a look at the fun side of the author's life, you can also "like" the Facebook page of my wife, Marcia, at www.facebook.com/theauthorswife.

Finally, if you enjoy my books, please post your reviews online at Goodreads, Amazon, Barnes & Noble, and other sites for book lovers—and spread the word to your reader friends. Thanks!

# ACKNOWLEDGMENTS

I work with a great team of people to bring you my Frost Easton novels.

Jessica Tribble at Thomas & Mercer led the way at every stage of making this book happen, from the initial proposal through the editorial work, production, and marketing strategies. She is what every author wants in an editor. It's been a great pleasure working with Charlotte Herscher on all the Frost books. Charlotte has a special gift as a developmental editor for helping an author see exactly what works and what doesn't in an early draft. Laura Petrella spots details as a copyeditor that no one else does. I'm a bit of a fanatic for turning in a clean book, but Laura always catches things I miss! The entire team at T & M are amazing professionals, and it's a privilege to work with them.

My first reader on every book is my wife, Marcia. She is wonderful at challenging my preconceived notions about the characters and the story, and she makes sure that my vision for the book makes it onto the page. My other advance reader is Ann Sullivan, who adds her own extremely helpful perspective on the first draft. Marcia and Ann both play a huge role in shaping the books.

My agent in New York, Deborah Schneider, has been a determined ally and advocate for the last fifteen years. I'm always grateful to her and her colleagues for helping me navigate the world of publishing.

Of course, I am especially grateful to *you*, the readers, for coming along with me on this ride and for taking Frost Easton, Jonathan Stride, Cab Bolton, and my other characters into your hearts. Thank you!

# ABOUT THE AUTHOR

*Photo © 2009 by Martin Hoffsten*

Brian Freeman is a bestselling author of psychological thrillers, including the Frost Easton and Jonathan Stride series. His books have been sold in forty-six countries and translated into twenty-two languages. His stand-alone thriller *Spilled Blood* was named Best Hardcover Novel in the International Thriller Writers Awards, and his novel *The Burying Place* was a finalist for the same honor. *The Night Bird*, the first book in the Frost Easton series, was one of the top twenty Kindle bestsellers of 2017. Brian is widely acclaimed for his vivid "you are there" settings, from San Francisco to the Midwest, and for his complex, engaging characters and twist-filled plots.

Brian lives in Minnesota with his wife, Marcia. For more information on the author and his books, visit www.bfreemanbooks.com.